Strip

Strip

Andrew Binks

Nightwood Editions
2013

Nightwood Editions
P.O. Box 1779
Gibsons, BC VON 1V0
Canada
www.nightwoodeditions.com

Nightwood Editions acknowledges financial support from the Government of Canada through the Canada Book Fund and the Canada Council for the Arts, and from the Province of British Columbia through the British Columbia Arts Council and the Book Publisher's Tax Credit.

This book has been produced on 100% post-consumer recycled, ancient-forest-free paper, processed chlorine-free and printed with vegetable-based dyes.

TYPESETTING & COVER DESIGN: Carleton Wilson
COVER PHOTOGRAPH: Graham Davies

Printed and bound in Canada.

LIBRARY AND ARCHIVES CANADA CATALOGUING IN PUBLICATION

Binks, Andrew, 1958–, author
Strip / Andrew Binks.

ISBN 978-0-88971-290-4 (pbk.)

I. Title.

PS8603.I56S87 2013   C813'.6   C2013-903131-6

For Bernard and Hugo

Mais tu restes muette, impassible, et, trop fière,
Tu te plais à me voir, sombre et désespéré,
Errer dans mon amour comme en un cimietière!

—Émile Nelligan (1879–1941)
from "Amour immaculé"

One

A DANCER'S FINGERTIPS—ETCHED with a language that is no long-er decipherable—tickle space, trace its volume, press, pull, contract, constrict, until they touch, grasp, hold and balance, shift what is on and off balance. They retreat, release, flick, dab. At careless times they graze. Graze nipples. Trace filaments across the skin. They touch the sternum and search for the heart.

A SLAMMED DOOR ECHOES up this stairwell from the floors below. Am I naked underneath this bedsheet? Is there bleeding? Blood. Re-assuring. It means I still have a heart. They say it's in our blood, this new disease. So far, they say, hundreds have died because of it. And my balls ache. My lip throbs. I taste the warm blood and my saliva mixed with something salty. There must be tears; I can barely see. There must be tears. If I had something in my stomach I would vomit. I remember Kent said our New Year's resolution was to make 1983 our year. "Here's to you and me in '83," he said. Helluva year it's turning out to be.

EVERYONE HAS A DANIEL, and, with luck, you'll have him early on, to break your heart to pieces and then get over it. Never make the same stupid goddamned mistake again. Funny how you can talk yourself into thinking the road less travelled will be a noble trip. I tripped on the road less travelled.

I haven't thought much about him recently, not his sharp chin or his Adam's apple with the tiny cleft of stray whiskers that his razor couldn't reach, or his long nose extending down from his forehead, making him look like the distant relative of the black and white television test-pattern Indian. He was superb and perfect, and he knew it. Someday someone might be inspired to stage a full-length ballet about nothing more than his eyebrows.

In this stairwell, in this light, Daniel is no more than a flicker. Through him I have come to understand lust, *désir*. Through Kent—love, *amour*. Lust singes the hairs on your hand, and can just as easily bite them with frost. Lust can kill quickly. Love tears your world asunder, then leaves you to die on the battlefield. But if I have to blame anyone (that is, anyone other than myself) I would start with Daniel. I could blame Kharkov, too, who brought in Daniel as a guest *répétiteur* at the end of our tour.

Montreal, our last stop on the homestretch of our first national tour as a big-league company. And 1982 was the Company's year; we premiered the full-length Prokofiev *Romeo and Juliet*. We were exhausted and bloated from too much road food. The ballerinas were thick around their middles—even the anorexics were struggling—from endless health muffins and Caesar salads with house dressing hold-the-croutons-in-the-name-of-the-diet, and late-night post-performance carrot cake, or the great fatigue fighter, chocolate, in its many evil forms. Cigarettes were no longer keeping the addicts thin. We ignored our colds and our injuries—women taped their toes, wrapped their ankles, and rinsed the blood from their shoes. Men danced through pulled groins, shin splints and torn Achilles tendons. We were sick from drafty buses, drafty hotel rooms, drafty rehearsal halls and each other. A few sought refuge in chamomile tea, steamy showers and naps. In the midst of it all I, too, needed a pick-me-up.

This malaise, this touring burnout didn't stop me, or anyone else from trying to impress the arrogant fuck, Daniel Tremaine, Montreal's ballet wunderkind, the teacher and choreographer you went to if you wanted to win a medal at a ballet competition. Deep in Place des Arts in the bright rehearsal hall, cavernous ceilings, mirrors for miles, Kharkov announced, "Monsieur Daniel Tremaine will be giving us company class while we are here in Montreal." Giving us? (Kharkov only took class in December when he faked his way through Drosselmeyer in *The Nutcracker*. Even then he usually just fumbled his way through barre.) Kharkov was nervous about impressing Montreal. Daniel would be his salvation. I looked around the studio. Some dropped their heads, pretending to limber their necks, others caught my eye. Some rewrapped their warm-up gear, leg warmers and sweaters, placing them strategically to hide the extra pounds.

Daniel Tremaine, the legend. People had compared him to Nijinsky, said he was built more like a bird than a human. But it didn't stop his very ethereal body from betraying him; as he rehearsed an understudy for Montreal's Conservatoire's production of *Swan Lake* in Glasgow, he tore his Achilles, badly. Therapy went well, but he fell on some stairs when wearing the cast, and ripped the healing, the muscle and the skin, even worse than the original injury. His dancing career went kaput, but it hasn't stopped anybody from wanting a piece of his greatness.

I tried to take it in stride as Daniel stooped—all six-foot-three of him—the top of his head, his thinning crown, next to my crotch, correcting my line and adjusting my instep. Oh sure, I have been nervous to the core with each new coach, teacher and choreographer, but when he touched me that first time, it hit me like the February wind at the corner of Portage and Main; my breath was shallow, my heart *frappéd* inside my rib cage, my ears rang and my vision went dim. I squeezed the barre, inhaled and fought a sudden numbness in my thighs. Like I said, it is the kind of attraction that will eventually destroy you.

He ignored me the rest of the class, thank God, but I couldn't stop looking at those big hands that had touched me, the broad feet that had walked in my direction, the same feet that had danced all the great roles at so young an age on international stages, and at the way he flicked his famous wrists as he dreamily explained something into the air. I suppose that blasé, unimpressed look was how he got dancers to push themselves; the dancer's ego is a frail and determined thing.

After class, in the bright hallway, while the others wandered ahead, I sensed him behind me and though I wanted to flee, something inside shouted, *Stop for God's sakes! Linger!* And I listened. Daniel Tremaine stopped me with a touch to my elbow. "You have a nice line," he told me, then he dropped his voice, "but the Company is destroying your technique and your body." Then he put his hand on my shoulder, looked into my eyes and smiled, daring me to be shocked, "You 'ave a nice ass," he said.

It seems my heart, as a muscle—pounding out beats and measures—is hardwired to that muscle between my legs. I had never felt so obvious. But I had never met a Daniel Tremaine. "Thank you."

"Would you like some private coaching?" But I couldn't speak. "I mean here, after class?"

Was I the only one who noticed the upper right corner of his mouth twist when he spoke English, and how it was met by a twitching at the corner of his right eye—as if it was painful to speak?

The rest of the day I wandered the tight neighbourhoods of the plateau, narrow streets of walk-ups pressed in on top of each other, iron stairways extending to the street, all punctuated by small cafés. But any place I came across seemed empty unless I could imagine myself there with him. My mind dipped in and out of what a professional coaching session with this man would involve—Daniel Tremaine having his way, a million different ways, with me. Why me? Second soloist? And only then, to fill the ranks.

After class the next morning, I lingered while he talked to his fawning fans—mostly Company members who would have killed for a coaching session—and a few notables such as the mayor and dance critics who were observing class. Daniel was a national treasure for Montreal. I continued to stretch until the room thinned out.

"Why don't we start with some jumps; I can see you are a jumper." This was true, although being a good jumper means you have to work on the weaknesses, and it forced me to perfect my turns. So I started with simple *changements*, to get some real height and momentum— and to hopefully impress. He stood close and calmly placed his hands on my shoulders, pressing against my lift, a logical action, but then he told me to stop. "Do you know what you're doing?"

"*Changements?*"

"Your fifth position is forced."

"I've always done it that way."

"How are your knees?"

"Tender, but…" One of Martha Graham's principal dancers told us we would never have a day without pain until we stop dancing. I had lumped all of my aches and pains under this noble disclaimer.

"You're forcing your fifth."

"The Company likes it that way."

"Why?"

I paused.

"See, you have no idea. Do you think people in the audience are going to notice? No, of course not. It hurts me to watch. I mean, your jump is good enough to distract you or anyone else from your bad technique. Your knees must stay over your metatarsals. Does that not make sense?"

I just stared at him. Of course he was right but it's like smoking, you know it's bad for you, but…

"Are you listening to me? Stop staring. Your knees are made to bend forward, not sideways. Turnout originates from the hip. Why are you forcing your fifth? Jump, in first, and do not force it."

As I jumped he walked around me, placing his hand on my lower back, on my stomach, on my upper chest. "How does that feel?"

I could have really told him, but all I said was, "Off balance."

"Of course. The rest of you will have to get used to doing it properly, not overcompensating. Soon it will be easy. Soon you'll understand a *sauté*."

We worked on several sequences from corner to corner, a bit of "Bluebird" from *Sleeping Beauty*, but to do it properly would be another story. Daniel walked beside me as I moved, occasionally taking my hands and throwing them skyward. "Think of your landings. Think of the in-between." But soon my legs turned to rubber. Why the hell were we doing a variation no one would ever give me a shot at?

"I want you to think of all of this tonight, when you sleep. I want you to see your body rearranging itself, changing the foundations, shifting to its core. But don't be mistaken, this won't happen overnight."

I left Place des Arts and vowed to keep my mouth shut as far as Daniel Tremaine was concerned. I had a hot bath, a nap, strong tea and an early dinner and went for Company warm-up. All I could think about was his firm touch. I worried that my dancing would be sloppy, but I was light. I was nimble. I was fuelled by something unexpected. The evening flew.

The next day, in class I became aware of others. They must have known about the coaching. I stayed at the back.

After, I lingered again, and when the groupies had dissipated Daniel approached me. He rolled his eyes at the departing stragglers. "Did you think about what I told you?"

I nodded, but my voice caught in my throat.

"Good. Let's learn a bit of *Le Spectre de la Rose*," something the Company was planning as part of next season. Again, a long shot for me, or was it? He walked me through the first bit, showed me the choreography, miming everything on a small scale as if having a conversation with himself, complete with arm movements. Soon I was flying across the studio. We worked mostly on the entrance and the *grand jeté*, and the *grand jeté en tournant*, but he seemed more concerned with my arms. Then he took hold of my waist on each jump, lifting me beyond what I was capable of. As I focused on the ceiling I'm sure he was focused right bang on my crotch. This required the utmost concentration.

Finally, I came to rest on terra firma. I searched his expression to decipher what he thought of my jumps. But I was preoccupied with the *why* of this. Why was he coaching me? Had Kharkov requested it? Was I due for another promotion? Or was it rather what I *suspected*— did he have, as my friend Rachelle liked to say, his compass pointing in my direction? I couldn't tell.

"Your legs are now throwing your arms off. You have to take risks now, and the arms have to go higher. Everything has to go up. Do you understand? You might as well be doing this with a walker. And for God's sake, do something with your eyes; they're absolutely blank. Look a little like you are enjoying it." But I was terrified. And I wanted so much to enjoy it. To be coached by one of Canada's great teachers, to imagine that one day "Bluebird" and *Le Spectre de la Rose* could be mine, was too much.

"My back?"

"Your everything."

I didn't have the strength for what he wanted.

"It will take a while to get your landings back. That's all. You've lost your centre of gravity. Now go and change. I'll wait."

I couldn't imagine what he would wait for. My blank stare? My vapid smile? My rotten jumps? These two days had presented the opportunity of a lifetime. He could have been working with the principals.

I washed layers of sweat, savoured the coolness of the water. I had a few hours to recover before our warm-up and performance. And I was keeping Daniel Tremaine waiting.

I stepped out of the shower, a little less defeated, taking a solitary moment to survey my naked form in the mirror—something less likely to be criticized. There, in the mirror's reflection, stood Daniel Tremaine. From his mouth tumbled the words, "Would you like to go for a coffee?" Dancer's language for everything from a mini-debrief to mini-therapy to gossip to foreplay. "Tomorrow?"

WASN'T THERE A CHORUS line of principals cuing up for him? All I had to offer was me, second soloist. Every guy, even the straight ones, and all the women in the studio followed my eye line the next morning. It was impossible and against the laws of the universe: Daniel and John. They must have laughed, but I was grinning behind that blank stare. Romeo and Juliet were nothing compared to this.

But, whatever else he may have been, Daniel Tremaine was a perfectionist, and did give two shits about my technique. I still believe that. No man had ever been as direct. When we went for that coffee on rue Saint-Denis (there are some perks to being a professional dancer: you have time off at odd hours of the day; you feel physical one hundred percent of the time; you can sit in a Montreal café with the famous Daniel Tremaine while the world buzzes around you; and you can dream), he told me more, in his killer kind of way. "If you want any kind of life as a dancer you must pay attention. You started late?"

"I swam competitively until about five years ago."

"So you're twenty?"

"No. I'm going on twenty-two. Swimming was boring."

"The dancer's friend."

"That's true." It had made me supple and strong, but I needed more than endless hours of lengths at 5:30 A.M., five mornings a week, and in Edmonton winters. "But when I started dancing..."

"It's no use starting late only to finish early. So they've given you a job after five years of this."

"A bit longer, I danced and swam..."

"Why second soloist?"

"I was next in line."

"You should be further along. You get paid a little more than corps. So what? If you stay on this path you'll be in a wheelchair by the time you are thirty, teaching little girls to point their toes for the rest of your life. You obviously have a gift. Don't abuse it." These were the first positive words I'd heard him say. "And don't be arrogant. They always need males, especially in the Company. The prairies are a wasteland. Males don't last there."

"They're born there."

"The prairies are too limiting, too Russian. Maybe Vaganova will make you strong, but your muscles will bulge and your joints will turn to putty."

I bit my lip, while he sneered. "You'll be bulky with t'ighs like the Winnipeg football team. What do you call them?"

"The Blue Bombers."

"The Blue Bombers—there'll be no difference, in their white tights and dance belts."

"Jockstraps."

The right corner of his mouth reached the far corner of his eye, as he stifled a laugh. "You must know *tu es adorable*." He flicked at a bag of sugar, "But your knees, *mon ami*, won't last."

"You're telling me to give up on second soloist?"

"The Company repertoire is tired and boring. *Romeo and Juliet* is their newest ballet in what, thirty years?"

"The Company's expanding."

"Not if they want to tour."

He was right; *Romeo and Juliet* had been a gamble that paid off.

And as far as my knees were concerned, he was right; they burned every time I stepped up onto the street curb, although they were fine in the studio. The hours I had spent dancing now rivalled all of my schooling, ever. As a child I badly wanted to get up on that stage with Nureyev and Fonteyn, even if I was going to be stuck beside the scenery or in the shadows, holding Rudi's cloak. No matter if it was *The Nutcracker*, *Rodeo* or *Swan Lake* that my mother took me to, sitting in the audience while the action was onstage was pointless.

Seven years ago I stopped twirling around the basement, slipping on the carpet, wearing holes in my socks. I stopped dreaming. In fact, it was a Thursday in early December that I took the leap and lied about a trip to the doctor for a flu shot. Yes, I climbed that same narrow staircase that led to our family doctor, but kept right on going. Up. Up to the place that made the high ceiling in the doctor's office throb and sent fine plaster dust snowing down during checkups. Six months earlier, on the staircase where I had previously seen only armies of young girls with tight buns on their heads, I saw two male dancers ascend. If there were other men dancing in Edmonton, I would, too, but it took six more months of dreaming, yearning, gathering my gumption.

Soon I lied about other things—swim practice, movies, getting together with friends. All traded for a dream. (Look at me now, lying about everything, to everyone, myself included—sitting in this stairwell, now, has nothing to do with the dream.) Up I went, like Alice following the rabbit down the hole, but in the other direction, to a wonderland of Chopin played on out-of-tune pianos, the thick scent of old lady perfume, sweat, talcum powder. Bodies wafted corner to corner across creaky floors, mirrors for walls, boxes of resin in room corners, people dashing from dressing rooms to studios, draped on the barre, sitting splayed in hallways, stretching, waiting for their class to begin. In the musty windowed office Lisa, my first teacher, looked over the class list. "Are you a football player?"

"I swim."

"We get football players. Their coach sends them. A few times and then they're gone. It can't be the tights, can it?" She smiled at me. I relaxed. "God, football. Football is some kind of abomination to human movement. It frightens me to see these guys with clunky feet and mitts for hands—banging their knees sideways. Funny, in the long run, ballet is probably going to do as much damage." She winked at me.

"I want to dance."

"Show up regularly and I won't charge you."

After the class, she stopped me at the door. "Will we see you again?" She smiled. My father could have adjusted her slightly protruding eye teeth. I could tell by her openness that she liked men, a lot. She said a lot of guys who started late had careers. I couldn't believe we were talking about free classes, talking about careers, like it was a possibility and not just a dream. My whole world was starting to shift. I was involved in something I absolutely loved.

"Keep swimming," Lisa said, "for now."

So there I was plié, *tendu* with the beginner adults, women and the two men I had seen on the stairs. Then Lisa threw me into a room of little girls balancing on tippytoes, learning the syllabus, for a moment, and after that into seasoned recreational adults with timid wrists and tight fingers, until she figured I could rub shoulders with those who had hoped to be dancers one day, and along with them classes of serious teens with talent, strength, discipline and their dreams still in front of them. This all meant that some nights I was at the studio for up to four hours. The girls needed a male partner for their exams, and the adults wanted partners to make class more challenging. And all I wanted to do was dance. A simple port de bras at the barre was enough to satisfy the craving. I couldn't wait to get to the studio, change, stretch the soreness out of my muscles and see how much further I could turn and how much more controlled I could be when I leapt. At night I dreamt I was so much better. When I swam I reached for the end of the pool; now when I danced, I reached for the heavens.

"Just turn," Lisa shouted, while I made myself dizzy with *tour en l'air*. "Worry about your technique later, just get around for God's sake. Be careless."

Classmates started to recognize me as a dancer. And if I recognized them on the street, they'd introduce me as "one of the dancers from the studio." It seemed unfair that because of my sex I was fast-tracked. Being called a dancer can be like a drug. Yet I didn't feel deserving of the title, not then.

Soon Lisa asked me to come and dance with a group of retired pros in the morning in the Company class. "Stay in the back," she told me, "and follow. You'll get it." I skipped school to make that class, and soon we were rehearsing for festivals as far away as Red Deer. Fantasy ballets. Ukrainian folk dancing—holding the girls by the waist on cue—them grabbing my arm, run here, run there. Jump. Kick. Wait for the applause. Bow. I begged off my parents' European tour (it was Mom who wanted me along, not Dad) with the excuse of a part-time job, but while they toured Europe, I toured the sun-baked stages at Alberta county fairs. Old ladies and the odd queer stage door Johnny off the farm were my fans. I looked like an honest-to-God dancer.

My body took to it. My brain. My balance. My thighs thickened, counterbalancing my aching butt. "You've got to stretch all the time," Lisa said, "especially in this heat—take advantage of the heat. You need strength up the back of your legs, too." My swimmer's shoulders screamed with each new partner I lifted. My lower back ached. And I couldn't keep my eyes off myself. I am still obsessed with the potential for beauty, proportion and line.

Lisa had said I wasn't too old, and when Madame Défilé, Lisa's wrinkled, stooping boss and mentor—and a Canadian dance icon whose old-woman perfume scent infused the place—learned I was serious, she challenged me, as if to prove Lisa wrong. "You're the swimmer," she said in fading Queen's English. "Maybe we can make a dancer out of you, but I doubt it." She would grab my leg at the top of a *grand battement* and push it higher, shoving her sharp nails into the back of my knee. "Don't cheat!" She shouted her commands. With her back to me she would pull my thigh from its joint, while leaning against me to keep my hip back, in a tug-of-war with my torso. Then she'd shake my arms. "You've got to press the weight of the world *down*. They aren't just there to hang off the side of your trunk. Now pressssssssss!"

To get what she wanted, she slapped me and screamed until her pale powdered face turned pink. From time to time she would throw me out of the class and then ask me what the hell I was doing sitting in the waiting area and "Get the bloody hell back in here you bloody son of a bitch, if you want to dance then bloody dance for the love of God. Show some spine." I suppose I was a whipping post for all the princes who had never courted her. Once and only once did she waver. We were facing the barre in arabesque and I tightened the hell out of my lower back while squeezing my butt to get my leg up, the muscles fighting each other to maintain the form, while stretching my leg through to the end of my foot. "Now John, that's good," she said. Did I hear that correctly? The pianist stopped playing, the other students fell silent.

"You others would do well to follow this young man's example. He's working bloody hard to make up for lost time and though he may not make it, I have a feeling he'll die trying." Her compliments were calculated and short-lived. "Swimming isn't enough. Do weights," she shouted. "Cans of soup if you must, lots of repetitions, until it burns. And push-ups. Drop and do forty. Now! You wait until you have a men's class, then tell me you want to dance. Swimmer ha! Have you thought of joining the army? It would be a hell of a lot easier." In spite of her reputation—she had garnered a Governor General's award bringing ballet to the prairies—she was slowly forgetting and being forgotten. It was obvious she would never get the perfection she demanded from anyone. In the end, I heard, she died alone.

Maybe I can blame this all on Lisa: she said I could do it.

BUT DANIEL DIDN'T HAVE time for these trivialities. "Everyone wants a kick at the can," he said. "You won't be pretty forever, you know. In the meantime… you can kiss me."

"Here?"

"You're in Montreal now."

"And?"

"You have a *look*."

"I scraped my nose on the bottom of the pool. I was fifteen."

He didn't care. "No. You are more than second soloist material. Any male can become a second soloist, if he has a pulse. You have line, proportion, height. You're already halfway there. But you could be a prince. You'll reach your prime a little later than normal but you were born to be a prince."

"That's my plan."

"Then you are going about it the wrong way. You'll be a shabby has-been—on the prairies—and that's all. You'll be bored to tears. How many times can you dance *Fall River Legend*, or *Rita Joe*? It's a small dusty repertoire of museum pieces."

I realized he was encouraging me to leave the Company; dancers never berated Agnes de Mille, or Vaganova or Russian technique for that matter. My head spun, this time without my body attached.

"Montreal can be your threshold to the bigger world of dance: the States, Europe." But I only wanted to go where he would be. "It's a nice nose, by the way," he said.

"Yours is nice, too." Actually, his was magnificent.

"It's one of my Mohawk parts. I'll show you the rest later." My heart swelled, my chest expanded, but it was my legs I had to squeeze tight. This was a head-to-toe solid dance master, a real man that, for some reason, I had all to myself.

I followed his steps closely. He took me back to his home, the kind of place where you're never sure if you're inside or out—loft, terrace, rooftops, skylights and trees—and that's where he wrapped his wiry arms around me. There was a ballet barre in his huge bedroom. I saw him moulding me into the next Godunov.

"Come here." He pulled me to his mattress on the floor.

"Baryshnikov sleeps on the floor, too, but without a mattress."

"Baryshnikov is nothing but bullshit stories about Baryshnikov."

Up to then, only six men had touched me, physically, in my life. And each time felt like the first, and freed me once again from all the years of indecision, confusion, questioning and holding back. It had been an adolescence marked by disappointment, pretence and fakery. The breakthrough came when the swim coach offered me his Speedo, the day I forgot mine. I knew my fate when I surreptitiously took it home to spend some alone time with it, later telling him that I rinsed it for him. Our eyes met when I handed it back to him early one morning. Then, on a subsequent out-of-town swim meet, he pretended to be tipsy (as I had done up to then, when it came to begging off kissing my latest girlfriend), but it was me who took advantage of him. Desire put me in the driver's seat, but he knew exactly what he was doing on that motel bed.

And though Daniel was number seven, that afternoon he took the number one spot as he ran his finger down my sternum. He pressed his palm onto my chest, as if he were trying to leave an imprint on my heart, and I let him. He tickled the ridge of my lips with his fingers until they twitched in anticipation of him touching his lips to mine. He worked on my flexibility, every night for a week after that first afternoon, stroking my inner thighs—to start with. As far as I could see, having him make love to me was the only thing that would cure that blankness he said he saw. I was still technically a virgin; I wanted Daniel to change that.

Sure I've had moments where I thought I could see what was going to save me, change me, open me up, turn me into a great dancer. I never believed it had anything to do with love. Every new teacher I encountered held new hope, and many of them fulfilled that hope, with a gem of their knowledge. I owed my *grand jeté* to these gems (think of jumping after you've left the ground; if that doesn't work think of a hot poker up your ass). Then, with another, my body changed its interpretation of a *tour en l'air* (think of one side of your body trying to catch up with the other, think of the stability of a brick shit-house). But after all is said and done, it's love that fills in all the empty spaces and makes you dance better, love that transcends the physical plane, love that couples the true material with the ethereal, joins the dance with desire. I became weightless for that week, and for weeks following the Company's departure. All I could think was, *This is my moment at last,* and *God, I am so ready for it—from now on, things will be perfect.* But it was lust, that's all. And I'm starting to think that the uplifting effects of lust, like caffeine, alcohol or cigarettes, eventually wear off and leave us feeling and looking like shit.

My Winnipeg roommates—hunky Peter, a solid and story-book-prince stunning Ukrainian, and the chain-smoking Rachelle (who was our landlady, also happened to be our roommate while on tour, and also happened to be a co-corps de ballet member, *pas de deux* partner and confidante)—both forced me to come clean in an empty coffee shop, one rainy morning on Rue Crescent. We sat in idle chat, commenting on stylish or down-and-out passers-by, dreading the matinee, until Rachelle spoke. "So? Come on. You've made up your mind haven't you? Is it love? Are you moving in with him?"

"It's time to move on," I said. "I can't get comfortable with the Company. I'll end up rotting on the prairie." I actually had myself convinced. Looking back I can see how easily I can make myself believe anything.

"Rotting on the prairie? Mr. Rottam is rotting? They're planning *The Rite of Spring* and *The Firebird* and you say rotting, Rottam?"

"They've been planning those for years. It's some kind of publicity stunt. Do you actually think they'll get around to it before we retire?"

"Kharkov has started running ideas for *Serenade*."

"More Tchaikovsky?" I teased Rachelle. She loved Tchaikovsky; so did I, but he became our whipping board for everything from music to sexuality. "Feh! If he were alive, he'd be writing movie music."

"So John Williams is a slouch? What the hell's wrong with movie music?"

But my leaving was a betrayal. Peter was mum, resting his chin on his hands like a scolded puppy, and most likely worrying about being an understudy that afternoon for an injured Paris. He'd rehearsed it to death and the dancing wasn't really that difficult. He just had to look good, which would be no problem. He finally spoke. "So, it's about dance? Or him?"

"I don't know. My mind is too crowded. There's him…"

"And all the thousand and one nights you've yet to spend with him." Rachelle said.

"And the possibility that I could be better than a soloist, with some good coaching. He really believes…"

"But do you? Come on, dig deep."

"You've seen me dancing these past few days."

"Yes, we all have." She droned, "*Big deal*."

"Big deal? I can do it. I am so centred right now. I turn on a dime, and just keep turning. Did you see me today? I turned five times…"

"I've turned seven, *and* on my dick, *and* with my eyes closed."

"Correction, Peter. You were *on* someone's dick."

"Hey. No potty mouth around me—you cocksuckers."

"...and then I just stood there on *demi-pointe* in a perfect *retiré* with everything so aligned. If it hadn't been for having to have coffee with you two I could still be there. And my *grand jeté* is ..."

"Yeah, we know, grand. We saw it. Come on. Cut this shit," she said, holding in a drag. "You're in love with that frog. Am I going to have to clean out your room back home? That's all I want to know." She paused for a moment savouring the smoke. "God, I love how everyone smokes here."

Rachelle had never babied me, not from the moment she parked herself outside our upstairs bathroom with a can of cleanser in one hand and a sponge in the other, telling me it was my turn to clean up the pubes in the bathtub. Peter could be as harsh, too, but he knew when to stop. He never let on if he had actually had sex with a man but he had become a friend after some fumbled attempts for us to be bed buddies. Not a good idea for roommates—we ended up just cuddling.

There is something like a double negative about doing it with someone you know, as a friend, who also happens to be a dancer; it takes an awful lot to become aroused, simply because you know all the ins and outs of their physique, mostly their flaws, and it is almost clinical as to how you know them. But he was definitely the hottest dancer I had seen that side of the Ontario–Manitoba border. As well as cuddling, we spent time physically close to each other, massaging shoulders, feet, ankles while watching whatever Rachelle and her husband wanted, usually *Wheel of Fortune*. Making it even less of an issue, we both talked about his body like it was a commodity we could both appreciate from the outside. We'd agreed that it was my weaknesses—low arch, tight tendons, feet that wouldn't stretch—that would make me a strong dancer. And it was his gifts—perfect feet, high arches, a beautiful line, flexibility for days and visible muscle beneath his paper-thin olive skin—that would get him to where he wanted to go.

But perfect feet and flexibility can be a curse; they can hinder your strength. He was the first one who enlightened me on that, after a particularly shitty day in the studio. I decided to walk home in the rain in order to catch terminal pneumonia, if possible, and he got off the passing bus to accompany me. With his great instinct for knowing when I needed a pick-me-up, he punched me in the shoulder and said, "It is your weaknesses that will make you a strong dancer." I've repeated it to myself a million times since. It became my mantra in class with every *tendu*, *developpé*, and every session with my feet locked under the nearest radiator to stretch my tendons. And the mantra worked. So there was something more lasting to our relationship than the physical. During rehearsals and before class we stretched each other incessantly to the point where we must have looked way too comfortable physically, like twin sisters, Siamese twins. And if that were the case then Rachelle was our den mother. Even so, Peter wasn't above being a bitch, especially now that I was smitten. "It sounds like this is your *big chance*."

"Let me ask one minor question here: has he even *asked* you to make the move?" Rachelle asked.

"Thank you, Ma'am!" Peter said. "You took the words out of my mouth."

"Do I detect a note of *sarcasm*, or is it jealousy?" Peter and I were drifting. I hadn't felt the same bond recently. Maybe we had had too many weeks on the road. He was odd, distant. Was I a threat? How could I be a threat? True, I had been promoted to second soloist just months before this tour, and he had stayed in the corps and we had it out over that—tears, the jealousy thing (although I had hoped he'd be a little more jealous for my own ego's sake). After sharing a litre of Mogen David in some snowbound stop on the northern Ontario leg of our tour, where we performed in a cold gymnasium and slept in bunk beds, we breathed heavily from our respective bunks and stared up into the darkness. He actually found the nerve to speak, however drunk: "It's politics; Kharkov has to show the board he doesn't play favourites."

"So Kharkov hates me? Is that what you're saying? And he *luuuuuuvs* you?"

"No love lost, let me put it that way."

Later, sober, I was more willing to consider it. But now, here in Montreal I, along with the whole company, was sure Peter was next on Kharkov's list of conquests. Kharkov promoted me because he had to; he would promote Peter because he wanted to. Peter was a shoo-in for a long career.

"No, he hasn't asked me. Not yet. It's strange, but I feel like meeting Daniel is my chance to really find myself, as a dancer." I actually believed this, then. Now, I'm not so sure I like what I've found.

It was Rachelle who persevered, "That's BS. It's the same BS I told myself when I married Gordon. Now look at me."

"You thought Gordon could teach you to dance? He's a... what the hell is he anyway?"

Gordon referred to himself as an engineer, but he was unlicensed jack-of-all-trades from plumbing to wiring. He'd wear his dirt-caked boots around the house. Rachelle would scream at him. He'd call us fairies. They'd slam the bedroom door and go at it—sexually—and Peter and I would turn up *Jeopardy* on the TV. It was almost like having a family.

"I meant being in love. Married. He would be my escape hatch."

"Wasn't he?"

Rachelle inhaled nicotine with every breath throughout her day when not dancing. She was sallow, her ridged teeth were tobacco stained, but every night, minutes before curtain in tights and tutu and tiara, she looked like the world's loveliest princess. She had the perfect Company body; Kharkov loved tits and hated thighs. It was a tough type to find, but any female with an ounce of meat on her thighs didn't stand a chance. Every company had its type.

"It's a pretty good sex life when you get home from tour, from what I hear on my side of the hall."

"If the sex weren't so..."

"Stellar?"

"It can help you ignore other things," she said. "That is something you should experience: Kharkov can be breathing down my neck all week, trying to crush me for the millionth time, and I think, *Who cares? I'm going home to get fucked, wildly, unapologetically and furiously*. And I know it pisses Kharkov off—royally."

"I hate you."

"Everyone needs an outlet. Looks like yours is going to be in

Montreal. Anyway it's not always perfect. What do you think hubby's been doing for the past seven weeks while we've been taking Barnum and Bailey's across the country?"

"Framing houses?"

"I don't care what the fuck you say—men, gay, straight, when it comes to love they're all assholes. With the exception of you two, my dear hearts."

"Who said anything about love?"

"Just make sure you have a plan—a Plan B."

"Plan BS. I need retraining according to him."

"Him? I'm sure you've discovered something more apropos to call *him*."

"Monsieur Tremaine."

"Oh, s'il vous plait."

"Okay, Daniel."

"Daniel. My sweetie. *Mon amour*." She smooched into the air.

"Great lips for a blow job. No wonder hubby sticks around."

"You pig. *Cochon*."

"Seriously. I can feel it—in my knees especially. Can't you? The Company forces everything—arches, knees, ankles. I'm surprised I can still walk."

"That's ballet, for shit's sake! I don't believe a word of it. You're just repeating a bunch of stuff he's told you."

I looked at Peter, who just stared open-jawed. People get antsy when they see someone genuinely happy. He finally spoke. "Maybe you just don't have a natural turnout."

"I think we've been down that road of me not having natural any-thing at this point, o perfect one."

"If the ballet slipper fits…"

"Of course Captain Bohunk here—and notice how I emphasize the *hunk*, dear—and his knees of steel from years of shumka-ing."

"You're just not as sturdy."

"True." I had to somehow prop Peter up, as if I were betraying him, which was absurd: we were all in it for ourselves and no one else. "Now if only we could get you to keep your shoulders down when you turn."

"So all of a sudden you've become Monsieur Tremaine's secretary? My shoulders are just fine without your help."

"Maybe you should relocate your tension."

"To my butt, like you?"

"You have *such* potential."

"Maybe Daniel is making you weak at the knees." He sounded deflated now, and distant. I would miss him, no doubt about it.

Rachelle picked up the slack. "Poor thing! You're letting this Daniel brainwash you. When you stop hurting, your joints I mean, you've stopped being a dancer. When your nuts have stopped hurting, which I'm sure they haven't since we got here, he'll break your heart. Trust me. Peter, tell him I'm right."

"She'll say anything to keep you."

"Of course I will."

"He sounds like a trophy, that's about it," Peter spoke, barely moving his lips.

"You're saying he's too good for me?"

"Get him to un-blank that stare of yours, then we'll talk."

"That blank stare is called concentration. Maybe you should try it."

"Yeah? Well you should be concentrating on your audience—or maybe you are—yourself and your big ego."

"Hey! No nut-cracking. Grow up. Both of you!" Rachelle turned to me. "The broken heart? It will make you a great dancer."

THAT NIGHT I PHONED Daniel from the stage door, between acts.

He said, "Just talking to you gives me a boner." And I danced act two with as much of an erection as a dance belt will allow.

I was hooked like Juliet, believing nothing would keep us apart. Not even the warring dance factions of the West versus the East, the Vaganovas versus the Cecchettis. It was a dream, me fleeing the Place des Arts fortress in a cab, through the lighted boulevards of Montreal. Prokofiev's music finally making sense. The ebb and flow of the lover's *pas de deux* went over and over in my head all the way to Daniel's place, where he met me at the door. He kissed me. "How was the show?"

"Fine. Peter was Paris. They loved him. He's on top of the world."

"He'll go far."

"He might," I said, but Daniel was already on his way up the stairs and all I could do was follow his broad smooth back, semi-naked ass in loose pyjama bottoms, and wide feet up the narrow stairs to the rooftop for Campari and soda mixed with foreplay. Why had he said that about Peter? Was I too easy? Or stupid? But Daniel's grasp reassured me. We had a hot nightcap and our own twisted *pas de deux* until the sheets of his bed were wet with sour Pierre Cardin–scented sweat. In the times to follow, it started with him heavy on my chest. The pressure of his growing erection would press up between us. I can't sit still when I think of it. (Evidently I have no trouble separating a broken heart from the sex.) Or he'd press his torso just below my rib cage, arch his back, raise his head and we'd wait and wait and drip and then he'd go tight and his thighs would tremble just before exploding—shooting up between us, onto my neck, the odd times stinging my eye. After, I wanted to own him; do something to show this was mine; write *I love you* with my tongue, tracing the silhouette of his back and spine, over his tailbone and into the softness of his dark barely hairy crack, down his thigh, back of the knee, vein-wrapped calf, the scar that had made him a legend, over heel to the rough part of his tarsal where the years of dancing could be counted by the shades and toughness of the skin. I wanted to devour him.

"Stay." He had said the magic word.

"Where?" I had acted surprised.

"Here, in Montreal. The Conservatoire isn't great, but it's not the prairies."

"It's been on my mind—six weeks of forty below zero, then the tour—besides Kharkov has gone off me."

"He'll use you up. Now is your chance. I'll find you work."

Somewhere there was a Romeo waxing poetic to the sun rising in the east as I got back to the hotel. As usual, Rachelle had built a giant nest of pillows in one bed with herself, the not-quite-dead dying swan, unglamorously earplugged, eye-masked, propped sound asleep and snoring with the TV still flickering. Prince Charming, even beautiful in his sleep, was in the other bed, which we normally shared. I was exhausted, confused and getting tired of listening to myself around these two, knowing they weren't convinced of my decision. My body ached, but I did something I hadn't done in ages. I crawled under the covers and held Peter tight.

He whispered, "Kharkov kissed me." Peter was awake.

"What?"

Peter turned. "He kissed me when I got back to the hotel. I was hoping for a new contract, to be honest, but he closed the door to his room and..."

"Fuck. That pig!" I surprised myself with my own feelings of jealousy. What was it I did not have? Peter always had admirers, and he never seemed moved by it.

"He was decent. Not piggish. Coy, I guess."

"Then?"

"I left. I mean what do you talk about with a Russian masochist whose English is limited?"

"Sounds like you're up next for soloist." So thrived Kharkov, and his habit of making appointments with the certainty of being thanked in a big way. Two of the principals had spent several years of their prime thanking him. Kharkov would find Peter delicious.

LATER THAT MORNING MY resolve was even greater. It was true: Daniel was showing me the way to my dreams, and reminding me not to sit back on the comfort of a Company contract. At the same time, I had fallen for him and all that goes along with it; it joined me to humanity, the universe and everything in between. Walls fell and I discovered a hidden energy. I became a greater dancer than I had ever dreamed of—jumped higher, turned faster, balanced longer. There was a completion to my technique. I believed in myself, one hundred percent, for the first time. In laymen's terms, if I were a secretary I'd type faster, burn through the filing system; a house painter, I'd end up with the Sistine Chapel in fifteen shades of neon; a bricklayer, I'd redo the pyramids with a smart Egyptian faux finish. It all became so easy, so effortless. My body was rubber for those weeks—pliable, solid, tensile—all with very little sleep. Supernatural. My knees? No idea. Ask any dancer who has had time to be in love. I shone in Company class, stood in the front, flew across the stage, intimidated the soloists and principals. I couldn't get enough of dance, or love. Did Daniel feel the same? I was too busy with all this to have any idea.

At the height of it, I gave my notice and final bow to the Company's repertoire. As Daniel said, "Why do they call it *repertoire*? It's been done, over and over and over: Tybalt, Romeo, *The Nutcracker* prince, any prince, anything dusted off and redone, from Ashton to Balanchine." So I stepped out of the royal storybook, to become a finer dancer. I traded that rush of a curtain call—opening my arms wide enough to embrace three or four thousand people, and then seeing, when the house lights went up, the faces whose collective breath I'd sensed throughout the performance, all of them cheering, as they stood in one motion—for a promise of even greater praise. Someday they would clap for me alone as I stepped forward out of the line. It was time to remind myself of that dream once again. So many times since then, I have forgotten the dream.

I vowed to excel and pay attention to my technique, establish a strong foundation and secure a long career, with Daniel's help, not to mention his international connections. This was so much more than the limited choice I had become so used to. I had come so close to being satisfied as a big swan in a small lake.

I met Kharkov in a makeshift office in Place des Arts, after company class, while I was still soaked and high from whatever it was that was forcing me to go beyond my limits. Kharkov was wearing a tailored Italian suit that he'd obviously picked up in Montreal. Everyone had been shopping their heads off before going back to Canada's breadbasket. "It's time to move on," I said.

Kharkov sat still, put his hand to his mouth. I could see the wheels turning. Finally he spoke. He told me I wasn't serious. He threatened that if I paused now, all the young dancers nipping at my ankles would finally overtake me. (*You don't cross Kharkov*, was a Company mantra.) "You aren't dancing well, you know. But I liked you. I think you know that." As with all the dancers, I hated his grip on us. In a flash he could praise you or put you down, leave you a crumpled heap of fucked-up-ness if you cared—the humiliation and manipulation, his temper, his mood swings. Ballerinas would be in tears one moment and hugging him the next. "Promise me you won't come back. I've seen so many dancers go after something, fail, wind up so far away from where they first started, I'll never understand—bank tellers, bored mothers, strippers even. And they somehow think I will take them back. This is final—enough of your stubbornness—the Company does not take lightly to this kind of thing. You are too young, too insignificant. Are you absolutely sure?" He needed to know. It always looked so much worse for Kharkov when he lost a dancer he hadn't fired or whose dismissal hadn't been discussed with the board. In fact he'd been known to strike deals of irreconcilable differences, so both could save face. "You have always lacked soul. There is nothing to see when I look in your eyes. I see nothing."

"Yes sir. Thank you, sir."

"Perhaps Monsieur Tremaine can teach you something." He knew. "Now get out of here before I do something both of us will regret."

I will never know what that something might have been. Would he have kissed me like he kissed Peter? I doubt it. Maybe he wanted to strangle me. That, we both would have regretted.

But I was full of the good dancing I was doing. I looked down at my thighs, my crotch, my feet, my hands hanging at my side, parts of me I only normally saw in a mirror. I was an asset—why wasn't he begging me to stay? I hated myself for having a brief moment of self-doubt. Although I wanted to leave with as little fanfare as possible, it would have been nice to have him regret losing me.

It was time to dance *and* love as others had done. I needed to keep following my heart. It was there, tucked inside Daniel's sternum. That's where I saw my future. I saw with conviction the rejigging of my technique, establishing myself in the East, and most of all, endless love.

I met Rachelle at Dunn's for one last cigarette and coffee. There, surrounded by busy waiters, customers lined up at the door and glass cases of cheesecakes, we tried our best not to get too sentimental. "I'll write to you about it."

"Just phone. How was Kharkov?"

"He squirmed. You know Kharkov."

Rachelle *mmmm*'d like she didn't believe a word. "Don't take any shit. The dance world doesn't like outsiders."

"The dance world *is* outsiders."

"Not to sound negative, but I hope your prince is all he's made out to be. You deserve it."

She had her prince, and I wanted mine. "Take care of Peter."

"You're leaving a trail of broken hearts."

"Peter? I think we sorted that out long ago."

"He's a sensitive boy."

"Kharkov likes sensitive."

"Sounds like he's up next for soloist." Rachelle was a perceptive girl.

"Did he tell you?"

"I heard you guys. I know all, see all. I am a woman, for God's sakes. I just ... I just don't believe it."

"Me neither."

"No. Honestly. This isn't you. It's like you've been brainwashed. Yes, you're dancing better because of all the endorphins in your systems, but it's making you crazy."

"Cake?"

"Oh God please no. My thighs are starting to squeak; I'll have to start greasing them."

When we were paying, I bought a whole cheesecake for later with Daniel. "It must be love." Rachelle jabbed me in the ribs, her momentary seal of approval.

After the show that night, I packed my things and Peter, Rachelle and I opened a much-needed bottle of champagne.

"Altogether now, you know it by heart: Give me Veuve or give me death."

"God, how many of my paycheques have gone up in bubbles since you two moved in?"

We drank it in a kind of noisy silence: Hotels doors banged, someone knocked on our door and an elevator bell kept dinging as if to mark the very last moments we would have together. But we sat, with our backs to it, in our own silence. "I can't talk or I'll cry," Rachelle said, breaking the silence.

"You'll probably get Tybalt," I said to Peter.

"No. Too good-looking," said Rachelle. "He'll get Paris and a really good role in something new."

"Something new?"

"Mark my words."

Soon my thoughts shifted to the future, my future. All I could think about was getting to Daniel, and sharing another celebratory bottle with him. I didn't want to drag this out any longer. Rachelle would get weepy if she had any more to drink—there was still a stocked mini-bar after all—and Peter was probably just thinking about his next role. I'm sure I'd already departed as far as they were concerned. We kissed, hugged, I took my bags and my cheesecake and tried not to run into anyone else, as I ran to him.

WHEN I GOT TO Daniel's, we celebrated the Company's departure and my new life. In the moonlight on the bed, after Daniel separated the seeds from the stems, we smoked and then we stuffed ourselves on cake and each other. We lay on our backs looking out into the treetops and he told me about an abusive father and a doting mother as he traced his fingers through the shadows above our heads. I told him about the big empty house in Edmonton and the anticipation of siblings who never arrived—how my father's family humiliated my mother until it was revealed it was father who was reproductively challenged. (Was I a one-shot deal? If not, who was my real father?) Father appeased his guilt, starting with her first mink coat and continuing with her very own convertible—that woman drove a shrewd bargain. As a result, my mother referred to me as her "perfect boy." The term was loaded with, "Since I can only have one, then he is perfect; in fact he is the only perfect male in this house ..."

There, in the dark, was something I had never shared with another person. We weren't hiding in a closet or a motel room. He stayed on the bed and I moved to the floor, leaning against the bed. He touched the top of my head with his long fingers. We were two men, two complete and naked physical beings, comfortable with ourselves.

"It's time," he said. "I want to make love to you, properly."

"Soon."

"I want to."

"Now?"

"You sound surprised."

I hoped the marijuana might make it easier, but the pain was excruciating. I always thought it would be so natural with the right person. But I ended up with my face pressed into the pillow, biting hard into it, trying to suppress a scream.

He gave up and dropped, deadweight, onto me. I whispered to him, "Thank you for being so understanding." Then he sighed and rolled off.

Old thoughts about my inadequacy now haunted me. My mother drove me, her perfect boy, in her new Cadillac to the doctor's office while I sat bent over, a seven-year-old with a searing pain in my abdomen like something was stuck inside. The pain stopped my breath, a herniated something, an incomplete something else, a testicle that hadn't dropped. It was a series of trips to the doctor and operations in hospitals.

It always started with me standing on a small box in the doctor's examination room, my pants around my ankles while one or two doctors poked my abdomen, stared at my penis, or shoved their dry fingers behind my scrotum and up into me so hard that they raised me up off my little snow-soaked socked feet. The efforts to find the source of that pain and rip it out blinded me. They laid their big fingers on my stomach and pressed here and there on my naked body, staring at my front, touching me.

I was innocent until a fifth visit and that one doctor looked up at my face and our eyes met. He looked like one of the ballet princes, and I retracted my hips as my penis began to stir for the first time I was aware of. While I was consumed with guilt, my mother was more concerned with her lipstick and the dashing doctors. A few years later, I was back to the doctor for another hernia, or was it bedwetting? I remember my mother had her hair done for the occasion. The doctor dug around in my underwear pressing on my abdomen, intestines, stomach, balls, pulling on them as I tried not to show spontaneous arousal. The thought of his staring, and rough pokes and soft lingering fingers, while I looked at the top of his head, sent a terrible thrill through me. Years later when I would dream of the visits to the doctor I would wet the bed, but not with piss.

WE LAY WITH THE streetlight and shadows playing across our skin. I vowed to give up anything for love.

Two

A DANCER'S BARE FEET approach the earth, toes extended. The soles, broad and thick, reach for the earth's membrane then cushion the impact, draw history and resonance through the weathered skin from core to core. The soul is shaken free of its trance. The body again ascends—as the feet beat back at the world with *entrechat* and *frappé*—to the stars.

A DOOR ABOVE ME slams and my clothes fly down the open space at my side. I rise, look down the twenty-two-odd flights as a stray sock spirals defiantly to the bottom. Something cracks onto the floor below, cufflinks or my watch. It doesn't matter. My belt buckle? And no one will come after me. I am in no man's land, in the shaft of the sleek condo where I got everything I had ever asked for, or deserved, in a matter of seconds.

Sunday morning came quietly in Daniel's tree house. We woke late, and there was no "the Company"; no daily rehearsal sheet slipped under the door; no Company class; no dour-faced dancers poking forks in lone grapes on breakfast plates and dreaming about their second cigarette of the day. Once again I was outside my safety zone. There would be no equity-minimum-for-second-soloist paycheque in two weeks. There would be no speculation on who would get what role in the coming season. Before, I had paid-for dreams and goals, but now they were replaced by free promises.

By now, the Company would be assembled in the hotel lobby for a bus to an early flight back to Winnipeg, welcoming a day off. They would later go for brunch and then put their fingers down their throats and puke, or sit in a movie theatre and worry about their 102 minutes of inactivity. Rachelle would read the Sunday *New York Times* Gordon had picked up earlier at the Fort Garry, spread on the floor (with the bright prairie afternoon sun filling the room, making it difficult to ignore the streaked window and the gathering dust bunnies) smoking something harsh, drinking pots of coffee, disappearing with Gordon to the bedroom at regular intervals, then making him dinner and curling up on the couch for hours of TV and wondering if the Company would make her a principal dancer someday—why hadn't they already?

Peter would be playing with himself in his room, thinking no one could tell, or maybe he'd have his perfect feet shoved under the radiator to make them even more perfect. God bless those poor overstretched tendons. Then he'd probably get together with a few of the dancers for coffee, and not so much a chat as a series of agreeable grunts. He was social that way. They'd have Monday morning off.

I wondered if my days off with Daniel would be like Rachelle's, until he whispered in my ear, "Come, we have a breakfast to go to."

"So early?"

"*Mon ami*, it is no longer early, we have slept late and will just make it."

When you get to know someone, you find out things about them that you overlooked—how they snore, chew, sip, wipe their nose with their knuckle, how sloppy they are or, in Daniel's case, how meticulous: his attention to the order he dressed himself—shirt first; how many times he washed his hands—frequently; when he washed his hands—always after touching me. What did he think of me, and the way I piled my clothes on the chair, and how my bed-head looked, and how my breath smelled and how the sheets had creased my face? Did he notice?

We rushed out the door, Daniel looking far more together than I felt.

"Welcome to your first day as an independent person, not following the pack."

"It feels strange."

"Good I hope."

"Good." But I felt like the prodigal son, again.

BACK AT THE BEGINNING of my big dreams, I had this groovy little dance bag I'd bought at Army & Navy. After a year of dancing, disguised as swim practice, it all came out. I was between swim practice and dance class, and I had come home to wolf down my dinner. I tossed the bag by the front door and, as bags do, it fell open. Dad came home a few mouthfuls into my meatloaf. After the called *Hi* and the requisite, *Do you want a drink?* he walked into the living room with the bag, threw it on the floor, where the contents spilled—the shoes, tights, leg warmers, the layers of ripped T-shirts and sweat socks and the dance belt. "What are these?" he asked. "Something for Halloween?"

Ballet slippers. For my father, I imagine this was something that only happened to other people's children, in other cities. This was something you only heard about and never, ever dreaded because it seemed so far-fetched.

"It's my dance stuff." It lay on the living room floor, deflated, dirty too.

"Dance stuff? What kind of dance stuff?"

"Shoes." (*Ballet slippers* caught in my throat.) "Slippers."

"Slippers. What the Christ?" he said. Well, wouldn't it have been an education to see me sew the elastics on them, and carefully sew exactly where the shoe folds down? You can't sew the elastic just anywhere, and if you want two elastics to hug the slipper to your foot, then you've got a little geometry to do.

"What's this?" he asked in a confident monotone, as if the battle had been won and he was simply making a point. "A bathing suit or some queer kind of jockstrap?"

"It's a dance belt."

"A what?"

I wanted so badly to tell it like this: tighter than a Speedo and smaller than one. It cuts up your ass-crack. You pull it on, then grab your nuts and dick and pull up. The old ladies in the audiences watching *The Nutcracker* for the umpteenth time say why do they have to have those horrid bulges? It's anatomy, honey. Arms, legs, boobs and cocks. They've been around for a while. So your nuts are crammed into these things because between your *entrechat* and anything else that slams your thighs together at the speed of light, if your nuts aren't out of the way, you could end up seeing stars. The only hazard when the equipment is out there is turning to your Swan or Princess or Sultana and in the midst of careless fouetté or pirouette having her knee whack your nuts. The pain. The numbing, bent-over-crippling, dizzying pain. It happens to all of us at least once.

"What else? A goddamn tutu?"

"A T-shirt." Something loose and rag-like, showing tendon. Muscle. Line. That's the dance bag. Maybe a skanky towel for the shower. "It's ballet dance stuff. Tights, too, for men. Black, is that okay? Male dancers wear them."

"Part of your school work?"

"No."

"And what about swimming?"

"I still swim."

"In your tights?"

"In my Speedo."

"How long has this been going on?"

"About a year."

"Where?"

"The studio—the one near your office. Madame..."

"Défilé?"

"How do you know?"

"She's been there for years. She came in for checkups—when she could afford it."

He turned to my mother. "How long have you known this?" But she just took a sip of her drink and went back to the kitchen.

"She didn't know," I said. He'd made his point and from that moment we rarely talked. I had wronged him and his dreams and his agenda. My mother stopped talking to either of us. She'd sit in the sewing room under her poster of Nureyev and Fonteyn. I imagined her weeping though I could never be sure. I had done enough to shame them for life. There was no turning back. The distance helped me find a kind of bravado, and as a result I made another magical leap toward becoming a competent dancer. I had little—even less—to lose anymore. During his pre-dinner, post-looking-in-people's-rotting-mouths drink, I'm sure I asked him why he was so against something so cultured, so refined, so creative. Maybe I just said, "Why do you hate that I dance?"

"I'll tell you something about Madame Défilé. She stopped coming to see me because she owed me so much. I gave up trying to get even a nickel out of her. Do you want to end up like that? Teaching little girls to point their toes. Worrying about when the power will be cut?"

"She danced with Les Ballets Russes."

"And she's going to die a poor, old lady."

"But I'm good. I really am."

"You don't have the talent. After one year, at your age?"

"I do."

"Fine. Do what you like, take up knitting for God's sake, as long as it doesn't interfere with school."

It was long overdue, this parting of ways, and after that I wondered if part of Madame Défilé's fiery temper tantrums toward me were for my father.

DANIEL'S WORDS BROKE MY reverie. "You will make your parents proud someday, and put that Company to shame. Believe me."

And the streets in Montreal were different now that I was free.

We went north along rue Berri, past rows of old walk-ups, and stopped in front of an iron staircase leading up to a massive flat. The stranger who answered the door raised his eyebrows to Daniel. Daniel touched the middle of my back and gently pressed me through the doorway. Six men sat on low plush couches and rat-a-tatted Québécois. One of them, who had the look of Hitler youth—good-looking but evil at the same time with a protruding brow and chin, and wavy, very bottle-blond hair—massaged my scalp and told me I was too tense. This was typical; I seemed to attract these kinds of comments. And the massage didn't surprise me as I am sure he had hoped it would, because Kharkov had reminded me more than once that as long as I remained an uptight Anglo-Saxon, I would be stuck in the corps, then after I became second soloist, it was forever second soloist, never principal as long as, and on and on...

The others ignored me.

We sat around a low table and alternated drinking mimosas with dark coffee and nibbling daintily on lox, cream cheese and bagels, which was heaven and hell for me: it was my day off and I needed to eat, but with reckless guilt-free abandon, not restrained bites. Sunday was time-out from diet, discipline and dance. For two hours, I nodded politely at their babble, but knew my cursed blank stare was most likely working against me. I understood them perfectly when they said I didn't understand French, which happened before and after pauses, but then their chattering would start up again. I so wanted to tell them I understood French quite well, but not Québécois.

None of them cared about the Company, or me, or dance at all for that matter. Not one of them had seen the show. In retrospect, Daniel must have had some disdain in socializing with dancers. Justifiably so—dancers could be crushingly boring to outsiders, never to themselves: when you are taught that what you do is the most important, difficult and disciplined work a human could ever do, what else can there possibly be to talk about? As for these guys, they were probably trading decorating tips, or who had winked at them in the past two days. I'll never know.

It was Sunday, our first whole day together. One of the men, Hugues, the Aryan who massaged my head, walked us to his place in the Old Port. I couldn't help dwelling on the idea that Hugues and Daniel had known each other much better than they let on. I was feeling more and more like the soft touch in this *pas de trois*. Regardless, he had the decency to point out places of interest, mostly historic buildings that housed restaurants where, he said, I might be able to get a job if my French was okay. I looked to Daniel, but he soldiered on, his royal highness deep in thought until he spoke. "It will be better for you to have your own space. There are too many distractions at my place. You will be staying with Hugues. He has an extra room."

"Of course. Perfect." I vividly remember that snubbed feeling, but I quickly displayed my bravado. "Now I don't have to look for a place."

"What about a job?" Hugues asked. "You can't work wit' no French. And you can't pay the rent wit' no work."

"I'll be dancing, that's my job, and mon français n'est pas parfait mais pas mal de tout, by the way." Hugues grinned. I looked to a distracted Daniel for support, but he had that distant look I had seen in the studio. I had resources to take me to the end of the summer.

"We will still have lots of time to spend together," Daniel assured me.

"Of course," I replied, as if it was I who was reassuring him.

Hugues' place was just so, all light maple and clean-cut corners that looked onto a neighbouring limestone wall in a narrow alley. At the far end of the alley, overfed tourists waddled up a cobblestone street eighteen hours a day—on the way from the metro to the crêperies of Old Montreal, and on toward the ice cream and beavertail booths of the Old Port, their floral prints and gaudy perma-press created a travelling kaleidoscopic parade of continuous colour in the distance. Fortunately the only sound that made it down the alley was the clicking of horses' hooves from the *calèche*. It was all a lifetime away from my room in Rachelle's house on the banks of the Assiniboine, in a city surrounded by infinity. I imagined Montreal throbbing with an energy of troubled cafés where lovers argued, and smoky bars where they made love in the dark corners.

Later that afternoon, leaving Hugues to his place, Daniel and I wandered silently along the Old Port to a precious gem store owned, he told me, by geologists. It was the kind of place where tiny lights in the ceiling focus on shiny chunks of polished stone, and people's whispers were swallowed by thick grey carpet. He asked me to wait outside. I was dying to see what it was he was buying for me. It was one of the most perfect afternoons I had known.

"Do you mind if I ask how it was for you, when you stopped?"

"Considering I had no choice, a relief. It is nice to go out on a high note. Of course it has taken me years to look at it that way. But that is the reality. Look at the icons. Marilyn. Judy. Piaf."

"You're an icon?"

"*Pas de tout*, but people who never saw me dance have turned me into a legend. To be honest, I miss it desperately. Watching you do

43

entrechat or *tour jetés* or anything eats me up inside. I was so much better."

"Will I ever be great?"

"You shouldn't have to ask such a question. Being a fine dancer is so much more than greatness will allow. To be great you need an ego, and you must be lacking a soul—like me." He laughed at this, but we knew it had an element of truth. "It will be up to you to be fine, but not great."

That week, we met for meals and sex and I took open class at the Conservatoire. I never stayed over at Daniel's again; he would come over to my place and then go home. We needed the time—a courtship, I told myself—to get to know each other.

He came over late on Saturday night, a week into my new life, after attending a closed rehearsal. Daniel lay on the bed staring at the ceiling, his nose whistling, after another sweaty attempt to penetrate me, while I sat on the toilet telling myself the pain would lapse.

"One week. It's been over one week," he said. "You're afraid to let go. You will never be free as an artist or a dancer if you can't let go. You will be nothing more than an uptight Anglo from the prairies." Then he left.

We were good with silences—connected enough to not need to speak. In spite of this little obstacle, I felt something was about to change with some kind of proposal. Then, with the little piece of polished rock he would give me, we would become the toast of the Montreal dance world. Our names, John and Daniel, would be on everyone's lips. I would be his protegé. He would be my master.

SITTING HERE ON THE stairs, even now, body as it is, bereft of tears, blood and sweat, it seems absurd to wonder how he saw me. What is a bad decision? What's the difference between a bad decision and adventure, or a good decision and boredom? Do all decisions make themselves? I haven't thought of him wistfully for months, almost a year. I haven't pined. You don't believe that? And I can't even remember the last time I got one hundred percent sentimental over him and had a good old-fashioned wine-soaked wallow. The cornerstone of lust holds up those castles in the sky.

It was after I bought Egyptian cotton sheets and pillowcases at Ogilvy's, and the salesman made a fuss over the thread count, something I'd never heard of, that Daniel became scarce. He was busy coaching, and when I pressed him for a rendezvous, he stopped returning my calls.

I'm no stalker, but love does strange things. I didn't want to sit in our café alone, wondering if he'd drop by, staring at a bunch of other sallow-faced intense couples. I didn't want to feel like my ass (the gluteus maximus part) was turning to putty either. I picked another café nearer to the Conservatoire, where he did most of his work, and drank endless refills of café au lait *en bol* and ate just one more *croissante au beurre* and listened to ballet brats complain about their bony knees or flat arches, and wondered just how much butter it would take to turn my obliques into love handles. I didn't want to forget what I was: a dancer, not just someone in love. It was every part of my life. It was me. I couldn't live without it. But it seemed the magic was slowly leaving my body.

I looked for him at Eddie Toussaint, but years ago they had banned him from their studios for artistic differences. Les Ballets Jazz was on a Central American tour. I finally got up the courage to inquire to the tight-lipped receptionist at the Conservatoire. She told me he dropped by sometimes, but only to use the space. She thought maybe he'd gone to New York, on invitation or on an emergency. Was it a family emergency and he couldn't get in touch with me before he left? Did he leave a message? Had there been some miscommunication? Was he too preoccupied to even talk to me? As Rachelle said, "If you believe that, you'll buy this watch."

When I asked Hugues, again, if there had been a message, he said the same thing, "Pas de message," imitating my harsh English accent. He was as helpful as his face was angelic. I knew he knew something, but he probably figured this *maudit anglais* didn't deserve a decent answer. He seemed permanently secretive. He said there was no word, not even from a friend who fed Daniel's cat. He had a cat?

"I talked to someone who talked to someone else who said d'ey saw him, said d'ey t'ought 'e was back," Hugues finally said.

"He's back?"

"Didn't you know he might have a job as a *répétiteur* in New York?" Hugues grinned. "You know him. 'e 'as lots of friends, you 'ave to share 'im, and you 'ave to enjoy him when 'e is around." After that, Hugues didn't speak English so well.

Add to this foundering romance the fact that there seemed no plan of attack for my physique, and I lost my footing. I had avoided the Conservatoire long enough. I started taking drop-in classes, hoping it would eventually lead me to him and be noticed at the same time. I could wait no longer for some kind of dream of a mentorship with Daniel. I couldn't dance in a bubble. I finally decided to audition for the Conservatoire, but no one took much notice, and one of their uptight *répétiteurs* had the gall to suggest I take a simpler class. I had gone from professional soloist, well second soloist, in the West to corps in the East. Dancers return to the basics occasionally, it does us good, so I took my training in hand and surrounded myself with summer students following a pounding drill by a Chanel No. 5–marinated, Gestapo torturess. The Conservatoire studios were legendary, but paid the price for their nastiness. Although their teachers had produced fine dancers, the best had gone off to New York and companies in Europe.

"Your technique has been forced," the torturess said. "You will 'ave to start over. You will 'ave to relearn."

Then another frustrated emaciated has-been picked up where the torturess left off, in a men's class. Between pliés we did the usual sets of push-ups, with her on our back, chin-ups with her pulling down on our ankles, and pliés with each of us sitting on a partner's shoulders, to make us solid. "Your plié is completely wrong." She pinched my lower back with her claws. I can still feel it.

The third blow came from a faded legend. Not a Daniel, but someone who owed his reputation to all of the years that had passed. The other dancers called him the "Sugar Plum Fairy" under their breath. He was an overgrown, over-the-hill, alcoholic *boy* whose shape changed between each binge and purge of booze and pizza, gravy-soaked frites and *Frusen Glädjé*, hold the waffle cone. He whined, "You just aren't serious enough."

I'd heard about his definition of serious: he went down on his knees to keep his job. But all he did was pray and cry and beg. I refused to beg, but returning to the basics for a while wouldn't hurt my technique. I had to trust what Daniel had said. So I ate less, drank more coffee, warmed up earlier, stayed later, took every class on the schedule. And I made sure to keep my appointment with Madame Ranoff, the artistic director, to make it clear what my plans were.

Madame's office was dark. The collected years of history crowded the atmosphere, robbed the air of oxygen, turned living beings to chalk. Madame looked as transparent as the ghosts in the photographs on her wall. Her old skin was waxworks smooth, her smile small, tight and forced. Every time she opened her mouth her dentures clicked. She had been making tough, do-or-die decisions for years to keep her dancers working. She was another who had danced with the Original Ballet Russes. And like the truly intimidating legends—Graham and Makarova—she had a rock-hard soul. Single-mindedness, time and obsession turned people like Madame Ranoff and the Sugar Plum Fairy into legends.

I didn't tell her I had cut my ties, or about my training in the West. I was a fool to think I could marry into the Montreal dance world. She must have known. They all must have thought I was an opportunist. When a dancer leaves a company, the news spreads like syphilis. And when a dancer takes up with the likes of a Daniel Tremaine there will be a price to pay. Besides, it had always been the West against the East. The West was viewed with disdain and mild curiosity, as was the East by the West, perhaps with a little more envy. "You must start over," she told me. "How long have you been dancing?" I thought she was being sarcastic or exaggerating but she meant every word as blankly and blandly as her lifeless face muttered it.

"Almost six years, and I used to swim..." My voice trailed off. She couldn't care less.

"You should be better than this," she said through a burgeoning fake smile.

"But Madame, I was soloist, second soloist, with the Company."

"The Company," she sighed. "They have a unique way of doing things. Not that I disagree, but they have their own set of laws." She precisely applied condescending laughter to underscore her comment: "You must forget what you learned."

I was a specimen: the boy from the West who now had no technique, from the Company that had no standards. This boosted the Conservatoire's collective ego. "I would like to audition for the Conservatoire."

"In due course."

Of course I hadn't kissed one ass since taking class. And as far as they were concerned I was no more than some star's arrogant bumboy. Tarnished goods. I had one disconnected connection. I had simply traded one set of lies for another. There were too many dancers in this city and not enough jobs.

Forget my knees or forced turnout, my heart had become the pulled muscle. I could point to the pain the way I could point to tendonitis or a strained groin. How could a few weeks of simple self-indulgent wallowing for a questionable love-of-my-life do so much physical damage, when it had taken me almost eight years to become a dancer? Something left my body as quickly as it had appeared. My spirit perhaps. I was lead. I had lost my centre of gravity. My limbs pulled me off my axis and had become my enemies. I was shocked at myself, and my clumsy appendages.

Booze helped. I drank in my room, and cried like Cleopatra into my Egyptian cotton pillowcases so Hugues wouldn't hear. I went out, too. I had never been to a bona fide gay club or bar. It just wasn't part of the discipline. There had been the odd outing with the corps to a questionable place called Tiffany's in downtown Winnipeg but then only for a birthday. No one tried to burn up the disco floor with so much classical technique running through their veins, and so many critical eyes watching. Besides, you needed to be at least tipsy to do so, and booze had calories. (I'll say it again, we are a boring lot.) It had always been bed by ten except on performance nights.

I unpacked a T-shirt, and the cowboy jeans for house parties. I must have been determined to re-fire the engine, get the drive back, find someone, find Daniel (I felt like he was always just around the next corner), who could make me whole again. I left home at eleven that night, after three hours sleep. I found the club off an alley of another alley. I didn't know what the hell I was doing there. Escaping the noise in my head and the heaviness in my heart? And every time someone started up a conversation I must have been pigeon-holed as that tight-assed Anglophone, or some American tourist looking for a real Frenchman. I couldn't hear French or English. I was caught in a twilight zone of smoking men who weren't interested in me, and whom I found unappealing. I skulked in the dark corners with my rum and Coke and dreamed of what I'd do with some guy dressed like a lumberjack, with hairy forearms the size of my thighs.

No one had ever appreciated me the way Daniel had, and no one then in that bar seemed to find me attractive at all. I seemed to be disintegrating, like the elastic in over-washed tights. I kept my eyes peeled for his dark profile to appear somewhere in the crowd. It was only him who had made me feel desirable—lips, nose and all. How could I have felt so good? The more of my body he appreciated, the more of me there seemed to exist. As if my physical self was gradually coming into being for the first time. I'd only ever known myself from the inside out and he made me aware of the weight of me—my mass and the space I was taking up on the planet, and in his eyes. But love and Daniel were nowhere to be found.

THERE GOES MY NOSE. Now I am bleeding from both ends. If someone comes into the stairwell I'll tell them I'm rehearsing a scene from Julius Caesar. Why Daniel? Why thoughts like this now? Am I not pummelled enough? My mind is searching independently for a resolution and it wants to start there, back in Montreal. I assure you I am not expecting that handsome prince at the end of this bloodletting. I would rather die.

IN TRUTH "HE" WAS a kind of demented self-flattery for me, as in, *How could someone so masculine and so commanding and so dashing, love someone so much less so (as I perceived myself to be)? That was it— Hey, everybody, look who loves me. I must be worthy.*

It was the kind of thought that kept me from doing a complete dying swan. I remember Kent once said maybe I really had been in love. He said that maybe I was being too hard on love and on myself.

He said I should give love more of a chance. Give myself more of a chance at being human and knowing what it is love can do. But it's still too soon to think about Kent; we've only just hit the concrete, and I'm still whimpering about Daniel. Kent, in his quiet, wise way, knew more about love than I ever will. He may have been right, but maybe I knew more about lust. For the truly hard-hearted, lust can paradoxically be safer; if beauty can be skin deep then lust can be a little deeper. But in those months, I found something that had only ever existed onstage—my ego.

Since men didn't seem to be swarming me like sylphs to a poet, my confidence dissipated proportionally. If I had pursued those strangers in the bar, they wouldn't have liked what they found: a tired dancer with a tight ass. "What a waste," they'd say. "You have such a nice ass." Maybe it was evident. This was the new meaning of "rock bottom."

Pride kept me from admitting that all Daniel wanted was my supple ass, and who knows for how long? Our survival instinct keeps us from such thoughts. In my room I drank my savings while I stared at that limestone wall. Lost sleep. Daniel had told me once in the early stages that I was sentimental "in a good way," spiritual too, and sensitive—meaning he believed he could pass judgement, meaning he was full of it, meaning I let him do so, meaning I was blinder than Alicia Alonso. Now I even recall on our last night in Hugues' living room, draped over the sedan, he had told Hugues he didn't really know where we were going. I pretended not to understand as I freely and stupidly blurted I was in love, in my *Le Spectre de la Rose*–tinted glasses.

AFTER DILUTING MY PRIDE with a gut-bloating six-pack and a few glasses of red wine, I made the call to Kharkov. Who knows? Maybe he'd think I could lure Daniel back to Winnipeg, and then he'd take me back no question.

Kharkov would not take my call, of course, but gave very specific instructions to his secretary Miss Friesen, a severe and uptight balletomane who got into ballet politics and mind games like a dirty shirt, and whose name provided no end of amusement for us more vengeful types. I was ready to grovel. "Can't I please speak with him?"

"Kharkov wanted me to pass along his regrets. I don't think it would make any difference. He has already signed on four very *strong* males—two from Texas and two of our apprentices. He has to start rehearsing them immediately for the coming season. I'm sorry."

Miss Freezin' was still so full of it. She couldn't have been happier to take my call. Kharkov would use it as an example to the Company as he had in the past. He'd gloat, then they'd gloat, thinking they had landed in the biggest pot of ballet honey around, but it just wasn't the truth. The truth was that they had a job.

I called Rachelle after finishing all the wine. Her voice grounded me. "Hello prodigal son. We miss you like stinkweed. You're drunk. Are you with your hubby? Are you coming back?"

"That's optimistic."

"Which one?"

"All of the above, although I am quite inebriated."

"A little game of hide and seek?"

"Good news travels fast."

"Never mind. Your big plunge has caused a wave of self-doubt. Three have taken offers to dance in Atlanta. You probably could have gone with them or negotiated something. And the empty spaces have all been filled in. It's all up-and-comers and new blood. Speaking of blood, Gordon and I are getting a divorce. Do you want an invitation to the un-wedding?"

"If I were married, we could have a double divorce." It's funny how the memory of replacing the receiver of a phone into its cradle lasts longer than the feeling left by the call. I have this long internal list of post–hang-up-the-phone feelings. Someone tells you they are sick, someone accepts an offer, someone says goodbye, maybe for the very last time. That moment after stamps itself forever onto your consciousness. It could be filled with silence, or a clock ticking in an empty room, or the swirl of life still continuing around you in a train station or an airport. The echoed ring from the receiver being slammed down. In this instance it was the sight of gob and tears that dripped from my face onto the floor, as I had a drunken weep. I was still on the same patch of floor the next morning, shivering, when

Hugues took pity and actually brought me a café au lait and wrapped me in a comforter.

September's cold, clear blue skies shone over everything: the city, the mountain—forcing everyone to be happy about good weather for sleeping, and a fresh start at school or work after their vacation. And me, hungover on a Monday morning with nothing to start. What now? Shop around? Find a small company? Which one? Les Ballets Jazz? Eddie Toussaint? I looked too desperate. I was dancing like a fucking broken nutcracker.

Things have been a little too stop-and-start recently for me to be a big believer in fate; doors slam in front of you or behind you. It ends up meaning the same thing. I wouldn't have described what happened next as luck, not then. In retrospect it brought a crazy dancer, Bertrand, into my life, to save me from my ennui, unclog the cogs and get the next part of my story unstuck. But it's not what it sounds like—not another man for my dance card. Yes, I found him attractive, but only because he was the only person I'd ever met who was as crazy and as cockeyed-optimistic—a truly nutty look in his eyes—as me.

He was passionate about dance, had a gorgeous big muscular ass and a generously loaded crotch. He was a tight package of male body odour and lean muscle ready to burst. I only mention these qualities because that is how he danced, with a suppressed energy, as if he and everything in his tights would explode in a second. His face was Depardieu before food—the meandering nose, slightly crooked teeth and wide jaw and a kind of indefinable handsome wild aura. He had studied at the Conservatoire for the summer and we exchanged glances and nods in the hall from time to time. I wondered if he was gay—he wasn't—and he probably wondered why the hell I was staring at his crotch. We shared a *pas de deux* partner, which is where our paths crossed, in repertoire class.

He seemed to be the only one left to impress, so I tried to hide my increasingly shitty attitude. My dancing sucked and as a result I'd put up a barrier protected by a severe pout, the kind that says I expect more from myself and have danced much better than this, and you can go fuck yourself.

His English was minimal, and most Francophones couldn't understand his backwoods French. We managed on a different level. I'd speak my proper French mixed with *Franglais*, and he would reply in his French or with halting, breathy English that made him sound like he needed oxygen. In *pas de deux* class he would mutter profanities under his breath. He could be so particular that you thought you'd met *the* most precious bitch. His criticism, if that's what it was, forced the girls to glare and huff and fold their arms. He always snapped back at temperamental ballerinas. They already hated themselves for any extra pounds or ounces gained, especially in the summer with ice cream and slushies on every corner. They'd take it out on the men, like we were the ones who had fucked up. If one had a tantrum, Bertrand would match it and not hesitate to knock her off her pointe. I found this bravado so refreshing.

But I didn't escape his sharp eye and tongue; one day he had a go at me. We were in the dressing room and I was towelling myself dry, wondering how I could make a quick exit without the administrator asking me to pay up. Bertrand interrupted this plan. He started scolding me while he stood naked in the shower (giving me a good solid excuse to pay attention). "Why do you bodder?" he searched for each word. "I am so sick of passionless dancers. What is it d'at you want?"

"I want to dance, to perform. I can't be in fucking class *pour le reste de ma vie.*"

"*Il faut choisir.* There is nothing 'ere for you. You come home wit' me tonight and we can talk."

He was boarding at his brother's, a beautiful space, and not something any dancer I knew could probably ever afford. Every apartment in that city was huge and unusual, whereas out west, they were standard cookie cutter. After no food and a gallon of wine from the *dépanneur* across the street I felt I knew him. And we didn't sit; dancers drape or lie, or squat or scrunch cross-legged on the floor. We knead our feet, open our legs as wide as possible, to not miss a moment of stretching. I lay on my front like a frog on a specimen tray and drank wine while I worked on my turnout, letting gravity and inebriation pull my hips to the floor while my knees splayed in opposite directions.

I sensed Bertrand was a rare gentleman. I poured my heart out: "Have I made a mistake? Am I really that bad? Why won't they take me seriously?" I cried for my dancing (but crying for Daniel was likely a large part of that). I was messy, not the tight-assed Anglophone others had accused me of being. Not tonight. If he didn't think I was crazy then, he never would. When I was finished, it was his turn and he wouldn't shut up. I couldn't figure out what he was saying but it was something about a ballet company in Quebec City. He was rat-a-tatting his Lévis French. "You-stay-in-Montreal-and-train-at-da-Conservatoire-always-'oping-like-the-rest, or-come-dance-with-us-in-Quebec. The Conservatoire? Pah."

That's what I figured he was saying. It's so much easier to comprehend a second language when you're drunk. He finished up with a question, looking at me in silence until I realized he had asked me something. "Why do you do it? Why are you 'ere?" he repeated. But I was numb by then. Why did I do it? I was starting to wonder. What was I in pursuit of? Fame? The perfect *fouetté*? The perfect body? Attention? Love from every one? Love from just one? How long could I go on blaming everyone else? I remember once upon a time it had felt so good.

That night we slept in Bertrand's older brother's big bed and he talked for another hour, face to the ceiling, eyes wide, before he fizzled. His solid body crawled across me to turn off the light. I could feel his warm red-wine breath. He knocked my alcoholic erection with that fat bulge he'd kept in his dance belt. Was this a last shot at getting me to dance with this Quebec company? He may have meant well, but my instincts told me not to touch. I'd seen him briefly with a woman at the Conservatoire, and something else said to wait, just a few more seconds, for Daniel and an answer. I so wanted to hold out for true love.

I rolled away from him and stared into the dark and saw a kid, me, being shipped off on a bus for a bilingual exchange. It was *une échange bilingue*. French immersion. Two weeks with a French family and then a boy my age with us for two weeks. I went to a town, Bonneville, in rural Alberta. Big farms and warm wooden houses under a sky so big and clouds so high it could make you say your prayers even if you never went to church. I stayed with a French Canadian family who laughed together, took pride in everything—their food, their children—asked me lots of questions, worried over me, the English kid. They joked that I was one of them. Their son came into my room during the lightning and thunder after a prairie summer day to hold me and never say or think anything about it again. I remember the sheen of his hair. He came back, for his two weeks, to our empty bungalow in Strathcona. How different he must have found us. Our humourless hand folding and knuckle wringing, the television news at the dinner table, the stiff coughs and icy smiles. We caught each other's eyes across that vast dinner table, but we were strangers.

Fortunately my instincts were correct. In the morning the girl-friend I had seen him with, Louise, came by for coffee before class. Sex with a man had probably never crossed Bertrand's ballet-obsessed mind. Anyway, the fantasy of it has gotten me some alone-time mileage. And Louise was built for men more than for dance. She must have made him very happy—and he, her, if she didn't find him too much. "You stayed over? Even I don't get that privilege. Don't want to dishonour the brother's bed." She put two *pain au chocolat* on the table. "Eat, eat," she said, and we all tore bits off. "He's told you about Madame?"

"Madame?"

"It's her company. The one in Quebec."

"He seems pretty excited about it."

"Madame is a genius," he blurted.

"What do you think of moving to Quebec City?"

"Really?"

"He won't shut up about you."

"But…"

"You have potential. I mean you're being a bit sloppy right now, but we all have our phases. You were second soloist. We saw you with the Company."

And I had seen her dance at the studio and, although she would never be part of a big company with a figure like hers (a woman's, not a ten-year-old anorexic boy's), she had a solid technique and strong natural instincts. For her to devote herself to this company in Quebec City, she must have been a believer.

"Wow, no one has said anything that nice since I got here. Shit, I'd be honoured." I was intrigued by the idea of running away, but I still had to convince myself that Daniel had run absolutely cold, for peace of mind.

After our first *café*, Bertrand started up again. "Our company is what dance is all about—we honour the dance—we don't let anyt'ing pass—we are not sloppy like the Conservatoire—they don't understand how to find the dancer within a person—we are only five—with you, we will be six—you will be dancing all the time—doing what you were meant to do—the big companies they only want paper dolls who have never had a period in their lives—am I right, Louise?"

She rolled her eyes—another of her big assets—brown and dark, arched eyebrows. She was the kind of woman that made you say, *If only I were straight…* "You see? We do need another male."

"We need a good male." Bertrand slammed his hand on the table. "'e's jealous."

"Of whom?"

"You're jealous of Jean-Marc, Madame's pet," she shouted back at him, as if jealous of his jealousy. She turned to me. "Madame would do anything for Jean-Marc."

Jean-Marc, the other male dancer, was their bone of contention. Bertrand obsessed about Jean-Marc. And Louise was miffed by Bertrand's obsession.

"We need another male for our New York tour."

"New York?" Music to my ears. Daniel would see.

Madame brought the rest of her little company to Montreal to see Le Ballet Naçional de Cuba at Place des Arts. The hall was filled with Montreal dancers from the Conservatoire, Eddie Toussaint, Les Ballets Jazz and any students who could afford it. I shared the row with Bertrand, Louise, Madame and the Quebec dancers. We waited for Alicia Alonso, the blind legend, to perform with lean, brown-skinned men who swirled around her, doubling as seeing-eye dogs. I closed my eyes, pretending to be meditating. Instead saw my young self in the audience one snowy Edmonton night.

BIG OLD CARS—CADILLACS, IMPALAS, Buicks—skid toward a downtown theatre. There I am, peering over the window's ledge into a continuous stream of snowflakes flying by the car. Bored voices from the front seat drop in and out of my little window-world, blankly telling me I am on my way to see something great, that I would probably never see again.

Ballet.

It's *your* father, (she calls him) who said, "I don't know why we had to bring him along, he won't remember."

Your mother, (he calls her) said, "It's easier than getting a sitter."

Bringing me along turned unlucky for him. I could have clung to her but, no, I hung on his jacket sleeves, and the curses he muttered under his breath. The theatre was velvety and everything swirled upward. The seats were soft enough to fart silently, unlike the harsh wood pews at Bellamy Baptist. In that world of gilt and gold and plush fabric, the smells were thick, too. A woman's powdery perfume drifted down her Dippity-do waves of hair, tumbling over the fur collar spread across the seatback, suffocating me, my throat collapsing involuntarily. And as the fur collar inched toward my little flannelled knees, I wondered if I would ever be a grown-up.

"Don't touch," Father scolded.

"Let him touch it, he's not bothering anybody. Besides," she whispered loudly, "it's only muskrat."

They never found out about the sticky mint I glued under that muskrat collar, in the dark, or the giant gumdrop I stuck to the back of some woman's ermine resting on the radiator. But that was when I didn't appreciate the price of fur.

People laugh and whisper, lips touch ears, heads tip toward me with that isn't-he-cute nod and wink, until the sounds fade with the lights and the heavy blood red curtains obey the jab of the conductor's baton and magically fold toward the corners of the proscenium.

And who gave a damn about the dancing back then? Anyone could do it—twirls and twiddles. I was more interested in the ballerinas looking like they had been dipped in icing sugar, and the feathers on their costumes that tickled the men's noses and clung to their sweaty foreheads when they all danced together. I wished, in that silent world, that someone would sneeze. But real swans were much more graceful, I told mother, and they had longer necks, and didn't clomp on tippytoe.

All those cotton candy distractions didn't compare to my fascination with the *danseurs*. I could see myself as one of these princes so much more easily than I could see myself wearing a charcoal suit and tie. These men were strong like I dreamed I would be. They had poise, and shoulders and thighs that looked like they were carved from ivory. They flew, lithe and nimble, through the air. Not like us kids who dropped from trees, twisted our ankles, scraped our shins, or awkwardly leapt across prairie ditches in the spring only to fall short of the opposite bank and have our boots fill with icy water. They only bowed to queens and kings. Their legs were smooth, save for a bulge at the top.

And how could this living statue love a large white bird, when he cared more about his hunting partner? Their big legs bounced them toward each other across the stage, twirled them, too. Then they whispered, touched their hearts and softly stroked each other's shoulders, like I had been taught not to do, one Edmonton summer afternoon on my way to the river. Benjamin Weinstein and I walked toward the water, and it was my father who shouted, "Boys don't put their arms around each other." So we let go and held hands. "And boys don't hold hands." We walked shoulder to shoulder, touching, but never again without shame. But the ballet proved me right; the prince and his buddy embraced each other in front of a whole audience, while the other handsome hunters stood like living statues—firm thighs, round butts and bulges—arms draped on one another's shoulders, waiting for their cue to join in the dance. They didn't mind showing their round butts, firm thighs and bulges.

"Why won't they talk?"

"Shhh!"

But how could anyone understand the story if no one talked? Or sang?

At the intermission women tipped their glasses of rye and ginger and carefully stuck their tongues in their glasses to keep their lipstick from caking, as my mother explained.

And people kept saying new-RAYE-ev and Fon-TAIN. The men talked, laughed, whispered and belched out words into their rum and Cokes and Scotches, words like *commie* and *ruskie, bohunk* and *fairy*.

"What's a commie? What's a ruskie?" I knew how to be a shit. The women ignored me and stroked my cheeks with the backs of their hands, and I knew, even then, that if I smiled they would say something. "Lovely new teeth—fitting for a dentist's son."

For better or worse, with no brothers or sisters I was the centre of their attention. Everyone said how fortunate my folks were to have such a handsome—blond-haired, blue-eyed and lovely lipped—and well-behaved young man.

"Your father says you won't remember, but I'm sure you will."

"Your mother has a thing for ruskie fairies." His jabs had a distinct tone; I knew what to ignore and when to pretend I didn't understand.

No one asked if I'd ever be the next New-RAYE-ev.

At home my mother tucked me into a grown-up bed in my big room, far away from theirs. Indian rugs covered the cold oak floors. They probably still do. You'd never know it was well below zero outside the walls of that big warm bungalow in Strathcona, Edmonton.

In my bedroom in the basement, I lay in the dark and wondered what it was they liked about going out. Was it the intermission? Seeing their friends? The same reasons they went to church? Or was it a chance to drink cocktails? I figured the husbands went to make the wives happy, and the wives went to dream of princes. As I dozed, I wished I lived in that world where no one spoke and everyone was beautiful. I slept and dreamt of feathers stuck to women, and closed lips miming secrets, while dancers with rock-hard thighs flew through the sky, their tights full of sticky mints.

INTERMISSIONS, FOR DANCERS WHO happen to be sitting in the audience, are the side-shows of life, where egos bow and grovel to be noticed. Since they aren't up onstage, they make sure everyone around knows they should be; the females wear their buns twice as tight, with enough makeup to ice a wedding cake, while the men wear corduroy pants just as tight, stretched over their butts, belts snug, and walk bolt upright, waddling with toes pointing in opposite directions like ducks. Then they'll voice their opinions, refer to the stars by nick-name—Misha, Rudi—and hope someone notices.

At intermission, Bertrand's much-spoken-about Madame, Madame Talegdi, reclined on a bench in the foyer, stretching like a Siamese cat and inhaling cigarette smoke to her toes. If there was attention to be had, it would have to find its way to her, as far as she was concerned. She looked me over like she was about to eat a big steak and didn't know where to begin. She was strong, lean and dark. With her dyed-black hair pulled tight to a knot, and her even, capped teeth, you could squint and believe she was a twenty-year-old señorita. Up close, she was an aging Hungarian woman, maybe with a dash of gypsy blood. But her presence filled the foyer. People pointed and whispered; whether they recognized her or not, she was alluring. Blowing that smoke everywhere, she made sure she was noticed. The attention was justified. When I saw her dance in Quebec City I understood. Her legs were rock hard, her ankles were a little thick from two infants and a newborn she hauled around. But she could stay on pointe forever. One afternoon the girls in her small company ran from the room, in tears, because she had shamed them by doing thirty-two fouettés without moving, not travelling so much as the diameter of a dime along the floor.

Louise and the girls sat at her feet and Bertrand and Jean-Marc, Bertrand's nemesis, sat beside her. Louise strained to maintain a graceful seated posture, despite her full chest. If she leaned forward she was just way too luscious—a no-no for dancers though no doubt pleasing for any civilian straight males in the theatre. Other, thinner dancers in the lobby would look down on her, but she would smirk because in the end she had the best of both worlds. The Company would have called her "heavy" until she showed signs of anorexia. Someday, in the real world, her body, and all the other shapely ballerina's bodies I had known, would be appreciated. Until then, they'd have to settle for some crazed taskmaster's petrified idea of beauty.

Next to Louise, the other girls appeared to be corpses. Maryse, a buck-toothed and anorexic stick, ignored me outright. Bertrand admitted she could dance but then mimicked her overbite when she turned her back to him. She was all knees, elbows, shoulder blades and grey skin. She snacked on raw celery out of a baggie.

The other female, Chantal, came across as stern. She looked in my direction, but her eye-line just managed to graze the top of my head. When I phoned Rachelle to fill her in on the Company, and described Chantal—legs crossed tight, back bolt upright—Rachelle predictably said Chantal needed to be fucked. This was her solution to most women's attitudes. Chantal had the perfect dancer's body and profile. She stretched her feet in her shoes, and showed off her perfect arches.

Jean-Marc, the one who had brought Bertrand and Louise head to head, sat beside Madame, and presented a huge, toothy, open smile when we were introduced. Bertrand's jealousy of Madame's attention to Jean-Marc showed up as disdain, and Louise's jealousy of Betrand's jealousy registered as fury. Jean-Marc was lean and muscular with veins splitting his biceps. Madame referred to them as his telephone cords. He had a big jaw, and a perfect space between his two front teeth. He looked around the room with eyebrows raised in a *Je suis innocent* way. With a body like that, I'm sure he's had no trouble making his way to the top. That didn't occur to me those few months ago. I still believed it was about talent.

Did Madame sense I would jump her protegé in a second? It turns women on, to think their man is attractive to boys like me. It can also be a big fat insult that no one, including their boyfriend, is noticing them.

Madame finally diverted her attention from her audience in the foyer of Place des Arts. She seemed content that she had been seen by all. "Bertrand tells me you would like to contribute your talents to our little company. He says you can dance."

Bertrand frowned, but I was growing used to having to prove myself.

"At last we can remount *Rimbaud*," Louise said. "Madame has created a ballet after the French poet."

"It's a masterpiece," Chantal added, toward the space above my head.

Madame pretended to have caught someone's eye. She drew on her cigarette, waved, and shook her head at Chantal's flattery. Like any faded ballerina, she would have killed to be back onstage at Place des Arts. You could almost taste the desire.

"We are taking *Rimbaud* to New York," said Madame. "Harlem. Three nights. It needs at least six strong dancers." Her exhaled smoke settled around our little group. "As usual Bertrand will partner Louise. He will be our Rimbaud. Jean-Marc will work with Maryse. They make an ideal match." Jean-Marc puffed up. "I think you might be a good partner for our Chantal," proclaimed Madame. "You would make a perfect Verlaine: jealous, in love and always in Rimbaud's shadow." Chantal tightened her knees, sat even straighter, and curled her lip as though the one person who could turn her into the next Alicia Alonso, and make her dreams come true with the snap of her fingers, had just cut an extremely foul *fromage*.

My time had finally come. This is what I had needed. Not a ballet factory like Montreal, but a small company where I had time to focus on being brilliant. Montreal was short-lived, perhaps another stepping stone along the way—the way to New York.

Three

THE ARMS EXTENDED JUST enough, relaxed never, are open to cradle the most precious air, like an angel holding the earth, or releasing what has entered the body—by way of the trunk and the back—through the arms and out the hands toward the heavens. To feel a mere fraction of this, for yourself, slowly push the air away with the back of your hand.

BERTRAND CALLED THEIR LITTLE group *un equipe*. Every time we met in Montreal, he never stopped his crazy chatter until he returned to Quebec. I didn't need convincing; I wanted to prove I could overcome anything. I tried not to think of Daniel over me, big hands on my back, soaking me with sweat on our second-last night. If he just got cold feet and planned to return, then the break would make our reunion that much better. And ignoring him would make him want me even more; he'd see what a hit our little company was—New York—and how I was not a threat to him, and how serious I really was about my dancing, then he'd want me. I wasn't going to mope around Montreal and envy the ones he danced with, choreographed for, had cigarettes with, disappeared for—or to—his fucks and tricks and protegés. I had my own life to live. I tried so hard not to think of Daniel.

Empty pockets, empty bank account, and stuffed on another bus with all my crap, I'd show him. Dry heater in my face. Frosty late September morning air, a prelude to winter, raced down from the *Les Laurentides* in the north and across the highway to Quebec City. On that ride I must have dozed. I saw the boy, me, walking through the ravine in a yellow raincoat, matching yellow hat, black galoshes, my

63

tight pink fists holding a crumpled painting of dancers, the colours running and fading in the rain. My mother told me to show the class what a wonderful artist I was. How proud I should be. The cold autumn sleet rushed me along, the wind splashed me into puddle after puddle. Coat, hat, boots filling with icy October water. Paint washed away. Up and rush. Hands red with blood and paint and chill and pebbles in the flesh. Up and rush. Up and rush. Hot and damp in yellow. The yard was empty. Everyone was dry in the warm brick building. The heavy door gave quickly and I tumbled into my seated teacher and class, gathered for their rainy day story. Bloody nose, snot and tears ran over my upside-down smile. My gasps were drowned by snorts and giggles, chortles of childish laughter from slouched kids as the plump teacher's ass sagged over the tiny seat of the wooden chair. I strangled the art.

IN QUEBEC CITY I stayed at Madame "Smoke-cough-ska's" house. I will never understand the link between the physical demands and stamina a dancer must have, and the ability to smoke in spite of it. Madame met my bus in her rusting crayon-orange Volvo station wagon that smelled a nauseating combination of fresh and stale cigarette smoke and rotting apple juice mingling with kiddy poop. Madame had dropped the posturing, let her hair down, but was in full makeup. Regardless of the filth, she had a pristine allure as if she had just stepped out of a *Blackglama* magazine ad. All she spoke of was Jean-Marc: "He's finally coming into his own."

We chugged into Sainte-Foy. "He's got charisma and energy like the dancers I knew in Hungary." We coasted up to her peeling bungalow, surrounded by yellow grass and no trees. I was starting to feel defeated and inadequate and I hadn't even so much as *sautéed* for Madame. I wondered if she had already started with the head games or if she was simply oblivious to my presence. "He's lean, handsome and hungry for it. I remember what that was like." The last sentence was another silent mantra that aging dancers lived by, usually followed by a wistful sigh, as they swallowed their bitterness back into their core and secretly prayed those nearby would whisper about their greatness in the past, saying things like, "She had amazing technique," or,

"His was the definitive Albrecht." I followed along the cracked walk-way, to the front door, as she shoved children's toys aside with her foot and cursed under her breath before announcing, "He will make our name in New York."

Was I surrounding myself with people obsessed with anyone but me? Everyone loves to talk about how much they are in love, or at-tracted to so-and-so. But I had been around enough male dancers who had impressed the pants off someone, and even been described as the next Godunov or Baryshnikov, and they wisely rode that wave of enthusiasm. Those were the ones who knew they had an ace in their pocket. Others had no faith in that allure and had slept with Kharkov, perish the thought, or his wife—which made Kharkov even happier—or with anyone who could help them along the way. And there were tons of Jean-Marcs to be obsessed about, which led inevit-ably to someone's heartache or break, while they forged their own route to the top.

Madame led me into the house, took off her coat, revealing her walking-anatomy-lesson taut torso and medium-sized breasts with no bra, amazing for a woman her age. She knew it. She dropped her coat, almost on a chair, and then rifled through her bag to finally find a cigarette, which she lit and took a drag on. She led me to the kitchen. The house itself looked like it had been ransacked and I was waiting for her reaction, but none was forthcoming. This mess was *de riguer*. In the kitchen, she leaned over the cluttered counter. "When I first saw you I wasn't sure. You have blankness in your eyes. Are you sad or just hesitant? And there is something very uneven about your face. Your nose." She grimaced as she choke-talked, "But now I see you again and I think maybe you are handsome."

"I banged it on the bottom of the pool."

"Playing pool? Hmmm."

"Not playing…"

"You could get it fixed."

"It hasn't affected my dancing."

She tapped her ashes effortlessly into the sink.

The studio was situated on a road that led toward the walled part of town. It was simply a sad fluorescent-lit, linoleum classroom on the top floor of a 1950s beige brick high school that had been converted to a clinic for mental patients. When the wind blew up the slope, the windows howled. No sprung wood floor. No showers; we changed in the bathroom across the hall. After class the girls used talcum. We used cologne; Jean-Marc shared his collection of Drakkar, Pierre Cardin and Christian Dior for our stinking armpits. Bells went off at weird times, people in white coveralls, lab coats, pyjamas or nothing at all ran down halls. Hortense, the pianist, arms like water balloons, hammered everything from Chopin to Delibes to Tchaikovsky with the same heavy hand.

I wanted to believe that Madame's classes were the best I had ever taken. I told myself that this was it. Yes, it was gruelling; my thighs screamed every moment with every plié. Madam had an incredible imagination when it came to putting together a class—the barre was intricate and rigorous, although she seemed to have a habit of forgetting what she had showed us. Regardless, it was hard: from a full plié in first position she would have us *développé* so that we were being supported by one fully bent leg. She seemed to do whatever she could to make our thighs scream and our calves seize up. I might have been starting to get my form back, feeling my legs stretch, feeling my arches once again, and starting to feel like everything was finding its former place within my body, but it seemed too ambitious, and I was too physically worn to sleep well. But I told myself—in the glow of the newness of the experience, and of Madame Talegdi's allure and charisma—that it would make me great.

The days were full. At nine in the morning the six of us had company class, with Hortense at the piano and Madame stomping out the beat for two hours. We extended our tired muscles and followed her commands through a series of pliés, *tendus, battements*, with the aid of a barre. "Don't hold the damn thing like you are trying to strangle a cat," she'd shout. I was developing bad habits all over again; I used to rest my hand lightly, if at all, on the barre, but now I needed it for most of my support. The second half of the class there was *adage* floor work, where we danced and danced and danced—worked on our jumps, turns and everything you could do from one corner to the other. Although there was an air of competition, I doubt they would have acknowledged it. Dancers watch not only themselves, but others, to measure their progress. Following this, Madame would alternate later mornings with a follow-up men's class—more thigh-bursting held pliés, Ukrainian kicks, Russian splits, endless leaps, *tours en l'air*, *grand jeté en tournante*, exercises that focused on male capabilities, designed to exploit the major muscle groups, all interspersed with endless sets of one-armed push-ups with the heal of her Capezio digging into our backs. (She knew how to work a man.) People say that a male dancer's role is to support the woman. Balanchine said ballet is purely a female thing. And I say it's not fair: go to any classical ballet and tell me the man doesn't fly or spin or become airborne for supernatural lengths of time, and I'll know you slept through it.

Madame had the good sense to alternate our men's class with women's pointe class every other day. Jean-Marc, Bertrand and I would watch the women's class closely, but during our class, Maryse, Chantal and Louise would talk in the lunchroom to the extent that Madame would have to shout for them to shut up. After lunch we would all have a short warm-up at the barre, then a *pas de deux* class. It was odd and good to have such a small group; the good being that we danced so much more than one would in a large group, the odd being that I knew my body was undergoing some fundamental changes and I wasn't really sure what my condition would be when I came out the other end.

To finish up the day, we rehearsed sections of repertoire, including Madame's ballets. I rest my case: if it looks like dancers work longer hours than athletes, that's because it's the truth—which is to a dancer's disadvantage. The body needs a sufficient amount of rest and recovery as well as nutrition when it is this active. The ballet world, built on obsession, competition and starvation will never figure this out. It is cemented into a tradition that involves an outdated work ethic. The dancer's fitness regimen involves hours of physically demanding repetition (why else would it look so easy onstage?), optional cigarettes, mixed with coffee and no food. The law of diminishing returns has never been read to the dance world.

Maryse and Chantal kept their noses turned up at me when I was partnering them, when I was beside them at the barre, when I was dancing next to them and when I was anywhere near them for that matter—fortunately it was perfect ballet posture. I had no qualms about staring at their chests, it made them horribly self-conscious—they needed to get out in the bigger world and see how far being a little league bitch would get them. And I noticed everything: when Maryse got thinner, Chantal seemed to put on weight, as if no stray pounds would leave our little company. But Maryse looked like death in this condition, which, paradoxically, made her perfect for the children's roles that called for waif-like fairies, sylphs, fireflies or something equally translucent. Chantal did her best to disguise her expanding thighs with a variety of sheer rehearsal skirts, and I had the misfortune of being her *pas de deux* partner while Jean-Marc partnered only the skeletal Maryse, making him look even more capable.

Sometimes Bertrand shared Louise with me. She was the only one who responded like a real performer. She had instinct, trust, generosity and perhaps even a crush on me; she always looked at me with a grin and a twinkle in her eye as though we were sharing a private joke. On this particular day we danced together rehearsing the *pas de deux* from Minkus's *Paquita*. Both of us knew the choreography more or less, although we had never danced it together. As Hortense crucified the music as if she were nailing Jesus to the cross and making damn sure he wouldn't get away, Louise and I flew beyond the staleness of that crummy little studio. Madame stood silent and the other two couples finally stopped their cumbersome, indulgent and weighty movements to watch as well. If Louise hadn't been Bertrand's woman, I would have made her my dance partner for life. There was a natural sensitivity in every move we made; every lift, every turn, we became one, and far more than one when we danced.

Later that week, we were to rehearse one of Madame's creations set to Debussy's "La Mer," and based on Grimm's *Little Mermaid*. Jean-Marc, her Neptune, was late and had not called in. Madame was visibly shaken by this lack of etiquette, so I stepped in. I took my place and watched Madame slide across the classroom, arms carving the air, her footwork an intricate swirl of triplets. She swam me from an imaginary giant clam, to Louise, *bourréeing* as Les Algues, an overgrown piece of seaweed. I followed slowly. We call it marking; in the whole ballet theatre world we call it marking. You rarely, if ever, dance full out when initially learning the choreography.

"You're not going to move like that!" she shouted after I traced the steps, head down, arms grasping the air, counting out the beats. "Of course not, Madame."

"Go and sit down." Madame choked, turned red, leaned on the barre.

Louise rat-a-tatted something to her and then muttered to me under her breath, "Madame hates marking. She'd rather see you get it wrong full-out, than have you mark it."

But Madame shouted back short and quick at Louise, "Mes nerfs!" She stood by the window and lit a cigarette.

Louise rolled her eyes then whispered, "Make her choreography look difficult. Does that make sense?"

It didn't matter. Even if I did pirouettes on my ear, Jean-Marc had stood her up.

Madame continued to make things more difficult. She altered the choreography, put in extra lifts, made them last longer. My repertoire became rife with adagios with laboriously slow lifts from Albinoni to Telemann. To my credit, Chantal and Louise appreciated a male who didn't gasp in a *presage* or a *cambré*.

Only one of them, Saint-Saëns's "The Carnival of the Animals," provided any real dancing challenges. My only other hope was a piece she was putting together to Holst's *The Planets*, but even then I had been assigned all adagios while Jean-Marc and Bertrand were allowed to allegro. True, adagios showed off my line, but I had the quickest *entre-chat*, and tighter and cleaner footwork. One bright spot remained—Chantal's bullying: if I placed my hands on her waist for a lift, she would dig her nails into my wrists, and on pointe she would shift aggressively to make it look like I didn't have her on her centre; she would pull at my arms, or go limp spontaneously, and Madame could see through it. If anyone were to shit on me it would be Madame and Madame alone. "Chantal you are dancing like a dead marionette. *Qu'est ce que vous faites?* Enough! Monsieur Rottam is a dancer, not a cheese-maker!" Thank God someone else had incurred Madame's wrath.

One Monday, after one too many lifts and not enough dancing, I pressed her, "Madame, when do we start rehearsing *Rimbaud*? Shouldn't we be rehearsing *Rimbaud*? And what are the exact dates? Which theatre in Harlem? The Apollo? The Company performed there. Before my time of course, but I've seen the pictures, just after the Apollo reopened and then closed."

"It's the Harlem School of Music."

"That's in Brooklyn. It's the Brooklyn Academy of Music."

"Harlem."

"But—the Dance Theatre of Harlem?"

"And unless you can convince me as Verlaine..."

At that point Chantal ran out of the room in tears.

"Chantal! Christ!"

Louise giggled. "Chantal's afraid of New York."

"Maybe she's afraid of herself," I added.

I'd taken a wrong turn. I started doubting Madame, and once I lose trust, I am gone; that's when my eyes go blank, I suppose. Slowly day by day, class by class, rehearsal after rehearsal, the thought crept over me that I had little to do but recover, get strong, get some cash and *then* get out of there.

The next day, I inquired about payday, with not much money to spare, and they laughed. We were on a break in the small kitchen off the classroom. As usual I was deaf to the Québécois rat-a-tatting going on around me. I had practised my question. "Et bien, quand est-ce que nous reçeverons nos salaire?"

"Didn't Bertrand tell you? The classes are our payment," said Maryse, in quite good English, which was a shock since she hadn't spoken to me since we first met. She obviously took great joy in being able to deliver such bad news. I had had enough free classes to know this was not a bonus. In smaller places, men's fees were always overlooked. Madame definitely owed us. Besides this, I started to see her innovative exercises as masochistic, designed to destroy line, over-build thighs, and make me strong, like Madame, but too tight. What had worked for her at the academy in Budapest wouldn't work for me. My legs were becoming bulky and overly muscular. She was one of those teachers who could only work from the perspective of their own body type, and although her strength had made her an anomaly and a legend, it hadn't made her a very good teacher. Her reputation was of no use to me. My pants were becoming tight on my thighs. I remember Kent, someone I was yet to meet, using the term *thunder thighs*. This turbulent honeymoon with Madame was over. It was worse than what I had left on the prairies.

Even though I was losing my line and my flexibility, I'd survive the misery she was dishing out. And I still wanted to prove myself before taking my final bow. This "fire walk" had happened with Kharkov and each one of the teachers in the Company's school. You either got no correction, or you got picked on by all the teachers, all at once. In both instances your head would be spinning after a few weeks of the treatment. And now it was happening with her.

I couldn't leave empty-handed, and without money. I also needed something—a role, a performance—for the resumé. I ruled out the idea that she might provide me with something good, a gem, a bit of conceited wisdom if possible, like most well-intentioned, yet fucked up, dance teachers I'd had. Perhaps the example of her strength and single-mindedness would be that gift. The way she taught made certain things more obvious: ballet was obviously unnatural and bad for the human form (unless, like Nijinsky or Daniel, you were born a freak of nature with legs and feet like a bird), not to mention it being invented by a mad French king who must have had some kind of strange foot-bondage fetish.

One night at her dinner table (an easy place to eat small portions after watching her snot-encrusted infants mash food through their angry little fists), over the last of some Hungarian wine, I mentioned that I would have to start looking for a job. She banged the dirty dishes into the sink and said, "You can stay here and pay me rent when you have it." With the offer she wobbled, then pressed her body close and smiled.

It was time to go.

None of the other dancers spoke about money. They boarded with siblings who had also left the folks out in the wilds of northern Quebec, but to brave the city as government clerks and bank tellers and house painters. If any of the dancers did have a job, it was part-time for pin money to buy tights and shoes, not rent and food. Madame spoke English very well when she was angry: "These other dancers are spoiled brats. They don't understand you need to work. How do you think I paid for my training in Budapest?" This she shouted in the studio for all to hear, exploiting my situation to put them all down, and for a moment Madame and I spoke the same angry language. She seemed excited at the idea of my life beyond the dance studio—as if her secure routine in the narrow world of ballet had become a bore. But it was all an act.

Right away I started looking for a place to live. I lost my patience; just being under the same roof ruined my sleep. The brat-and-baby noises started early and went late. Every noise started a disturbance in another part of the house, and all of it overlapped, stopped for a moment, and then started up again.

I lost my precious sleep. As well as needing sleep to recover physically, it was the only escape from my problems. In the meantime, Madame took another boarder, her cousin Milosz, a Hungarian cellist looking to move to Canada. Every day by the time we got home, the old guy had left the kitchen a mess: daily disasters included burned spaghetti, plate upon plate of crusted dried food and one of the kid's plastic toys used as a coaster for the hot espresso pot, which adhered to the toy and in turn to the counter. She'd swear up a storm, which was interspersed with her fawning over Jean-Marc, then she'd scream at the baby, and cough from imminent lung cancer. She'd fly around the kitchen like Giselle gone mad: "Jean-Marc/ that bastard Milosz/ oh but Jean-Marc/ look what that fool Milosz has done/ Jean-Marc is so, so.../ goddammit, can you believe this idiot cellist?" All I knew was that I couldn't dance tired, look for a job, find money and an apartment. I couldn't even afford the dumps with pink walls, orange shag carpet and dusty macramé hangings covering the holes in the walls.

That night I lay in my room, the world of ugly apartments and the mayhem of Madame's home on the other side of the door. I stared at the ceiling thinking that maybe *Romeo and Juliet* in Montreal had been my swan song and the best I would ever dance. I had stepped out at the wrong time entirely. These dancers in Quebec had dreams and futures different from mine. Madame had a home, albeit in a hurricane zone. With kids, a husband and a ballet school, she had much to fall back on. I had little, verging on nothing. I was living someone else's plan. I had strayed so far from thinking I would be settling in with a beautiful man and dancing like a prince. I was in the wrong ballet, one for which I hadn't learned the steps.

The next afternoon Bertrand stared me down. I'm not sure why, but it was too late to bother convincing me of anything. After, in the dressing room he approached me. "Now you fight. Il faut que Madame sache que tu es mieux que Jean-Marc. I saw at the Conservatoire. Mais avance, comme les Mongoliens."

Bertrand saw me dance when I was *in love*. "Mongolians?"

"Magyars," added Louise. "That's what Madame said."

I had no idea what they were talking about and it could very well have been lost in his translation or hers, but he persevered. "Mais, quel obstacle t'arrête?"

"Rien. Nothing is stopping me, but I can't go back."

"Ces chances-là n'arrivent qu'une fois." A polite way of telling me this is my last chance.

I argued, "Vous etes fou! Madame aime Jean-Marc! Christ! Louise, tell him. Madame doesn't like men like me. I don't look at her the way she wants. I don't give a shit about Jean-Marc, which bothers her even more. Explique-lui, s'il vous plait!"

I DON'T BELIEVE IN grace—maybe disgrace; I've never thought my useless prayers deserved to be answered over anyone else's. However there is something to be said about finally knocking on the right door (after slamming my head repeatedly against the wrong one), and feeling slightly blessed, even if the blessings are small. After a lacklustre class with Madame (in which she attempted to distract us from the doubts that she was less than brilliant by spontaneously breaking into a series of fouettés, once again, and I started to see her as a fearful, insecure spoiled brat, unfulfilled and desperate for attention from six equally desperate dancers) I wandered up toward the Old Town, delaying the return to Madame's bedlam of burned food and broken toys. I was empty of Daniel, dance, energy, inspiration and direction; and especially sick of Bertrand's psychotic enthusiasm. My body was rebelling. My lower back, which had never been a problem, was locked up tight as if a metal corset were clamped around my torso, from all the lifting she had me do. Therefore, even if I had wanted to stoop so low, I could no longer hope to impress Madame in class. In the mornings, I walked like my grandfather in his last years, and stared at the ground until I became limber and warm. She had proven to me that I was not worthy, nor capable, of any roles of substance in her repertoire. I thought of that pathetic dance teacher in Montreal who used to beg for his job on his knees. I wanted to fall to my knees and beg, but my knees ached and my faith was questionable.

When I finally got to the Old Town I wandered up the cobblestone rue Sainte-Ursule—one of the first streets after the stone gate of Port St. Louis. Despite just a mild incline, my ass fought against each step. The street was four-hundred-year-old limestone storybook scenic. Windows with blinds half-drawn like droopy eyelids looked out onto the street, mindlessly watching. Maybe I could find some doorway or alcove among these eyes, where I could sit and have a good old-fashioned, self-indulgent cry.

In a café window, a bright orange LOCAL A LOUER sign caught my eye. Anything in the Old Town would be a fortune, but I needed to stand in a warm empty apartment for a few minutes and entertain my fantasies. Maybe the owner would offer me tea, and I would have a moment to chat with someone other than this tiny, nasty company of masochists. In the café, a guy in an ironed plaid shirt with the wholesomeness of a carpenter told me, "Deux-cent-quarante-cinq." What had I lost in the translation that made this sound like two hundred and forty-five? Thousand? A day? A month? Was it the shed around back? Unheated? No running water? What could possibly cost two hundred and forty-five, when twice that amount got rust-and-avocado shag? He led me out of the café and stepped into the street, walked a few steps, then through another door and up some stairs leading above the café. The two rooms were huge: one with a yawning blocked fireplace, and the other with a small open kitchen in the corner by the window. Both had windows at least eight feet high, two looking over the café terrace in the back and two facing onto the street below.

"It was our office, but we move everyt'ing next door."

I took a risk and let the landlord know, "Je suis danseur," which either garners a little respect and intrigue, or reluctance. But he seemed unmoved, still pleasant. Either he took a liking to me or just wanted to live dangerously.

"Je suis Luc. Vous êtes bienvenue," he said. He was my lucky Luc. He had to be because I didn't tell him I was working for nothing and that my bank account was almost as empty as I was—enough for first month's rent and groceries to get me to the weekend.

It had been so long since I had been in training as a student, and the memories of those days of scrimping seemed to want to vanish with my first real paycheque. Sure the scholarship came in very handy, but I still needed to eat and sleep. After three years of being a bad waiter by night (being fired from almost every eatery in Winnipeg) and a struggling dancer by day, you can bet that I jumped at that Company offer. But for those three years I learned how to be thrifty, and knew that plain spaghetti and a jar of dill pickles, mixed with whatever I could pilfer from whatever restaurant I happened to be working at, went the farthest on a dollar, and still left me with coffee money, which was a staple.

It was a deal. I was now free of the worst of Madame. The surroundings would help immensely. It was the difference between Prokofiev and Elgar, order and dissonance, Odette and Odile. I loved my little empty space. I could grasp the window frames and lean forward into the most painfully satisfying arabesques. I could dance around the space to my heart's content. I could shove my feet under the radiators until I turned blue.

The first call on my new phone was to Daniel's answering machine. After all, I couldn't be that intimidating if I had moved all the way to Quebec and now had my own place. It was a short message, "Hi, it's John, here's my number. I'm in Quebec City," in the best matter-of-fact-I-don't-give-fuck voice I could muster. That's what being in love with someone who, well, isn't where you are emotionally, forces you to; it makes you a damn good actor. *Was he out? Or still in New York?*

I gave him the benefit of the doubt. Then it was me I doubted. *Did I sound blasé enough? Too blasé?* My phone didn't ring. Being my Pollyanna self, I thought it was broken and kept picking up the receiver to listen for the dial tone—until Friday night. I know this next bit couldn't happen according to the laws of physics, but in retrospect, and according to the laws of dance, which often break any physical laws—demanding us to leap even after we have left the ground, for which, yes, we've all heard it, ad nauseam, Baryshnikov is famous: I leapt fifteen feet through the air, flying to answer the phone.

This next part did happen:

"My name is Kent. Daniel gave me your number."

"How is he? Is he there? Did he get my message?"

"Message? Here? No. I'm in Quebec."

"Is he all right? Is there some problem?"

"I think he's fine. He called and gave me your number."

"Is he still in New York?"

"He never mentioned New York."

My head roared, my heart was beating so fast. Daniel knew where I was. He'd gotten my message. Was this his way of telling me he wanted to get together again? Was he testing the water? Was the next move up to me?

"What did he say?"

"Nothing, he just gave me your number. I barely know the guy."

Barely know *the guy*? So not only did Daniel dump me, but he dumped me on someone he barely knew. Did he see me as some kind of pathetic charity case? Was I to be a consolation prize? Was this guy another version of me? "So?"

"Well let me give you my number," said the voice named Kent.

"I don't have a pen." Was Kent some gesture to absolve Daniel of any guilt (which I doubt he felt)?

"What's your address?" Kent persisted.

"I'm in the Old Town."

"There are lots of streets in the Old Town."

"Sainte-Ursule."

"Above a café?"

"Café Latin."

"The apartment that was for rent?"

"Yes."

"I live next door. Hey, I bet you're the one I saw on the street. You're blond right?"

"Dirty blond. I moved in yesterday."

"Nice butt."

"Pardon?"

"And legs. But you're a dancer, so it figures."

How did they know each other, Kent and Daniel—and how did they know each other *not that well*? I had wondered this with everyone I'd met who was connected in any way to him, until it burned me deep down. How could they know him casually, without falling for him, like I had? How dare they not fall for him? Who could know Daniel like I did? Love him like I had? Did Daniel have a network of guys across *entière monde*? I was just *plat du jour* in Montreal. One long audition, to Daniel, and I didn't make the final cut. So much for gut-rotting bitterness. Jealousy.

Daniel had reintroduced me to jealousy. It was something I had lived with every day since I had taken my dance career seriously, and then almost boiled over, in my last year, before being invited to dance with the Company. They played us off until we practically devoured each other with hatred—our saving grace was our collective hatred of nasty faculty head-trips. It was ass-kissing to get whomever I wanted—Miss Friesen—to do whatever I wanted: give me a private meeting with Kharkov to let him know how devoted I was to the Company, and that I would do whatever it took to get in (except sleep with his wife). It was what brought out the best and worst in dancers.

"What are the chances of two WASPs living side by side in Old Quebec?" Kent said.

I forced my disheartened self to sound interested. "Where are you from?"

"Toronto, mostly. Hey, I'll be right over. We can do this in person." He didn't give me a chance to reply. A moment later I heard a door slam out on the street. His door. Then another slam. Mine. Then I heard him on the stairs.

When I opened the door, I saw a smallish figure in a white T-shirt and jeans, Levis, with an obvious bulge in his button crotch. *Hopeful* is the only word I can use to describe my first impression of him. He looked like he had been in the no-one-to-talk-to desert way too long. His eyes were sunken and searching. He wasn't like Daniel at all. Daniel had hair. Daniel had perfect teeth. Daniel was taller. But this guy, Kent, was making up for it by his openness and his crooked, hopeful smile. His young old-man's face. I imagined his better days had seen lots of sun, cigarettes and drinks. But now his deep eyes drooped, just a little, with a sparkle. Come to think of it, Daniel probably wouldn't have liked that. Dancers live in fear of aging; it's all they talk about. They live their lives in dog years. Yet they do everything to bring it on: chain smoke, starve themselves, dwell on their short-lived careers and say things like "I'm old."

Kent had a small hard body. Daniel *would* have liked that. Kent definitely wasn't a dancer. Daniel might have liked that. He stood at the door in nothing more than that worn white T-shirt and faded-in-the-right-spots blue jeans. "Come on in, you're shivering."

He stood close. A nervous energy radiated off him and my nipples hardened and the hair on my arms stood up in some kind of response.

"Henri's at home, so I thought I'd come over."

The smell of stale smoke was on his breath and his skin.

"Who's Henri?"

"My roommate. He's uptight about company." Kent looked around the empty room. "Is this it? Where's your stuff?"

"This is it."

"I guess it didn't take you long to move in. Luc take a liking to you?"

"Maybe I was looking a little desperate. I've seen so many dumps."

"Someone made a fortune in pea-soup shag."

"Pea-soup toilets, yellow sinks, pink bathtubs. Ugh."

"You're in *la belle province*. It's pea soup from here on in. You lucked out. I don't know, but if you want some furniture, some cat-house neighbours had to make a quick exit and left enough stuff to furnish this place. And it's all in our basement."

Right away, just like that, he said it: "You want some company?"

THE STAIRWELL WAS SILENT before, and will be silent again, after I leave, but right now it is crowded with the noise in my head, like a corps of swans running into place for the final curtain, pointe shoes tapping the stage. I just heard a door slam way below. The laundry room must be down there somewhere. But I'm paralyzed. I sit here with my hands shoved between my thighs, I can still flex them tight enough to crack nuts if need be.

THERE WAS THAT OFFER of the hookers' furniture. Kent always stood so close. "I mean we're practically buddies, we both know Daniel—I could just sleep beside you— shit, is that where you sleep?" He laughed out loud when he saw a sleeping bag on the floor by the fireplace. "You dancers are gluttons for punishment. I hear Baryshnikov sleeps on the floor."

"Baryshnikov is nothing but..."

"...bullshit stories about Baryshnikov. You dancers..."

"Well I'm saving myself," I said. "Maybe that sounds old-fashioned to you."

"For a mattress? I'll get you one."

"That's not what I meant."

"I'll get you one anyway."

"A hooker's mattress? I'll pass."

"No. Something new. I have a friend at Kresge's. He owes me a favour." He looked me over. "So you're saving yourself? Does he live in the neighbourhood? Have we met?"

I'd be damned if I'd tell him it was Daniel. "Montreal."

"Lucky guy. Can't believe your type still exists. You're pretty. You sure you don't want me to stay, anyway?"

I'LL START WALKING. I can keep my back against the cool concrete. For fuck's sake, I have a bedsheet on. How discrete is that? It's not like I'm naked. I'll start moving. I have to move. Down is easy. I'll say I'm doing a booze run for a toga party. My clothes are down there somewhere. What the hell has come between me and happiness?

NEXT MORNING KENT WAS on the sidewalk in front of the door that led to the cellar, between his place and the café. He was hopping around still in that white T-shirt trying to keep warm, hands tucked under his arms, making his lean biceps taut, cigarette tucked in the side of his mouth. I'll never forget the damned cigarette. "Where's my cig'rets?" he'd say. *Cig'rets.*

He scraped open the door, and we stepped down centuries-old limestone block steps into a still life of recent bordello history, Quebec, circa God knows when. Dusty light flooded in behind us, as well as in from a narrow window in the back, which provided enough light to see things I didn't have any use for: torn red silken lamps with black fringe, fake tropical plants with big dusty leaves, French provincial end-tables, mauve rattan dressing tables and matching purple headboards.

Kent convinced me to drag a few buried items up to my place. We made a couple of trips, exchanging glances each time we passed. Smiling. Wondering. Searching. Counting my lucky stars. Suddenly I had a furnished apartment: cutlery for ten, a toaster, pots, foam mats for a bed and more foam padding in the corner to recline on, a glass-top, gold-framed ice cream parlour table and two matching chairs to put by the window where I could sit and look into the street. And I had a friend, Kent, my real live fairy godmother.

Kent's enthusiasm didn't waver. "I'll cash in on that Kresge's favour and get you a mattress." And he was gone.

I looked around the room. I was alone. There would be no forced-polite sharing that came with roommates: not like living at Rachelle's or Hugues' or Madame's. It was all mine, at least for the moment. For now it was my own quiet space that no one would walk through on their way to the bathroom or kitchen, with their hair up in a towel, or shout from another room that the phone is for you. No noise or babies or smokers or someone else's dirty dishes or anyone bitching about mine not being done.

There was a cobblestone street under my nose and a café terrace beneath the back windows, and lots of room to dance. Under me, four-hundred-year-old stone and timber, and I was surrounded by feet-thick walls. There is something about space, creating it and owning it—in a ballet class, onstage, sitting quietly in a corner on the floor of your room. I didn't want to move. I wanted to sit on the floor for maybe a day or more, and not think. I had been desperate for this. I remembered security in the past: the smell of my mother's cologne—Calèche, coincidentally—saturating her mink coat, Christmas lights, knowing that Benjamin Weinstein's mother would always break the rules and give us cola on a school day, a warm theatre seat, my own apartment, payday, a full fridge and finally an offer to dance with the Company—one paycheque and only one job to do—and finally, thinking for a moment that Daniel was all mine.

Late in the afternoon, a cab with a mattress sticking out of the trunk pulled up, and out stepped Kent. In a minute we had it upstairs and into my room. "Happy housewarming. We'll try this out sometime. Take it for a test run around your place. Put it into high gear, burn some rubber, when you aren't saving yourself."

"You're optimistic."

"No. You are."

I made tea and we sat by the front windows on my Marie Antoinette dining set.

He broke the silence. "Would you like to come for dinner?"

"I can't remember the last time someone asked me for dinner. I'm sure it's happened. I guess we ate…"

"Who?"

"Nothing. No one."

"Mister No One."

"Yes. I suppose."

"Well, I am asking you for dinner. One of us will pretend it's a date. Most likely, me. Now get some rest. You look pooped." He rose and kissed my cheeks, first one, then the other—"Hey we're in Quebec now"—then he quickly left. I lay on the new mattress, stared at the ceiling and wondered what favour he had called in to get it.

I dozed and when I woke it took a moment to remember where I was—the room was dark and the streetlight fell across the floor. My body ached from finally relaxing into a quiet place. As I got dressed I got caught up in the occasion of it. I made a point of wearing my party T-shirt—tight on the biceps, worn silky thin. I'd worn it to the disco in Montreal. No underwear: when you spend as many hours as I have in a dance belt, you relish the pleasures of not being confined.

Something about being physically close to Kent made me feel sexy—a natural physical response that was new to me, and not just a hard-on. It turned me on to know I turned Kent on, knowing that he was watching me with one thing on his mind. He had become my "mirror mirror on the wall," making me believe I was sexy. It wasn't like my attraction to Daniel, who excited me because of his own sexiness. It occurred to me that I needed to be desired.

His apartment was old mixed with new: a pine loft furnished with French Canadian antiques, settled, mature, not like this dancer's make-do of hooker hand-me-downs on the other side of the wall. Kent kissed me like he had been on a desert island for a spell—long and big and juicy. I sat on the instinct to pull away.

Kent was whipping up an honest-to-God grown-up meal that would scare any ballerina. It included spaghetti with homemade sauce, bread and real-France French red wine most likely out of my price range: Chateau something-sur-something. He plunked it on the counter and twisted the corkscrew showing off the working tendons and ligaments beneath his fine this skin. "That *mis en bouteille au chateau* phrase on the label means it should be good. I mean it better be good."

"Because of what you paid?"

"No, because tonight is special. It's kind of an anniversary I guess, a celebration of our first dinner together. The wine should be special. If it isn't I'll go get something else. Although I'm warning you I bought a few."

"So what about the *mis en bouteille* thing?"

"It just means they squeezed the grapes..." Here, he paused.

"Isn't that how you make wine?" I wondered if it had been just plain stupid to dress like this. I mean what the hell was I trying to show here? At this rate we wouldn't make it to dinner. "Go on."

"...on their own property, and then bottled it there."

I shivered. I drained my first glass of wine.

"So much for savouring the wine," he said.

"It has a nice aftertaste."

"I'll teach you how to taste wine."

"There's a trick?"

"A technique."

My head was spinning from an empty stomach. "I guess I should have eaten today."

"What is it with dancers? Are you all on self-destruct?"

"I'll make up for it. This looks amazing—enough to make a ballerina binge, then purge."

"Let's eat," he said, carefully loading the plates.

I led the way to the table while he followed, hoped his eyes might be taking in some part of my anatomy. I sat down and tucked my napkin into my T-shirt.

"Now, what I'm dying to know…" he asked (my mind kept filling in the blanks at ninety miles an hour, saying things like, *know if I'll sleep with you*), "…is whether all male dancers are gay?"

"Are you kidding?" I had the feeling he was leading me on.

"Well?"

"Of course not," I said, pacing myself on my second glass of wine. "I mean, I wish. But it isn't fair to all the heterosexual dancers to say something like that."

"You wish?" He grinned. "How so?"

"Well who hasn't?"

"Fantasies are different."

"Well I mean everyone probably thinks we're all blowing each other in the wings before going on."

His knees touched mine under the table. I took a bigger swig of wine. "Go on."

I sighed. He wanted a story. "Well, I mean, when I was a teenager I spent days fantasizing about the male corps of the Caracas Ballet, the Eliot Feld Ballet, the Dance Theatre of Harlem."

"What were they doing in your fantasies?"

"Mostly dancing naked, you know complicated lifts, lots of body contact." My heart was racing. "It's hot in here." Anxiety was overwhelming me. I couldn't stop smiling. I drew a breath. "The sad truth is that dancers have too many body image hang-ups to be that open. I've heard it's the opera singers who like to eat and have sex with abandon. What about you?" I gulped and hoped he would do all the talking, so I could settle.

"My fantasies? Or do I like to eat and fuck with abandon?"

"Oh, well, your anything. Past? I feel like we've met before."

"I get that feeling with you."

"Funny."

Now my feet were twitching. Meanwhile we polished off the wine and he opened another. I was trying not to look like a glutton, but I was always hungry, recently of limited means, and always in a hurry. And he was lean, a little gaunt maybe, or maybe just overworked.

"I've never seen a dancer eat so much. Do you purge?"

"God no. I just binge and starve, kind of like a cobra or something. When I was in school the more I worried about my weight the worse I looked. Now I eat when I'm hungry. Swimming taught me nutrition." Now I was blathering. "You have to keep your strength up. Good nutrition is kind of a hobby—too bad I can't afford it. I mean..."

"You're a dancer. Say no more."

I wished I hadn't shown up empty-handed. "God you just can't escape the food thing as a dancer, can you? Everyone is fascinated by it."

"It's refreshing to see someone eat."

"I hope I'm not making a pig of myself." At least eating kept me occupied. "This wine has gone to my head."

"We can only hope."

"You can."

"Yep. So. What brought you to the land of poutine and pea soup?"

"Just looking for better opportunities, better training for my body. I'm working with an extremely talented woman now."

"Your body looks fine to me."

"I could have stayed with the Company. I was second soloist, but the training was... oh forget it." Of course I'd stopped believing this long ago, but it was the official story.

"It seems a big risk to take. This woman must be something."

"She was a principal with the Hungarian State and a soloist with the Royal before immigrating." I wrapped the spaghetti on my spoon and tried not to think of her filthy kitchen, enough to spoil a healthy appetite, and hoped he wouldn't ask much more about her. I didn't want to have to start lying on our first date.

"As in London's Royal Ballet?"

"Mmm hmm."

He looked at me like he understood this world of the gypsy and the circus, something most non-dancers do not get. "I've never had an artistic outlet," he said. "I've never felt the urge." He poured another glass of wine. "I love wine, I love music, love dance but don't have an expressive bone in my body. Well, maybe one. And to give it credit, it is quite expressive and come to think of it, it has urges."

"Your outlet."

"Definitely."

"I get the point."

"You will."

I giggled the way I hate to do.

"Oh, I've known a few dancers. In Toronto mainly. The National—among others."

"So maybe that's your expression—doing dancers." My nervousness was replaced with regret for this last comment, like a bucket of cold water thrown on the conversation. How could I compare with all of everything he had heard, seen and tasted of the dance world in Toronto? I held up my glass for a refill. He touched my fingers. When he took the glass I noticed how thick and rough his hands were. He steadied the glass and poured.

"Dancers don't strike me as risk-takers."

"No? With a lifespan less than a moth to a flame? That's not a risk?"

"Well, not once they have a job. You've taken a leap into the unknown, which this place certainly is. I'm surprised you left. You're brave."

"Or naive?"

"Optimistic."

"Stupid?"

"Idealistic?"

"I wish I could look at it that way."

"You'll see—someday." He clinked his glass against mine.

I swallowed a small burp. "You're drunk."

"It takes a lot more than this to get me drunk."

"Well not me. I guess I should have eaten something today." I pushed back from the table. (It's amazing how satisfied you feel after a meal cooked with care, not just thrown together for sustenance, mixed with paranoia that there might be one calorie too many.) I got up and plunked into an old velvety easy chair. Kent filled our glasses and returned to sit at my feet.

"Speaking of dancers, you ever hear from that guy, Daniel?" I tried desperately to sound matter-of-fact.

"God, no! I don't keep in touch with every trick I have, although I'm pretty good about it. But Daniel, he seems like he's all over the place. Who could keep up with him? Though I gave him my number, I didn't think he'd call. But he did. About you."

"What did he say?"

"Nothing. Said you were a dancer. Said he coached you. That's about it. Nothing special. You know. Nothing extraordinary. Don't pout. You know how he feels about dancers. You two have a thing? That why you're asking?" Kent pulled on my pant leg then quickly reached up and undid my belt. "You still saving yourself for that guy in Montreal?"

Kent was fast, but I liked his bravado. His fingers fumbled around to get my fly half-open and pull my pants below my waist, before I pushed his hands away. God I needed to be touched.

When Daniel vanished so did my confidence. Kent somehow stirred those ideas that I might be an attractive being. Not to mention the fact that he continued at my leg with the earnestness and openness of a horny dog; you can so easily forgive them as you affectionately slap them away, believing they chose you specifically, but knowing it is merely physical. I couldn't help but laugh, and with his innuendo and my drunkenness I couldn't take it seriously.

He sat back and started to untuck his shirt. "This room gets so hot," he said. After two bottles of wine, this was true. When he pulled his shirt over his head I saw that he was just lean, wound muscle, like someone whose metabolism was working overtime.

He unzipped his pants. "Do you like getting fucked? If you know Daniel, then you like getting fucked."

"But…"

"Just kidding."

Now I had to part the clouds of inebriation to make some sense of where it was all going. His desperation was driving me nuts, and although I didn't want to disappoint, I did not want to start something. I remember hearing "like sticks with like" when I was growing up—the Ukes, the Scots, the Anglos—for some unknown reason, and now we fairies had to as well. Anyway, I couldn't figure out what Daniel and Kent really had in common to bring them together, if in fact they were both tops. Then I saw Kent's penis—a huge sloppy thing, like Daniel's but circumcised. They were card-carrying members of the big cock club.

"Don't move for a minute. I have to take this all in." Just looking wasn't complicated. I wouldn't have to explain myself. "You have an amazing body." Even if I wasn't prepared to partake, I could at least enjoy the view and maybe be truthful about it.

"Well? *Have* you?"

"Hmmmm?"

"Have you ever been fucked?"

"No. Don't see how I'd enjoy it anyway."

"So you're a top?"

"I don't know. I do like sex if that's what you want to know."

"I can't believe, with an ass like that, you've never been fucked."

"Never had the opportunity."

"It's an amazing feeling."

"For you?"

"For you."

He lunged. You could forgive kissing, but I bit through the lip lock. "I have to go."

"You're joking."

"I wish I was. I can't do this tonight."

"You can stay. We don't have to have sex, or I can come over, give you some company. We could cuddle."

"No. I need to sleep. I'm just… I can't."

"More wine?"

"No, really. I better go. To be honest, I've only slept with about seven people—and only sort of."

"In your whole life?"

"It's been kind of a no man's land down there. I think it had to do with a couple of undescended balls and a hernia."

"Well, everything looks well descended now. Jeez, you're practically a virgin. I've been with upwards of two thousand. Maybe only seven today…"

"Sex, never mind fucking, is one of the most pleasurable experiences for a man, any man." And with this comment I was flooded with a mixture of humiliation and what I knew to be a fear of not being good enough.

"You sound pretty committed to the cause." Kent was obviously a sexual athlete. I didn't just want to be number two thousand and one.

"You're saving yourself for someone in Montreal?"

"You might say I'm old-fashioned."

"Sex and love go hand in hand for someone like you."

"And someone like me is what?"

"You're a romantic. You're hopeful. You're a dreamer or you wouldn't be here. I told you I know dancers, and I'd say you have taken a hefty risk."

"Sex and love."

"That's why you're here. Don't worry. You'll find both. Together. At the same time."

"It's not like I grew up in a hotbed of sexual activity."

"You probably just had no idea. What's the worst that could happen?"

I thought of our last tour when some guy in Thunder Bay asked if I wanted to go on a date. He said, "Look I don't want to marry you I just asked you for a date." I realized after that, that the other six guys weren't like me. They weren't looking for love.

"I guess I'm hung up on the love part."

"Maybe you should fall in love a little more often."

"With you?"

"Not with me. God. Just, you know, loosen up. You're a dancer. There are things you have to cultivate—your instincts for one, an appreciation and knowledge of good wine for another. Sex, too."

"Hah."

"Sex is an incredible gift. Don't waste it on some moral high ground. You can eat spaghetti alone, which is fine, or you can share it with a friend or even a stranger or with someone you love, slathered with sauce and good, fresh parmesan. Each time it's unique and good in its own way. Tell me this is bland."

"This is definitely spaghetti with sauce."

"God you're a baby, but you like me don't you?"

"Daniel tried to…"

"Daniel? Daniel? That's who you're saving yourself for?"

"Shit."

"Don't worry. Unfortunately the world's full of Daniels. If that's what you're pining, I mean waiting for, good luck. I've had a few."

"A few thousand."

"No, you count those types on one hand. You'll get over him—I guess you know he liked fucking, by the way."

"Is that what you did?"

"Not really. We are both after the same kind of thing. Anyway you, my dear, have some growing up to do. I've always thought dancers were a little on the thick side." Kent's tone had changed. I had offended him. "They can't really help it with the protected lives they lead. One thing you should know, though, is that a guy like Daniel will never save himself for another man."

"We'll see."

"You better start enjoying sex for what it is. Love will happen. I fall in love ten times a day." Kent slowly got up, went to the window.

I had spoiled the evening by talking too much, by being too much of an innocent—or at least presenting myself that way.

CERTAIN IMAGES COME BACK to me, as easily as torn bits of folded paper with fading phone numbers, or a silken business card I keep pulling out of a wallet, too worn to use, but reminding me of something. You know exactly where it is if you need it. It might show up unannounced or it might be lost forever.

I see a child running naked into the street. The street is in front of me because I am that child. Afraid of what goes on inside—of me. Inside, I'm broken. Afraid of pained urine, an aching abdomen. Afraid I was broken like my mother. To make it better she took me for tea at Eaton's. I was always well enough for tea. She dressed me in patent leather shoes, a little black velvet cap and a tweed coat. I always sat on the banquette and she faced me so she could look past her teacup and over my head to watch the reflections of those who came and went. I asked her once if I could have a brother or sister. I thought it was that easy. Like asking Santa for presents. She squeezed my hand, looked at me and smiled. I thought she was going to laugh, so I smiled, too, but she started to cry. "It's not up to us."

"Who then?"

"God. Sometimes God sees that people are so happy with one child that he sends more to another family. God will give us different gifts. You'll see."

That afternoon my mother surprised me. After tea she said we should get some groceries but she took me to my first movie. We sat in the theatre and watched *The King and I*, my mother's second-favourite movie after *The Red Shoes* (which, she said, I was too young for) and my first homoerotic experience: Yul Brenner dancing barefoot, with a woman who looked like my mother.

I figured that since she couldn't have children, she got different gifts. God had sent her a black mink coat and a black convertible Pontiac Parisienne, no station wagon for her, not like the other mothers. And the rooms in our home stayed empty, the boys' bathroom became the men's cloakroom and the girls' bathroom, the ladies' powder room. And my room stayed my room. And I just wanted to play outdoors with brothers and sisters. Instead I wandered in the dry prairie heat, hoped no one would know I had a scar. Prayed for the broken part to go away, no matter what the cost. I knew she was broken, too, and that God's wishes were as strange as Santa's. All I prayed for was to not be like her, or worse, like him. I wanted to leave myself, like a prairie rattlesnake shimmies out of his skin.

KENT STOOD NAKED IN the light. His body small, hard from the vertebrae under his skin to his tight ass to the veins under his calf muscles. "This has been such a good night," he said. What was it that made me trust him? He moved the curtain aside and looked down on the street. "There's a gay bar outside the gate, on the way to Lower Town," he said. "If you're ever looking for love, and Daniel doesn't come through, it's called Le Cirque—or you can pay me a visit."

"I'm going to go back this weekend," I said, "and stay with him."

"Good luck. You can sleep here you know. You don't need to try out your new mattress tonight."

"No. I think I need to be alone. Thanks anyway."

Later, when I was dressing, he squeezed some bills in my hand. "For the bus," he said, "to Montreal."

Back in my apartment, I lay on my new mattress. I stayed dressed to keep the chill away. I woke the next morning, having had one of my deepest sleeps in months, and got myself ready for the bus ride back to Montreal.

IT WASN'T UNTIL I was on the back of this bus, in a drooling dry-aired reverie, that certain things became a little more obvious. First, Kent must have thought I was a masochist. Second, I had arrived at a jobless, moneyless dead end.

Hugues had moved or was away. Phone numbers had been changed. I walked to the Old Port—walked past the jewellers where I had believed he was buying my engagement rock, and stopped and waited—as if a magic portal would open and I would be transported back to that day. I was a mess of instincts and fantasies. I wandered Montreal and ended up outside his place, waiting for him to answer the door. There was no "I know you're up there." I'd done that as a kid—tried to wrangle my way into someone's tree fort.

I spent the rest of that night on a bench at the bus station while the winners in Montreal filled the clubs, and glistening cars and cabs left the rest of us to sleep on our broken dreams. I dreamt he came to the bus station, and we cuddled and ate *croque monsieur* and drank red wine out of a thermos. We even had sex. He left with no messages of how to meet, ever again. I woke with that familiar stickiness in my crotch and a stained zipper. As I tried to dry myself at 5:45 A.M. in the can some old guy wagged his dick at the urinal for me. There's always someone around to make you feel wanted.

That morning, dirty, stained and tired I got the bus back to Quebec City; the ride took forever. There were some gigglers and partiers who had been up all night and were making the fun last as long as possible. Fatigue won out, for all of us, and the bus droned silently along the highway. I thought of my parents and wondered if they were thinking about me.

I dragged myself off the bus and up to the Old Town. As I walked up Sainte-Ursule I fought the urge to ring Kent's bell. But he stepped out his door and draped his arm over my shoulder. "Welcome home." Over café au lait and croissant, which he treated me to, he told me how he finally let the guy at Kresge's suck him off for my mattress, and throughout the conversation, with the tact of someone consoling someone at a funeral, he had the decency not to ask me how Montreal went.

THE LAST OF MY money went to the first month's rent and security deposit. At the end of each day of bad dancing I wandered restaurant foyers and hotel lobbies looking for work. Wasn't this a tourist town, for God's sake? Employers weren't impressed with my French, but hell, weren't the tourists English? It didn't matter; no business in Quebec City would hire a WASP with high school French. The slim and slimy maître d' at the Chateau Frontenac curled his upper lip as if I had just shit in the foyer. (Believe me, no matter how quaint the lobby of a hotel or the dining room of a restaurant, you can be sure that the personnel office stinks of leftover food, cigarette smoke and butts older than rotting leftovers, and anything else dried up, crusted, forgotten, tossed over or snatched from the kitchen.) Meanwhile others brushed me off with a single wave of the hand, with no more effort than you would use for a housefly.

How would I survive in a fairy-tale town with a four-hundred-year-old wall around it, nursing a broken heart and a broken ego? One fucking *Oui* to a job could have changed my life. On the other hand, it might have meant that I would still be working at the Chateau Frontenac. I wanted another meal with Kent that night, just to be able to share my exasperation, but there was no answer at his door and the lights were off. I had a full set of cutlery at home, chairs and a table, and while I could have returned to my standby of pickles and spaghetti, I used my savings to buy a large bottle of red. I sat at the table and looked out the window—perhaps I'd see Kent come down the street.

I MAKE MY WAY to the ground floor of this white tower, hoping that, by some miracle, my clothes will still be waiting for me. I freeze when I hear a door open, hear voices, car keys jingling, and sigh when I hear it shut. I still curse those bastards and the doors slammed in my face; why the hell was it so hard to hire an Anglophone? In the Canadian public school system you may learn that there are two official languages but, *mon ami*, halting classroom French isn't one of them.

My high school French teacher, Monsieur Laflamme, pointer in hand, prodded the language out of us. I sat in the second desk for an undetected crotch view. He was cute; a dark testosterone machine, *coureurs-de-bois* with the trimmed beard and big butt in hug-your-ass Hudson Bay Co. wool blends. Thick stubby fingers. Against the rules for him to teach *Joual*. You know: *ouai* instead of *oui*, *Chez-K* for K-mart, *Chez Kreszh* for Kresge's, Pepsi for Coke, *tabarnak* for whatever, *trou-de-cul* for asshole, *tapette* for homo, et-cet-e-ra, et-cet-e-ra, et-cet-e-ra. I worshipped him—my study partner and I set elaborate costumed dialogues based on ballets. We draped the desks, wore costumes. None of it made sense. My speech centres were frozen but my brain was popping with inspiration. Laflamme stood back and watched open-mouthed as I haltingly played to him.

After I graduated, I heard that my study partner had made a different career choice: to dance at a bar downtown. Then he got a government job, and they paid him to study French full-time for two years so he could lick envelopes in our two official languages. Where is he now?

If you can afford it, red wine is good at a dead end, and it might be your only option. I was so sure Kent would wander up Sainte-Ursule that night but I woke, tumbling off of the chair.

Four

A DANCER'S LEGS CURVE like a gentle "S" reaching from the base of the back, around and under the buttocks, the front of the thigh, through the knee and into the calf, folding then extending into a *développé*—presenting itself like a meal to be served—or a *battement*—the swinging pendulum from a body that is solid and unmoving. To plié, the muscles release, as if in agreement that—as supple and controlled as they must be—they will lower and then return you to the stature of a mythical god. To *sauté*, there is an explosive power, rock solid if trained properly, that slingshots the dancer into a precise trajectory, the sum of body, mind and instinct, as the knee recoils and summons all available physical elements to order. The thigh, the calf, each joint, each tendon, each tissue rallies to elevate the privileged being to a place of otherworldly experience and expression, before becoming earthbound once more.

KENT'S FRENCH WAS REALLY no better than mine and yet he had found a job. But a little voice in the back of my mind told me that he had that rare gift called *charm*. My famous blank stare revealed my lack of charm and enthusiasm at the prospect of more restaurant schlepping. I was transparent. Kent had met a couple that found his accent quaint and they admired his effort to speak, no matter how badly. He ended up waiting tables in their small restaurant. It was a hole in the wall where the furnishings hadn't changed in four hundred years and the food was "exquisite," according to him. I prayed his luck might rub off on me.

I could never have walked into a gig like that, let alone find it. And though there is something to be said for dedication and perseverance, the chances of getting work do not increase per miles searched.

Late Friday afternoon, I sat on my floor beside a phone that had forgotten how to ring, leafing through *Le Soleil*, making no money by the hour. The last dollars had been spent to and from Montreal, and the last spare change spent on a café au lait to weep into, leaving a jar full of pennies standing between me and a beer in which to drown my final sorrows. My father had made it clear after I dropped out of pre-med that there was no road home, and though we had reconciled when I proved that I could do it, and proved him wrong—I'd made it clear I would never again need their help—there was no way now to eat crow and phone home for a loan. If they knew what I had done to pummel my career they would be dumbfounded, and rightly so.

A newspaper ad for a nightclub, showing leggy feathery girls, à la Las Vegas revue, surrounding a guy who had way too much hair on his head, caught my eye, and I considered my chances of serving drinks there. Maybe they attracted tourists, and needed an English-speaking waiter.

What the hell had gotten into me? It was a cabaret. They dance there. Dance. I dance. Was I blind? They advertised this place with showgirls in silver sequined G-strings, feathers shooting out the tops of their heads, a big-haired guy in the front with two more hot guys in the back in glove-tight pants. It all looked so polished, so French, so cosmopolitan, so *Folies Bergères*, so alluring, so damn exotic for this boy from Strathcona, Edmonton. It would be a job related to my chosen profession, *mon métier*. I had the same skill set for this job. And you don't have to know how to conjugate verbs to dance in faux *Moulin Rouge*—you don't even have to speak. Dance, like music, is the international language, spanning borders, cultures and millennia. If some woman is waggling her tail feathers in your face, I think we know what she's trying to say (get me outta here and get me some money). No question, I wouldn't need a translator.

I called the club and repeated the two most important words: *travail* and *danseur*. Above a noisy background and a throbbing bass, someone shouted in French and told me to call *Agence en Vedette*. There was more incomprehensible squaggling. Some guy shouted the phone number at me, which I didn't understand, and then I let my crossed fingers do the walking through the yellow pages.

I paid a visit on Friday to the *Agence*, after class. It was on my route home. At the agency, a woman, Martine, with cigarette-rotted teeth and hair that had had way too much attention and looked similar to a rusty, teased bird's nest, chattered in a smoky, cluttered office with two tough guys. She waved me in and stood up behind her desk, revealing most of herself in a tight leather vest and leather miniskirt.

"Je cherche travail comme danseur," I ventured.

She babbled something back at me that was very quick and incomprehensible, but for some reason we knew we were speaking the same language. I had a product that she seemed to be in need of, which was a far cry from the past few months of rejections. She smiled, too, and in spite of the bad teeth, it was endearing, confident and open. I couldn't help feeling like the two guys she was entertaining were thugs, but for now she liked me, and all seemed to be well with them. From her desk she took a business card that shimmered red and gold 3-D and swirled depending on the angle you looked at it. On the back she scribbled the number and name of someone: Marcel Missoni. It seemed it was his show. He must have been the big-haired one I'd seen in the paper. She told me to give him a call on Monday.

I wanted to skip all the way home at the prospect of having some cash come in, and also because she had been so damn nice. When I got home, I called Kent to see if he could lend me twenty dollars, but not before telling him my good news, so he would know he'd get paid back.

"You can have it if you let me blow you. Why do you need twenty dollars?"

"For the weekend."

"The whole weekend? You can survive a weekend on twenty dollars?"

"I'm thrifty." The hole in the wall at the end of the street sold pints to locals for two dollars, and I was rich—I had a jar of pickles and some spaghetti to last me for the weekend.

"Sounds like someone needs taking care of. Let me buy you a beer or two."

And from that moment on, Kent called me every day. Funny how comforting that ringing phone became.

MY JOB FOLLOW-UP WAS limited to later that moody Monday, after Madame had a run at us, leaving our spirits even less intact than our bodies. Her bad mood reflected an especially pissed off state, which I figured was because of my good mood at demonstrating some grain of independence and successfully finding a home I referred to as *spectaculaire*, and my job prospects, and as a result out-dancing everyone that day.

I raced home with the single thought that the nightclub would work out. I called Marcel Missoni before I'd even dropped my dance bag, and he told me in perfect English, spiced with some kind of Franco-Italian accent, to come to the club that night. This request involved the hunt for bus fare. I mean, *fucking bus fare*. Pocket bottoms. Jacket liners. I cursed having spent all of Kent's twenty. But I hit the jackpot: a fiver in some trashy cut-offs I wore two summers ago up on Lake Winnipeg, long before poverty had set in.

Which bus? On the phone Marcel couldn't say because he'd never taken one. Who does? I wandered around the *carrefour* outside the city gates to find the bus to rue Lévesque, a sweaty ride in the back corner out to the Chez Moritz that busy September rush hour. An Indian summer had nosed its way in from New England for a moment. Could things get any better? Free transportation—Company buses, planes, trains, taxis and limos—was a thing of the past. This idea of me riding out to the suburbs of Quebec to work in a tits-and-feathers show would have disappointed anyone who had invested their hopes and efforts in my career, but fortunately there weren't many. Not fair I suppose: Lisa, my first teacher, as well as my ex-roommates Peter and Rachelle, and the kind souls Bertrand and Louise, and others I have most likely and selfishly overlooked, played a role. Still, I was blindly optimistic.

Small-town Canada had been a family curse for several generations: Great Grampa Ramsbottom became Rottam. Dad showed them, and moved to a plusher place, got a college education, turned to dentistry—big money in big mouths. Big house. Only one kid, leading to suburban slanderous whispers of what a wife does alone; then years later what their son had being doing at a ballet studio. They tried their best: Dad with hockey, Mom with ballet and symphony. And I took my little opera glasses everywhere. At the hockey games, I watched the half-time figure skaters, while Dad and the men left their seats to drain their beer-bloated bladders in the common urinals and return with hot dogs.

Even at the ballet it was tough to conceal an appreciation of the human form. Timing with opera glasses was everything. My mom knew I loved the ballet but it was unheard of to have a son learn ballet. I would be the prisoner of a lumpy seat, an observer. She dreamed, too; when we weren't at the ballet, my mother spent time in her sewing room, talking to my aunt on the phone while mending my socks and trousers, under that framed poster of Nureyev and Fonteyn on the wall above her, with classical music on a portable record player. "Swan Lake" crackled endlessly; "The Nutcracker" at Christmas— mostly things by Tchaikovsky and the Russians. When it was a ballet or a concerto, I fell asleep with patterns dancing in my head. My escape to university in another town brought freedom—and gave my parents the prestige they craved—but I surrounded myself with the familiar, the music mostly.

God. Family history flashing before my eyes on a desperate bus ride to the suburbs of Quebec by the only Rottam son (of the only Rottam son), who would most likely never carry on the family name. Shame does that. I stared at the backs of heads, wondered for a moment what was driving me forward, but knew the answer so well. By the time I got to rue Lévesque, the bus was almost empty and all I could see was the Chez Moritz standing out on the edge of the highway next to a motel, like the last remaining bulb in a dressing room mirror. That was it. No trees. No Dairy Queen. No Country Time donuts on Pembina Highway running south to the American border. No nothing. Just land ugly enough to be developed. The bus stopped midway along that nothingness. A stop made for the future inhabitants of dream homes.

The bus driver must have known why I got off there. I was reeking of lost soul. I risked being a statistic to walk the highway where there was no shoulder. The club probably had windows in a previous life. Maybe it had been a restaurant where people went for Sunday dinner. But now there were only frames surrounding boarded-up sections of wall with metal-screen grating nailed to that, all coated in matching flat brown paint—one nasty-looking compound. A neon sign spelled out the name, c-h-e-z m-o-r-i-t-z, letter by letter, with a cancan dancer whose one functioning pink leg flickered spastically from behind. I hauled open the door.

In the dark, I noticed the thick smell of beer and cigarettes first, then recognized the shape of that head of hair I'd seen in the paper. "Mister Missoni?"

He sat at the bar, looked over his shoulder. "Marcel, please, Marcel." He was Louis xiv from a children's book: very froofy, with glistening curly black locks, a near-handlebar moustache, great nose and chin. Handsome. He had a mouth that read slightly disgusted with everything. His small and slightly effeminate manner—like a tropical bird preening while clucking to himself—betrayed his masculine looks. He wore tight, black pants, and a vest over a dress shirt that made him look like a matador. Nothing seemed to be said or thought without a coif adjustment. He stirred a tall drink with a swizzle stick, his wrist bent at a ninety-degree angle. "You must be John. Have a seat."

I sat on the stool beside him. He clicked his fingernails on the bar and the bartender quickly slid a beer in front of me. He must have seen my concern at not being able to pay, and winked. The bar extended from just beyond the front door and curved toward the back. Marcel sat closest to the door. As my eyes adjusted to the darkness behind him, silhouettes of bodies became women on small boxes dancing for slouching men at small tables. And soon I saw the bodies were naked—moving like wild animals on their stoops at the circus. I see them all now as I steady myself. I control this step by step to the bottom floor of no man's land. I remember thinking it was like a kind of hell on earth, and here I am in this stairwell.

The naked bodies danced like they were in love with themselves. The agency never mentioned that part. Did they think I wouldn't be interested? It wasn't the chic nightclub of my fantasies. Still, bills had to be paid; I couldn't ask for a twenty from Kent each time I needed to eat. I had rent to pay. In restaurants, booze prices carry the food losses. At the Chez Moritz I'd say the table dancers paid the bills, and the feathers-and-sequins burlesque passed things off as wholesome family entertainment. In the dark, men in the audience could have been dead for all I knew. But there was a stage against one wall where the legitimate *spectacle*, that I had come to be part of, happened. "We do three shows a night," said Marcel, "at 10:30, midnight and 1:30." He spoke perfect English with that hint of an accent. "You can come back tonight and see if you like it. Watch the show. Did you say you studied at the Conservatoire?"

"A little. Don't hold it against me. I mean I can easily do this kind of..."

"Then we're family. Best years of my life."

"I was just there this summer. Before that..." I didn't tell him before that. And I could tell he was one of those whose world only existed between Quebec and Montreal. The country was full of them, whether it was knowing just Toronto or just Edmonton or just Van-couver, Sudbury, Fredericton, Wawa or Medicine Hat, and believing that your place was the centre of the universe. Besides I didn't want him to know what I'd left, or how promising I once thought I was.

"And now?"

"I've always wanted to do the Vegas thing" (but I didn't think the "Vegas thing" would happen so soon). Many retired ballet dancers had gone on to Vegas to dance or to choreograph or even run casinos, but they had already taken a few kicks at the ballet can (and it had kicked back). Had I sounded insincere?

"We have some good people. Talented." He definitely sounded like he was exaggerating.

"Great."

"Don't you want to know how much we pay?"

"You're making me an offer?"

"Come to my office for the paperwork."

I followed him around the bar and down the back stairs. Girls coming up. Girls going down. A few of them nodded at him, touched his shoulder. No one noticed me. I got the feeling that drugs and booze were the big thrill on both levels, probably softening the rough edges, caked makeup, sweat and running mascara. As for me, I still had my days to get through, and since my body was my temple, I couldn't afford much more than the odd beer. I would have to be fit to lead this double life.

He took me into an over-large makeshift bathroom—concrete floor, particleboard walls—with a grungy mothball shower. "I'm sure you can dance if you've been at the Conservatoire but I need to see your behind," he said. "We wear G-strings. I make most of the costumes. Assless chaps, stuff like that. I just want to see your butt. Know how it will look—know your measurements."

I figured it out.

Turn around.

Undo belt.

Drop pants.

Expose ass.

Wait for it. Whatever it might be.

"Dancer's butt. Madame Talegdi find you?" he said.

"Yes."

"I thought she might. She's mad you know."

"Crazy."

"How are your thighs?"

"Stiff, tight. Too big."

"They look great. Splits?"

"Both ways."

He touched my behind, which felt good. But that was my problem. Then he reached around to my front. "Nice," he said, gripping me. I exhaled. "This package will look fantastic in a G-string. I'll need to make a generous pouch. You'll do well here." He let out an audible shiver.

"Was that my audition?"

"One of my guys just quit."

"Right place at the right time?"

"Fifty bucks a night for the three shows. Plus tips."

One week's work would pay my rent. "Tips?"

"Bonuses. You don't do drugs do you?"

"No."

"I didn't think so. Well in that case you'll make some money. Just be careful here. There's always lots to walk in on. You don't want to get under anybody's skin. And watch your money, your tips."

"I'm in?"

"You're in. So come back tonight. See if it suits you."

He was genuinely cute, with a twinkle in his eye; he was almost bashful, harmless and completely innocent. I remember that look— he looked up at me like we'd done something naughty.

OUTSIDE THE CHEZ MORITZ, the remains of the Indian summer clung to the end of the day, and a pale October sun turned the flat brown walls of the club orange. There was no going home for dinner and then coming back in the evening. I was confined to public transit and poverty. If I went home now, I would never return. I walked past an adjoining dump of a motel next door to the Chez Moritz and wondered who could stay in a dive like that.

As I walked I hummed that song. The one from the Disney movie. Something about how your dreams really do come true. Look at me: the poster child for following dreams. There I was following my dream, which had shrunk down to getting a coffee with extra cream at a truck stop out near a strip club that looked like an Armageddon bunker where the daily special was abuse and torture. I ended up about a mile down the road at a diner and spent two hours in a booth with a jukebox (which was useless without an extra quarter), stretching out a free refill of coffee and dreaming about the sugar pie in the display case. Dancers' naive conversations about the difference between a fat calorie and a carbohydrate were a thing of the past.

Things had to get better. Did the truckers at the counter and their girlfriends ever go to the club? Maybe their girlfriends were those dancers I'd seen moving in the dark. Would I see these guys back there later on? Or did they have more important things to do than drink and watch strippers? And did I look out of place? Did I look like a westerner? Or like a chorus boy? How many John Rottams came in every week? On tours some waitress would always ask if you were with the Company, even if they'd never been in a real theatre in their lives. They recognized us. They fed us, and our egos. But now I was so far away from that, and even further from anything I knew. Maybe the waitress would ask if I worked in that bunker over there.

There was a fancy diner that my parents took me to on Sunday nights for roast chicken and mashed potatoes. I would sit hands crossed. "Quit staring," Dad would say. But my heart would go out to any sad, old cowboy sitting alone eating a hamburger. I imagined that if the rustler's cheeks weren't full, or if he swallowed, he might cry. The same went for a homely girl alone in a booth with puckered lips peeking into a compact, trying to look pretty, pretending she was waiting for someone. I wanted to tell them it was okay. I was sure I knew exactly how they felt. But they had their own stories, they'd get by, create a story to keep them from going crazy, like I had. Me and the lonely cowboy and the homely girl were in it together. It had something to do with comments at school, mostly about being the only one.

We sat in that fancy diner, and I stared at my parents and they stared out the window at our Cadillac. I wondered why they wouldn't look at each other. What had I done? Was it really my fault that there were no other kids? Maybe God thought I was enough. How could I convince them that I was? Did everyone wonder why I didn't have a sister at the table with me? I had to know. "Did you ask for more kids, Dad?"

"Ask who?"

"Ask God."

"It's not up to God."

"Then who?"

"No one. Kids just happen, like accidents. No one can know when they will happen."

"That's nonsense. What your father meant was that they happen like surprises."

"Do all these people have kids?"

"Doesn't look like it."

"So not everyone has kids?"

"No."

"But..."

"There's only one thing that matters in your life and that's to keep good care of your teeth. You can worry about kids when you get older."

"Brothers and sisters?"

"Sons and daughters."

I could go insane wondering why I was sitting in a diner on rue Lévesque. I was beyond the point of no return. If Lisa had invested her time and attention in my beginnings as a dancer, she must have believed in me; she was my first ballet teacher and she said I could do it. She was the very first to say I could be a real honest-to-God dancer. After all, she had danced with the Company in the corps. True, it was short-lived; her centre of gravity was too low and her thighs too big. Any dancer would know she'd never be a principal or a soloist. Still, an ovation was due for any female who got that far, and with her handicaps. The competition among women to make their lifelong dream to be a princess come true is nothing a man, other than one like myself, can ever comprehend. To want to be a ballerina must be the most alluring and devastating dream in the world—other than maybe the dream of having your own pony. Every woman wants to be a ballerina at some point—it demands absolute pristine and holy perfection—and if they don't make it, they can be satisfied that everything else will always be second best.

I left Lisa and the hometown studio. University in Saskatoon, the alibi, appeased my parents and off-campus I tracked down a brooding dancer, Drake, from the Company days gone by, who taught me how to dance like a man, between screaming at the little girls with bun-pulled faces. I took his classes six days a week. "You don't have to worry, you won't be paying."

To add to it, I found a group of extremely talented ex-ballerinas in the campus gym—most within a whisper of having made their dreams come true. But circumstances, family, genetics—their bodies hadn't been perfect enough, arches high enough, chests flat enough, hips boyish enough, nothing proportioned *enough*—decided for them. Now they danced for the love of it they'd lost, along the way,

among the competition and heartbreak. I danced with them in a
brand new vacant studio used for nothing other than cheerleading
practices between scheduled lectures in dim auditoriums and naps
in the stale library. They were pushy and demanding, pre-law and
pre-med, and I was so grateful. I stretched my arches under radiators
until they stung. Forced splits in my doorway. Dared my hamstrings
to snap. Ate, slept and dreamed dance. Took class with tight-lipped
Drake. Learned what male dancers do on the ground and in the air. I
had somehow pulled together a homemade full-time dance schedule.
Now, in Quebec, I was cobbling together another life.

I finished my bottomless refill of day-old coffee, wiped my mouth,
wiped my mind clean of these characters, paid, stepped outside, inhaled, pressed my shoulders back, ignored my growling stomach,
stuck out my chest, made like I was a star and headed back along the
edge of the highway, into the dusk and onto a bar stool to wait for the
show to begin.

I ordered water and got beer.

Two big guys in charcoal suits slid on and off bar stools to the
door and back, flexed their shoulders and cracked their knuckles.
They looked like a genetic twins experiment gone wrong. Both
probably weighed the same but were completely different shapes
and composed of very different body mass. They were dark, Greek
maybe—"He's Vasili."

"No, he's Vasili. I'm Mihalis."

"No, I'm…" And on and on. The heavy one joking that he could be
mistaken for his brother, the muscular one. The other one, too thick
to figure it out. Vasili must have weighed in at a sloppy three hundred
pounds—white shirt untucked, hairy belly hanging over his belt. He
kept tucking himself in, like he was trying to carry rising bread dough
from one place to another. A few days' growth of whiskers covered his
double chins, and ringlets of hair shone on his oval head. Everything
about him said grease. He was chowing down on a bag of poutine,
which he tried to share.

Mihalis was big, too, but it was three hundred pounds of triple-
A prime Greek muscle, a former Mr. Canada contender. When he
shook my hand I held on tight. Biceps practically split the sleeves of

his suit. Shoulders like an ox. Face like an ox, too. Forehead tilted like a Neanderthal, as if the supplements were going wonky, or he'd been hit by a truck. I was curious about these muscle-bound types. They had some sense of aesthetic. Was it anything like mine? Mihalis had a dream. He owned a gym in Lower Town. That was his passion. So he must have understood if I stared a bit, since it was the nature of his career, and mine too. Both of us were exhibitionists; we had a connection to physical pain, narcissism, single-mindedness, perfection, dissatisfaction and being familiar with every inch of our bodies. Was there truly no line between the dancer and the dance? Was my need to dance coupled with my need to embody and possess the human form in all its potential sensual and sexual beauty? Most would not think a monster like Mihalis beautiful but so many, Michelangelo for instance, had tried and captured it.

Vasili came over, licked the grease off his fingers, and stuffed his shirt in his pants. "Come I introduce you to da girls," he said.

I followed him to the jukebox where some of the girls were sitting, feet up on the edge of the stage. A small one in a white fur bikini, high white leather boots and blonde hair down to her behind was someone's little-girl fantasy. Mihalis called her *Chaton*. We were ignored by a tall s&m dominatrix in leather hot pants, breasts stuffed into a matching tube top, straight black hair, dark narrow eyes. Then there was one who looked as wholesome as an old-fashioned Hollywood starlet. Her hair was pressed into curls. Her name was Nadine but I'd say she was more Rita Hayworth. She wore a white blouse and a pleated plaid miniskirt. She took my arm and pulled me toward her, whispered something in my ear and laughed. Vasili rolled his eyes and told me she was crazy. "Poor Nadine," he said. "Her 'eart was broke ten years ago and she's still not over it. She should be teaching kindergarten." Then he said something to them and they giggled. The blonde little-girl Chaton nodded toward me, said something, and they laughed some more.

I took my place back at the bar and during three more complimentary beers I watched as after-work businessmen trailed in and slid over to the vacant tables. A few of the girls were dancing on boxes. One was in chain mail, one in a leopard and fishnet bikini and one in a black unitard, with her spandexed bum in some guy's face. They had a routine: pose, run their hands up and down their thighs, squat, take off their tops and then tickle their nipples.

And every time a waitress went by she checked me out, like she wanted to see what *the new guy* was like. Soon they were winking at me while they were shoving their rear end in some guy's face.

Meanwhile Chaton, now up on the stage in her white fur, was in a state. She yelled to anyone paying attention, "*Cureees.*" She was stuck, and looked like she was trapped in a poodle outfit, squirming and tearing at her zipper like she had fleas.

I stayed at the end of the bar and leaned against the wall. Another beer came. I sat. I stared at the rim of the glass.

Marcel's voice pulled me out of my reverie as he announced "*le premier spectacle du monde,*" backed by a bum-bada-bum disco beat. Four leggy showgirls, like giant peacocks, heavy with silver sequined harnesses that pulled trailing rainbow feather tails, swayed corner to corner. They balanced glittering headdresses, sometimes tipping and getting stuck on ceiling lights or each other. The Rita Hayworth girl, Nadine, spent most of her time scowling. Then Marcel made his entrance in a one-piece bodysuit split down the chest and opened around the top of the bum. I swear his head of hair was bigger than Gino Vanelli's, which made him look even shorter. He lip-synced Chevalier's gravelly "Le Temps" while the girls posed at either corner of the stage. He was convincing. He took himself seriously, and he'd done his homework. And the show wasn't bad; it was genuine glitz. But it wasn't dance.

After the intro two guys—smooth-muscled, tanned torsos—strutted on (clumsy too, like they were trying to remember which foot goes next) in stretchy bell-bottoms to escort the girls in huge circles around the edge of the stage. They were easy on the eyes, and that's what this show was about—costumes and titillation. Their main assets were their chests, arms and behinds. But most of the show was about Marcel lip-syncing and the girls posing in different costumes with deer-in-the-headlights, I-hope-my-tiara-stays-on looks.

Finally everyone disappeared and Marcel's voice piped up: "*le meilleur ... le premiere.*"

Then an old guy in a trench coat and bent flower in a broken top
hat wandered onstage to do a couple of naughty pranks: you know,
flash his boxer shorts, wear a dildo on his sunglasses while he had another one sticking out of his shorts—*that* kind of naughty. He set up
his card table and did some bad magic with Nadine as his assistant.
He was so bad I thought it was on purpose. The show finally ended
with more fanfare and all of the performers taking a bow. It was over,
the whole thing taking about thirty minutes. The only applause came
from an old guy sitting at the edge of the stage.

After that, the other girls, the strippers, got back to lugging the
boxes they table danced on, above their heads, over to the clients'
tables and plunking them down to start work again. They also took
turns choosing a few songs on the jukebox, getting up on the stage,
and stripping.

Then Marcel was back, sashaying through the room in a noisy
chiffon dressing gown and swishing onto a stool at the bar beside me.

"What did you think?"

"C'est fantastique." I could tell that this whole thing, for Marcel,
was high art. It was art he would suffer for. It had a very particular aesthetic that was soaked headfirst in absolute unapologetic tackiness.

"You speak French? You won't need it here."

"It can't hurt."

"I gave Patrice, our magician, the gig to keep him off the streets
and out of public washrooms."

"Well don't do me any favours."

"You'll be taking Luc's place."

"He's good." (I meant to look at. He could barely walk, let alone
dance.)

"He's going to Montreal. The money's way better, but it's more of
a head trip."

I had missed an important connection. How could a klutz, never
mind a hot one, make it in Montreal? Was I really that clued out?
"Head trip?"

"The money, the free jewellery, the come-ons—*if* you're stripping
in a gay place. But he who pays the stripper calls the tunes."

"So he strips?"

"You should have seen his finale on Saturday night."

"So guys strip here?"

"Usually two of them during the week. You'll meet Bobby tomorrow night."

"Who do they strip for?"

"Oh. Not for men. Well maybe, but not specifically. Not specifically for anyone specific, I guess you could say. A few women come in during the week, either in groups or with their boyfriends. Weekends it's all couples, and pretty middle class—Shriners, Kiwanis, you name it. I still don't get it and I've lived here most of my life. Anyway that's something you don't need to worry about. Come back tomorrow night and we'll walk you through some of this stuff before we go on. The second show's different but I think you'll pick it up. You don't have to stay tonight. You might as well get some rest while you can."

"I can't believe this but I left my wallet at home. Can you lend me bus fare?"

He must have heard the desperation. But I could tell, the way he glanced up from under his eyebrows and big hair, and his gentle manner, that he was a gentleman. He slipped me twenty. "You can pay me back when you hit the big time." Lending me bus fare was barely a sacrifice when the show must go on.

Miraculously a bus did come before too long. On the way home, staring out the window at a landscape of electric light and the reflections of car lots and warehouses I found myself humming that song Shirley MacLaine had sung in *Sweet Charity*, "If They Could See Me Now." Those who wouldn't get it if they saw me then or now were those from a few years earlier in the ballet studio at the university, the girls who demanded no less of me than the Kharkovs and Kozachenkos had. They were a collected wealth of ballet know-how. They showed me how to partner, again and again—which finger to offer for a *fouetté*—how to keep them *en pointe*—find their centre of gravity—control their centrifugal force. It was like learning how to drive without power steering; their ballast had increased since they had left the severe world of training and starvation. It forced strength upon me, control, and the kind of listening that the body has to do. I learned how to trust them through a turn. They told me to be more "zen" in what I did—remain rooted in the moment and trust the instinct of knowing when it was time to stop the turns.

All of them helped me. They knew the advantage I had of being a male in the dance world. They generously passed on their tricks like a flock of mother swans. I wondered if any of us stop doing what we love without a fight, including these women. I found out the answer when I offered to choreograph them—put the designs that were swirling in my mind to music and into a pattern on paper, and from paper onto bodies and all of it onto the stage. There was no question they would perform. It was in their blood. They offered me their trust for one more chance. Did they think about that first dream? Did they wish it for their daughters?

And soon everyone at the university heard about a dance extrava-ganza—from the jocks too thick to recognize the fantasies of a cre-ative fruit, to their girlfriends who dragged them into the theatre to relive some childhood dream. I was a freak running from cheerlead-ing practice to Drake's ballet school in town to more ballet with the women in the gymnasium. If they could see me now. But when I told Kent, he didn't bat an eye.

"It's going to be like a real job—money, hours, even a real pay-cheque," I told him on the phone. "What have you been up to?"

"Just doing the town."

"Be careful doing the town."

THE NEXT NIGHT MY grand entrance was a matter of squeezing be-tween the front door and an obliging Vasili, who opened it for me now that I was on the payroll. He made a big deal of treating the employees well; he'd wink and share a private joke, though I didn't understand any of it.

Marcel was waiting at his spot at the bar, where I'd left him the night before, now in a kimono, hair in a plastic cap, traces of cold cream on his face. He was tapping his nails on the bar. He said we needed to have a talk then whistled a long sigh through the hair under his nose. From the look on his face, I was sure he was about to fire me. "Louis, the owner, won't put you on the payroll just to do the show. You'll have to wait tables, too, between shows."

"Tips are okay—aren't they? But I'm a crappy waiter."

"Oh sure, tips can be good I imagine..."

"He's been warned..."

"That won't matter as much, but you have to dance. Strip. Table dance."

"Sounds like I have no choice." Drunkenly stripping down to my boxer shorts as a cheerleader at a university football game was one thing, but to stare down a room full of paying customers? I suppose it wasn't so much about my body doing something as it was about my body being a certain way. I was starting to feel more and more like a commodity to help others tell their own story or create their own art. Clearly I was not in my own driver's seat. Was this my new path, from the Company to the Conservatoire to Madame Talegdi's to flashing my harnessed ass at the Chez Moritz to sugar-daddy-dom at some dark strip club in Montreal? What a thought. "Okay."

"You don't have to worry. You have a nice ass and the rest is obvious. Are you okay with that?"

"I won't argue."

"Have you ever stripped?" he said.

"At football games."

"Football games?"

I was caught between wanting to brag about it, and the urge to deny. "From college days, I had a routine."

True, the idea was titillating, and challenging, but I couldn't imagine how it would all come together, the mechanics of it—standing on a box or being on a stage—being watched *closely*. Until recently, nakedness was confined to the dressing room, although I had had fantasies that involved being naked with strangers. It didn't matter. I had to keep moving forward, and anything that involved a paycheque at this point was a move forward.

I climbed up on the stool beside Marcel and ran my fingers along the edge of the bar as I thought of all the reasons why I was destined to pull it off. I thought of all of the sittings for all the photographers when I was that kid. I was the only child with no siblings on either side. I was all blond, all blue-eyed with a pout to bring you to tears. They said things like, "What perfection, a perfect boy, he always,

always, *always* smiles," which was fitting for the son of a dentist. I
was a walking advertisement; I was well behaved, I never argued,
was never contrary, ornery or selfish. I was unspoiled, perfect, angelic, cherubic with "cheeks like ground soapstone." And it didn't
end in kindergarten. I stayed the favourite and when that wore off
I learned how to be the teacher's pet. I knew what and how much
it took to get by. I developed a "lip" repertoire: the pout, the "poor
me" look, forgotten, adorable, even able to make myself look like I
was thinking deep thoughts. I was quite the actor until the blankness set in.

The first year of junior high, "teacher's pet" lost its allure. There
were too many teachers—too many students—too much competition. My attempts to fit in ended in sprained ankles from volleyball
tryouts, a bloody eye from basketball. The truth hit me by the time
I reached high school that I was merely anonymous, and teacher's
pet died as fast as it had arrived. Real pets had real brains, talent,
cutthroat popularity, muscles, moustaches, sneers, breasts, makeup,
cigarettes, annoyed glances and character, not pimples and Acne-B-
Gone, a bird's nest of chlorine-damaged straw hair, textbooks held
tight against the chest, crushes on other boys and a jarring nothingness to their stare. The only place for approval was at the pool, or
alone, locked tight in the huge basement bathroom after the snow
had been shovelled, Tchaikovsky's pained violin concerto sifting
through the air duct, my torso twisted to the mirror and my back
round like the forest creature in *L'apres midi d'un faun*, and only then
did I know I was good enough, even if no one had any idea what was
meant by beauty other than peach fuzz and rusty cars. I stood on my
toes and reached my arms to the mirror like the dancers I had seen,
which led to thoughts of lean long thighs, flexed calves, round bums
and possible stardom.

Marcel touched my hand and took me back over to the girls. It
was early. They were sitting by the jukebox flicking their nails, smoking, looking bored and bothered, but looking sober enough, while
they waited for clients or anyone to come into the dark. Chaton, the
tiny one with blonde hair down her behind in a fun-fur bikini—the
hysterical poodle in her own little cloud of anger—smoked, away

from us. Nadine, Rita Hayworth, now wore a sixties knitted bikini, the top suspended by breasts that defied gravity—looking elegant— probably still thinking of what went wrong to end that relationship ten years earlier.

There were two new ones sitting in the group. One was a tall woman, long straight black hair, I'd seen at a distance the night before, in suede fringe and feathers smoking one of those elegant non-cigars: "Smoking deez always makes me busy, every time I light one up someone wants me to dance and I have to ditch it. Like waiting for da *maudite* bus. Then it comes just when I light one." And the other was Suzette, a freckled, outdoorsy, chubby girl-next-door you could have a beer and an arm wrestle with, in peek-a-boo lace baby-dolls, rough and tumble, leaning forward, legs splayed, confiding that she was a bitch and didn't know why she was a mother (she was pregnant again), while her cigarette drooped from the corner of her mouth.

They all said *"B'jour,"* or *"Salut,"* like, *We saw you already last night, so what?* But when Marcel told them I'd be stripping as well as doing the burlesque show, they perked up. Suzette guffawed something in French and then asked if I'd ever stripped before.

I looked at Marcel. "Not in a club," I said.

"Don't worry," said Suzette. "We show you da ropes, *mon ami.*" She turned to the other girls to translate and they looked at me with no more interest than they might the neighbouring cigarette machine, with their eyes at the same level as the knobs. I doubt anyone had time to show me the ropes.

Again, Marcel led me down to the basement, his cover-up billowing around him. There were two makeshift dressing rooms, huge sheets of plywood for walls. One was for all of the strippers, both sexes, and the other was an empty room reserved for any featured *en vedette* performer.

A hall beyond the rooms led to a bigger space where the cast of the *spectacle* changed: a few scattered chairs, ashtrays, empty and half-full drink glasses, and a rack of elaborate costumes for the show.

"I make all the costumes for all of the shows," he told me.

Despite my amusement at the missing essentials, like seats missing from pants, necklines plunging to the crotch, or openings where skin could show through, I noticed the variety of texture and colour forming the most elaborate patterns.

"Those are from albino peacocks." He carefully touched a clump of white feathers drooping from the back of one of the outfits. Who'd have thought? He flew them in from Honduras. Why didn't the Company's costume department know about these?

"I'll introduce you to Bobby when he gets here. He's in the show and he strips as well. He can help you," Marcel brushed his hand across my behind, "with the stripping part." This was going to be good. I'd finally get to add a new fantasy to my repertoire: me being trained by a male stripper.

In the corner of the basement the magician, Patrice, was trying to tie a long narrow balloon into a shape, but when he looked up at me, it fluttered away in an extended fart. The showgirls wandered into the area one by one. Suzette and Nadine, the only ones who stripped and did the *spectacle* as well, had large assets compared to the other two showgirls who were pretty, slim and small-breasted. "I've got a family to support," Suzette whined, then repeated that she had a bun in the oven. "Dat's why d'ey love my tits."

A little guy—sagging face, bumpy complexion—rushed in when we were all in the final stages of getting decked out and ready to go. "John, Bobby (Marcel pronounced his name with the emphasis on the second syllable BawBEE), Bobby, John, introduce yourselves later. You can zip John in for now." I recognized him from the night before, but he looked so much better onstage. In the harsh lights of the basement he looked more like an old hippie than a stripper, but he filled out the bell-bottoms. There I was, checking out the competition.

We lined up one by one as soon as we were in costume. The girls balanced their headpieces and held their tails up off the ground. The top of Bobby's bare rear end stuck out of his pants. I hoped mine was as alluring. We followed Marcel single file, my nose next to Bobby's butt, up a narrow spiral staircase to the stage. The girls brushed stray feathers and lint off of their behinds, breasts and cleavage like they were flicking mosquitoes. There was nothing sexual about those moments before, and not much sexual about the backstage—compared to the dim lights upstairs forming shafts through the smoke-filled air, coating everyone in a filmy translucence while music oozed and throbbed beneath every curve and shadow, lulling the clientele into an open-wallet trance.

There was the familiar recorded announcement from the night before, on a loud and scratchy sound system, and then we were on. I remembered most of what I'd seen. Walk, walk, walk. Suzette partnered with me most of the time, talking over the music and chewing on her gum. Donna Summer was deafening. We walked, stood, posed. "Relax," she said. "This isn't the *maudite* ballet." I tried to be more casual with my movements. I held out my arm and escorted two girls around the edge of the stage. The lights made it difficult to see anything including the audience. Suzette started to smile. "That's better." She seemed happy to have a guy who knew how to walk. I was completely relaxed—weird to be onstage and not have adrenalin giving you an edge. It was fun, but it was flat; there was no tension, no stakes, which allowed for moments throughout to think of just how pathetic it all was. This was my bread and butter.

We did the first show to an empty house. The only hard part was the costume changes. Some disappeared down the narrow spiral stairwell connecting the stage to the basement—plumage, sequins and crinoline disappearing through a hole in the floor—while others made their way up. Breasts and bums, crotches and bulges in each others' faces, meeting, passing, squeezing to avoid getting stuck to each other, tugging here, squashing there, in a most unflattering way, the likes of which a ballet dancer with the Company may have never seen.

It was over quickly and then we were changing out of our costumes. "How was that?" Marcel asked.

"He's a ballet boy," Suzette said, her hands on my shoulders, "but we can fix that."

"Suzette was a dancer at the Conservatoire."

"A lifetime ago. And I have life now. It's not like I miss it." She was like the Mother Earth of this place. I could see her baking marijuana birthday cupcakes decorated with pills, and encouraging everyone with smiles, winks and hugs. She grunted, and squeezed back into her baby dolls for another round upstairs. Her English was good, and usually to the point. "My days are numbered."

I turned to Marcel. "Well?"

"Fine," Marcel said.

Nadine and Suzette and the two other girls clapped like they'd just seen a toy poodle in a tutu do a back flip.

A fresh-faced guy with curly blond hair à la Christopher Atkins out of *Blue Lagoon* stuck his head into our change area. "How was that?"

"A bit loud for the first show. There's still no one out there. Steve, this is our new guy, John," Marcel said. "Steve's our DJ."

"You'll do great." Steve raised his eyebrows, gave my crotch an intense eyeballing, then spoke. "There's already a table of women—it should get busy."

I wavered and felt a twinge of anticipation. I had protected myself, in the world of fantasy, dreams and the puffed-up superhuman skills that ballet was. You could thrive in that closed world if you gave your soul to it, and never have your feet touch the earth. But now that I had lost the keys to the magic kingdom, I had to pay the price and wallow in mediocrity while Kharkov and my mentors stared down, without pity, from on high.

"Are they drinking?" Bobby asked.

"Nuns." Steve unlatched his gaze. "Drunken nuns." He tossed his golden curls, turned and left.

"Bobby, take him upstairs. Louis says he has to wait tables and strip."

I don't know if I was more nervous about understanding raw Québécois drink orders or getting naked, but everyone else seemed blasé about it. I figured no one would be breathing down my neck telling me I was doing it wrong.

"Now?" Bobby said.

"Every night. Show him the drill. You could use a little competition."

Bobby turned to me. "What have you got to wear?"

"Jeans?"

"Button or zip?"

"Zip."

"You'll learn. Just unzip slowly. I have a tank top you can borrow."

"Silk boxers?" I offered.

"They'll have to do."

It's funny. I braced myself the way I probably did when I first performed, years ago. The spectacle was nothing, but this would be different. Nervous energy and anticipation sustained me through that first evening. The challenge. I got dressed in the main strippers' tight and cozy change room. I wore a tank top, boxers under my jeans, a tie. Bobby took me upstairs to the bar and gave me a tray. "Just float. We don't have sections. If someone wants a drink or a dance, they'll get your attention. The girls can be pushy about the drinks. If you see them going for a table, don't tangle with them." He called to the old guy behind the bar who gave me the free beers the night before: "Hey, Hubert, be nice to the new guy." Then he turned to me. "Hubert's an angel. It's pretty hard to piss him off. You can drink as much Pepsi as you like, and just tip him nicely for anything else he puts in it."

There were a few men sitting alone and that table of eight women Steve had referred to as nuns, who came in while we had been downstairs changing. I wandered the room, wondered how to look busy while Suzette danced on the stage. Bobby shadowed me. We stood in the dark by the far wall. "Official strip. It means they have to dance for three songs they pick on the jukebox. Everyone has to do it. Everyone hates it, too," Bobby said. "It means three songs when you aren't getting tips for drink orders or making money from table dances."

But the room was bare.

"The first song is usually up-tempo and can be pretty boring because they don't take anything off. Most of them just walk around to the music. Just a minute." Then Bobby disappeared toward the bar.

I was all eyes. Suzette, stuffed into her lace baby dolls, strutted around to "Maneater." She was larger than life with an "I don't give a shit" look about it and her main activity seemed to be chewing gum, twirling her hair in her fingers and squinting into the crowd. There was something mesmerizing about her doing this, perhaps because she didn't care. It's not as if the girls had years of formal training— learning was watching and copying—yet every move was hypnotic.

Just in front of the stage was that table of women looking like what I imagined a bank-teller girls' night out to be. Bobby ran toward their table to deliver a tray of tall drinks decorated with fruit and little umbrellas, and then returned to the table carrying his box high over head. While I had been staring at Suzette, he was the quick one, keeping an eye on the room, and had picked up on their cue. Just as well. I wondered if I'd manage to get on the ball and become a competitive player. I had missed that step once already, and now it would be all I could do to keep up here.

Bobby took his cue from the beginning of Suzette's second song, "Bette Davis Eyes," slow and mellow, still with a beat, and when the first familiar notes played, he got up on his box and the ladies hooted. At the same time, onstage, Suzette squatted—difficult as it might be for a pregnant woman—and rocked her hips a little but still looked more involved playing with her hair and chewing her gum. Even when she finally started to stroke her breasts and her nipples, it was done as if she were intent on ignoring a scolding parent. She tried to coax a breast close to her mouth but the most she could do was mime licking it. I laughed at the fact that she just wasn't all that into it.

"They're too sensitive," she shouted toward me. The lyrics to the song described Suzette's cockiness well. Meanwhile Bobby had to get everything off before the song ended. When he was finally standing there naked, again he looked better than what I'd seen in the change room. I didn't want to look too obvious checking him out, but the dim lights washed him in a powdery orange glow, took away his rough complexion. I'll say it again: he had a beautiful behind. I imagine Marcel had enjoyed taking measurements. Judging by the expressions on the women's faces, I'm sure what they could see from the front was just as pleasing.

When Suzette started grinding on all fours, her breasts jiggled like upside-down Jell-O being shaken from a mould. The song ended and she awkwardly clambered back up onto her heals. This meant Bobby's table dance was finished, and he started accepting bills the girls were holding out toward him. Then he sat on his box and chatted and laughed while he dressed. Finally he got up, left the box by the table and came over to me. "They're going to want you in a minute," he said. "Wait till Suzette's finished her third dance and then go over. Fifty bucks. They're fun."

Meanwhile Suzette had thrown a blanket on the floor for her third and final song of the official strip, and was getting all wound up to Kim Carnes, again—which seemed to show a lack of imagination or incredible originality, I'm still not sure—wailing "Miss You Tonite." She wiggled out of her lace bottoms but didn't take the naughty route. She was more like a naked kid at the beach trying to get undressed than a woman stripping. Maybe that was her gimmick: to look innocent and leave them wanting. What the hell was I going to do up there? I didn't have any props, blankets or a routine.

I thought of the ballerinas, struggling to find the sexuality for parts in *Boléro*, or as the Black Swan or even Juliet, and the deep soul searching that was involved. Here the women climbed on the stage, or on a box, shoved a stick of Juicy Fruit in their mouths, and that was it.

An old guy by the side of the stage from the previous night was back for another night of bliss-filled voyeurism. He clapped. Suzette got to her feet, wavering in her heels and ignoring the limited applause, pulled on her bottoms and top, and stomped down the three little steps between the stage and the jukebox. She sat at a table with her feet up on a chair and lit a du Maurier. Bobby caught my eye and nodded toward the ladies' table.

I wandered over and the women clapped a little. Steve said something over the speakers—what sounded like *Le Grand Blond*—and the girls hooted. I looked around and Steve was in his booth smiling like the Cheshire Cat. I pointed to the jukebox but Steve shook his head and lifted his arms and pointed, with large movements so I could see him, down toward the turntable. And then that familiar scratchy and oh so familiar intro to "In the Summer Time" came on. It's not a song I would have chosen, ever, with its hokey beat and tune. I planned to kill Steve in exactly three minutes. I nodded at the smiling women and climbed on the box. For the time being, I had no choice but to start undressing. I played with my tie until it was noose-tight, and I was more obsessed with breathing than seducing. When I was able to rip it off, I twirled it over my head, tossed it somewhere and that was the last I ever saw of it. Rachelle had given it to me as a novelty gift for a birthday. It was gone. It's probably still there, in the club, shoved under a table or stuck to the floor with spilled cola.

I looked at the women, trying to make the best of Steve's bad choice, and cut the beats in half to get into a slower, more comfortable rhythm—in ballet it could be described as dancing through the music. I then slowly slid Bobby's loaned tank top over my head. The women looked up at me. They wanted to look into my eyes; they didn't care about what my body was doing, not then. I ran my hands up my stomach and squeezed my chest, which ended up feeling like the funky chicken. But the girls still stared. I held my belt, pulled at it, twisted a little, ground a bit; I realized I was holding onto a useful prop that was full of possibilities. I unzipped my jeans, slowly—remembering Bobby's instructions to take my time—and pushed them down to my knees. I tried to focus on the girls. I tried to project sex and allure, but my mind raced. What were they thinking? Did they speak English? What if I had to talk to them? Was I smiling too much? What did I look like? How much money would I get?

I pushed my jeans the rest of the way, untied my shoes in a panic, and finally stepped out. My silk boxers, a gimmick from my cheerleading strip, were sure to get a smile. But they weren't looking where I thought they should. When I pushed the boxers down, the girls continued to look intently into my eyes, but now I got the feeling it was because there was not much else to look at. I ran my hands down my front, but was hesitant to touch myself. Finally I squatted, and a quick glance at myself revealed that nerves and too much attention had shrivelled me up and I couldn't think my way into anything larger; couldn't tactfully grab it, pull it or give it a shake.

My life-saving smile barely hid my embarrassment. I wanted to crawl under their table, admit defeat, wave a white tissue and then flee. Some of them smiled sympathetically, and the others looked away. The song ended. No one spoke to me. Some of them spoke to each other. Then one of them handed me five bucks. All I wanted to do was apologize. Even worse, Louis, the owner, was sitting at the bar watching. "You 'aaave to do somet'ing about your dick. Marcel, he tell me you 'aaave a nice dick." Black light made his false teeth look yellow.

"I do."

"Somet'ing like dat costs *me* you know. You, too. I can't afford dat. Doz girls pay my mortgage every time they order another round of drinks. Be dirty. You gotta be dirty."

I didn't think that I would have more worries here. Ballet was worth obsessing over, not stripping.

The rest of the audience was made up of men. The women had left quickly and quietly—definitely not contributing to Louis's mortgage—probably to be up early for work, and to tell everyone at the bank about the shrivelled dancer. I didn't end up table dancing again that night. Bobby said guy strippers were busier on the weekends, with couples and women in groups. Part of me wanted to rise to the challenge, and the other part wanted to take a flying leap off the honeymoon parapet of the Chateau Frontenac.

Then Steve was at my shoulder. "Sorry about the song."

"Why did you do that?"

"It's short, that's all."

"Not the only thing that's short. It took forever."

"I didn't want you to suffer your first time out."

"It just didn't inspire."

"Don't worry gorgeous. I had a good time, all alone in that booth. Know what I mean? Every first timer goes through it. Don't worry." He patted me on the back. "You're a fresh one. And the sooner you stop worrying about your dick the better. Your dick is your friend. That's my only piece of advice. Make it everybody's friend. It all comes from there, buddy: before, during and after. All you have to do is smile, maybe give them a bit of Bette Davis eyes. Get it?"

Downstairs the others walked me through Marcel's steps for the second show. By now all of my co-workers had seen most of my white butt and some of the rest of me or no doubt heard about it—I avoided eye contact. No one seemed to care. It was time for another costume change tornado of spandex, Mylar, sequins and feathers. The second show was completely different, but just as gaudy. The third, at 1:30, was a repeat of the first. Since the room was almost empty by then,

I ended up playing it to Steve in his booth. He was my biggest fan at this point. His bleached curls and capped teeth glowed every time he leaned near the black light—the mysterious non-light that was the enemy of falseness. Later most of the girls started looking tired, drunk or stoned, although they still managed on their heels, except Nadine, who collapsed on the back staircase with her drink, leaving a mess of blood and spilled vodka on her legs and hands, crying and babbling. Vasili hoisted her into the change room.

By 3:30 A.M. we had all changed, girls had wiped their mascaraed eyes, makeup cases were shut, outfits hung. Boyfriends and tricks showed up and the last of the drunks were digging absent-mindedly for their car keys in the lining of their coats. When the bar lights went on, the spell was broken; the room was a sea of chipped tables and scratched worn chairs, the girls were pink-eyed and pasty. I had no idea what I looked like, but it couldn't have been much different.

Suzette's guy showed up in leather and a motorcycle helmet with a little boy, maybe six or seven years old, in leather, too. "These are my babies," Suzette squealed. "I thank the Mother of God he didn't destroy my career at childbirth. Thank the blessed Virgin my tits don't sag, though God knows he sucked hard enough on them, harder than you, eh, *ma beau*? Can't believe I'm putting myself t'ru it all again."

Marcel told me that Patrice, the magician, would drive me home. "It's murder getting a cab out here, and it's expensive." But with no tips I wouldn't have had to worry about a cab because I would have been walking.

"It sucked tonight," Marcel said.

I gave Marcel a light kiss on the cheek, trying to avoid a mouthful of hair—"I'll see you tomorrow night"—and followed Patrice out to his waiting carriage. We only spoke French, and then only minimally, since we both may have feared being misunderstood. Conversations grew in length as we got to know each other. "Une belle soirée."

"As-tu passé une bonne soirée?"

"Ah oui, mais les clients ce soir étaient tellement tranquilles." Gradually some of the French I heard, seeming at first incomprehensible, started to sink in. Phrases would come up at the oddest times—calice, tabarnak, tabarnouche. I had no idea what they meant but curiosity sent me running to a dictionary or to ask someone at the club. Grammar was out of the question as far as anyone helping me; you just said what you said and they'd figure it out. Most of the time we just said fuck, or *ça va*, as a question or a comment.

Patrice could have been Liberace's long-lost poor cousin. His teeth were big, like Louis the owner's—big capped ones. (Dad could have cleaned up in this town.) Patrice's streetwear was a step up from his costume, minus the squirting plastic flower and the extra wide tie. He wore a white leather go-go cap, à la Petula Clark, from the sixties. On his pointy manicured fingers, all ten of which clutched and kneaded at the steering wheel, he wore big, showy rings with huge rhinestones. This was all brought together with a white leather bomber, not the trench coat, and a scarf. Whenever I looked over at him while he peered into the dark empty route, I saw something sad, protected and fragile about him.

He ended up driving me home every night, and one night we stopped at his tiny house (even in the dark I could see it was fuchsia and lime green, with a Virgin Mary in an upright bathtub in the front yard) to meet his mother who didn't go to bed until he rolled in, but was happy to sit in the kitchen smoking, stroking their hairy cat Pirate ("pee-rat") and listening to the radio. I realized this was the obligatory meeting for a one-sided courtship. She looked at me with the same enthusiasm one does at a vase full of flowers well past their prime. Here it was, four in the morning, when the entire company back in the West was resting from a full day of repertoire, lovers all over the world were entwined in one another's bodies, dancers were swatting suitors away like flies, and I somehow found myself auditioning for some sixties gender-blur's vicious mother in Vanier.

Sometimes we'd stop at a diner, Le Rosier Flamant, with a burned-out buzzing pink flower above the door. I guess my companionship was my payment for the drive home, and though I felt like a hostage at 4 A.M., he'd usually buy me a banana split (I didn't mind the extra calories as I had been on my feet for at least eight hours) while he nursed a cigarette. The first time we went there he read my palm. Held it. Tickled it. I wished he'd stop. I wasn't going to sleep with him for a free ride.

Anyway, he managed to read my palm and tell my fortune. He saw that someday I would have money. In slow French he told me my past and my future: "Tu étais une danseuse Russe…" He said I was a Russian ballet dancer in a past life. A female, a ballerina. That's why my expectations of a lover were very high. And my father in that life was a domineering tyrant—wanted me to be a star more than I ever did. That's why I have had trouble with male authority figures. I didn't need a past life for that kind of insight. "Mais c'est l'amour, qui vous donnerais de la peine…" But it's love that will cause me much pain and sadness. He told me I would be at my best when I had love, and even better when it came from one person, a man, and not just an audience. He said I was smart, sensitive and I worried too much, and I tried too hard to analyze my life. He scolded me, too: "Don't t'ink so much about your dick."

At home, I wondered if Kent was tucked in on the other side of that four-foot-thick, four-hundred-year-old wall as I washed the lay-ers of smoke and sweat off of my body, working my way down from my stiff hair, my clogged nose and ears, my sticky ass (I must have sat in something at some point), arms, legs—disgusting and so satis-fying at the same time. Many nights I was a little drunk and always dead tired, and would be hypnotized by the water swirling around my black swollen feet. The only time I ran a bath was when I figured I wouldn't fall asleep in it and drown. After I scrubbed myself clean, I left the tub coated with a brown filthy film.

My one prayer before bedtime was that the sky would stay dark until I fell asleep, but the world was already into a new day as the old, ragged, sweat-soaked, sometimes bloody and tear-filled night vanished into the shadows. There was always the music coming through the floor from the café downstairs while they were baking for the morning, twisting *pain au chocolat* and croissants—letting the baguette dough rise near the warm hearth, then punching it down.

Five

A DANCER'S BACK FORMS the part of the core that embraces and defines space and negative space. On the way down, the spine can curve into itself or reach to superhuman degrees, carrying the trunk to the earth to fold the torso against the legs, and then roll up again in one fluid motion, while the blood rushes back to the dancer's head. Then the hand, joined by an invisible thread above the centre of the sternum guides the spine back, while the trunk, bracing to hold the curve, opens the chest to the heavens.

AT EIGHT, THE ALARM ripped into a sleep where I was dreaming I was trapped onstage in one of Madame's ballets, wandering aimlessly with dancers dressed as squirrels, chipmunks and skunks, all with bare bums showing through their costumes. I was naked and the audience was laughing me offstage. I knew Madame would tear me apart when I returned to the wings, so I started to dress onstage.

I picked myself up off the mattress after barely four hours of too deep of a sleep. I showered again. Cold. Hot. Cold. My head spun and my heart banged. Although I walked to the studio to warm my muscles, it didn't matter, Madame immediately saw how tired I was and gave all of us one of her killer classes—an old trick, not just limited to Madame: the more tired you are, the more complicated and strenuous they (regisseurs, ballet masters and mistresses) will make it. I tried to ignore everything about Madame—her mood, her games, her shouts—except her instructions. With my fatigue I had lost all patience for her temper. But I had also lost my sense of balance: my back was full of knots, my hips and hamstrings ached, and my calves and Achilles tendons rebelled. If she wanted me to think I was a shitty dancer, less capable than her Jean-Marc, then she was right and for once I didn't care. I had to survive; Madame was no longer necessary for that survival, so I ignored her.

That afternoon we rehearsed *Pinocchio*, the lead played by Bertrand with me as Geppetto, a role that demanded I lift Bertrand over my head in joy as he becomes a boy. But hoisting Bertrand's 160 solid pounds over my head finally finished me off. It was three o'clock, the end of our day, when he was over my head and when my back froze. Madame got the last word; she told me to stay and take a class with the little girls who come in after school—an offer that mixed me with joy and panic. How would I teach these girls and also squeeze in some rest before the club? Would I be able to quit the club and teach regularly? It never rains but it pours. Why had I thought she hated me when she was offering me this?

"It will do you good to return to the basics." When I realized she didn't want me to teach the class, I swallowed a "Fuck off," to the linoleum floor.

I walked back toward the Old Town, hoping to loosen up before I got home. I limped through the gates, slowly climbed rue Sainte-Ursule, passed Kent's door, passed the café, prayed for the day when I could sit there again and have whatever the hell I wanted—café au lait, hot chocolate, sugar pie—and just stare at the wall for a very long time.

At four I put my head on the pillow and closed my eyes until the alarm went off four hours later, at 8 P.M. I reached the phone and called Kent. "Can you come over?"

"Should I bring wine?"

"Something stronger. I have to work and I can't get up."

I crawled to the door to unlock it and lay there until he arrived. "I brought rum."

"Walk on my back."

"Naked or..."

"Barefoot, and all your weight."

"I didn't know you were into this."

"Lots you don't know. Oh my GOD that feels good."

"You sure you're okay? What happened anyway?"

"Pinocchio needs to learn to jump up, not on."

"Sounds dirty. Did you know the feet and dick brain functions are very closely related? Probably why you love dancing, come to think of it. We'll have to put that theory to the test, um, to the testes."

"Please don't make me laugh in this condition. Do you know that in just a few months I've gone from thinking about penises the average amount of times in a day…"

"Six thousand?"

"I didn't tell you I have to strip."

"You sound like you didn't expect it."

"I didn't."

Kent sat beside me, his white, veined feet close to my face. "It wasn't obvious?"

"Well it's a disaster. I shrivel up whenever I have to get naked. I'm going to get fired from a last-resort job."

"Can you call in sick? I'd give you *un massage*." He squatted, and I pulled myself up his backside. "Be careful, we both don't need bad backs." I hung onto his shoulders and he walked me to the shower.

"First you need a rum and Coke and then you need something to perk you up. He fixed us each a strong drink and then he rummaged through my summer stuff, grabbed some painter pants and a billowy striped shirt, all stuff I had thrown together for the act.

"Where'd you get this stuff? It is so *rummage sale*. I love it."

"Sally Ann. For emergencies. Parties I'll never get invited to."

"I knew a woman called Sally Ann. Imagine naming your kid that. Anyway, get rid of it. You don't want lice. You can go through my closets. You'll find a thing or two from my clubbing days. Wait a minute, these are my clubbing days. What the hell am I doing here? The eighties were supposed to be my decade. But then again, so were the seventies."

He walked me to the bus. "I think we need to talk about this as a career choice, and why it might not be a good idea."

I leaned on him and wanted to cry. "Some other time."

"Now don't worry about your cock. Just don't do any coke. It'll make those gorgeous big balls dry up like raisins—in your case, prunes."

"Maybe it's you who should strip. Heck, I'd watch."

"And if this is what you want then you better stop walking like a dancer."

"But my back."

When your back is better, relax your chest, your back, your ass, your dick. You dancers are such an uptight bunch. It's like everyone has to know that you're a dancer. Why? I mean look at Daniel. I hate to say it…"

"I already told myself that, and now I can't walk at all. And what do you mean *if this is what I want*?"

"It's just that you seem pretty tied up in this new job. Don't you want to dance?"

This was the first time I'd felt really humiliated since I'd stripped for that table of eight women. Something or someone always manages to force you to stop and take a good long look at yourself when you least expect it.

"Spend the bus ride thinking about me locked to your dick."

"I'll get a hard-on."

"Exactly."

"I can't table dance with a boner."

"Why not?"

"It's against the rules."

"You just have to take advantage of that lead in your pencil."

"You're an angel."

He waited for the bus to leave. He shoved his tongue in his cheek, mimed a blow job. I forced a grin, ignored onlookers—he had meant well.

You need talent for many things, especially to sleep well on a bus. If you arrange your bones and muscles in a certain way, you won't wake up with a stiff neck. I bent my elbow so my head rested against the wedge it created, with my forehead pressed to the window. It was a job, for Christ's sake. I didn't want to do anything at this point other than survive. I closed my eyes on that bus ride—thought about my body, my ass, my cock—while the rum went to work. I saw the colour red flowing into my crotch and burning up into my back and down into my thighs. I relaxed my stomach for the first time in years and breathed deeply. I thought of what Kent said, thought of my posture—saw myself walking like the oafish football players from the university—feet turned in, shoulders hunched—stubby hands on each other's asses. That got me hard. I thought my way into Bobby's body: his walk, his posture, his confidence. I thought of Madame's girls and Bertrand and Jean-Marc. I thought of all of the dancers I'd ever seen walking down the sidewalk, flocks of them, eating in restaurants, sitting in the audience on an off-night, backs straight, eyebrows raised, as if a conductor's baton had accidentally been shoved up their asses to their stubborn thick skulls.

As a dancer I have always used the mirror—checking my arches in any position, assessing my line with quadriceps flexed, gauging the degree to which I can turn my thigh in my pelvis to keep my lines long and flowing. All of those things dancers obsess over and hate because they are never good enough. Now, before going off to my night job, I would have to look at myself from every other angle. How to stand? Pelvis forward? Legs turned in? Or better, the bas-relief of Nijinsky's *Sacre de Printemps*—if Nijinksy did it, surely I could, for part of my waking hours. I would have to relax all the parts of me that were so tightly held and held together, as a dancer. I would present the hips and relax the shoulders to create bulk in my chest and accentuate the width of my back; cave in so that everything was drawn toward the earth. But in the morning when I woke I would have to rise as a dancer again, with everything corporeal the exact opposite, pointing toward the heavens. From now on, I vowed, I would leave the dancer at home every night, and take the stripper to the Chez Moritz.

AT THE CLUB, MARCEL supplied sympathy and Scotch and Coke. Most of the other dancers were already well into the more sophisticated substances. Some of them, especially the circuit girls who stayed at the motel next door, showed up at work in bad condition, and Louis would send them away if he happened to notice.

Tonight everyone seemed to want to get involved with me: Mer*la*, a seamstress, showed up once or twice a week in our change room with an open suitcase full of outfits—latex, spandex, neon and fish-net—bikinis, G-strings, fun-fur stockings, boas—wraparound, pull-away, Velcro or zippered—micro-minis to body stockings. Early that evening, the girls surrounded me, wide-eyed, and presented me with one of Merla's G-strings. It was metallic black with shiny scallop shell sequins, the size of fingernails, on the front. There were small hooks and eyes on the side for quick removal.

Merla's assistance reminded me of my mom. Once when my uni-versity football team had an away game in my hometown, I got to come home as a cheerleader, doing my folks proud as the successful son home from university for the weekend. I slept off one too many vodkas and orange juice in my room while my mother stitched to the classics. When I left on Sunday she gave me my cheerleading uni-form cleaned, and with the stripes Velcroed back on. The stripes had shrunk in the wash, bunching where they were attached to the pants. But now, thanks to the Velcro, the stripes could be pulled away before going in the wash, or as part of my act.

That night, over Merla's G-string, I wore the bleached painter pants from the Sally Ann and the wide, blue-striped dress shirt from Goodwill that made me look like a popcorn vendor. It went with my white jazz shoes, borrowed but never returned from a humpy, clos-eted Company-wannabe we had all taken bets on to see how long until he came out. He left in a huff when I became soloist, but I later heard he saw the big pink light and is living it up in Manhattan, trying to get into the Joffrey.

Over the next three nights, my back loosened up. I slept in four-hour shifts and dreamt only of more sleeping. One night when I got home there was a pair of leather shorts and a studded wristband hanging on my door handle, and another night some dumbbells, courtesy of Kent's connection at Kresge's no doubt. I guess everyone knew the rule of thumb: stripping was just costume changes to get to the goods. It certainly wasn't cheerleading, where I drank with the guys, slapped their backs and their asses, wore a uniform—the crest, the banner, the sweater—and jumped around trying to convince myself I cared about the green and white. All I actually cared about then was the booze, and with enough early morning Saskatchewan

Sunrises it was easy. I cheered my pompoms off, popped around the field, carried the girls, made pyramids, human caterpillars, bridges, bad gymnastics, you name it, all done half-drunk.

But that one time I pulled off my sweater to cool down, a wolf whistle combined with two or three half-time Saskatoon Berry Purple Jesuses were all it took to get me going. The band woke up and played a spirited rendition of that old standard, "The Stripper." Off came the tie, the shirt, the pennant. My belt, oooh. I shook my pompoms between my legs. My shoes arced through the air. Who gave a fuck about the game? We were all dizzy drunk, laughing at my pink body steaming in the cold, and I had their attention for a whole minute. My clothes lay in a clump. I was small-town famous.

When football season finally ended, I sobered up and spent cold Saturdays after dance class walking along the river. I had had one awkward time with Drake, the ballet master. We never talked about it, and barely looked at each other because of it. He lived in a small wood bungalow on the outskirts of a suburb that stared onto blank prairie, with his policeman paying him visits from Regina most weekends. And I preferred to be alone, hoping some confused jock would give in to his urges. Then, as now, I wanted to lie next to someone.

I tried to squeeze into the leather shorts Kent had left late that night, and the wristband, and strutted around my place half done up before falling onto the mattress.

SATURDAYS MEANT TWO EXTRA hours of sleep before going to Mihalis's gym in Lower Town and being surrounded by deformed mammoth men who walked as if they were balancing trays on their chests, even when they were relaxed. (This was not a posture to which I would aspire.) It was my day to blast my stripper muscles with bench presses for my chest, chin-ups, dips and curls for my arms. The lower half had the day off. My thighs, rump and calves were the envy of the gym. But watching this parade of guys around me, climbing on each other to squeeze out one last calf raise was an education. It was all form, size and shape, hindering any type of function. The change room dynamic was unlike any other: eyes met eyes, eyes roved over body parts to openly appreciate, compare and admire. It was as if they wanted me to stare.

Every night before heading off I had a strong coffee and one of Kent's magic diet pills, and then used my own weights, some killer sets of push-ups, chin-ups on the door frame, sit-ups with arches stretched under the radiator and curls to get me warmed up for what was to come.

That weekend, like most of them, the crowd was couples: Monsieur and Madame Suburbia. Heavy smoking everywhere. In the audience they didn't have to worry, smoke can't stain your dentures, and backstage the counter in the dressing room was one long line of burnt edging. More strippers showed up on weekends, too, like fruit flies, and my instincts told me to stand back and let them have their way. I still managed to fuck up about half my drink orders, mistaking rum and Coke for Ricard to not understanding *sur glace*, which in those moments when I could hear, Hubert the bartender hollered, "Wit' ice?"

Heavy trays full of drinks, cocktails, bottles of beer and empties teetered above our heads. Waitresses used their T and A to push between customers and get up to the bar. They made great money. Two hundred was a bad night if you were female. What I could have done with some real cash. Most of theirs supported bad habits.

There was also another male stripper on the floor that night. The guy was a useless phobic fuck, pardon my French, but he didn't have the decency to look my way, as if he might catch something. Not a team player. He was a muscle-bound no-neck, all shoulders—just my type. I saw some penis action during his official strip and figured the steroids had done their damage, which may have been why he wouldn't look my way. But he had the oafish strut. He kept his ass cheeks squeezed and his pelvis tucked and crotch shoved forward, putting the goods out front. Textbook. He kept his shoulders forward and down, not up and back, and tightened his six-pack. No wonder Kent thought I had a pickle up my ass. And like Patrice said, it was all about cock: put the goods there as if you were serving someone dinner, or trying to suck yourself off.

Marcel was propped at the bar, hoping to be noticed by everyone and anyone. He introduced me to François, who worked as an extra bartender. François was Marcel's guy—news to me. I wondered if François knew that Marcel took special measurements during interviews? Did they have an agreement? Could I partake? Did I have "naive" tattooed in both official languages on my forehead? François, with his brown curls, heavy eyelids, and face like the sweetest, smoothest *crème caramel*, slipped a nice strong Scotch and Coke my way.

That was the night I did my first official strip. I should have looked at the song list on the jukebox earlier. Steve didn't deejay for anyone's official strip. He just got his thrills watching. And, discovering how much of an exhibitionist I really was, I got a thrill knowing he was watching me. Since "Maneater" had that great beat, I chose it for my first song, but on the opening beats Suzette—box parked between two tables and the stage—gave me the finger because it was her song. It didn't matter; it bombed. It was a lady's song. I hoped she wasn't going to take this into the dressing room. I hated to be on anyone's bad side, especially when they had a shellacked French manicure.

I walked across the stage, untied my shirt, put my hands on my hips, relaxed my shoulders, ground a little. Then a thrust. Hands on thighs. Then ass. I took off my shirt and rocked it between my legs like I was towel-drying my crotch. I ran it side to side across my behind. Then I fell to my knees for some women at the side of the stage. I lay back, stared at the lights revolving in the ceiling, and pressed my pelvis into the air until the song ended.

Things could only get better with the next two songs: Laura Branigan's "Gloria," and Phil Collins' "In the Air Tonight." I got up and spun (in ballet lingo *chêné*) from one side of the stage to the other to "Gloria." I felt like I had to shake off my straitjacket. It was time to have some fun. Kent's medicine, and my Scotch cocktail, kicked in. "Gloria" took over. My head and hips whipped and I didn't care that my hair was stinging my eyes and blinding me. I could see wave after wave of sweat-spray fly away from me as it caught the light. I forced some tight quick turns in a low *a la seconde*, with no idea what that was in strip-dancing lingo. I sped up my pirouettes, kept my legs low and tight. My heart pounded. The room was spinning with streamers of neon and mirror ball pinpoints. I finished by carelessly slamming a not-bad Russian-splits onto the stage.

Then it was time for "In the Air Tonight."

I was already down so all I had to do was unzip and lean back with a slow easy grind, my hips gyrating. My hair was stuck to my forehead. I couldn't see for the sweat, and tears now, too—they caught me by surprise—my gasps were mixed with something else. I was outside of myself. I was indulging in a moment of self-pity. I needed to cry, but not with an audience. All I could see was a room of swollen stars. But something pushed at me to go on; what mattered to me was that I had to be good, even here. I lay on the floor and kicked off my shoes. I snaked out of my pants leaving only my scalloped G-string between me and the audience—and me and the floor. Steve changed the lights until I was washed in a cool blue. Everything got quiet—the audience, other strippers—and I became the focal point in a hypnotic tantric ceremony. I stayed low, undid the G-string and tugged at the sides. I pressed my hips into the cold, hard stage—made sure everyone got a nice long look at this dancer's behind. I ground my pelvis into the floor until I felt arousal. I rolled over, reached for the ceiling, rocked up and down, up and down, and then I stood, running my hands over my torso, my thighs. I shoved and it was Kent's mouth I saw in front of me. Just as I relaxed into the blue light, the music ended.

I grabbed my stuff off the stage and made a quick exit. The next dancer ground her cigarette into the carpet, sneered at me as I passed her at the foot of the steps.

Steve was by the jukebox. "You can dance. That *will* get you far."

I was still trying to catch my breath, wipe the sweat out of my eyes. "That was the idea."

"Louis won't care, though. He'll want to see even more of you. You have a nice one. You don't usually find cut ones in these parts. Total turn-on. It looks great like that, you know soft and fat, and those balls, too, man they're full, but Louis thinks the women want you almost hard." It sounded like he was talking about how to boil an egg, the way he went on. "You know. *Gonflé. Grossir.* Swollen. Inflamed. Louis's willing to take a chance. *Hard* might be against the law but not *almost* hard. Guy, my Guy, he's coming from Montreal to dance next week. Says Montreal is getting to him. You watch what he does and I'll help you, too."

SUNDAY MORNING AFTER FIVE more hours of sleep I rolled onto the floor. My mind wouldn't shut up from seven crazy hours in the club. I kept seeing women stuffed around the bar like piglets breastfeeding with their pink behinds wagging, and the blood vessalled faces of old men smiling, sweating and drinking *un Ricard* or *un whisky sur glaçe*. When I finally woke I kept going over my strip. Was it good? Where could it have been better? It went over and over and over in my head. I needed to move, to talk to someone, to shake it off or maybe brag a little. Opening nights were like that—you needed to bask in it for a while. But at Kent's there was no answer when I rang.

I had a few hours of sanity before going to meet Madame and the group for our Sunday afternoon *Pinocchio*. I looked for an open coffee shop but even with my extra hour of sleep I was up earlier than anyone in town. The search for I-don't-know-what led me into a cobblestone square. It was there I followed organ music up the steps of a grey, stone church. Would my evil body go up in flames if I went in? Was my survival a sin? I'd thought about it and came to the conclusion that everyone solicits different parts of themselves: minds, muscles, talent, knowledge and skills. (I seemed to be repeating that to myself frequently.) My skill set was specific, that's all. I leaned against the door and it gave way.

It was strange; the minister spoke English to a small congregation—a secret society of Protestants in a land where people build bathtub shrines to the Virgin Mary, in front of their fuchsia and lime-green shacks. Strathcona Baptist was about just showing up. The grey flannels. The little navy blazer with a crest on the pocket. The tartan tie and everyone patting my head with their swollen hands smelling of Aqua Velva and Shalimar. I had no idea what I had ever gained from those Sunday mornings other than a sense of guilt.

That Sunday morning, there was something right about wearing tight jeans, no underwear and a bomber jacket in the holy place. It was what I was becoming—a projection upon which the audience could unload their sexual fantasies. We were all so much more entwined than we chose to believe. A member of last night's audience could have been there in the congregation. I placed a fistful of tip money in the collection plate; it wasn't mine to keep. I scuttled out before the service ended. My real church was somewhere in the back pew of the city bus: that is where I had time to examine my reflection. I didn't lack faith. Faith was all around me now: I had a home, a job and a neighbour.

After the warmth of several hotel lobbies where I lingered, some cheap coffee and a freezing stroll along the promenade above the St. Lawrence, I met Kent on the street on his way home. He was silent and looking wounded, but I kissed him on the cheek. We went into our café downstairs and I bought him sugar pie and a café au lait. Kent usually reported on his sexual scores. And he wasn't really emotional about his tricks. He might occasionally claim to be in love— but never in a way that knocked him off his feet for more than a week. I got the feeling there had been a break-up, but then Kent always looked like his nights-before had been harder on him than mine were on me. I figured he just wasn't a morning person.

He finally broke the silence. "Have you tried the leather shorts?"

"My ass is too big."

"Don't whine. How about the cock ring?"

"Cock ring? I thought it was a bracelet."

"Get someone at the club to show you how to use it. Oh God, I can't believe no one has showed you how to use a cock ring. I'll show you. You are so naive I can't believe it."

"It's been touched upon. I guess the competition just isn't interested in showing me."

"It works wonders. Put it on while you're soft..."

"I'm sure I can figure it out."

"... play with yourself or jerk off, whatever, leave it on, it will stay swollen until you take it off. You'll bowl them over."

There wasn't much more time for chat. By early afternoon Madame had us performing *Pinocchio* in some theatre an hour from town. We stuffed ourselves—parkas, scarves, mitts and toques—into the freezing van jammed to the top with sets, costumes and props.

It was our first chance to feel like we were dancers on tour—different from life with the Company where we used big warm coaches on non-stop night drives north of Superior, through the Rockies or criss-crossing south of the border along Route 66. If we were lucky we flew, while trucks carried our sets to meet us. But now we schlepped huge, badly painted panels, tables, chairs and cots through the first freezing days of winter.

Our destination was an old movie palace. Our route was of interest because it took us along rue Lévesque and right past the Chez Moritz. I stared straight ahead but there was an odd silence in the van and Jean-Marc jabbed me in the ribs, raised his eyebrows and winked as we passed the deserted compound, its light flickering EN VEDETTE.

Madame had booked us into an empty—as in no audience—theatre. Not that the dates were wrong, but the publicity machine hadn't been well oiled. I didn't bother to ask what it was or who our audience would be. On the stage, behind the curtain, Madame took us through a warm-up and my Achilles tendons stung from the cold van ride. The maple floor was too hard—maybe concrete underneath—and varnished to a high gloss that made the girls skid on their pointe shoes. My thighs swelled like two water balloons as I pliéd.

"Monsieur Muscle," she said and then pretended she was a body-builder posing. To a regular human this would be a compliment, but to a dancer it was as bad as saying you were fat. I had already started to fill out after only a few weeks of my stripper regimen. My shoulders were building up, and though it might have been pleasing in a tank top at a strip bar, in ballet it was limiting and distracting.

My body, once a supple lengthening rubber band, was nothing but volume. Madame continued her rare cocky mood and joined in our warm-up instead of barking out orders. The training that had given her a deep-seated strength and technique was always there for her—she could hold *developpé en pointe* forever, which she wanted us to know. She could out-turn, out-extend, out-jump and out-dance any of us. But this forced emphasis on strength was destroying my line. Yes, I could jump; yes, I could *retiré en pointe* for ages now. I was stronger, but the added bulk worked against me when I was tired: I continued to lose my axis, my balance, and like she said, I was starting to look more like a bodybuilder. The girls at the club said I had *cuisses de grenouille*. But on the good side, I could jump higher than I ever had and I didn't look bad naked.

After our warm-up I burned my mouth on *chocolat chaud instanta-née* prepared by Madame. It seemed like a peace offering. I guess she wanted some good feeling on our debut.

Bertrand winked at me. "Come 'ave a look at da 'ouse." And we headed back to the stage to look through the curtains into the audience. Our audience, somewhere out there, breathed. There may have been a woman with a child. I'm sure I heard someone cough. I realized I wanted anything but to be in that theatre. Fatigue hit me. I didn't have the strength to dance to an empty house. I wanted to sit in my café with Kent. That's all. I had lost my dedication. The only pay-off that day (and it was cruel but I had to laugh) was the look on Madame's face when she realized what had happened. When the curtain finally rose, it did so to a house that coldly echoed every sour note of music, played on an out-of-tune piano, every step and every breath.

When it came time for me, as Geppetto, to lie down for my choreographed nap while the Blue Fairy, Maryse (whose severe makeup was more suggestive of an evil indigo fairy), kept falling off her points, trying to grant Pinocchio's wish to become a boy, I fell into a sound sleep. Bertrand's larger-than-life Pinocchio finally jabbed me, his poor father Geppetto who was trying to get forty winks from all his wood-carving, whittling and late-night stripping. I woke, startled, to Bertrand improvising laughter and some very silly dancing, which put us miles behind the music and gave us both a harsh fit of onstage giggles.

As we packed the van, Bertrand tapped me on the shoulder and pointed to a woman holding a little boy, both in matching down and leather. It was Suzette. "Hey *ma beau*, you danced well. *Hien, mon p'tit*, he danced well, didn't he? You recognize him from the club?" Clouds of still vapour hung. I was happy to see Suzette. She somehow reminded me that a real world existed somewhere. The real world, where I started to see that everything was on the outside, the opposite of ballet.

I laughed. "So, that was you at the back!"

"There were a few of us. Don't be so hard on yourself. See you Monday." She was a rosy-cheeked vision of motherhood and all that is good and wholesome in the world. I knew then that I needed a hot meal when I got home. And some company.

After the miserable walk from the school, I stepped into a time warp. Belle Époque, around the corner from my place, would be my church of choice for a moment on this grey day—a warm pub carved into the wall three hundred years ago and filled with cranky ghosts. I would let Kent recuperate from his night before, his latest broken heart. From my alcove I offered up more of my tips from the Chez Moritz and took communion in the form of the sacred barley brew of Brador while I watched the world start to tie itself into knots, and my ghosts—present, past and future—take form and then vaporize through clouds of cigarette smoke. This is where I came to seek refuge and ponder what had become of me. There seemed so little left. But I could crawl outside of myself and observe as if I were a character in a storybook, and by doing so I was able to take myself less seriously. Now, that has become impossible. I am clawing my way to the bottom of a stairwell in a bloody toga, all the while promising myself, and God, that I will never be so stupid as to come to this again.

LATER, SURROUNDED BY THE longed-for warmth of Kent's place, we had dinner. We sat in the easy chairs this time.

"Spaghetti, again?"

"Seems like you need your carbs."

"This is fantastic." He'd had a lot of wine, and I'd had sufficient beer by the time I got to his place, and couldn't stop laughing when I told him my falling-asleep story. It was good to be warm, really warm, and with him. I didn't have to impress him. He'd seen me at my worst in a very short period of time. "Can you imagine? I could still be asleep on that stage. I'd wake up and wonder where the hell I was."

"Is this a habit or a tradition?" He looked at me. "It's our third dinner together."

"Second one here." Why was I trying to steer away from the obvious?

"Third if you count takeout pizza at your place and a few hundred with coffees downstairs, but who's counting?"

"It's good to touch base, in case one of us falls asleep onstage…"

"Or the other disappears into the wilds of northern Quebec, hot on the trail of some lumberjack." I waved my finger at him. He had to know I'd registered his absences.

"I have a lumberjack friend. I could introduce you."

"I'll pass."

"Daniel? Still? Is that why you haven't…"

"Been laid?" I said. "Shit no!"

"…been good old, cock-slapping, body-fluidy, gooey, slippery-slidey and anonymously laid. You know, not just a naughty public shower game of peek-a-boo, but some sex. Call it lovemaking if you want."

"I've had my moments. You know, before I finally gave up pre-med, I organized the university dance club and choreographed the ex-ballerinas into a recital."

"This was a moment?"

"I'll get to it." I had wanted to tell Kent about the two male dancers, and our curtain call, but the whole event came flooding back. He had to know I was more than this. "It was hours of tapping out the 'Merry Widow Waltz,' recorded off a cracked thirty-three. The girls, all bobbing boobs and big behinds, leapt across the stage. Rehearsal skirts snagged, ripped, flowed, but they did it over and over until it was perfect. They ignored the bunions, the calluses, tendonitis and all the other reasons dance could be hell."

"You had sex with them?"

"Of course not."

"But you had sex."

"Indulge me."

"Go on."

"It was trial by fire. I was the novice. But it was my idea so they gave me their attention just because, you know, ballet: stern, unforgiving, repressed, autocratic."

"Get to the sex part."

"We sold tickets. I invited two male dancers from the Company as our guest artists."

"Finally."

"Not yet. I paid a groupie to make posters. We booked an old lecture hall. Classmates set lights. I scavenged backdrops: classical, fake flowers and columns. The girls sewed tutus. They made themselves up as only a ballerina can, you know, thick eyeliner above and below, extending at least halfway to the moon, angling up to the temple. Thick eyeshadow, too. Pinkish rouge, and contour until they looked like Bambi's cousin."

"The buildup is killing me."

I got up and strutted around Kent's place, arms flowing in the air. "I copied Balanchine-esque port de bras arms, studied Labanotation and choreographed patterns that came from hours of listening to music over and over again. I even created my own *pas de deux* with one of the smaller girls, to something slow by Vivaldi. They congratulated me, used words like *choreographer* and *dancer, director* and *producer*."

"Your point being that all this was better than sex?"

"It was the two guests..."

"At last!"

"...who came all the way from the Company for a credit on their resumés, past protegés of my teacher, Drake. The two men had such grace, such posture, such asses."

"Assets? I see where this is going and I am shocked."

"I'd seen them in the change room and I swear there was a tendon and a muscle for every single step they took. There was strength and grace I'd never seen in a man. I was so ashamed in their presence that I downplayed my crazy dream to be a dancer. But on our way through that frozen prairie air to the after-party that night they told me to go for it. They were both late starters, too, but did it, and after that my dreams and imagination went wild."

"Did you orgasm?"

"When we got to the party it was kudos for all. Glory for the girls. Glory for the boys. Real honest-to-God professional dancers and fans cooing over us."

"To make a long story short?"

"To make a long story short the men begged me to come to the

Company, somewhat drunkenly. And later that night, for the first time in my life I had intercourse."

"You fucked?"

"I fucked them both."

"That's more like it."

"But even then, the next morning I hoped some kind of bonding had taken place but I was wrong. It was just sex, again. Get-dressed, put-on-your-socks sex."

"I've never heard you brag about yourself. You should do it more often."

"I was already hooked, but it was those two men who finally opened the door by saying I should do it *now*."

"No doubts?"

"I jumped from the ivory tower without a net. Freedom. I left them all—the ladies at the barre to continue their pliés, *tendus, rond de jambes*, fouettés. They had their Tuesdays and Thursdays. I left Drake teaching the little girls to get it right on Mondays, Wednesdays and Saturdays. They would either quit or continue, be told they were the wrong shape or be cursed with perfect proportions. They were at the beginning and I was at a place where I had to know how much more it could hurt. That one night was worth it to see smiles between swigs of Mogen David and ginger ale. Bouquets. Boyfriends. Talking dance. Basking. We were hopelessly confident for one night. We did it. In spite of the odds, their soft shapes rivalled the beauty of Degas' dancers. But then they talked of other dreams—degrees, professions, law, medicine, nursing, archaeology, motherhood, children, homes and real lives without dance. I was about to depart on a journey they would only ever dream about, with their blessings; I would have a career because there were so few princes. I was more hooked than ever. They left, weeping, laughing, in a giggly cloud of cheap wine."

"And now?"

"I'm in a giggly cloud of cheap wine."

"Not *cheap*."

"To answer your question. I am a sinking star, no, pin of light on the horizon, faded to the point where you aren't sure if you can see me at all."

"Come on, you're young—you're drunk, too, by the way. I like it when you're like this: you have a dream, you have drive. But those two guys—number five and number six? So few. I mean what a waste."

"Too many warnings when I was young. We lived by a ravine full of evil men exposing themselves, offering candy and molesting wayward children."

"Now you're full of it."

"And swimming lessons at the Y."

"Continue."

"As of now, I am just way too tired to even get it up, and as of right now way too drunk."

"That was an option?"

"Could have had a big bag of candy by now. I guess I was holding out for Prince Charming…"

"Daniel."

"Now all I want is the sleep that even he can't wake me from."

"You're still young."

"Middle-aged in dancer years, and feeling very old."

"Dancers. You're nuts."

I flopped back into my chair. Performance over. I wondered if he cared about any of this—he got up and came around the table, squeezed my shoulder. I didn't feel like a target this time. "Just one more mouthful of spaghetti?"

"You can finish it later. I promise."

"I'll hold you to it."

"So I take it your bottom is still undiscovered territory."

"My *bottom*. We are polite, aren't we?"

"You call it bottom."

"I call it behind."

"Fine, so your ass…"

"Things don't work so well down there."

"Maybe you just need the right person. How about a massage?"

"Do you realize you just used the massage line?"

"But I meant it."

He got up and went to the kitchen. "A little olive oil? A couple of fingers? Maybe a tongue." He pulled his shirt off, let his jeans drop to the floor.

"This isn't exactly how I saw our evening playing out."

"You have a beautiful body, and I want you to understand what it feels like to have a beautiful bum. You'll thank me. Take off your clothes."

As he returned, I took in his very un-dancer physique. I had grown so used to supple, defined, slender and overworked—and here was something so tight and beautifully proportioned, and so real. .

Kent squatted and rubbed my inner thighs and looked at me as though he was taking in the view.

"I'm not kidding when I say…"

"Sit here, on the floor, face me, relax, just relax and enjoy the ride. I promise I won't hurt you."

THIS STAIRWELL CANNOT TAKE me away from what just happened up there. Some might say I am in shock. Some might say so what, I had it coming to me. The idea of two men having intercourse might force some to turn away. The idea of a man being raped might do so to others. I can do my best to turn away, run, block it out, but something is in the way.

I WANTED TO TELL Kent that I'd heard the "I won't hurt you" line before. But I trusted him. His straightforwardness demanded the same of me. There were no games, no second-guesses, no ulterior motives. My whole professional world was one big theatrical facade, and now here I was naked before him, in body and soul. I sat cross-legged on the floor in front of the chair, while Kent gently touched me—my inner thighs, my testicles. Then he slipped his hand underneath and gently tickled his stubby fingers into me. "We have all the time in the world."

We sat face to face.

"Think of your ass as a big beautiful white moon. Pretend you're me, looking at it. Pretend you know my desire." I wondered if Kent's desire verged on desperation. Did he desire all of me? Did he want things to go a lot faster than they did? No. He ended up being the most patient person I have ever met. It was the first time anyone had ever taken the time—and it happened. There was such a release in just having someone touch me after so many weeks of living in a straitjacket with the psychotic Madame—her band of crazy dancers—endless schlepping across the Lower Town of Quebec to make a little money—and after leaving Daniel far behind. I had to turn my mind off that other world and just be here in the room, on the floor, face to face. I was being cleansed. Reminded of my sexual self. "Relax." The lights were on, not off, and we were staring into each other's eyes. "You feel so good." He pressed farther, until I tingled inside… "Three fingers," he said. "How does that feel?"

"Three fingers in my bum!?"

"In your bum? No. Up your ass, yes."

"Close to amazing," is most likely what I said. He was so close and we were so slow that I could watch his pupils dilate. I inhaled his breath.

"That's your prostate," he whispered.

"It's like I have two penises—one on the inside the other on the outside."

"If that's how it feels, you're a bottom." He pushed harder, rocking my pelvis. And each time, our eyes stayed locked.

I barely knew what was happening with me, inside me, inside my head, my heart. I didn't want to think. About Daniel. My new self. I hated myself for thinking this.

We sat like naked children facing each other, Kent's penis pressed against my leg. It was absurd, him in rapture like this, all the while talking me through it. Why Kent? Why no embarrassment? Why so easy?

I broke the rhythm.

"Here, I'm going to withdraw. My fingers are starting to fall asleep. You are so tight. And that's not a bad thing."

"For *you*."

After that we lay on the floor and held each other, falling in and out of sleep, slowly exploring each other with our hands. It was so good to press against a body. His body. He was one of the most sensitive men I've ever touched. Even when we kissed he seemed to be in some kind of rapture. I dreamt of the North Saskatchewan River that runs through the city where I was born, like it did into my bathing trunks as a kid. I loosened them a little and then a little more until they accidentally fell away with a kick and my shrivelled dink puckered in the icy currents. There was no beach, just a grassy bank, and no one came there to swim. There was a man, standing in the grass with his fly open. The red sun burned across the valley. I woke not knowing if it was a dream or a memory. We kept holding each other. An urge flooded me, which Kent sensed and satisfied, and then the closer he got to climaxing, the harder I had to hold onto him as his body trembled and convulsed. He bit, squeezed, dug in—whatever he had to do to keep from flying through the roof.

I LEFT EARLY FOR the studio. There were reports of a blizzard already shutting down Montreal and making its way to us, causing havoc on the highway, jackknifed transports, whiteouts, hundreds of cars in the ditches. At the ballet studio, despite my morning-after inner grin, everyone was silent. This was no victory morning; the sounds of Sunday afternoon's applause did not echo. The scent of incompetence was still fresh. Madame Talegdi was losing support; she had lost our trust. Layers of discontent and blame crowded the studio. Bertrand refused to talk to Maryse. He said she couldn't dance, was all over the place, sliding *en pointe, trop sauvage*. He called her anorexic—which she was—and too weak to do anything. She wouldn't speak to me, nor would Chantal.

The sky grew eerily dark in the west, as if our foul moods fed the tempest. The radiators clanged and Madame shouted and clapped out the beat, since Hortense was ill. We all stood frozen at attention, shoulders around our ears and not looking at Madame, even Jean-Marc. She finally had her own version of a fit. She stopped the class, slammed her hands on the barre and then stomped out of the room.

Then it was Louise's turn. She coldly started her own barre while the others stretched and continued their warm-ups. When I joined Louise, she turned and stomped across the studio to the kitchen and slammed the door behind her. She had always been warm—her big eyes, her endearing shoves. But having designs on a gay man, if you're a woman, can be a challenge. In the Company, more than once a female best friend ended up in tears because her "just friends" gay male buddy had snubbed her when she got too close. I felt it from Rachelle, and even from the girls at the club: possibilities reflected in their gaze. And in the linoleum kitchen off the studio, after I opened the slammed-in-my-face door, Louise lunged—her hips square against mine, with nowhere for the family jewels to go. Louise's physique, her being, in fact everything about her, was lovely. You don't need to be made of stone to appreciate a mountain. Forcing herself against me, she spoke in a loud whisper, "Who do you think you are?"

"What do you want?"

"I don't believe this. After all the flirting, and you're playing hard to get? I know exactly what you do."

"Chorus boy?"

"You strip for women."

"They pay me, that's all. You know what I am."

"But you're not interested in me?"

"Is *chère amie* not good enough?"

Louise relaxed her hold, but she squeezed my arms with affection and perhaps a measure of sensuousness. Maybe she saw me treading water until someone threw me a life vest, or until I drifted into a current that would carry me far away.

"What are you doing here?"

"*Je fais rien.* This has all gone wrong."

The following weeks Madame played Bertrand off Louise by giving Louise the attention and ignoring Bertrand. But all he cared about was dance, and his too-honest face gave away everything he felt for Madame. I could also tell that he saw from my weak dancing that, pretty as I was, I was no longer competition for Jean-Marc.

WITH THE BLIZZARD, I felt like Christmas had arrived. Everything was coated in frosting and the Old Town looked even more like a fairy tale. But major roads were cleared and work was still on. At the club, in the strippers' dressing room Suzette wouldn't stop. "*Il danse. Le Grand Blond danse, vraiment. Il est danseur. B'en je n'ai jamais imagine.* Hey, what the hell are you doing in a dump like this?" The girls all seemed so impressed; if I had been keeping a pregnancy a secret, they couldn't have been more pleased. But it didn't matter. The idea of becoming a fine dancer was fading for the moment. I just wanted sanity and simplicity.

That night I decided on the songs for my official strip, with "Gloria" as my first song. It was about someone living in a world where no one calls, no matter how important you feel or how many people you think want you. And I danced to it, full out until my eyes stung, my heart pounded and my throat burned from the stale, smoke-laden air. Me, the star of my own little world.

Then Toto's "Africa," which made me think of the kind of freedom I had never known, while I caught my breath, got grounded and started taking most of my clothes off. It was perfect timing for undoing buttons, zippers, ties and belts. After that, Suzette ran up to the stage, waving me over. "Did you pick your t'rd song?"

"Not yet."

"Can I?"

"As long as it's not 'In the Summer Time.'"

She laughed and dropped the coins in the machine and looked at me as she punched the buttons, like she knew exactly which buttons to push.

The music started slow with a guitar strumming and then notes on what sounded like and electric organ and a woman singing in a whispery voice, "*Je t'aime,*" while a man replied, "*Moi non plus.*" The song put me right in the bedroom it was so sensuous and sexy. As for the words, it could have been me singing to Daniel, *Je t'aime,* and Daniel replying, *Moi non plus.* But it took me to better places in my imagination—a loft in Paris—and then, being naked on the stage seemed more reverential than simply eyes staring at me in the dark. It gave me a greater understanding of the effect my sexual body could have and what I was capable of. The emotion coupled so easily with what I was doing. I had never given myself to the emotion onstage. I had never found it, and now it was so simple. My body was the song.

Suzette was waiting for me after the spell was broken. "Just remember, you have to like your songs, because you'll have to listen to them a thousand times."

"Thank you for that one."

"It used to be mine, but I don't know, it got too personal. I want you to have it."

When I went back downstairs, Guy, Steve's Guy, was in the dressing room. The girls loved him. Unlike the buff muscle-head who had done us a big favour with his uptight visit between bench presses the week before, Guy was everyone's friend. Guy had a face like a lion—big-boned, big-muscled; the only thing fake was his perfect tan. Even though he didn't have much to say, he had a huge, open, I-won't-hurt-you smile. He even tried to speak English. He got a kick out of me watching him get naked and getting a load of his goods. That's what men do at urinals, in showers, change rooms and anywhere we can have a look and compare. It was circumcised, and if only one word described it that would be *heavy*, with one pronounced blue vein along the shaft. I stared because he clipped something on, around the base of the shaft. I thought it was a decoration or an ornament, but it was a leather band that held everything up and out.

And later when Guy was dancing up on his box, this thing did the job. *Don't stare at Guy*, I told myself. Staring was bad for business—I was supposed to be interested in the female clientele (though they like it if you stare at their dates).

I was a better dancer, but he had the moves. Really, you only need to dance so well… dance any better and it's the law of diminishing returns: people wonder what the hell you're doing. He didn't spin around or do anything fancy; he just worked it. And he had that Lou Rawls heavy balls energy. He had personality, too, which you can never have too much of. As a club favourite, he didn't have to drum up any business. He just kept his regulars happy going from table to table and making some good money. Although the business went to him, my tips were always great on a night he worked.

Steve took advantage of the fact that his boyfriend was busy, and made his move when Guy was up on the stage for his three dances. I was on my way downstairs for our first feathers show of the night, our 9:30, when Steve caught up and nudged me into the wall on the landing. He took my hand and led me down to the bathroom. I figured he was going to ask me to smoke with him or try something more daring, which I would have declined, already deciding I would tell him it didn't react well with me. But he shut the door, pushed me up against the wall and started kissing me with his cigarette-and-mint-gum flavoured lips and tongue. He pushed his palm into my crotch and yes, I responded. It was the first real reaction I'd had since I started working there; too many things on my mind: when to dance, when to sleep, who to please. Even the calm bartender-granddaddy of the place, Hubert, without a mean bone in his body, had me on edge on busy nights, like he was surveying the horizon for inadequate phalluses. The noise stopped for me for maybe a minute—Steve had a secure grip on me. He stroked through my pants. He spit out his gum, got down on his knees and unzipped me, then himself. He squeezed himself with one hand, me with the other. "Nice."

There was that feeling of giving over that finally comes with know-ing that you are on your way into some guy's mouth. He pulled on my balls until they hurt, before he pressed me to the back of his throat. Then he got into a slow rhythm that matched my own and I got closer to exploding each time he went deeper. I was on the verge and the top of his head was bobbing up and down, slurping—the noises he made fed the feeling—eyes peering up, me so hard I felt as if I could barely fit in his mouth. I was on my toes, calves cramping, and I held on tight. I was in some kind of eyes-rolled-back-in-my-head-this-is-ecstasy kind of place. I didn't care if anyone banged down the door; I was beyond the point of no return. And he loved it. He knew how to hold me, when to pull back, let go, and how to make the most of the explosion. Now, here in the stairwell thinking of him hungry for it, still makes me hard. How could I have ever let guilt get in the way of something so good?

"You 'ave to wear this now—" he said, "a cock ring like Guy has."

"This?" I held out my wrist with the bracelet Kent had given me. Sweat covered my arms, dripped off my nose.

"Yes. Put it on." I unsnapped it and looped it around everything, the way Guy had. "Now it will stay nice and big, like my boyfriend's." The strap had a row of snaps all along it. "Dat's how you keep busy all night. I can't believe no one told you" We both looked at it.

"I guess I needed the demo." I couldn't believe it took this long to figure it out. Now I was one of the guys. I had to tuck strategically to get it all into the G-string and even then I could barely zip up my pants.

"You jerk off if I'm not here." He leaned over the sink and rinsed his face. My quest to find true love had been temporarily delayed. Of course Patrice was right there outside the door, drooping flower on his fedora—*trés blasé*—and it was obvious. I hoped it wouldn't tarnish our rides home.

After that it was a fast change into tits-and-ass attire and upstairs for some walk-walk-walk-turn and repeat. Steve was back in his booth waving. I looked at the others, then back at Steve and he was pointing for me to look down at my crotch. Was he trying to tell everyone in the whole place what had just happened by pointing to his own? But it was Suzette's dramatic glance at my crotch—I thought she was marvelling at the bulge—that gave it away. There was a wet spot on my pants; the pipes weren't empty when I dressed and it had soaked through my spandex pants and was glowing under the black lights like radioactive goo.

Later I danced for some English exchange girls from Laval University—blouses buttoned to the throat, hair perfect, house wine. I wanted to show my new toy off to the room—co-workers included. Off came the vest, down came the pants, I unclipped the G-string, felt myself flop out. Now, I was friendly competition for Guy, thanks to his boyfriend. But when I searched for amazed stares at the wonder between my legs, the exchange students didn't care; they wanted to have a talk after I was dressed. It may have looked like I was going to be getting a few more dances, since spontaneous conversations usually meant just that, but the conversation turned awkward.

"Was it a wise choice to be in a place like this?" A fresh brunette asked me. She could have made some good money here. Her friend advised me, "Never turn gay," and another, "How can you work in such a hole and not have a life plan?" then said, "You're a beautiful man." I tried to laugh it off: unless they were ready to offer me food and rent money, this was where I'd be staying for the time being. True though, they did almost get to me, as in *What* am *I doing in a dump like this?* Having others' pity can be like a drug. But that night, I didn't care. With my cock ring I had finally graduated and was giving the competition a run for the money.

Patrice drove me home without a word. I think he and Steve shared something themselves in the can, either sex or coke. When I got home I gave Patrice a peck on the cheek to secure a few more rides at least, and the feeling that my good fortune was wearing thin disappeared when I saw a reluctant and dirty grin flash across his face.

I put Kent's bracelet beside the bed, and wondered when he would have used it.

THE NEXT FOUR HOURS barely helped, and my new bad habits—too many push-ups, chin-ups, curls, trays of booze held high—and sleeping on a cold floor at night, left my spine lopsided for the first thirty minutes of any day. My body was a battleground between Madame's masochism and my job. Class wasn't going to happen that day. I couldn't let Madame see me so exhausted. I rolled over, fondled the cock ring, remembering the night before, and thought of my new magical powers before falling back to sleep.

At noon, I stepped out onto Sainte-Ursule with a pocket full of tips to get some leather or latex, a vest, pants, anything that could pass as sexy. But in the touristy Old Town, not one place specialized even remotely in sleaze, other than your basic tacky gift shop with edible panties, booby beer mugs and whoopee cushions.

I went back home to bed and didn't wake up until six—fortunately my back came around just in time. The sleep had done me some good. I put on the cock ring and called Kent to come over. I answered the door with my new prize. "Steve blew me yesterday and then I…"

"Blew you?"

"Said the man who's had ten thousand."

"Two thousand. Don't take this thing too seriously."

"Look who's talking."

"You're serious?"

"It's your fault. You gave me the magic amulet. You, more than anyone, know its hidden powers." He touched his lips to quiet me.

"Look I don't have time to be guilty. Will you give me a quick massage?"

"As in..."

"My back is in knots, lots of small ones compared to just one big one, that's all. I almost feel normal."

"You almost look normal. You've been working out?"

"As much as I can."

"You took the pickle out of your ass."

"You did."

You could say I had something new to put in my dance bag.

SEVERAL NIGHTS, ON THE way to the Chez Moritz, I sat diagonally from a guy with a weak chin and a perfect rim of hair like a monk's, but obviously dyed a colour that had turned yellow. We'd done this ride before. He was built; the sleeves of his jacket were tight on him. On one of those rides we played peek-a-boo through the suburbs and into the dark, until the glow from the Chez Moritz came up on the right. When I got up he frowned, but that's life. I remember so wanting anonymous warmth.

As I walked the last hundred yards of freezing highway and watched the bus disappear, I thought about all of us, connected by a place where there was absolutely nothing but a small paycheque and tips. And then we all leave at 3 A.M. Again I wondered what the hell I was doing. Each week I was getting further and further away from a technique that I had been so privileged to acquire, and to acquire so rapidly. At 9 P.M. I should have been getting ready for bed with a cup of warm milk and a biography of Diaghilev or Nijinsky, maybe stretching my hamstrings while I waited for the news to come on, or stepping onto a real stage with a real audience, where the show ends at eleven. But now I felt like I had the flexibility of a quarterback and gait of a thug, out on a fucking highway to nowhere.

Did anyone, other than Kent, know where the hell I was at that moment? My parents believed, as had I, that I was working with a small independent company that paid me real money. They'd figure out something respectable to tell their friends as they guzzled their rye and Cokes. If a truck or car clipped me right then and turfed me into the ditch, sometime during the following spring people would have wondered how the hell I got there. They might see the club a half a mile away and put the pieces together. But they would never know it was where I found the spotlight, money, costumes, great music, eye candy and easy sex.

But the thrill of easy sex had risks, like losing my ride home with Patrice. I couldn't get beyond the hand touching, kiss-on-the-cheek stage that he was forcing on me. Like me, he wanted capital-L love and I just wasn't interested. He could tell, and made me wait longer and longer for my ride—he'd have a nightcap, laugh with the bartender, or get into a deep conversation of palm reading with one of the girls—as a punishment. Lucky him, he had nothing to do all day but sleep.

One night after he'd had many drinks, he read my palm and told me that I had to "embrace my stardom." He said most people have to leave it behind, forget their ego, learn humility, but he said I had to take hold of my star and soar. He said I had to stop hiding within myself. He told me not to give up. I was too young to throw it all away on the circus. Then he placed his hands over mine.

THE NEXT DAY, FREEZING rain turned into hard snow whipping down Sainte-Ursule. Kent and I sat by my window at the hookers' wrought-iron dining ensemble. Recently Kent never seemed at ease—as if he couldn't sit completely still—until he was in the dark corner of a club and he'd had a beer or two.

"I have tea." I wondered if his agitation was because sex with me was on his mind. It was on my mind: I finally felt ready to have some fun and easy sex, but I wasn't good with advances.

"Tea would be great." We stared out the window. I told Kent about Louise throwing herself at me. He told me I was too concerned about them. But I went on. I told him everything was getting to me: Madame's moods, the tight-lipped ballerinas, Bertrand's wackiness, then about the club and Patrice's cold shoulder, pre-show blow jobs, drinks, drunkenness, the cock rings...

"No one likes advice, but you know..."

"Shoot."

"You seem disconnected. It's kind of weird, I mean, you, your language, you said *penis* when I first met you and now it's all *cock* and *ass*. What the fuck? Everything about you is changing."

"I've only said *cock* once."

"That's one hundred percent more than you did before."

"And that's not good? Didn't you say I should grow up? I mean I have to say *ass*. *Behind* sounds like a jelly dessert or something."

"I did not say you should grow up. Your innocence is endearing. Was."

"Well, I'm sure you thought it. I mean, my God, *penis* sounds like it should be wearing a doily, a periwig and a ruffled collar, a tutu or something."

"It's not even in your nature to grow up."

"You want to keep me naive?"

"Forget it. You could at least use the word, *tool*."

"Tool's loaded. I'm a tool. I feel like I've been a tool for years, in someone else's ballet. I've been useful to others. That's *tool* to me."

"Fine, you've made your point, had your rant."

There was nothing but silence and the wind whistling forlornly at the window.

"I'm bringing my bosses, Brigitte and her husband Alex tonight. They're driving me. They've been before. Don't worry. They know what it's like. You'll be a celebrity yet."

"Don't forget your opera glasses."

"I won't need them if you wear that cock ring."

That night, because of the weather, the place was almost empty. We did our show and Kent's bosses, Brigitte and Alex, loved meeting a real live *étoile de spectacle* star as much as Kent liked introducing me. He smiled like a proud parent.

I danced a string of songs for them. Alex had no reservations about staring at me, while Brigitte seemed preoccupied with women dancing at neighbouring tables. We chatted while I squatted and rubbed my thighs. Kent related my company gossip to them, told them about the hopeful Louise, the narcissistic Madame. I'm not sure what he said when I wasn't there, but I had the feeling he was bragging.

They left after midnight and Kent took up a seat in the dark against the wall. He didn't mind staying until the end of my shift, and I was glad to have him there. He smoked, drank a lot, was quiet and watched me. I danced for him a few times and each time he gave me a different compliment; he mentioned my innocent allure, my Ivy League persona, my strengths, good proportions, my weaknesses, a tendency to retreat into myself... He called me *Doc Sauvage. Flash Gordon.*

"What about the you-know-what?"

"Cock looks *formidable,*" he told me.

"Penis, please."

He touched me in the dark, whispered, "Shit, I'm getting turned on." Girls were fired for less.

"I confess, I gave it a pre-show workout." But he knew I was lying; Steve had been the one to do that. I continued, "I just make sure it's not illegally hard. But you know, ballet leaves way more to the imagination, though it is hard to ignore the Bluebird in *Sleeping Beauty,* flying through the air, all gold leaf and blue feathers, checking to see if it's a pickle or a sausage in his codpiece."

"Ballet it ain't," he said. But his mood had changed.

THAT NIGHT KENT PAID for our cab ride home. I didn't have to think about Patrice's silence and the debt I owed him. Kent was silent. The roads were being cleared of snow—orange and yellow flashed through the cab, across the snowbanks, out into the darkness, and the streetlights reflected off the clouds above, making it an eerily yellow early morning—as we sat staring in opposite directions.

Finally he broke the silence. "It's not exactly the New York City Ballet. You can't do it forever," he said.

"You're not impressed?"

"It's stripping."

"And for once it's good enough, even if it is a little side-show shit attraction." I went on; his attitude had provoked me. "Fuck, it is like some idea of perfection has hounded me all my life. I couldn't please my father so what do I do? Go headfirst into an art form that is all about perfection, all of the time. It was my escape. I'm not perfect—

not for the Company or Daniel. Now I'm stuck trying to please you, a stranger, mere months ago. What is going on?" I was drunk, tired and my guard was down. Those were the facts. "I can run, but I can't fucking hide."

"That's not a bad thing," Kent said.

"Well it seems I've never pleased anyone."

"You poor thing."

"I'll disappoint you, too." At this point I had slowed down.

"You won't."

"Other than a swollen dick and a fake blond swoosh, there's not much to me. I have all the attention I want. No one to say I'm so much better than this, other than those self-righteous bitches, or that I'm above it. Truth is that I am no better than this."

"Fake blond swoosh?" Kent started to chuckle.

"Yes, and taking off my clothes."

"Won't you have to make some decisions eventually?"

"About my abs and chest?"

"You know what I mean."

"You've changed your tune."

"No. You might as well be good at what you're doing. That's fine. But you do have a future. Believe me. The voice of oldness, if not wisdom. Where to next? Is there a next? I can't see you becoming an aging stripper in *vieux* Quebec. Even I have a Plan B."

"I used to think I had a career."

"Are you too proud to go back?"

"Are you pissed because of my pre-show blow job?"

"I'd give you a medal if I had one."

"Then Daniel?"

"Daniel's a loser."

"Well then?"

"Well then. What next?" I was surprised that he cared.

"Maybe this will be all I ever have to offer this fucked up world."

"That's just laughable.

"Recently it's what I tell myself."

"Well I, for one, wouldn't let you. You have no idea what you are capable of."

"Why is it so important to you, anyway?" But I already thought I knew the answer. And maybe that wasn't so bad.

"Sometime I want to show you something at my place," he said. The cab turned up Sainte-Ursule and he fell against me, reaching for his pocket to get some cash

"You can show me now."

THAT WEEKEND I RAN my ass off between shows. It excited my customers to have a half-erect man a touch away. The whole thing had finally become easy. I wished that table of bank tellers from my first night would come back.

Six

THE POWER DRAWN FROM a dancer's gluteus maximus enables everything from a strong port de bras during reverence to providing the source for the *sauté* or a simple *tombé*. The gluteus maximus maintains the line when a dancer does a *tour jeté* or a *saut de basque*. The gluteus maximus is responsible for holding the leg, pressed against a solid lower back, for a remarkable arabesque. The gluteus maximus provides the resistance needed to create momentum throughout a turn. The gluteus maximus curves away from the back to begin defining the lines of the leg. When the male dancer stands with his back to the audience, his right arm extended to support his partner's grip as she *developpés à la second*, they are looking at his gluteus maximus.

WHAT THE REMOVABLE STRIPES did for my cheerleading, what Kent's cock ring did for my allure, what "Je T'aime… Moi Non Plus" did for my centre, is what Brittany Barrymore did for everything else: the loose ends, the showmanship, the spaces in between. Brittany put the icing on this stripper's cake.

The news on Thursday was that our featured dancer would be Brittany Barrymore. Most of her name was on the Marquis—Br'tny B'more EN VEDETTE. And by late Friday afternoon the parking lot was full. Men had left work early, called their wives to say they were held up at the office, or picked them up on the way out here and brought them along. Brittany was the draw. One of the circuit girls, she toured the northeast US and the Great Lakes while most girls only came from Montreal for the week, and others were stuck with rural Quebec—every town from Lac St. Jean to Trois-Rivières to Iberville to Chicoutimi to Rouyn-Noranda. The circuit girls usually had better moves, music and costumes, though it all got copied, borrowed or stolen. They stayed at the welcome-as-a-bomb-shelter motel beside the Chez Moritz, which was useful since they'd be wasted by the end of the night—a crawl back to their rooms was all they could manage. The only part of day they ever saw, if they were lucky, was sunset after they woke.

Starring—*en vedette*—that week was the perennial favourite, Brittany. She had driven all the way from Detroit in her white Cadillac, following a feature circuit she had blazed for herself. The place was buzzing with waitresses shuttling full trays of drinks from the bar to the floor, as if the demand never subsided. And middle-aged, middle-class couples, some in their Kiwanis and Shriners vests, occupied almost every seat not taken by the nightly regulars. The corps de ballets (as I started to call my co-workers) were happy there was less of their time wasted onstage and more time spent on the floor, and with everyone drinking more than usual, they were making good tips.

There was a mild commotion at the door. I laid down my last tray of empties to take a breather before heading downstairs for our first show. Vasili entered the club, hugging a huge fuzzy cushion, him all puffed up, leading Brittany through the room with a stuffed garment bag over her arm, blonde hair glowing the same unnatural shade as her fake fur jacket. Her small face was lost in all that plush.

In the basement she had the dressing room next to ours. Dressing room? Stained counter. Chipped mirror. Cold concrete floor. A suspended rod of wire hangers. She had respect downstairs, and the girls gave her space. It seemed not one of those women could compete with Brittany, so they made friends with her, trading drugs like baseball cards, with stoned promises of post-show companionship, too.

When I saw her onstage I understood the fuss: Steve announced her to the house, *en vedette*, like a circus emcee, announcing her most recent list of accomplishments: "*Partymag*'s Miss January"; performances "live from Detroit via Cleveland, Buffalo, Rochester, Sherbrooke"; and attributes—"the lovely, trés sexy, bad-girl-gone-good, girl-next-door"—as the tiny follow spot swirled across the stage. After the noise subsided and Steve had caught everyone's attention, the rhythmic intro to George Benson's "Turn Your Love Around" filled the room and Brittany Barrymore slipped one long, smooth leg from behind the slit in the red velvet curtain (that curtain hid a space big enough for one stripper or a pile of discarded clothes). She twisted into the light in a tight-fitting blue sequined gown slit to her hip. The whole outfit was lined with silver and was probably worth more than all of the bikinis, G-strings, leather miniskirts, hot pants and thongs put together at the Chez Moritz. Every turn, the slit in her skirt flashed the line of her waxworks-perfect legs. In her open-toed Cinderella acrylic stilettos, she floated over the stage, and Steve shone a milky light that made her look like some kind of striptease angel, skin powdery and white.

After all these weeks of slowly becoming more and more used to my lacklustre routine, I finally saw some true professional showmanship. She put us all to shame, but I was the only one who cared. She'd skip a little, or stop and then pull back in her hips, knees together, as much as her tight dress would allow. She made you think she needed someone to satisfy her immediately, but didn't want to give it away to just anyone. She made you think it was you who could save her. She strutted over to some guy at the edge of the stage and got him to reach up to unclip the side of her dress, then she got some other guy to unzip one of the seams until, with a little shimmy, the dress dropped to the ground to show her marble-white body from her tiny round tummy and breasts, to her perfect bum and thighs, to her toes. In a microscopic fringed bikini and still in her heels she stepped out of the pile of dress at her feet, knowing that doing very little was doing enough.

When the music changed to "Still" by The Commodores, you knew you were under her spell. Her hair tumbled off her shoulders, hiding that small face and upturned nose. The paleness of her skin and the white lights Steve used combined to make it seem like she was carved out of the softest marble. She unclipped the centre of her bikini top as she tossed her hair, with perfect timing, to fall over her breasts and her small red nipples. She kicked her large white cushion forward and then relaxed onto it, lying on her front, twisting her legs, knees bent, ankles crossed. She tugged at the tiny elastic of her

G-string, pulling it down her thighs and calves, and finally over her feet. All this with shoes still on, and the guys up front staring right between her legs. Why not?

All the strippers were staring. The room was mesmerized with this living statue. Finally she kicked off her shoes and playfully wrestled with the cushion. Everything about Brittany was holy. She took you away from your surroundings to a place where sex was pure and fun, and after that you could show her off at the finest of places, in her beautiful sequined dress, not that you would ever be able to. She wasn't like the others. She never got involved with her body. No poking fingers, squeezing breasts or crude clinical examinations with legs wide open. She was as respectful of her beauty as she wanted you to be. At least that's what she wanted you to think. The lights went down and came up again and she was gone.

She brought down the house. Brittany was a *goddess*.

For Brittany's later number she donned a nurse's outfit, with stethoscope and fishnets, to "Doctor's Orders." But some of the girls had already tired of the Brittany hoopla and were back on their boxes before she even finished.

Brittany revived herself in the in-between time with a cocktail or two, or she'd disappear. Soon the girls were in and out of her room one after the other, not even bothering to hide their nasty habits in the can—hits and lines—while everything got a little messier on those stairs: twisted ankles, broken glass, spilled booze running down bloody legs, over caesarean scars, stretch marks and bruises.

When I got up on the stage, I could just make out Brittany's bleached hair glowing in the shadows at the back of the room. I sensed she was watching, like every ballet teacher who had psyched me out at one time or another. But it didn't matter because the music took over and I had my cock ring. I had "Gloria," my life's soundtrack. My eyes stung late in the set, when I finally spun myself into that booze-induced trance. But I was sober enough to want to impress her and have her know I was on her team, the team that took itself seriously. But by song three the high was gone and I was trying to remember where I had thrown my clothes. And by the time I had collected everything—a woman holding my new tie in her mouth and someone waving my shirt at the edge of the stage—it was time to race downstairs and get ready for the second feathers show.

Brittany was back downstairs, too. She called out from her room, slurring her words, saying I was really good, saying I had to go for it, not be afraid. I knew what she was saying—only I was hoping she wouldn't have noticed. It's what had held me back, for every moment up to then, from punching Daniel's beautiful nose sideways, to kicking Madame Talegdi's ballerina ass. It's probably what kept me from staying with the Company. It was the decision to stare blankly, or take flight, rather than stay true and focus and fight.

Brittany slurred more, said she had some chocolate. Said she was "not supposed to… eat chocolate." It didn't agree with her. And as the night went on she sounded more and more wasted, but after our show she was back up there onstage in a Catwoman body stocking for her last number. She earned her pay, goddess that she was, and then went back to being messed up in her room—crawling across the floor looking for her glasses. "I h-a-a-a-d some shoclut. I'm-m-m n-n-n-n-n-not shupposhed to ha-a-a-ve shoclut." I guess Vasili took her back to her room that night at the motel. I didn't think I'd see her again.

THE NEXT DAY, SATURDAY, I arrived early. They'd aired out the place so now it still smelled as bad, but it was cold. Marcel's humpy bartender-boyfriend, François, was wiping glasses and had hockey on a television by the bar. The place was empty. Downstairs Marcel was fretting about the choreography for one of our numbers. He said he was getting lost onstage. Could I help it if the man was short? He squeezed my forearm. "We should have dinner sometime, talk about the Conservatoire."

"You're inviting me to dinner, while François is upstairs?"

"It's just dinner."

Marcel was cute, like dolls are cute. I wondered if I could go for him. He was a classic nice guy with a squeaky-clean dirty side. What is it with nice guys? The nasty ones are the ones we all end up falling for. The Daniels. From now on there would never be another nasty one. Daniels were made to break hearts. Daniels never belonged to anyone.

BRITTANY WAS EARLY THAT Saturday night, at the bar in her faux fur. She drank a soda water, spoke clearly and didn't slur. She didn't even seem to remember the night before, about being out of it, or the chocolate. "I saw your strip last night—on the stage. You were really good."

"You're the pro." I knew how to flatter a star. I'd had practice.

She moved closer, all small face and hair, lowered her voice. "But just go for it. Don't be scared of them. Don't hesitate. You're good, but you stand in your way. God I sound like a preacher. But I mean it. Look them in the eye. Tease the bastards. Because that's what they are, bastards. Kill them. Do it *for* them though. You're being selfish, you're holding back. It's not just about your dick. That's what you guys think. You have to scare the audience with commitment. No one here is going to tell you how to be better. They don't give a shit. But I do."

I nodded. I knew what she was saying. I just didn't want to believe it.

"You're so much like I was." she said. "Be the fucking master. Don't worry. You'll always do well in a place like this. But you have to be more than just good enough. That's all this place is about. Remember, not just for yourself. Share."

Kent had said something about good enough, too. It seems that the world gets by on good enough, and I'd stepped into something where good enough wasn't enough for me. She asked me, "Do you still dance?"

"I'm trying."

"I danced for thirteen years, was in the corps in Pittsburgh. Look at me. Go ahead." Instead I looked at my fingers weaving and tapping the bar. "No, I mean it. Closely. Literally. Look at my mouth. Look at my teeth. My fingernails." Her lower teeth glowed in the black light. "Go on, say it. Don't hold back." He fingernails were shellacked a hard, dark colour.

"I don't know what you mean," I lied.

"Perfect?"

"Yes."

"You've been here long enough to know what perfect teeth mean."

"I have an unfair advantage. My father is a dentist."

"This face isn't mine."

"The teeth?"

"The face." She reached out, touched my tapping fingers. "I was in a car accident, years ago now. Rebuilt." She laughed. "Like the bionic woman. Down to my pretty little fingertips. Believe it or not, I don't actually have nails."

I didn't know what to say. "Prettier than the bionic woman."

"It's funny, those sayings, every face tells a story, and eyes are the windows of the soul. But not this face—it's wiped clean. But my eyes are my windows, that part is true."

Why would anyone lie about such a thing? I found it hard to believe.

"I've always thought all those damn wrinkles and spots are what tells your story. Dancers fear aging, yet they embrace it like it's their cross to bear. It's all they talk about. Look how fast it happens. The diet. The smoking. We all look like shit by thirty—it doesn't matter— now I'm the one who's ageless."

"You're beautiful up there."

"You think so? Christ, even these tits aren't mine. Everything was smashed, inside and out. I hate to say it, but the 'after' shot ended up being better than the 'before'—I never had this figure with my old body, I was more of a square frame. Another price to pay is I can't eat certain things, chocolate for example, because of my intestines. I'm not supposed to drink, or eat fatty foods. The good side is I never get very hungry. And I call the shots—no overbearing directors or choreographers." She laughed lightly. "You understand. But it's a trap."

"It is easy."

"Too easy. Do you have a friend?"

I had the impulse to whine about the bastard Daniel, but that was making me sick. I thought about Kent. He had become my guardian, if I didn't check in. "Not really. Well. No. You?"

"Not with this schedule. Well maybe a few, you know, spread out rather than one. One who took off to the coast. Anyway, forget that."

"Took off? Yeah that's my story, too."

"You're pretty. It won't take long. Now, tonight I want to see you work with what you've got. You've got lots, but you can't take forever to figure it out. The world won't wait." She smiled. Touched my chin. "Come down to my dressing room tonight."

"You know I'm not *that* way."

"Well if you were we'd be back at my room at the motel, right now—anyway nothing has really worked too well since the accident."

I thought about my mother and how she had probably spoken similar words to someone at some point in her life. Then Brittany nudged me the way a sister would. "Cheer up, I get my kicks." She draped her arm over my shoulder and gave me a squeeze.

LATER, AFTER WE HAD driven Marcel's new choreography into the ground and into our skulls, I knocked on Brittany's door frame.

"I ate some shhhocolate." She slurred her words.

"Okay. Don't eat any more chocolate."

"I can't eat shhhocolate."

"I remember, you told me."

"I want you to put this on." But she just stared at me, as if trying to assess something, my height, my personality, who the hell I was.

She wasn't in her heels. Just barefoot on the concrete. She wavered, and everything from her breasts to her behind seemed to be sagging. Not what I saw onstage. She padded away from me, to that bar draped in costumes, hanging from the ceiling. She pulled something down, and tore the dry-cleaning plastic away. A short jacket and pants glowed like the inside of an oyster shell, trimmed in a gold-and-silver sequined swirl. Gold fringe dangled from the sleeves of the jacket and swished down the outer edge of the pant legs. It looked like some spaced-out cowboy costume shimmering with an otherworldly incandescence.

"Now, this is not just any costume."

I thought she was going to tell me it had magical powers but that I would turn into a pumpkin after midnight, which didn't leave us much time. She had a warning nevertheless.

"You have got to be careful." She slowly regained some clarity. "If you get any hair or skin caught in the zippers it will hurt like hell."

Then she ran the glimmering oyster sleeves over my hands and they expanded and stretched up my arms. She continued and pulled the jacket over my back. "Spandex," she said, "the stripper's friend." She zipped the front to just below my chest.

"Whose is it?"

"The Italian Stallion."

"A boyfriend?"

"You ever hear of him? Actually he was Romanian—Ionelo—stupid name for a stripper. And yeah, he was one of the ones who said he loved me, but in the end got pissed off with my plumbing. He took off. I think he's out in LA. Who wouldn't be? The Northeast is such a slog. Damn cold, too." We were silent. Our only warmth came from that smoky den upstairs where we wandered around half-naked.

Brittany fidgeted with the zips at the wrists and the tangled fringe. "I keep thinking I'll see him in a Chippendale calendar. Maybe he's doing porn. I don't know. I don't really give a shit. As long as he's alive."

I wanted to say something about Daniel, like *I know what you mean*, or *I hear you*, or even go on and on about my stupid broken heart, but why bother. Brittany was tough. I could be tough, too.

"Take off your pants." She turned and pulled the slick pants off the hanger.

I waited in my scalloped sequined G-string. Both of us barefoot.

"Your scallop shells are a nice touch, but they could be trouble." She crouched at my ankles, futzing with the zippered seams before I put on the pants. She really was plain, not the Brittany Barrymore I had seen upstairs. The lights and costumes hid the roots and the flaws, her splayed toes, bony spine and washed-out skin. Funny how alluring it all is and, when you think of it, you have to find more than perfect breasts and soft skin to love about a person. Her posture, her charisma and her spirit made it all come together in some kind of magical way. But that fantasy had vanished and Brittany was at my feet pumped full of coke and cocoa.

"You know, they say when you die your life flashes before your eyes. But I don't remember that. I remember thinking, what a stupid way to die and then I thought about all the things I wanted to do. All the roles I hadn't performed, how I wanted to be an actress when my dance career was up, all the possibilities waiting for me when I finally stopped dancing. I believed in my future as a non-dancer, which was weird. Most dancers live in denial, as if they'll never be non-dancers, and then when they stop dancing it's all such a big goddamn surprise, and they act like they are magically deserving of a new and promising future. Deer in the headlights, and those headlights are attached to the front of a fucking eighteen-wheeler towing a great big question mark." Without losing a beat she went on. "And please don't tell me this is your future."

I didn't have anything to say. I wanted to see myself in the costume for the future that existed for the next few hours. "Tell me this is a sideline to something greater." But this had taken over everything and Madame's group, my big dream, seemed so inconsequential.

She fidgeted with a stubborn clip on the pant leg. "I also remembered all the emotions in those seconds, every single one I ever had in my life, and every moment that they were created. I felt it all right here." She tapped her sternum. "That's all that there was for me." She looked up at me. "It didn't seem like there was a present at all or if there was, that it just wasn't as important as the past. I still don't know if that's good or bad."

Still I couldn't speak.

"This is the tricky part." She was clear when she had to be. I placed my feet into the pant legs and she started helping while I shifted. From there she began to slowly zip, one finger between my skin and the zipper. "So the hair on your leg won't catch. God he was hairy—Ionelo—IO for short. Yeah he owes me all right. Talk about being used. Good thing I had this dry cleaned. Talk about hair in the zippers." I tried to follow with the zip on the other leg but it was impossible without flexing my legs. She took over and the pant leg clung, like a second skin, and moulded tightly onto my cock ringed, scalloped-shelled crotch as she pulled the zip. "Whoah, that should make some guy happy," she said and then she flicked my basket with her knuckle.

I stepped into my shoes and she tied them for me. She took a cowboy hat out of a cardboard box, pulled away the plastic and handed it to me. "The hat will fit. It never fit him, his head was too small. No brains for one thing. Go on. Look in the mirror."

And it all came together when I put on the hat.

"Hey, I think we've gotten rid of his sour aftertaste for good."

My blond lock fell over one eye and I pressed my chin down. Nose. Lips. Eyes. This could be my night.

And the next moment she was blathering, "Ooooh, I had some shhhhocolate."

"Go sit down."

She disappeared into herself. Collapsed back on her ass on the floor. "G'wan upstairs."

With every step on those back stairways this second skin expanded and contracted. So much better than that crummy ballet company tickle trunk, staying awake as Geppetto in a gunny sack or inside a fucking mouldy foam tree. I climbed slowly, relishing the fabric on my bare ass, the squeeze and release—my balls, too—all so invigorating. The scallops on the G-string pinched, and my crotch responded with the rubbing between thigh and fabric, thigh and fabric. I became so aware of my body. My chest. My back. My thighs. I took up space now. I couldn't hide. I'd have to live up to this look. It wasn't jeans and a tank top. It was what it should have always been.

I punched in my three songs and stepped up to the stage. Steve waved from the booth and whooped. Then there were whoops from all over the club. The girls stopped in mid-serve, mid-grind. Everyone was watching.

"Gloria" plunged into the room and it was loud. Steve cranked the sound. You couldn't ignore me. There was nothing I could not do.

It was my song, and it made sense to me as I grabbed my hat and shot it to the back of the room—take that, Laura Branigan, I do think I'm pretty fucking important after all. My arms flew, one after the other; my hips followed; then my spine, my neck, my head—all flew with the fringe and then I spun as every bit of spandex kept me in a tight orbit on the stage. I blazed—in flames—and the crowd was high, too. I caught their eyes for split seconds, and exhaled their stale sick smoke that plugged my throat, blinded me, smothered me and drugged me. I owned them. They were in me. The girls didn't move.

Brittany surfaced in her kimono, became part of the smoky audience. I was on fire and they were there with me. I was a combination of years of technique and that moment of inspiration. They all knew then. I was a real dancer. For all the regimented crap, I was finally letting the dancer out.

For "Africa," I unzipped and ground. I peeled the jacket down my arms, over my back, and back and forth over my ass. I flung it behind me. Women stood and reached up to caress my chest, lightly touch it. Then it was time for my pants. I could undo the zippers on the seams and the pants would stay clipped at the top and Velcroed at the bottom. At the edge of the stage, I coaxed women to stand, then pull down my zippers; I pointed to them, and then to the zipper. They didn't catch on at first so I just kept doing it à la Brittany. Point to them, then to the zipper, them and the zipper, them and the zipper. They'd play coy: *What should I do?* Maybe they were shy. It was an act. It was all an act; their act, too. I held the clip at the top—they undid the zippers, both sides at two different times. Two different women.

Then I spun into the middle of the stage, unclipped the pants at the top, held them tight, pulled and, *poof*, they were gone (a disappearing act that even Patrice couldn't rival), and I was in my G-string. I decided to leave "Je T'aime… Moi Non Plus," for now and use a song I had heard frequently in the café under my place, French singer Diane Tell singing "On a Beau." There was something about her vulnerable voice and I could almost understand the lyrics. It was then that I felt as if the audience embraced me. I wasn't grinding to top-forty. I was actually moving to something they knew and cared about. I kneeled at the edge of the stage, leaned way back with nothing between my ass and the cold floor but peach fuzz and scalloped sequins. I rolled over and ground the stage while sweat ran into my eyes, and my body felt slick with it. I rolled again, with fingers down my torso and through the hair. They thought it was ecstasy and bliss. Bliss for all, we were all enjoying me—lips, chest, nipples, stomach, ass, on and off while the hips pumped.

And off came the G-string, both sides unclipped, like the pants. It all flopped out, the whole package, dangled two feet from some couple's faces. I was down again and then I rolled up and over to a different table. Faces looked up to me. Take that, I thought. Only the terrified stared past. I was still swollen, but it was my ass the women wanted to see. Run their hands on and over and down to my knees and up to my crotch.

And it was my cock for the straight men, too, comparing like we do. But we all enjoyed me. This was what Brittany had meant.

Then the lights were out.

Cheers drowned the house music. People looked around with *What happened?* on their faces.

My head roared and my body was numb. The adrenalin left me weak. It was the night I became, to myself, *Le Grand Blond*, the night I let loose and put the icing on the big blond cake. I was high and my mind raced. Sure I'd had the rush as part of the Company, the overwhelming applause that turns swans into swine in seconds, making egos swell almost as fast as my cock in Steve's mouth. And yet, all it took was a masochistic ballet master, or mistress-on-the-rag to bring you back down to earth, tell you that you were shit. Ego. Go to the newsstand and you'll see what it does to those with perfumes named after them, or their own lines of designer jeans. They may be on their way out but they've tasted it, soiled their soul. Can't ever turn back, will do whatever it takes to stay there, even if it means dropping dead. It's one of the most powerful forces in the world and leaves nothing in its path. It's so good to ride it while you can. All of the love you never gave yourself is finally screaming to get in.

BUT THAT WAS THEN, in Quebec. In this stairwell, if I survive, I will only ever indulge in small doses. I am to ego what Brittany is to chocolate.

THE GIRLS STOPPED ME, touched my shoulder and babbled about my act. Laughed, too. They used words like *franchement beau* and *tellement sexy*. *Trés* this and *trés* that, and I knew what they meant. I guess my French was getting better. One of them said it and the others repeated it: *Le Grand Blond*. Not "Flash" or "Rod," or "Streak." That night, j'étais *Le Grand Blond*. Je suis devenu *Le Grand Blond*.

Downstairs, Brittany was trying to stay upright in her chair. There were tears in her eyes. Her head shook when she spoke. "Never let them say you can't. Don't let them take it away from you. You can't keep it to yourself anymore." I knew what she meant but I feared it was a one-shot deal. How could I ever bring it all together like that again?

I got dressed and went back upstairs. Steve rushed out of his booth, took his gum out of his mouth and gave me a big wet congratulatory kiss. Guy gripped my ass and I'm still not sure if he was pissed or pleased. Marcel said I shone. For a few minutes everyone loved me. Had I been that bland before? Later Brittany was up on the stage. Perfect. It seemed the only thing that fed her were the lights and the attention of the crowd.

THAT NIGHT I DREAMT about the little boy with soapstone cheeks running through the backyard as a bloodstained cowboy. The best-dressed only child on the street. Falling through the hedge. No one but me cared if it was real rawhide. No one had time for my chrome-plated pistols. As a sharpshooter, I lied my way into friendships. Showed up unannounced, saying we had promised to play Cowboys and Indians. No kid liked dentists, or this dentist kid. Real chaps and fringe couldn't compete with imagination.

One Easter, I wore that cowboy outfit into the ravine near our house. The puddles were still deep from spring runoff. Some boys stood in a group, some I thought were friends. The pug-faced leader said I'd stolen Benjamin Weinstein's girlfriend. But Benjamin Weinstein never had a girlfriend. I did. Rebecca Lefebvre—blonde hair, Chiclet teeth. We spent Saturday afternoon matinees holding hands. They said I'd stolen her from Benjamin. When I figured out that the ravine wasn't a safe place to be and tried to run, it was obvious that running in cowboy gear wasn't easy. A horse would have come in handy.

The thuggish guy from the nearby Catholic school pushed me face down into my two-gallon hat. He leapt on my back and punched until I was numb. The others pulled off my chaps, my vest, my pants, my underwear and threw everything in a tree. The oaf on my back grabbed my head; when one of his fingers popped into my mouth, I chomped down with every last bit of cowboy energy, right though to the fucking bone. He was off me in a flash, his band of no-goods trailing after him like little lemmings. I climbed the tree ripping my cold skin, tugging at the authentic leather piece by piece. Dressed. Told no one. That outfit was worth everything to me.

SHE MUST HAVE LEFT the next day, Sunday. On Monday Steve said he had something for me. Brittany had left the costume behind.

Seven

THE THREE HEADS OF deltoid shape a dancer's shoulder into one thick orb of strength. No matter the power of the arms, the shoulders have to bear the burden and support the arms. You see the shape there, distracting if overdeveloped and hindering the line if overlooked. It is fragile and essential for the *danseur* to make the ballerina appear to float through a supported *grand jété*, suspended about his head in a *pressage* or lifted throughout a *pas de chat* or any of a million moments the hands touch the body. A shoulder is there to fall upon, swing from, roll on or cry upon.

FIRST IT WAS LOVE I sought, then I settled for admiration, then some attention and as a result, soon I wanted anyone. Some are fulfilled on the stage, even in the wings, but I carried my needs, kicking and screaming, out the stage door. I was dying for something. You've seen my type in the cafés, eyes searching, saying, *Notice me for Christ's sake.* Unfortunately, this kind of behaviour snagged me an English-French transplant student from Winnipeg living in the Old Town, who saw me strip and then days later followed me home from the bus stop. He was angry and into my pants because no one wanted him—he shoved his pelvis at me, ground me, kneaded my ass with a bruising enthusiasm. I shut my eyes against his conquest. Maybe he thought I was falling in love, but I was falling asleep in the lukewarmness of the moment. I'm sure I hoped Daniel could have loved me with as much zeal. I don't remember. I do remember this one had the face of a hungry monk, thinning hair and a bony body lean where there was flesh. Just get it over with for God's sake and let me sleep. But sex was air to him. And I was in his lungs, as a real live dancer who stripped. The idea fed his arrogance, and I had little to do with that high. How did he make those aerobics happen—get our hips to the ceiling, our nuts banging their numb way into each other? How did he do it—it couldn't have been that much fun—but oh no, he was frothing at my buffet, high on sex and ended up unloading himself onto the nape of my neck and across my shoulders. And why, after a too-long smoky Saturday night, was he once again breaking down my door and my back on Sunday morning with a well-meaning café au lait and *pain au chocolat* fresh from downstairs when all I wanted was to sleep right through to eternity? "I am Jonathan," he said.

I was beside myself with fatigue. I broke down and bragged a little. Told him I had been with the Company.

"Really?" he said. "But I'm from Winnipeg. When did you leave?"

"Less than a year ago."

"I remember you! I saw you in lots of things. I thought you were familiar. *Études*, my God your ass in those white tights—what the hell are you stripping for?"

"Well I'm just doing some research for a new ballet. I've decided to go it alone."

He didn't believe that for a moment.

And after two more hours of pelvis slapping, I sent him on his way. I hoped he registered my indifference and irritation and would get the message. I collapsed, but the café au lait turned it into a troubled sleep. I wanted rest, and love that didn't come with sex attached like an oversized game-show price tag. Look what you win! Sex! With a stripper!

In the early afternoon I crept, unnoticed I hoped, to my watering hole Belle Époque, where I drank alone and stared at the wall. It was a luxury to afford beer and have a moment to feel sorry for myself and feel as important as "Gloria," my song. Poor me. But I couldn't bear anyone pulling at my leg or grinding his bony pelvis into me for a desperate one-off, locked in his own bubble of ecstasy. When I got home, I phoned Kent to share a delivered pizza.

Before pizza we hugged and he pressed hard against my crotch with his own. Even though it excited me—just being next to him and his hands, and all that his hands could do—I needed to be held. "They're dying in New York," he said.

"Who?"

"Gay men are dying."

"Why?"

"No idea. You're not planning a trip to New York?"

"Not anymore. Can we relax for a minute? Maybe change the subject?"

"Are you okay?"

"I just need to connect, right now, with more than my cock."

"I've created a monster?"

"The cock ring works fine if that's what you want to know."

"What about the big, friendly stripper, the one whose boyfriend keeps blowing you? He sounds nice. Why don't you connect with him?" All of this said with heavily weighted stresses of sarcasm, driven into the conversation like the jabs of a conductor's baton during the key change denoting betrayal in *Swan Lake*.

"You're jealous."

"Don't flatter yourself." And with his tone of voice I knew someone was hurt. "I'm just curious about your principles. But in the meantime, if you don't meet anyone, you can stay at my place whenever you want, you know, for whatever, to be close, cuddle, get your rocks off. It won't destroy your principles." Kent held the pizza in trembling fingers, and I wanted to hug him. I don't know why. I wasn't sure if he was nervous or upset, if he'd had too much coffee, or if he found the pizza too hot. "So much for holding out for true love."

"Is it worth it?"

"I'm starting to think most people try *not* to be in love. It's terrifying. It requires energy. They get hitched and they get mean."

"You sound pretty jaded for someone with so little experience."

"Do you think that once you create love you can never destroy it? It won't go away? That's what I believe. Call me naive."

I told Kent about the Winnipeg guy who wouldn't quit bugging me, but he'd already had him, it turned out. I suppose he was working his way up the street. I was learning not to show my surprise. "I didn't really like him."

"You'll have to learn to say no. You can't mercy fuck everyone."

"Are you implying something here?"

"I don't need your mercy."

"You won't get any." I hated myself. The more I wanted to hold him, the harder I seemed to get.

"I was there, you know—had my pick of the National Ballet, was Zaitsev's bumboy for months until he found out that other celebs were dipping into his candy bowl." Kent licked his fingers. Looked up at me. Wanted to see how I'd take the news. "I was like you, couldn't say yes, couldn't say no."

"Zaitsev? He's a legend—my hero for a while. God, I am a dope."

"You're young."

"You've come down in the world and I've never even gotten up."

"Maybe I'm the sorry one, not believing there are genuinely good people in the world, like you."

"Good isn't a word that I would use right now. It's all *formidable, trés* sexy, *beau*…"

"Let's go find true love."

"I'll be your escort, but I'm through with the love crap, for to-day anyway." Kent licked his fingers, and then I licked them, too. He leaned across and we kissed and then laughed. We decided to go to Le Cirque. Kent had wanted me to go. Get picked up. Sleaze around. He said it would be good for me to have some dirty, rough sex and up my total. We walked through the stone archway out of the Old Town and along the battlements to a door. Our breath hung in clouds; more snow was definitely on the way. I could smell it.

We had gotten there way too early—the dance floor was empty—so I ordered a beer and Kent bought a chaser of some syrupy liqueur with gold flecks in it. Patrice was doing the weekly magic act he per-formed every Sunday night at Le Cirque while lone men stood in the shadows. They could have been the straight ones, the daddies, as Kent called them. No one clapped for Patrice except me. He shrugged, said something to us as if no one else could hear. I didn't understand him. I figure he was pissed off to see I had come with a friend.

My eye was drawn to a well-built guy, something I've never gone after because I figured I didn't stand a chance. This one was in jeans with a faded crotch, a shirt and pullover probably knitted by his wife. I imagined him in a penthouse overlooking the St. Lawrence—a big bed for me. He definitely spent time at a gym. He was aloof. So what? It was probably his first time there. That, we had in common. "I think I've found true love."

"Go for it." Kent delivered another shooter and then went into the shadows.

I made eye contact. I figured everyone was watching to see how this would play out. I felt bad for the ones who weren't as lucky. I got my coat from the coat check, enough done, enough said, I didn't have to wait all night. It was obvious he was interested. He would follow. I walked by and he leaned into the wall. I went down the stairs and opened the door onto the square. It had started to snow. Other than that, it was empty and quiet. I listened for him to follow. I waited, but no one came out the door.

I couldn't go back. Everyone in that meagre crowd would know. After a few more minutes the wind had changed and the snow started blowing in from the river. I wondered why, with all this beauty—the wind, the crisp air, the snow blowing past the streetlamps—I was trying to drag a stranger home from a smoky club. Was it the idea of another lonely night with nothing to look forward to but a bad ballet class in the morning?

But a touch on my shoulder stopped that chatter: a light tap, and a startled, hopeful, ready-for-it look. He had to be a local. He was small, with a face like pudding. You know: pale skin, dark eyes. A soft nose and an upper lip twisted slightly in the middle. "I'm Philippe," he said.

He wasn't what I had been looking for. I remember purposely ignoring him in the bar. Making sure not to catch his eye. He'd seen whom I was in pursuit of, but wasn't going to give up. I wondered how people in that position had the perseverance. I failed to realize that I was no different.

There is a kind of thrill of going to a place like Le Cirque and not knowing what grab bag you will come out with, if any, and I suppose it is that thrill of the unknown that drove Kent, and that finally pushed me to invite this guy back to my place. In my kitchen we unscrewed a gallon bottle of wine and talked in French, English and Franglais, mostly short sentences about the weather. We both loved snowfalls, before Christmas especially—not in April specifically, or any later than April—bad or good wine, candles, softness, holding, hungry sex throughout the night and sleep. Thank God Philippe loved to sleep. He got on his knees, hands on my thighs, not to do anything other than to woo. He was gentle and a better bet than what I'd hoped for.

Most of the time I stayed over at his place. He said he just wanted to love me, but I couldn't love him back. He spoiled me, and I pitied him. He wanted what we all want and what I wanted so badly. I gave over to being an object of his affection, and the one to later break his heart. I often thought of Kent. Who was he with? Was he thinking about me? Missing him started to feel like homesickness.

I USED TO WONDER why adults said Christmas was a hard season. How could presents be unpleasant, or the ballet, and the pantomime, and a million other distractions until Santa arrived? But soon Christmas stirred up a sore stomach because of its quiet brevity. Christmas would have been better in my absence, for two people with nothing much to say. My parents performed their own pantomime at every Christmas party and I had a supporting role that involved a lot of smiling. During university years, excuses were easy to come by, and welcomed with well-rehearsed concern. And then, with the Company, well, it was our busy season.

AS CHRISTMAS APPROACHED, THE crowds grew until every night was like a busy Saturday. I thrived at the club, and wilted at the ballet studio. One day my moonlighting was no longer a secret.

"It's good you have these other talents…" said Madame Talegdi. I felt a rush of embarrassment. Of course she knew. And she was right; anything to pay the rent, after lifting Bertrand (who was starting to thicken around the middle by the way) as Pinocchio for free, for her psychotic ego. As long as the pre-showtime booze and painkillers kicked in by 9 P.M., I'd be fine. I found comfort in knowing that my tight muscles looked great, naked, on a box, in perpetual twilight, even if they were worth shit to me as a dancer. Of course I was of no use in that studio. My toe was blue from *The Nutcracker* choreography she was setting on us. "…because," she continued her subtle assault in the flat matter-of-fact way she used when delivering an insult, "you will never be a really great dancer," while we all sat in our warm-ups eating our lunch in the kitchen off the studio. Bertrand picked up on her digs and asked me how my job was going with a nudge and a wink, but with Madame's nasty comment, I helped fill in the blanks.

"The job is a bitch," I said. "Une beetch. Chienne. Travailler comme un stripper c'est difficile, toujour les femmes essayent de me touché." I didn't know how bad my French was, but I tried to hit all the key words. "Les femmes aiment les gars comme moi. You must come and watch some night. Le spectacle est fun avec les filles et gars seminudes, tits and ass, poitrines est derrières." Madame turned about fifteen shades of blueberry while Bertrand bent over and pretended to adjust his ballet shoes. He trembled with laughter. Louise clenched her jaw; the corners of her mouth turned up.

Chantal and Maryse stopped eating their celery and carrots and looked into their Tupperware. I had nothing to lose. I could smack my head on Madame's wall for the rest of my life, but I had learned from Kharkov when to play and when to give in. It was time to use the secret weapon. The truth. "Of course I will never really become une étoile comme Jean-Marc, even though, like Jean-Marc I have les relations avec la directeur de Chez Moritz, et what do you know, Jean-Marc fait la meme chose avec vous, Madame. Jean-Marc est comme une amant pour vous. Je ne peux pas gagner ici. No one can, personne non plus, pas comme Jean-Marc. But no one loves me like you love Jean-Marc, Madame. Tu dois aimer la sex avec lui. I would. He's very sexy. Trés sexy, Jean-Marc. Yes Madame Jean-Marc this and Jean-Marc that. Jean-Marc is the end of the fucking world. Three cheers for Jean-Marc, the second fucking coming. Fucking merci Jean-Marc!" And Jean-Marc looked like a stunned horse, as usual. I went on: "He'd make a great stripper, with that bulge."

But Madame cut me off. "Shut up you, shut up now and leave here or I will call the police. How dare you insult my girls, my dancers or Jean-Marc." Madame came after me swatting me on the head, and then drove me hard in the gut. She had it in her to do much worse. I couldn't breathe, but I grabbed my things. The truth was out. The girls ran across the hall to the washroom and I heard Madame's shouts echo down the hall. I changed in the stairwell and left.

Once upon a time I had wanted to like Madame. If she had been more generous she could have made us all great dancers. But the ego can do horrible things to remain intact. Bertrand and Louise had also grown tired of her after their summer and being exposed to something greater in Montreal. They had outgrown her. Staying there would never have worked for them. Madame could only take them so far. I hoped for them that real exposure would take them to the next level.

MEANWHILE THE CHEZ MORITZ had another guest—not a circuit girl nor a drag queen—this one only to watch the show. I grew up with Marilyn Monroe in my soul even if she was wary of my type. Her beauty cast a spell over so many and her pain made us forgive. How many fruitcakes have told me that Marilyn Monroe was their real mother? Somehow it never adds up with the lie they tell me about their age. I swear to you that that Christmas, Marilyn Monroe dropped by the Chez Moritz. I saw her from the stage. There was a fuss at the front door. I thought maybe Vasili was giving someone the heave-ho. But a bubble of blonde was the focal point, being swarmed. Soon men in dark coats and sunglasses were shifting chairs at the back and Vasili was helping seat them. I wanted to believe what I was seeing. Steve was at her table, waved me down after my set ended. "You must meet my friend, Marilyn Monroe."

"I thought she was dead."

"It was all a lie to get her out of the public eye. Don't speak to her. She can't speak English."

"She hasn't aged much."

"Men buy her things: minks, jewels, cheekbones, the perfect nose. She'd like you to dance for us."

Other than batting her eyes to get me going, she didn't pay me any attention. She and her gang made sure they were being noticed. I just danced in the shadows with not much commitment. I was not the centre of attention by any means. When Louis joined the group, the men moved into a tight circle around him. Louis smiled too much. I'd never seen him smile like that. He dabbed his brow. He seemed nervous, and it wasn't to do with the size of my cock. Steve watched me with his back to them like a cat waiting to pounce on a moving target. Since no one was watching him watching me, he decided to add a little spice to his evening and stir up some trouble. He was smoking, chewing his gum, one eye on his booth, checking the room to make sure no one was going to run out of music and, during all of this, sitting close to my crotch and staring longingly at my dick.

I started to get hard. I had to stay in a squat, which pleased Steve even more with this private show happening between my thighs. I was Pavlov's dog, having been trained in the basement washroom. Marilyn was too busy sipping from a straw to notice. And her entourage popped their heads out of the clutch momentarily to catch an eyeful of tit. So this little porn-fest went on while I was trapped with a hard-on. Steve made this look like a conversation; between big chews of gum he talked about Marilyn, saying she ducked out of the stripper circuit early, before she got to be known as one.

I wanted to interrupt, find out what was going on with Louis and the men—it looked like he was about to be lynched—but he went on, "Now she really thinks she is Marilyn." He rested his hands on my knees all the while taking in the view, which seemed simple enough, but it was torture. "And she wants everyone else to think so, too, and treat her like Marilyn." He said she wouldn't last, just like the real Marilyn—she'd never be satisfied—showing up at clubs around Quebec for some attention and the odd newspaper photo op. Her Montreal mob husband had created a monster. It's funny that fine line between having a talent and having huge amounts of attention for nothing in particular. You have to work hard at both. At the end of the song, I left the table with my jeans tight over my crotch.

Later, when Steve had told all the girls in the change room about my woody, it got not much more than a chuckle. Steve's Guy didn't laugh. But all I could think of was Louis's smiling sweating face and wrinkled brow.

MADAME TALEGDI BROUGHT ME in for performances of her *Nutcracker*, since we were locked into a performance schedule. This meant playing the Mouse King and more small roles—from Dros-selmeyer to the Christmas Tree—than anyone double-cast in the Company could imagine in their worst dancer nightmares. After tripping over all of the junior school dancers in their homemade cos-tumes onstage and having Madame barking and stamping at all of us, even the youngest, I was ready to toss in my dance belt for good.

At night it was the Chez Moritz disco version of *The Nutcracker*. Marcel had better costumes; tits and bums unbound and glazed in coloured glitter like overgrown sugarplums. My sheer white leotards hid nothing. The roles were better too: I got to be the Nutcracker and the Prince. Marcel let me make up most of my own choreography so I twirled and fouettéed my way into the Christmas spirits of the audience—who, probably along with their kids, saw me by day in Madame's sloppy recital.

We were all relieved that the final performance was done. "No New Year's this year," Marcel shouted over the chatter. I looked up, not sure what he meant by it. "Louis wants just the girls for New Year's." There could have been some good money for New Year's for all of us. "I'll see you on the second. We have a new show to get go-ing."

Out west, *Nutcrackers* were followed by the obligatory family vis-it. But with a little cash and pre-Christmas tip money, I got it together to make my own plans to help me get through the time following Christmas by booking a last-minute flight to the tropics. Five nights, Quebecair, nothing included, paid for with a fist full of tips. I needed something to look forward to. I'd leave on Boxing Day. Keep it a se-cret from my parents—and from angel-face Philippe.

BEFORE HE HEADED UP to Rouyn-Noranda for *Noël* with his huge family, I told Philippe I didn't want to continue. "It's me, I'm just not ready for a commitment."

"We can still be friends."

"I just don't think I have time." It occurred to me that any time spent with someone I didn't care about created a horrible feeling of claustrophobia, as if my life really was being wasted. He gave me a little music box he'd bought at an antique store, insisted I have it, and a small box of cookies. I was such a shit. I said goodbye at my front door as he got a cab to the bus depot to be with his family in time for mass. Christmas Eve wasn't a time of year or of my life that I wanted to lie; I couldn't pretend any longer. I had bought a monstrous tourtière, but a silent meal between the two of us would have been farcical compared to what he would have with his family. I sat in the silence, eating the cookies, watching flakes of snow glisten in the chill outside my window as the tiny music box played "Waltz of the Snowflakes" from *The Nutcracker*. I suppose I should have at least appreciated someone who liked me so much.

At noon on Christmas Day my parents called, and while we talked I stared at the tourtière wondering how to dress it up. Vegetables? Cranberry? What did these people do? My mother was choked up as always, whether I was there or here. "Will we be seeing you over the holidays?"

"I don't think I can get away."

"Your father said you might surprise us."

"I wish I could." I knew he only said this to keep her from going on about me not coming home. My presence was the last thing they needed for a merry Christmas. I could hear my father talking in the background. "He says to say merry... oh for heaven's sake, this is ridiculous, just wait."

There was the obvious shifting and shunting of phone from hand to hand and then my father's voice in deep, stark contrast to my mother's. "Hi son, do you have someone there to spend Christmas with?"

This shocked me, but what the hell. "Yes, I have a neighbour coming over for dinner. We're having tourtière, since I'm living in Quebec now." But I'd lost Dad at the word neighbour, it was too much of a reminder of who I was: a person, not a projection. I picked up the slack. "You two have a merry Christmas and I'll see you in the New Year. I promise."

But it was my mother's voice that replied. "You have a merry Christmas too, and we'll talk soon"—something we often said when we knew it would be some time before another call.

After the call I went back to bed. The quiet sounds made it feel more like home than ever. I managed to wake in time to get the tour-

tière in the oven, potatoes boiling and squash boiling, too—a ballerina's nightmare meal—before Kent showed up, and when he did,
he looked oh so good. I'd never seen in him anything other than a
T-shirt, a parka or his birthday suit. He wore a red shimmering dress
shirt and a green bowtie he'd made from ribbon. When I saw him
standing there at the door with his bottle of bubbly, I could have eaten
him. "Real French champagne," he said. "Méthode champenoise." He
raised his eyebrows. "Can I come in?"

"Life should always be so fine," I said, following him to the
kitchen. He seemed so self-assured from the back, kind of strutting.
I loved that about him. Everything, the nastiness of the Company,
the distracted pressure of the club, the guilt over having more or less
dumped someone on Christmas Eve, vanished.

"It is fine, this very moment. I have something for you." He turned,
held up a small, wrapped package. "Open it."

"Oh, why did you do that? I completely... I was so concerned
with my own..."

"Just open it."

It was funny to think that not only had he gotten me something,
but that he had taken the time to wrap it.

"A book of..."

"Dancers should read. You should read. This."

"It looks French."

"Every word of it. It is French. It's the poems of Émile Nelligan.
You're living in his province so you should read something by him.
I'm sure you know enough words—*amour, mort*—to get the gist."

"I'll read it, you'll see. I *can* read. Thank you. *Merci, mon ami.*"

"De rien."

"You look like the biggest Christmas cracker I've ever seen."

"Pull me. There's a big surprise waiting for you."

"You may have been celebrating all day, but I've been in a coma."

Kent relaxed, let out his inner flamboyance, which made him
that much more endearing. He hummed a few carols with a resonant
basso profundo, and then sang a very fruity version of "I'll Be Homo
for Christmas." I was so used to him being the tough guy with his
short, quick movements and a voice that held no hint of affectation.

Often, recently, we'd had so little time together. It would be a blessing to sit down for more than one course. He wandered the place and hummed while I fussed at the stove and turned the table into a tableau dripping with Christmas sentiment, from candles to crackers to fake holly. It occurred to me then, with him keeping himself busy, that I had more than the usual good feelings for him. I was full of good feelings. But I think, for me at least, those kinds of feelings were the elephant in the room.

We sat at the table, tucked our napkins, pulled crackers and uncorked the champagne. I unloaded huge servings of tourtière, he served up my effort at vegetables. I lit candles and we both looked out at snow falling on the empty street, and listened to the silence. Golden light glowed behind drawn curtains up and down the sidewalk. At last a holiness had descended, and I still had time to make the peace of the Christmas my own. I watched him closely and differently than I had before, as he talked about Christmases with friends in Toronto and his reluctance to participate in family Christmases in Windsor since leaving home. His family turned their backs on him. They thought they were sleuths discovering he had no girlfriend. He said his leanings were more obvious with his too-fabulous blond hair, when he had hair, and very expensive taste when he was with someone who could support it. You could shut gay behaviour in a closet or excuse it away as "ladies man," "bachelor" or "loner," or just turn your back on all of it. Kent's family hadn't talked to him in years.

"It will be nice for you to catch up with friends in Montreal."

I knew he wanted more of what he was looking for—Quebec City was too small and too much work for him. "Don't let me know if you run into you-know-who."

"See? You've already forgotten his name. You might not even remember mine by the time you get back from down south." I untied his bowtie, and he tossed his shirt by my mattress, pretending for once that he was the stripper. He did a very endearing routine with a lit cigarette, mimicking yours truly, and then we got under the sheets, me in his tight grip. We watched the candles flicker and die on the table while the snow fell outside and then we fell asleep, naked, together.

AS I SLEPT I saw the snow bringing neighbours like us together. Then I dreamt of the land down south where the heat opens every pore, and feeds this man's testosterone like a leaky faucet. A pleasurable torture if you know how to control it. I saw the pale adolescent I was, my first and only Christmas in the tropical sun. We were two travel days away from Edmonton, Alberta, but all the same old faces had come along.

Sometimes a breeze pushed away the heat. But I learned the effects of sun on a man's back all day, the steam from the shower and my own light touch. There was a man on the beach who reminded me of Mister Clean—bald-headed and bulges of muscle as he flexed his crossed arms. Something stirred in me. The Edmontonians chuckled to each other at the small black Speedo that covered Mister Clean's family jewels and perfect ass. I watched them try not to look. I hoped the same firmness would find me someday. Could I ever hope to look like that? What would muscles look like on me? Would muscles grow? He was perfect. Why did the pear-shaped, soft-assed, sunburnt dentists laugh at this living statue? In an answer to a prayer, two more lean bodies, brothers or best friends, came down the beach in briefs. I made sure to spread out my beach towel in their path, but they didn't notice a horny prepubescent as they spoke a foreign language and stared into each other's eyes.

In contrast to this I noticed imperfections, peeling burns, wrinkled thighs, varicose veins, horny discoloured toenails at the end of crooked toes from a lifetime of badly fitting shoes. I saw everything and my senses exploded like the flowers blooming off the walls, over doorways, everywhere there was moisture, sun, rain, hummingbirds darting, cats in heat by night and dogs humping any old time. Black men wandered from shore to high-tide mark looking for something, full lips smiling, or puckered or squeezed. I experimented with my own lips in the mirror: withheld, wondering, coy, pouting.

I watched the natives as they gathered in groups along the shore casting their nets, bathing their bony cows. Dicks flopped in frayed loose wet boxers. I was dizzy wondering what they did in the heat of the day. I spent hours in the steamy bathroom (while my parents glugged sea breezes, daiquiris, mai-tais and Cuba libres). I hoped that someday I would be as big and as free as these men.

Tidy white men appeared for happy hour. "The boys," whispered someone's wife—echoed, with raised eyebrows, by someone's husband as if these well-dressed men were freaks, doing something wrong because they weren't with women. "The boys" sipping their cocktails in their cruise-wear, espadrilles, flip-flops, tanned feet and pedicures. They laughed as I nursed a ginger beer, then a fruit punch, while other conversations flew past me. Someone said they were fruits. And why did they care? Were they as bad as commies? Why wouldn't the fruits look my way? Why was it only the husbands and wives and other tourists in prints and patterns who doted on me and then ignored me?

"I'm not with them," I wanted to scream to those beautiful men. Why wouldn't they rescue me? Someday I vowed they would, or I would return alone, and never have to go back to the snow. Someday with my strong feet locked to the floor, a chest for a shield, a pelvis like stone, legs of steel and my dick shoved in my swimsuit, cocked like a pistol with a hair trigger, lips turned up in a sneer, I would return and no one would ever again, ever ignore me.

NO MATTER HOW CHARMED your life, winter in the East means a fuck of a lot of trudging, weighed down by layers of soaking Gore-Tex, wool, fleece and feathers—or fighting your way through a blizzard, or to a bus, or to a plane that is still whining miles above you in absolute zero. But the tropics mean wandering half-naked along the warm shores of the Caribbean with nothing but a few ounces of drip-dry nylon to care about.

In the morning Kent had coffee ready and got me in a cab and off to the airport without a hitch. "I'll do the dishes."

"See you," I replied. "And save New Year's Eve for us." If there was a knife in my gut I couldn't have felt it more sharply; I didn't want to leave him behind. I smiled bravely, and somewhat falsely. He could see it in my eyes. I know.

In several hours, I found the richness, the thick air that floods into the plane as the doors open, the heat, the bright sun, the blue sky and white clouds close enough to touch, the intense colours and the sound of the sea. All that I was looking for. I was a free man, living in a little rented shack, one of a few that had seen far better days, by the sea. Ignore the cockroaches at night and the bedsprings and it was bliss. The beach as I remembered it hadn't changed much since I was a kid. I hadn't been alone like this in a long time—if ever—with only my thoughts for company. That first afternoon was spent thinking about Kent, and wishing that Christmas night could have lasted for another week.

The men still wandered the beach, thank God. The tourists ignored me; husbands looked at me with curiosity, perhaps longing. I hoped to spend uncharted hours trying, with the help of planter's punches, to gain back the sleep I had lost in the past months. At a nearby hotel, a fat Frankfurter bought me martinis. Said I was his friend. I was drunk enough to excuse the next part. I could never catch up to Kent's numbers in so brief a time, and the most I could do was fantasize about Mr. Clean from a decade ago—and those Latin lovers, or were they brothers? Where had they all gone? Where were the boys in their pastels?

I followed the chubby *Mein Herr* to an abandoned house blasted by the sea, which at night must have been home for the black magic of the beach. A stained mattress with a hole burned in it, hanging over the sill of a window, presided over bits of animal bone, iguana skin and feathers while stray dogs and feral cats cowered among the dried palm fronds and coconut shells. Everything was in a state of decay. We only made it to the middle of the dark driveway hidden by this tropical excrement, rotting fruit, more dried leaves and dog crap. We fell on this, and as I serviced him, his swollen face turned pink with pleasure. The next day he was by the bar with wife and kids in tow, and I knew the hangover he was concealing. He pretended he didn't recognize me. He looked far worse sober, like every other hot and bothered dad.

I was sitting on the steps of my shack when a bony West Indian man in a knitted cap came by, reached under my sarong, cupped my nether regions—or whatever Kent thought a decent white boy like me should call it—in his hand and we watched those regions swell.

He smiled a mouth of gaps and gold. He turned and wandered under the trees along the road, and I caught up at the same ruined house from the night before. Pebbles pierced my feet. From the road, the house was faded corals and blues and the tourists wandered up to take photos of its quaintness through the chicken wire. If you squinted it could be the backdrop of many a travel brochure. He banged the walls to scare out the stray rats, cats and vagrants. Inside was worse. Rags of pillows and leftover mouldy mattresses along with more animal crap were rammed into the corners.

I followed him room by room through this bad dream, through a door to what once must have been a bathroom but was now a piss-stinking, toilet-less closet with a rotting hole in the floor. I couldn't see his face anymore. He was a skeleton to the touch, the same as his narrow, bone-stiff stubborn, coat-hanger dick that jabbed my thigh. I opened the fold in my sarong. "Here, hold my cock," I said, but he shoved my head down to his smelling-like-shit spindle for me to gag on. Which I did. I had to. His knuckles burned my skull until he was satisfied. As I had been taught, I feared for my life.

I ran from the house retching, spitting, wiping. Anything to take this foul moment away, subtract it, make it not have happened. He shouted that I broke the law. "Faggot! Faggot!" he yelled after me.

The next night, out on the road, after having vowed a conditional, self-imposed celibacy until I went home—and truly engrossed in a very dark and velvety night sky—a carload of well-dressed white boys pulled up and asked me which way to town.

As *if* they didn't know.

I pointed. The car headed up to the main road. I watched the lights fade under that vast tropical starry night. Take me, I thought, returning to my sky. But no sooner than I sorted Orion's Belt from the Sword of Damocles, did they make a U-turn, come back full speed, pull up and stop. The well-fed one in the driver's seat stared at my crotch and asked me if I wanted to come along. Sure. These were the boys, the ones from years ago. They hadn't aged. They never would.

"I'm Dennis," said the driver.

"John. Pleased to meet you guys." But the seconds remained stilted, so I went on, "I mean gays." The ice was broken and there was no doubt about me, not that I wasn't screaming it in bleached pink and turquoise. We drove and laughed and they slipped words in that Kent had introduced me to, like "Mary" and "sister" and "girlfriend." Soon I felt comfort in missing Kent. I was with family. We were a whole new generation of cocktail-hour, pastel, argyle and espadrilled homos ready to be hooted at or hated. In town we settled into the only questionable bar in the West Indies. Christmas lights doubled for disco lights.

A gorgeous black man took me up and ground his groin into me on the postage-stamp dance floor. A gentleman, too. I sweated something furious, and wondered if I could absorb his African gyrations. It was so simple and so powerful. He kissed me and went back to the dark side of the room. I wondered how all of this could someday be integrated into a dance—the heat, the slow intoxicating rhythm. We drank in our respective corners and I learned my new friends were all junior bankers, junior accountants, junior this and that office workers from Toronto. You know, some of them pudgy and well fed, some losing hair, all of them with a paycheque and a mortgage. Grown-ups in training only a few years older than me—covering their sunburnt bellies in a beach ensemble or perma-pressed cruise wear with nothing torn, cut off, open-toed, bleached or bare. Socks definitely midcalf in the summer and knee-height any other time of life. Everything tucked in and belted. How fascinating. I wanted so badly to be on the other side of the room.

"You dance well," said the chubby one.

"Well, I'm a dancer."

"Oh? Who with?"

"The Company, Winnipeg, but now I'm living in Quebec, working with a small company there." I was drunk enough to go on, and he didn't seem to be listening anyway. "I have to moonlight in a club."

"You strip?"

"Well..."

"I knew it!" His chubby face glowed at the discovery, his eyes popped open. "Hey, guys, he's a stripper. An honest-to-God stripper. I knew it."

I felt good. I felt bad. Crotch-driven gyrating and fudged dance steps had won out over ballet. And there I was—summed up in one word by this earnest accountant called Dennis—*stripper*. Javex-straw blond. Shaved chest. Cancerously brown. Tank top this. Sleeveless that. Thong this. Ripped that. Untucked. Disillusioned. Sallow. A pouter. Now they had a story to take back to the water cooler. Their friends would be jealous. They told me to come to Toronto for a visit. Dennis seemed to want to take me under his wing, in a big sister way. "There's no way you won't be moving to Toronto at some point. Give me a call. Look me up. I'm serious." But Toronto seemed to be nowhere on my horizon. I told them all to come to Quebec for Carnival, and that they could sleep on my floor. Then later that night it was drunken sex with someone's boyfriend by mistake on the beach, under a tree, in the night rain (when we were all supposed to be having a walk under the starlit sky), followed by an intense brief skin rash. I had tried to imagine I was having sex with Mr. Clean but it was not the case. "Look me up in Toronto," the nameless boyfriend said. He might have been cute but I couldn't see him.

Eight

A DANCER'S CHEST IS the first and most accessible conduit to the universe, from which a dancer can express himself, and from which the universe receives the message that a corporeal story is in the process of being told. The centre of the sternum rises skyward, tugged at by angels. Once you have experienced weightlessness you can never tell yourself that you will be content to be earthbound, ever again. The upper back follows, the torso narrows, the heels rise and soon barely the toes touch the edges of earth.

I GOT KENT'S MESSAGE from Quebecair's humpy tropical tourist rep, too late to be of any help. As for the rep, he stood at the gate of my compound (looking more like a tennis coach), bemused at my sparse accommodation. I wondered about him, too. How someone could be so satisfied with such a simple existence. Was I, alone, in love with martyrdom?

I only had hours to wonder about Kent's call before it was time to head to the airport. The message was to call collect, but I was coming home, which he had likely forgotten. Had my place burned down? His? Had all my stuff—leotards, dance belts, spandex, Mylar and hooker furniture gone up in an acrid, synthetic and sweat-stained smoke? Had someone died? I couldn't imagine my parents dead. And, as for Kent, at least he was well enough to get a message to me, that's what I told myself through many mini-bottles of bad wine as we flew north over the Bermuda Triangle, and frost gathered in the corners of the window panes, my tanned skin starting to crack like the bed of an emptied lake.

My flight was rerouted to join the last of stranded passengers, from a week of heavy snowfall and cancelled flights, draped on seats, luggage and corridors, at the airport in Montreal. People were arriving from the great beyond, as well as through the front doors, stuffing the departures and arrivals with bundled bodies. It was then I saw the profiles of two good-looking, freshly tanned males stepping off the Jetway of a Varig 707 shrouded in the weakening blizzard, all the way from Rio. They glistened. Their hair was touched, with help, by the sun. They looked superb and sleek in matching leather bomber jackets, worth more than everything I owned put together. Their shoulders jostled each other, they chattered and took no heed of the tired throngs. One was Daniel.

It's funny how cruel we can be toward our own selves in split seconds. It seemed farcical that I had ever thought the two of us made some kind of match, and so obvious that we were from completely different levels in the hierarchy. My life was an angry dance that was frantically whipping about this terrestrial stage, crashing into the edge of the proscenium, pulling on the flies, the curtain, the backdrop for support, putting other dancers on edge, at risk; Daniel's dance was order, perfection and a soulless, heavenly world of impressive accomplishments. What cruel entity had arranged this near-rendezvous, or collision? My throat contracted, my face heated, and I stifled a natural response to follow, shocked that I didn't care much that it was Daniel. And shocked, too, that I was experiencing nothing toward him more than disdain, not even hate. Okay maybe a little heartbrokenness, but the whole picture of two men, so apparently enamoured with each other, was what hit me. I certainly didn't want to spoil it.

Meanwhile *la belle province* was buried under a week of snow. There was nothing to do but sit and wait and then find out that New Year's would be spent in the airport. Hotels were all full and the best they could do was a bus to the train in the morning. I called Kent, his mysterious emergency still on my mind. He answered on the first ring. "Are you okay?"

"Oh sure, I was just checking in with you."

"Oh God. I thought there was an emergency."

"Are you back?"

"I'm at the airport, in Montreal, or somewhere near Montreal. Looks like you'll have to make other plans for New Year's."

"Well, here's to you and me in '83—we'll toast for real tomorrow, all right?"

I felt like I'd been away for years. "I miss you."

"Yeah, I could say the same thing at this end."

I found a corner of floor. Floor is familiar for dancers—although I prefer sprung maple to terrazzo—and got as comfortable as possible. I had my book of Nelligan poems, the one Kent gave me, and slowly leafed through it thinking I was making sense of the verse. There was great comfort in having something of his with me. I opened it to a poem, "Soir d'hiver," appropriately about lots of snow, and the pain of life as well, from what I could tell. Another, "Amour immaculé," about loving someone, a saint perhaps, who remains silent, impassive and proud. Who would do such a thing? Vaguely familiar. I wondered about what Nelligan had suffered as I drifted into a deep sleep. Midnight I was woken by brief whoops and then dozed for the next six hours.

On the train, I stared through a smudge of coconut oil my forehead left on the window, at clouds of churned-up snow blowing past us, wondering about Kent, wondering about Daniel, his friend—why they would fly from Rio on New Year's; did they have something better planned? I even wondered about the clean-cut employee who had told me about Kent's phone call. My head was spinning. What would Daniel have thought if he had seen me tanned, fit, blond, experienced, jaded, older and nastier? I still would have been no more than a morsel to be tasted.

I knew then, in that instant, that it had been lust—it was so mixed up with hate and apathy that it couldn't have been love at any time. It was obvious. I prayed Nelligan and I were free of our bad memories, *notre désir* at last. I was forgiven. It all made sense. The shame at my obsessive behaviour was gone in the blink of an eye. There was nothing that would ever connect us to each other ever again. I was starting to understand what love was: generosity, patience and care, for now. I dozed as the dry air pulled at my skin. I woke to a split second of Daniel vanishing forever, being swallowed up in the funnel of snow that swirled in the path of the train. I was full of thoughts of seeing Kent. In fact I was dying to see him.

The cab skidded from the station and finally gave up at the gates of the old city. I walked up Sainte-Ursule and saw from the street that my apartment was still intact, so before dumping everything I knocked on Kent's door. I knew Kent was where I could find refuge. There was a long silence, but lights said that someone was home, then a bang on the stairs, several uneven thumps on the stairs and the door opened.

"Surprise, *mon ami*. I came back just for you." Kent's broken up face greeted me: a plum-blue shiner streaked all the way down his nose. A swollen upper lip. He was leaning on a cane. "What the fuck?"

"There's not much left of me to come back to."

He lunged onto me for a quick and awkward hug. I heard him sniff and knew he was crying. He sniffed and pulled away. "Fuck, you look good enough to eat. Through a straw is how I'll have to do it." He turned and led me silently, half-step by half-step, up the stairs and into the living room. He said he fell down the stairs the day before, just after getting back from Montreal, and panicked, which was why he phoned me—said he just wanted to hear my voice and he didn't know when I was coming back. He denied he left a message about an emergency, says maybe it got mixed up in the translation. (From English to English?)

God, it was still winter and now things had gone from bad to worse, no club in flames, no job offer from the Paris Opera or the Moulin Rouge, not to forget the New York City Ballet. And these other pieces didn't seem to fit; he looked beaten up. When I joked that he needed someone to take care of him all the time, he broke down. He said crying hurt his ribs, said he had truly missed me. I sat with my arm carefully over his shoulder, for a long time. I wanted to undress him and make love to him for the simple reason that he was so vulnerable, less of a predator than I perceived him to be.

"Maybe you could take care of me," he said.

"I'll be your nurse. I'm sure I can find a costume at the club."

"I might need more."

"I'll sleep on your couch if Henri doesn't mind."

He was silent as he sat slumped with his hands clasped.

"Can I make some tea?" I went to the kitchen to fill the kettle.

"I had a fight with Henri." He didn't cry as he spoke, but tears were flowing. "He's gone to Montreal and wants me out in the next few days. I was phoning to ask if I could move my stuff into your place."

"He did this to you?"

"It was mostly an accident. I tripped. Thank God I was drunk." But I had the feeling it was as simple and nasty as Henri shoving him down the stairs.

FROM THIS STAIRWELL AND all that has happened since I got here, I can say with some certainty that gay men don't have roommates. They are either together or ex-something-elses—ex-lovers or ex-tricks—and if they aren't, then one of the two has a fantasy that their roommate is, or will be, the man of their dreams. Then, I had a feeling that there was much more to this than Kent was letting on. Prove me wrong. I'd like nothing more.

KENT ASKED ME AGAIN about us being roommates.

"I'm always on the other side of the wall."

"Maybe we need to be closer."

"We'd drive each other crazy." I wanted to protect what we had. "I don't want us at each other's throats because we're cramped."

"We have different schedules. I have lots of places to go when you need your space."

"Okay," I was hesitant. "As long as you don't smoke."

So, for the next two days Kent directed the move, sometimes from his place and sometimes from under a blanket and leaning on a cane, in the falling snow. Most of the furnishings were Henri's, thank God. I hauled all of his things—grocery bags stuffed with clothes, some bedding, some dishes, his dismantled bed—past the Café Latin and up to my place, until it looked like Madame Talegdi's garage. But I worked swiftly to change that.

"Time for bubbly."

"I'm on painkillers."

"So I have to drink this by myself?"

"God no. Painkillers and booze, it'll be great. Here's to you and me in '83."

I'd assembled his bed in the kitchen half of the place and we set up a little nest in the sheets, got naked and toasted everything we could think of. Counted all of our blessings, the roof over our head, each other, and the fact that 1983 started out so badly that it couldn't possibly get any worse.

Kent hobbled and chain-smoked along the hall outside the apartment as part of our fresh air agreement. "I don't know how you can do this to me, when you come home every night smelling worse than an ashtray."

"Then you won't mind if I don't have a shower," I said.

"Then I could taste you."

I could taste the smoke when he kissed me. I can taste it now.

THE NEXT AFTERNOON I left Kent to recover at our place while I took the bus out to Ancienne Lorette, staring at grey car-lots and strip malls, wondering why I had come back from the over-sexed, over-sensual, sinfully fertile tropics to this never-ending eyesore. Loyalty? To Marcel? To Kent? To a bad dream? I had less and less to lose. Not coming back didn't really seem so strange a concept. Why not run away?

The snow started to slice past the windows and soon we were riding on the driver's instincts more than the ruts in the road. The ride became quiet and slow. Did normal people do this? Didn't they stay home with a book or a good show on television? I was really starting to drift in terms of motivation.

When I finally got to the club it was to Marcel's news that we had guest showgirls from Montreal. Real professionals. I walked toward the stairs. Some of the girls had taken holidays and looked strange, un-made up, well rested and needing to readjust back into the nocturnal life-under-a-rock world of Chez Moritz. Something was different. They were sharing a joke, a secret. Had someone died? Was Brittany back? Was it my birthday and there was a huge cake in the basement, from which some fabulous guy saying he was all mine, and holding a one-way ticket back to the tropics, would leap? When I got to the change area this playful atmosphere of giggles and glances all became clear: at a new makeshift dressing table complete with lights and a wide mirror with a hunk out of the corner sat two over-the-top drag queens that gave off absolute sweetie-I-love-you-but-don't-fuck-with-me-or-I'll-rip-your-head-off vibes—Mesdames *Bichon Frissé* and *Tarte au Sucre*. "Call me Sugar—Brown Sugar." Bichon was lean and tall, and Sugar was as black as Grace Jones with a beautiful set of tight pink lips that she pressed when she meant business. They got up and stood on either side of me, looking me over with their hungry gazes. They must have each been about a foot taller than me. Sugar's bustier was folded down revealing curly tufts of black hair on a firm chest. Bichon's shoulders would have put any footballer to shame. These women were all men. But I couldn't be anyone else's appetizer. "Bitch, we struck it rich," said Sugar.

"'e's mine," said Bichon.

"'e's everybody's from what I hear. And you know—good news travels fast. And by God, 'e is good news. *Chèri*, if you gonna dance wit' us, you got to help us into our wigs, that's the deal. If you know what I mean."

"I hear he's a handy man." Sugar laid her muscled arm across my shoulder, but I had to look up, way up. Her hands and wrists were fine and long, and they twitched as she spoke. "You come wit' a best-before date, handsome? Can I call you handsome?"

"I'm known as *Le Grand Blond*."

"But I'm grander and blonder, no kidding, but you can see for yourself some udder time."

"You call me whatever you want. I was taught not to argue with the ladies."

"Oh so we're ladies? She, my dear, is no lady," Bichon waggled a plum-coloured nail in my face, "but she is all woman, I can tell you dat."

Beneath the costume jewellery-encrusted exterior of these two Amazon showstopper toughies, there was warmth and vulnerability.

"We dreamt of being dancers,"

"Once upon a time. Ballerinas, too, you bitch."

"But I craved Mylar instead of…"

"...nylon. Feathers from swallows instead of..."

"...swans. Stilettos instead of..."

"...pointe shoes. *Crêpe de Chine* instead of..."

"...shep de creen, um I forget, o yeah, tulle. Muumuus instead of..."

"...tutus. Carrot cake instead of..."

"...carrots."

I was witnessing part of a comic routine, complete with special attention to the wistful movement of lipstick-laden lips, bejewelled wrists to foreheads, performed somewhere and filed away but, more or less, based on good information.

Marcel hadn't mentioned them before I left, and yet they'd already started rehearsing and would be performing with us immediately. We had more in common than anyone would think: our shared dance background, and I could understand them, sort of. I mean I didn't have to pretend I could understand them. They were perfectly bilingual; their potty-mouth English was as jarring as their twanging Québécois.

Marcel was distant through all this, and I was finally starting to feel like the honeymoon was over, and that I, as flavour of the month, had gone sour. Running hot, then cold. It reminded me of the Company, my second-guessing, unchecked jealousies, need for attention, and how praise was erratically doled out, then rapidly retrieved. Was Marcel jealous of something? Had I disappointed him?

We all had an early night, and because of the blizzard, Marcel and François drove me back to their place in a warm Mercedes—opera lights, warm leather seats—to where they lived with Marcel's mother. I could barely understand François' French. Occasionally Marcel would translate when there was a pause. But François insisted on turning and talking to me the whole way, wanting to know what it was like to live on the prairies, as if to live in English Canada was another continent.

Camp with a capital "C" came naturally to Marcel. His penthouse walls were covered with leopard wallpaper. Sofas and ottomans were upholstered in cougar and fake tiger. The broadloom was thick, and stereo electronics flickered on the far wall. It was a collision of luxury and tack. He went home in a cozy car to this plush womb every night.

There were mirrors everywhere and a reflection from Marcel's mother's boudoir is how I first saw her. Looking like a retired showgirl, she wore full makeup on a snowbound Monday night in Sainte-Foy, sitting at her dressing table brushing her silver hair and calling out, across two thousand square feet of high-rise cushy penthouse, the news of the day: the blizzard will be getting worse, she warns, and then sobs telling the news of an uncle in Paris finally dying. Marcel reminds her that the uncle was ninety-three. She dabs her eyes and nods, "Quand même, quand même, et pourtant, je te demande."

It made sense that the sets and décor at the club, and all the exotic costumes were backed by her. The only tits-and-feathers cabaret between Montreal and the Moulin Rouge, the Chez Moritz was her plaything. Her martinis took the chill away and connected me to a place I'd given up—the security of my parent's home. We sat in the expansive living room, a fire blazing in the hearth, while the blizzard blew all around us. We sipped our martinis. Kent would have already bedded down, probably snoring. Bare as it may have seemed in comparison, I wanted to be back in my own place with him. Marcel and François curled into each other in the opposite sofa. François stared at me like the dumb cute hunk that he was. Looking good was what he did best.

Marcel sipped his martini and spoke, "Mom danced with the Lido."

"In Paris?"

"She met her husband—not my father—there. He made her a wealthy ex-showgirl." Marcel looked toward the bedroom. "Isn't that right, Mom?"—as if this was an ongoing patter between the two of them. "She made sure it stayed that way when she met my father. They were barely married long enough to conceive me. He's dead. We think. Or wandering around the woods of northern Quebec wrestling moose or bear or whatever."

As I lay down to sleep on a sofa that seemed to have more square footage than my apartment, I prayed for luxury. I was now officially sick of dumps. If I couldn't have the satisfaction of being a true artist and a dancer, then why the hell be poor? I was starting to see why my father had been so against my choice. He seemed to understand that comfort had a price, and once you knew comfort, you had no choice but to afford that price.

"What's this?" he had said about the dance bag, ensuring he would never know about me training with the women at the university, or having pointe shoes, rarely worn by men, custom-made to strengthen my arches. He would never know that my feet would end up as veined muscle, feeling like tenderized beef, or that I shoved my feet under radiators, pried at the cartilage for an unnatural stretch, or that Lisa, Madame Défilé and Drake made sure I learned depth from all the masters—Vaganova, Cecchetti, Bournonville, Cunningham, Graham—and the vast breadth of dance from flamenco to foxtrot to czardas. All he needed to know was that I had finally left pre-med for full-time dance, supported by part-time jobs.

That summer after my first year at university, my objective was to make money, enough to make my own decisions. I worked on an uncle's farm late spring into early summer and prayed my technique wouldn't leave me. Then, with twelve weeks of uncle's pay for chucking an early harvest of alfalfa by late June—and calloused hands, hardened biceps, a tight back, a butt that even dancers would envy—I made my announcement as we sat on the screened-in porch eating our berries and cream.

"The Company in Winnipeg has a summer program that they use as an audition for their full-time training," I began.

Mother left the table, sat in the cool living room with her *Vogue*. My father spoke. "Why not dance in the summer and do school in the winter?" I admired his inartistic logic. He had tried to see this madness from my point of view.

"A dancer can't dance part-time."

"But you're not a dancer. You have no idea what you're in for."

"I know exactly." My secrets had worked against me. Of course the idea seemed crazy. "I have been dancing now for years."

"What do you mean?"

"I am good. I've had good teachers…"

"Behind our backs?"

"It was all free. Lisa says I could dance professionally."

"Lisa?"

"She danced with the Company. She knows."

"I thought this was just some crazy hobby. I won't support you, you know. You can do it on your own."

"I will."

"I doubt you'll make it past the audition, anyway, but if you want to waste the rest of your summer, go ahead."

My mother wept; I could hear the sniffing and nose-blowing coming from the living room. I wondered what it was. Did she want me to escape, or follow my dream? Did it strike a chord in her?

I don't recall much else except that he stamped and shouted his way through the house and then simply abandoned me, told me during those last days that I was a talentless dreamer. He said I'd be back and that I had never taken care of myself and had no idea what the real world was like.

He was right. I had no idea how I would end up—all day long on foot, seven hours of dancing, lying about my work history to get another seven hours serving food at night, cleaning slop and filth at the Club Rococo on Portage, ashes and plates full of flu germs, fevers and sore throats. I served Scotch and Coke, a combination my parents would have sneered at. Waitered talentlessly at five different dumps: empty steakhouses, geriatric-crowded English tearooms, a dinner theatre of Hollywood has-beens and a trendy Jewish lox café where I couldn't keep up. All this for a dream. But the dream had a price—poverty, being fired, losing the race, fatigue, sharing one cup of coffee and calling it a date. My tendons, knees and ankles crackled when I finally put my legs up.

The perks along the way were: the hopes of a scholarship once the trial period was over; the leftovers the restaurants sent me home with; the clients' intrigue at having a dancer serve them food; and the rare, "Well done, John," after a perfect pirouette—music to this dancer's ears.

I justified sleeping on the floor by saying Baryshnikov had done the same thing. My desire to suffer for art was strong. This was the dream—to do something as simple as move my body to music. Just move. Colleagues, even the jealous ones, started saying I'd make it happen—out of all of them, I would be the one. Me and Leslie Browne in *The Turning Point*. That important. I was on scholarship just enough to remain poor, not destitute. They needed to break me, but maybe I was just too pliable to begin with, and after two years of gritting my teeth through assessments, Kharkov took a temporary shine to me and in a moment of weakness—when I was doing a particularly spot-on double *saut de basques*—he took me off the golden egg of scholarship and offered to put me on the payroll as an apprentice.

I couldn't share the joy; peers were now officially jealous and parents silent. And from the corps de ballet I watched and learned *La Bayadère, Paquita, Le Corsaire, Sleeping Beauty, Romeo and Juliet, Les Sylphides, Rodeo, The Nutcracker*. I rode the Company buses, planes, blizzards and tornados from Minneapolis to New Orleans, from Seattle to Atlanta, hoping that someone would injure themselves. But it was there on the stage in my hometown I finally appreciated that my dream had come true. I was on the very stage where Nureyev and Fonteyn had danced.

My doubtful parents appeared when the circus came to town. But still, they needed to be convinced. And I had to please someone other than myself. It was bittersweet, not being able to say, *I told you so*. Knowing they were in the audience made me swell with pride, but I wondered if they knew how hard it had been for me to get there. I desperately wanted them to see how good I was—what a different person I was. How all they had planned for me was so much less than all that I was at that moment, revolving onstage, leaping, flying to Agnes de Mille's steps and Aaron Copeland's music. During curtain call I tried to look for them in the audience. Surely they saw how happy I was, and how good I was at something I loved. I hoped they saw my talent. My mother had seen so much dance she must have known the good from the not so good.

We went to Hy's Steakhouse that night, our regular place for birthdays, graduations and prime Alberta beef—dark enough to recede into shadows when you'd had enough of anyone's company. My mother reached across the table and held my hand. I think it meant she was proud. We chatted quietly about the neighbours, the neighbours' kids, their cars, renovations, scandals. For a moment I felt I was being treated as an adult, with a career and a life, until I realized we were talking about everything but my accomplishments and my short life in the ballet studio.

On our drive home, my father did his best to act sober after three double ryes. "You've done us proud," he said. "I knew whatever you tried you would be successful, that was never a question." He still managed to get his point across. I slept in my room in the basement that night.

It boiled down to years of pain, victory and vindication in the Company's main rehearsal studio, where posters of the Company's pioneers looked down on me. Two years of intensive learning, following, copying, mimicking, forming, graduating, understudying and finally performing. Two more years hoping to move out of the corps, until the offer of a second soloist contract, and then Montreal, which clobbered me.

WHEN I WOKE AT Marcel's the next morning, the impact of the distance I had strayed hit me. In that luxurious Sainte-Foy penthouse, after bubble-bathing in the boys' tub and leaving an oily ring of tanned sloughed skin in their Jacuzzi, I looked out at the white rooftops to the frozen St. Lawrence and sipped *un bol de café au lait*. I had to believe that this alone wasn't what I honestly aspired to.

The boys drove me downtown, back along the same route I took to Madame's studio. I doubted there would be anyone there today. Madame's crap car wouldn't have made it through that snow. At last I could take a legitimate snow day and not feel guilty about it. It was much more fabulous to cruise into the Old Town in Marcel's mother's cozy Mercedes than to slouch back after a day of Madame's abuse, or be dropped off in the wee hours by Patrice and his New Yorker. It was odd, the silence in that car; we didn't talk about anything important or anything at all. The snow raised the level of tension just enough to make us believe we had to concentrate on the ride. Marcel smiled when he dropped me off, winked too, then they both cruised on to a meeting at the Château Frontenac—something about us doing a hair show.

My place was not a Sainte-Foy condo, but it was home and it was warm. Up I went, eager to tell Kent I had a night off, but he wasn't there. I thought he'd have been waiting by the window, drinking coffee, thinking about sneaking a cigarette inside rather than hobbling around in the cold hallway.

The weights sat by the wall. My sleeping mat lay still on the floor. Empty beer cases were stacked neatly. Kent's bed was parked by the kitchen. Boxes sat unopened, bags untouched. Quietness was smothering the room, while snow fell silently outside the windows. Loneliness showed up more often now, and it showed up at times like this. I was starting to find comfort in company and especially in Kent's company. Where the hell was he? He was in no shape to be out. I flopped onto my mat and for the first time in ages my back relaxed. The deep sleep on Marcel's sofa and a week of lying on the warm sand had softened me up.

Why had I turned away from the easy life? If I'd listened to my father, I could be cozy in a university residence right now with the promise of a couple of years more education before the guarantee of transferring—feet never touching the ground—to a secure life that rewarded its devotees with endless distractions: vacations, cars, sound systems and alcoholic downtime. Or if I had been really clever, I would have figured a way into that Sainte-Foy penthouse, no matter what.

The blanket of quiet had turned the Old Town into a ghost town and my heart leapt when the buzzer went. But the even thudding up the stairs was too heavy to be Kent's, and I opened the door to a bundled Bertrand. He'd taken the early ferry from Lévis and since there was no class, he decided to pay a visit.

"*Je peux vous offrir un boisson?*"

"*Bière?*"

"*Le matin?*"

"*Comme tu veux.*"

Beer before nine—he had come over to the dark side—meanwhile I made some tea.

"'ow are you?"

"Fine. Your English is better."

"Louise."

I gathered that meant she was teaching him. We hadn't actually spoken much for the last couple of months. All I'd done was lift him, and almost crush a few vertebrae in the process.

"Chantal, Maryse no more dance. Is finished."

"*Pourquoi?*"

He laughed out loud and a big smile came across his face like I had never seen. "You," he said. "You burlesque. You said Madame and Jean-Marc…"

"Ah."

"Louise. Me. Maybe we will go. I am sorry for that. I bring Louise to tell you about this." He swigged his beer. "I go to see Louise now." At least he had something good to do instead of class this morning, I thought as I watched him disappear down Sainte-Ursule into the blowing snow.

The phone rang, which it rarely did since Kent had moved in, and it was one of the bankers from Toronto. "We're coming down for Carnival. Is the offer still open? It's just for a night or two."

"Sure, just call before you get here. How many?"

"About five." Simple as that.

By the afternoon, the blowing had settled and left the Old Town looking like an overgrown Pavlova—not the dancer, the dessert; lots of stiff peaks of meringue with me as the fruit centre. I had some time to myself in my place and I took it as a chance to leaf through Kent's porn, mixed in with his *New Yorkers*, *Saturday Nights* and *L'actualité*. Kent liked to read, and to look at naughty pictures. It was funny to look at these guys, from the sublime (posed and beyond perfection) to the ridiculous (not posed, bad lighting, bad skin and pretty unflattering). I was a little bemused; Kent had set the bar way too high in terms of sexual gratification.

Bichon and Sugar came by, hesitantly clumping up the stairs. I was sure it was a couple of drunks. I opened the door to pseudo-drag—though if you saw them you would think there go two lovely, tall women—and we all headed out into the winter wonderland. We rendezvoused with Marcel and François after their meeting with the hair show people, and drank champagne at the

Clarendon. There was some levity, and for a moment I felt like I could have a little community here, and some security. From there we split up, and the girls and I stumbled into the snow, giggling and tipsy. In a consignment store in some ancient cellar they convinced me to buy a used *rat sauvage* fur coat for three hundred dollars, a good week's tips. The girls lived like stars and spent that way, too.

"Marcel hates me," I said. "Ever since I got back from down south, he's had a big goddamned hate on for me."

"Sweetie pie, you are teen beat-me-off property," Bichon started in her rocky French Canadian. "No one could possibly 'ate you—more than I do, anyway. God, I 'ate you. You're so cute." She hollered, "I 'ate him!"

"You ate him?" said Sugar.

"No I 'ate 'im," said Bichon.

"Did you mean dat you did eat 'im. Dat's what I want to know."

"Oh shaddup, you big old bitch."

"You bitch in stitches."

"More like d' opposite," Sugar said. "I think Marcel 'as da 'ots for you."

"He's in love with me?"

"Not love for Christ sake. Did I say love? *Tabarnak.*" We all tittered at the same time because it sounded so damn stupid. Although, it wouldn't have been that bad. I could still carve out a comfortable, if dull, life in that penthouse. The mom would have to go, and François would have to stay. "There's something you should know," Sugar went on.

"François knows about the audition?" I said.

"What audition? What the 'ell are you talking about now? I'm not so sure I like you no more."

"Nothing. Go on. What were you saying?"

"Louis told Marcel it's curtains for certain. Marcel says its da Mafia want to run the place, dey say too many dancers getting in da way—not enough T and A. 'e's pissed off. That's why we're here—we came as a favour. Wanted to help him go out wit' a bang. 'e's always been so good to us."

"You're doing him a favour? But you just said tits and ass."

"Is this not an ass, you twat? Anyway, 'e's always been good to us. 'e's always kept us working, between our Montreal gigs."

"Why the silent treatment?"

"He didn't want to hurt you. He likes you. We all do. 'e's confused."

"Merci. Je vous aime aussi."

Bichon turned to Sugar and wagged his finger. "I told you 'e speaks French. Now he knows all da shit we said about 'im."

"Marcel is sad?"

"'e knows you won't stay. So yeah, I guess he likes 'aving you around."

AND THAT NIGHT, AFTER our run-through, and before I put on my eyeliner, our cozy life went sequined-pasties-on-your-nipples up. Marcel, his eyes glistening, told us, "This will be it. Enjoy your last few weeks, it's all we've got. From now on, it's strippers, *les étoiles* and Patrice. Maybe we should have applied for a Canada Council grant." But no one laughed. Meanwhile the rest of the girls—the strippers— kept raking it in and the club paid us less than a round of drinks, fifty bucks a night, to do our three shows.

So that was it. I suppose I wasn't going to carve out an existence as a bad stripper in an obscure part of an obscure city. And I wasn't going to strip in Montreal, where I'd already made enough of a fool of myself. What a laugh. I could see Daniel's brunch buddies show- ing up for a freebie. Anyway I could now say Daniel was an asshole, out loud too, if I had to think of him at all. I wasn't going to go back to Montreal to dance either, in crappy shape, and as everyone in the Company said, the Conservatoire was a joke, only made great by its dancers, most of whom had gotten their start with other compan- ies. Their company promised what their training program couldn't deliver.

So, now that both my technique and my bank account sucked badly enough that I wasn't in any shape for a fresh start, with strip- per muscles in my chest and shoulders, Madame's contribution to my thunder thighs, a new centre of gravity somewhere between the moon and Uranus, and a lower back tough as an overdone pot roast, and the rest of me wondering which end was up, was I no longer a real dancer?

Go back to university? Why was I so stubborn about doing what I wanted to do? I just knew that I couldn't sit still in a lecture hall, alive from the neck up, knowing that my whole body had become such a large part of my life. I would be betraying something that on some level I knew I could still be good at.

Follow Brittany in her Cadillac? Start doing the circuit? Find her ex? Give him back his outfit? Was a legit dancing career entirely over? Time to take steroids and hit the gym daily? Hope my nuts didn't shrink and that I would bulk up? Dumb down? Be a fitness model? A hooker? Pose in porn out in California? Take the money and run? The world was no longer the oyster I wanted it to be.

Kent was still awake when I got home and I was surprised at how happy I was to smell relatively fresh smoke in the hallway. He reclined on a stack of pillows, on his bed. "Where the hell have you been?"

"Did you miss me?"

"You're in no condition to do whatever it was you were doing. You're practically an invalid. The show is ending, by the way."

"Which one?"

"The one between my legs."

Kent clambered out of bed and hobbled to the fridge. "I need the exercise," he said. He opened beers for the two of us. We sat on the bed. "You know, you're young, but you're not that young."

"What do you mean by that?"

"You should be happy that the decision was made that easily. Time to change gears."

"I know, but it doesn't seem to matter anymore."

"So, where's the dream at?"

"The dream?"

"To be a dancer. You had me convinced that was the master plan."

"I don't know. I'm scattered. I'm high one minute and in the depths of it all the next. It's cotton candy and anything you want, against drill sergeants and riding crops."

"Well, what started it all?"

"Dance?"

"Dance."

"Just plain old love for everything: the beauty, the aesthetic, the bodies, the art form—the feeling mostly—the music. Have you ever listened to Chopin's nocturnes or a bit of Debussy or Ravel? I mean, how can a body not respond? It's organic. It feels so good. It still can, I know that."

"That's it?"

"Isn't that enough?"

"Well it is reassuring that it's not just Gloria Gaynor and Heart. So that's encouraging."

"Who made you career monitor of Sainte-Ursule?"

"Tell me, what it is you have to offer—as a dancer?"

"Myself."

"*Myself* is vague."

"And I'm vague."

"Don't feel sorry for yourself."

"Okay, you're being tough, but I can take it. Let's see. I have to offer my joy of doing it?"

"Don't look at me for an answer. I don't know. It's not a quiz. You just don't sound convincing. Think about it."

I sipped my beer.

"Wait a minute."

"What?"

"One more time—you and me in '83."

"Et vous aussi, chèr ami. Hey, it rhymes. Now, don't change the subject."

"New Year's. Ha. You were icing bruises, and I was watching the skin peel off my arms. Fuck. Let's change the subject."

"Things can only get better."

"I'm with you," I said, and then in my harshest French, "Je suis en accord avec voooo!"

After I showered, I squeezed into Kent's bed and, in retrospect, I see now that that evening, for the first time in my life, I made love to another man. Real love. We were naked against each other and I kissed his beer-and-cigarette-scented mouth so deeply that I barely knew where he started and I stopped. I was hungry for his closeness.

Would he know this was love, or just think I was improving my technique?

When I woke in the morning, I lay quietly with him beside me and thought about the previous evening. I believed the dream to be a dancer had finally left me. Kent was right, I had nothing to offer and my dreams were rooted in a selfish ego. I had put in my time, deservedly and passively hoping I'd move up the ladder, but maybe my motives had never been clear enough, or had gotten sidetracked. Did I want to impress someone other than myself? Did I have to prove something? I really was my blank stare. Kent snored, and I slipped downstairs to buy a normal coffee among normal people, like a normal person.

THAT NIGHT, STEVE WANTED to have a meeting in the washroom. "What's the matter, *chèri*? This isn't like you."

"I'm tired. I'm tired of everything—winter, cold floors, city buses, four-hour sleeps, this shit-stubborn back, having to find another job, again—and not even being..."

"Excited? About this?"

It felt so wrong. I had become a different person overnight. I had no idea who the new person was, but he seemed to see the old one quite clearly.

To add to the confusion, when we left the can, Guy, Steve's Guy, was waiting in his Iroquois costume. He was a truly gorgeous man, not a bathroom thrills slut kind of guy that I had become. He didn't say anything. He didn't have to. It was simple. I was evil and he wasn't.

So the two of them went off to have their own drama, leaving me to get into the new costumes Marcel had made: velvet lapels and cuffs for me, and dyed-black wild turkey feathers for Bichon and Sugar. He had obviously pulled out all the stops, gone way over-budget as they say.

Bichon and Sugar, the two of them looking like a cross between Marie Antoinette and Big Bird's widow, pecked away at our situation like it was the end of the world, taking it to heart when they didn't have to worry because they'd be back in Montreal in a few weeks. Perhaps they cared about Marcel in a way I could not. When they

212

finally tired of creating alternatives and options for Marcel's future, they focused on me with advice and warnings. "You can't forget your technique," Bichon said. "Watch out for the talkers," Sugar advised.

"Stalkers?" said Bichon, face scrunched in misunderstanding.

"Talkers, for shit's sakes. And don't do that to your face, it cakes your foundation. The talkers will still be talking fifty years from now, about dreams and plans, and watching like hawks to see what everyone else is up to."

"Even if you never get back into the ballet," Sugar said, "you make great chorus boy material. Can you sing?"

"I don't know."

"But you have a dream?"

"Do you?"

"Well, but yes, of course. I am auditioning for *Trockadero*, and Sugar is going to audition for *Caracas*. I mean shit, she's the right colour."

"Really? But you two said you weren't suited for it."

"Baby, that's our shtick. And this is just a shtick shtop, a favour."

But my auditioning for anything didn't make sense since my new revelation. And add to that the fact that the whole new show had an overriding feeling of darkness, and I might as well have called everything quits; the lights were dark, the costumes were blacks and reds like a dark Marie Antoinette meets Darth Vader to both go to hell, with Bichon in a huge black hoop skirt covered in feathers, looking more like a beaver lodge than a showgirl. Everyone was glum, Marcel was still sour, Sugar was still pissed at Marcel for constantly pouting, and everybody bickered.

Fortunately we all started drinking during the shows, heavily, thanks to an old regular. He'd send trays of cognac downstairs. Some nights we ended up doing the whole show just for him—and do it drunk. He'd toss us flowers. We'd clap for him. He'd clap for us. He'd send down more drinks, and when he forgot to oblige us, we would treat ourselves. Soon word got out that the show was closing, and everyone started buying us drinks. Things got messier, though it didn't matter, since no one in the club seemed to notice us; we were background noise as far as the strippers and Louis the owner were concerned.

The low point of it all was the night I slipped under Bichon's immense igloo dress before she went onstage. She made her entrance, curtsied, and then I grabbed her fishnet thigh causing her to jump out of her skin, and the audience to wake up and laugh. But she didn't laugh. In fact she belted me in the chin hard enough for me to hear and feel my jaw compress, see stars and taste blood. "Don't ever startle me onstage. I don't care what we do back here, surprises are fine, but a drag queen with a broken heel is gonna be hell for you. I'm just warning you. I can't audition for the *Troc* with a broken ankle." With her permission, the number turned into an even sloppier and predictable piece after that—lacking originality—with me ogling from under her skirt and usually tumbling out eating something, like a banana. Like life, it wasn't that much fun without the spontaneity. And, like life, we never really enjoyed working together after that faux pas. We both knew I'd been careless.

A week later our contract was firmed up for the *Soirée Chartreuse*, an international hairdressers' convention at the Chateau Frontenac. It was also the weekend of the Canadian Dental Association's annual general meeting. My parents, with little warning, decided to pay a visit. They had called when I wasn't home and Kent had provided enough vague information to keep questions at bay but to make them sufficiently curious. He said he was my roommate, he said I was extremely busy with two jobs.

At ten there was a knock on the door, and heart blasting at the thought that it was my parents, even though I told them I would meet them at their hotel, I pulled myself together while Kent hid in the bathroom. I hit the buzzer and opened the door to run downstairs to be met by seven fresh-faced, snow-covered bankers and accountants stomping up from street level. "We drove all night," said the chubby one who led the way. Until that moment I had completely forgotten the call, or even what day it was. "Where's your tan?" the first one asked. I couldn't recognize them in their parkas, since I had earmarked each one by a specific fashion faux pas.

"I'll show you."

I explained it all to Kent once they'd dumped their stuff and gone out to be tourists. His only reply: "You met seven men and not one of them looks fuck-able, how do you do it? No wonder you've only had six in your life."

As for my parents, they stayed in a big hotel a stone's throw outside the wall, close to that locale where I had spent a majority of my time—the bus stop. Dad was busy all day with seminars at Laval and interviewing possibilities for a few Edmonton residency spaces. Mom slept. I made reservations for the two of them at the restaurant Kent worked at, and to keep things animated, made a big deal about the *Internationale Soirée Chartreuse* the next night. While I was getting ready to head out to work I asked Kent to take good care of them. "Could you get them a bottle of champagne or something, not too pricey? I'll pay."

"If I can go in on it with you, I'll get them pricey. How's that? Life is too short, you know…"

"Will you be waiting on them?"

"You are looking at the wait staff."

"Good luck. I hope they stock rye. My dad gets ugly without a warm-up cocktail or two."

"Good rye."

"He likes the cheap stuff."

"Now you go be cheap and stop worrying."

Kent was a charming man when it came to socializing, and, although they had some pretty ingrained prejudices—male roommate was suspect—I was sure he would charm them.

He must have won them over, because that night just as I was packing up from a table dance for the seven Caribbean carnival–goers boarding *chez moi*, who had arrived early—still on Toronto time—to get a good seat, Kent and my parents, having dined and amply wined, showed up.

Kent wasn't all bad; he made sure word spread throughout the club—faster than you can translate venereal warts—that my parents were in the house. I packed up my drink tray and my box and got my G-stringed ass off the floor. I vowed to murder Kent, but only after he paid me what he owed me in lost tips that night. I joined the three of them in the audience and from there, with my behind actually on a chair, and fabric between my bum and the fake leather seat, I noticed how bland and sedate a Saturday night crowd really was. All the activity must have only been going on in my self-centred mind. It was a backwash of middle-aged women in wigs, dentures, slacks and blouses, and men in cardigans and grey flannels. They all looked so much more sinister when you were over them or getting drinks or dancing at their tables. And among them sat my parents looking like the Duke and Duchess of Strathcona. But when I noticed my father's teeth glowing, I realized that for all those years, the man who I thought had perfect teeth was a capped and crowned fraud. How obvious. Under those many nights of black lights, I had learned the truth about fakery, as my mother's hair glowed green.

"I can see his thing," my mother giggled. "Oh my goodness." She took out a tissue and wiped her nose. Yes, she saw Guy's thing, and yes, oh my goodness, even though it wasn't hard, it wasn't hard to miss halfway across the room. This seemed to give her the upper hand in a silent war with my father.

Fortunately Kent made sure they continued to have lots of liquor, suggesting with some intent that I fetch a bottle of bubbly in an ice bucket. When we did our show, with them as drunk as us, they probably didn't recognize me or even know I was on the stage at all. Besides there were better things to look at; my father sat open-mouthed and wide-eyed as the girls showed their goods to neighbouring tables. I should have introduced the entire corps de ballet to him. He would have appreciated that. He may have secretly hoped these women would turn me into a red-blooded male.

Marcel and Louis both stopped by to share a drink. Marcel had a way with people's mothers, and ordered another bottle of bubbly. He was an approval suck and my mother, no different from anyone else who enjoyed being the centre of attention, responded. If anything could have devastated her that night it would be the vague connection between her own broken dreams and whatever the fuck it was I was doing. Soon a naked yet supple rear end got dangerously close to my father, and it was time to have Kent take them home.

"It's burlesque," I told them, breaking the silence, "like you'd see in a Parisian music hall." (I had no idea.) I shivered, waiting with them for a cab. Couldn't they just admit they'd had a bit of fun, even if it was at my expense?

"Nothing like it where we're from."

"You wanted to be a dancer," my mother said, as if she understood, more so than I, that this was part of the deal; satisfied that I would see the light as I dug myself out of this hole.

I shivered, rubbed the goosebumps on my arms, and watched the cab skid away. As I went back inside it struck me what made working in there tolerable: the touches, the smiles, the passing nudges, the pats on the back when I was exhausted at the end of the night or at the beginning of a shift. Mihalis winked at me as I squeezed past him.

As I looked across the smoke-filled room, busy and noisy now that alcohol had softened everyone up, I could easily have driven myself crazy if I had looked at this place, not to mention my life, with my parents' perspective. How could they ever understand a moment of my happiness, or one of my small victories?

After cabbing it home with the boys, and everyone getting tucked in, sharing the floor, the mattress and the foam, and dousing the flames of the one I may have had sex with on the beach, and taking in stride all of the lewd comments the others were making in the hopes of having a story to take home about a wild orgy with a stripper in Quebec City, I crawled in with Kent. The next morning the apartment looked like the end of Act One of *Sleeping Beauty*, with all the lords-in-waiting snoring up a storm in various stages of sobriety. Without disturbing any of my suitors, I called my parents who miraculously hadn't immediately left town, and met them for brunch at their hotel. On the phone my father said, "Don't bring him." Well that was fine because "him" was still asleep, after I had given "him" an early morning beneath-the-sheets morning glory while others slept on. I ran cold water on my head, tried to take down the swollen eyes of a deep, short sleep, stepped among the revellers, and headed over to the hotel.

We sat at a banquette and served ourselves Sunday brunch. I noticed their clothes. I had become so used to makeshift and second-hand and moth-eaten. They wore first-hand cashmere, wool, tweed, lovely new threads from stores where you could eat off the floor—

Holt Renfrew. I thought of that musty *rat sauvage* coat that I was so proud to find. After mopping up hollandaise with a bit of English muffin, my mother finally broke the silence. "Don't they have any self-respect?"

"Some of them are paying their way through college," I said, and it was no lie—there was at least one girl I knew of who would come down from Montreal one or two weeks a month and use the money to pay for her studies in anthropology. But I knew they didn't believe me; people had very specific ideas about strippers. I went on. "When you find what you really want to do, you'll do it, no matter the cost, even if no one offers support." I wondered if they made the connection. "Some are mothers. One is even pregnant."

"The shrimp salad is lovely," my mother interrupted. "Do you want another mimosa?"

"I'll coast."

"This room is really elegant. The French have such taste."

But I'm sure it was cookie cutter American Hilton. "It's nice."

"Now if you two excuse me while I powder my nose, you can get caught up."

After my mother excused herself, I felt no need to explain anything to my father, but I knew that he knew. In fact he probably imagined much worse. We sat in silence. All he could do was bite his lip and keep from asking the too intimate, *Are you happy*? "Don't worry about her," he said, then he smiled to himself.

"Any prospective residencies? How did your interviews go?" He knew what I thought of his so-called interns. They were always young and attractive. He raised his eyebrows, looked thoughtful, but didn't speak.

After long moments of playing with the stem of my glass, I watched my mother weave her way back to the table.

"Tonight should be fun," I said. "There will be fashion, press, lots to drink."

THAT AFTERNOON I PLAYED tour guide for them, on foot, exhausting them with walks up and down the narrow streets. There was a thaw, and we stepped over melting snowbanks and around puddles.

We finally stopped for tea at the Clarendon, which became drinks at the Clarendon, and out of the silence my mother spoke, "Kent seems nice." This was my mother's seal of approval for at least one part of my life. Nice people were important to her; it meant they would see her for the long-suffering good person she was.

"He is. He is a genuinely nice person." And for the first time in months, I felt proud of making a good decision. My father took a newspaper off a neighbouring table, looked down at it. Did he notice it was in French?

"Why is he here?" she continued. "Kent, I mean."

"Like me, Mom, it's a step along the way. He got tired of the direction things were going for him."

"It's a step? This is a step?"

"You'll see."

Later the two of them dined at the Chateau Frontenac—where once upon a time I had dreamed of being a busboy—while I got ready for the show.

THE MONTREAL MODELS DIDN'T like how much our group was drinking—with regular deliveries from the bar coordinated by Bichon and Sugar—compared to their one complimentary glass of champagne. But two drinks might have floored their fragile frames. They refused to share changing space and frankly, we didn't want to, after one of their light bulbs blew up because one of the model-idiots had thrown a wet facecloth on it. We were worlds apart. They were vapid, high heel chic, and we were barefoot in tribal wear and seething with drama. Nadine didn't show up, which put a hole in things, but we faked our way through Marcel's choreography exactly like all his other numbers: walk, walk, walk, turn, pose, *pas de bourée*, pivot step, pivot step etc. etc. etc. I wore one of Mer*la*'s leopard G-strings and a deafening and blinding crêpe paper lion's headdress, while the Amazons, Bichon and Sugar, stood over me in stilettos and latex. My father must have approved. Even I had trouble believing they weren't female. They didn't have to do much to pull focus.

Guy ambled like the sex god he was, as Tarzan in an eye-catching, jam-packed G-string and not much else, and used his prop—a papier-mâché spear—to accidentally (he said) draw my blood. By the look on his face he did register some surprise, but I had it coming to me.

Regardless of the fun onstage, the audience was too busy checking each other out to care. The seven bankers, eager for some fun, sat next to my parents, and my parents stared blankly at the runway in front of them, not knowing what the hell to expect. The time change, drag queens, drinks and dinner had all worked to slowly soften their composure: father probably pretending he didn't want to have a go at one of the tigresses or angry French models; both of them inwardly hoping that the other must be angry as hell that their only child turned out this way. Sadly, that concern combined with *What will our friends and neighbours think?* was their world. Were the Rottams cursed? Was I continuing to tarnish our name? Meanwhile, where was that waiter with the chartreuse 'tinis?

I pitied the three of us, stuck in the land of what was supposed to be. First grandpa, a gentleman farmer in the Wild West, betraying his name. Then Dad, turning perfectly good teeth into movie star fangs. And his disappointed wife, Barbie doll–perfect, surviving treacherous Edmonton winters by golfing in Phoenix. And lastly, a son who got the genetics all wrong, who loved being a man and loved having one. Had I done this to make their lives difficult? Was it a conspiracy? That's what the chartreuse was saying by the end of the night.

In the lobby bar at the Chateau—over Manhattans for me and my mother, and a double rye and ginger for Dad—with traces of cold cream and stray bits of mascara burning my eyes, I tried to put it all into black and white. "Once the show ends, I'll start auditioning again. I had some offers in Montreal but I didn't want to let Marcel down. Do you know that his mother danced in the original *Lido*? You should see their place. It's a palace. A shrine to kitsch. This has all been a great experience. Marcel is a great choreographer and Madame has given me so much. But it's time to move on." I forced an optimistic note.

"Those boys..."

"Yes?"

"Those friends of yours from Toronto."

"Yes," I said, thinking the inclusion of seven standard junior executives would finally present some legitimacy and hope to my life.

"They said they met you down south. When?"

My father conveniently excused himself "to settle up the tab, we have an early checkout."

"Oh, you know, a few weeks ago."

"Did you go with Kent?"

"No. Not really. No."

"Alone."

"I'm sorry I..."

"I don't blame you. I can't forgive you right now, but I don't blame you." My mother sipped her drink, then cleared her throat, changed her tone. "The Company was in town."

"Did you go?"

"Of course, well, I did. Your father..."

"Had to work late?"

"No. He had a conference to go to."

"What did they dance?"

"A mixed repertoire. I think we'd seen it before. You know, de Mille, Balanchine." She paused. "I was so sure I saw you up there." She cleared her throat.

Part of me desperately wanted to say I was sorry, and then wave my magic wand and go back to being in the Company, being the son she was proud of. But life wasn't like that. To say I was sorry would have been admitting defeat halfway through what had become a huge battle. The best I could muster was a reassuring, "Well don't worry about me, I'll be fine." Then I got them a cab and said I'd walk home to get some fresh air.

FROM THIS STAIRWELL I can say that I have become familiar with the stages of imminent death, and of a few of the stages following death. And when our big event was finished, it seemed that we had entered into a period of mourning that comprised of cloudy bad decisions, vague incomplete actions—trying to kill the beast quickly, but carelessly prolonging its suffering.

I CAUGHT UP WITH Marcel and the group at the Clarendon for a fun, funny and drunken moment—the way life should be. I heaved a huge sigh that my parents would be heading to the airport for an early flight. (I took great comfort in knowing that they would probably spend the next few weeks shaking off this experience with endless golf in Phoenix, and the past few days would end up being no more than a distant nightmare.)

Like all after-show parties, we behaved like self-centred brats. I showed Guy the mark from his spear, fumbling to untuck my shirt. Then, in bad drunken French I slurred something like, "Tarzan, what big tits you have—what a jaw—and that dick," and I shoved my hand between his thighs. Guy was from *petite ville* Quebec where they still had small-town manners, but with one beer too many he took my face in one big hand, squeezed my cheeks so my lips opened like a snap dragon, and when I thought he was going to snap my neck in two, he openly kissed me—hard and for all, including Steve, to see. He took his revenge, and I took my punishment like a man.

After hours of table-hopping, bathroom visits to pee the gallons of liquid imbibed—while others giggled as they inhaled, sniffed, snorted, dropped or tasted various substances—and more yattering, weeping and laughter, everyone faded. Familiar faces, Bichon and Sugar, kissed goodbye through tears and promises. It had been the kind of night I wanted the rest of my life to be—eternal irresponsibility—and so I asked Marcel in a haze of drunkenness to come back to my place for a nightcap.

We had the apartment to ourselves. The accountant-types weren't back. Kent wasn't home. It was too late to still be at the restaurant, so he must have been with someone. If he came in, he'd understand; once again I told myself he'd had his two thousand and I had to catch up. It was almost as simple as that. Almost.

Marcel and I stumbled onto the queen-sized foam. He kissed me and then made a kind of whimpering sound. And he was soft like his nature—the smoothest skin I'd ever felt. When you feel a body like that, you swear they never had it tough. No calluses on his hands, soft feet. Hadn't he danced? He was a true softie, hoping to be cuddled and coddled. As we lay there, he asked me not to tell François, whom he said he loved like a brother.

I guess I'd had big plans for that night. I wanted a grand finale, but as I touched Marcel all I could think of was Kent and of all the times I had touched him and how electric that touch was. I was sad that he was not home.

And yes, I know Kent taught me, *Sex is sex, and cock is cock*—but I'd say that when you finally get taken, and fall in love, it's the heart that really gets fucked. Without noticing, Daniel had come to resemble my warning flag against bad choices. He was a lesson in what not to do ever again.

THE PHONE RANG WAY too early that next morning and I noticed Kent was back in his bed-in-the-kitchen, snoring loudly—which meant he'd probably taken a sleeping pill or been very drunk—and Marcel had me in his arms. What *had* I done? I answered the phone and it was François. He knew Marcel had spent the night there but didn't suspect anything, since François was a good person, and good people don't suspect things. Someone sleeping in the kitchen, and seven on the floor, would be my alibi if pressed. "Can I speak with Marcel?"

"*Il dort encore.* He's still asleep. What is it? You sound flustered."

"Flustered?"

"Oh God, um, oh yeah, *enerver.*"

"Oh, yes, well I 'ave some bad news. Nadine, she kill 'erself. Last night. She wasn't at da *spectacle.*"

"No."

"Yes. She took pills."

Beautiful Rita Hayworth was dead because of a ten-year-old broken heart.

My head throbbed, Kent and Marcel both snored. I sat in the kitchen, made coffee and watched Kent. When would the running in and out of this place like it was a bus depot ever stop? Would we ever unpack and have a goddamn schedule? Would we die like Nadine before we had a chance to be sane with each other?

If I hadn't filled my life with these oddballs, I might have done the same thing to myself. Pills and booze. But most of the time I saw a death beyond my control, something more dramatic: sliding under a bus, freezing to death on the way to the club, having a stage light fall on my head, having a heart attack during pre-show sex. It would be *too* pathetic to die on that queen-sized foam matt on the floor in front of the sealed fireplace, at the foot of Kent's bed. It didn't have the prestige of dying of consumption in a Parisian garret. There, they had working fireplaces but couldn't afford wood. How about dying at the Chateau Frontenac in that Monroe-in-the-sheets pose? I could get them back for not hiring me for that busboy position. I could run a tab, stuff myself on room service, *Chateau-briande, Chateau-neuf du Pape, gateau de Chateau*, before doing the deed. I'd pre-choreograph the wake, down the street at Belle Époque. I had to at least give my parents' friends and relatives something respectable to utter behind their backs next Christmas. I didn't want to go alone like Nadine. I knew whose arms I wanted to be in.

THE REMAINDER OF THE shows seemed a battle against the gloom; we held a memorial for Nadine in the club a few nights later, and everyone arrived early. Bichon and Sugar wore black chiffon to cover their faces. In the concrete basement we lit candles, Marcel put André Gagnon on his boom box, and we created a little shrine with a photo someone took of all of us, surrounded by pieces of feathers and sequins. We took turns saying things about Nadine; some I understood, some I didn't. The girls who had worked with her for years were devastated. The rest of us were simply in shock. We all cried and then we laughed. I prayed the spirit of Nadine would know true love.

After that, all I could think of was the closing of the show. Bichon and Sugar would be gone. The world of the show would be a memory. Someone might ask if they didn't used to have a show.

I always say I'll see people again, to make the leaving not as painful. In this case it was ridiculous: I would never again see the bitchy Chaton in her tiny fun-fur bikini; my fan Suzette, the pregnant mother with a Harley escort; my driver Patrice; Mihalis the fit and Vasili the not-as-fit; and their stupid *parole*. They weren't showmen; they would still be there.

The second-last night of a run of any show, whether it's with a prairie ballet recital or with the Company, is always the toughest. I find myself blinking back tears and swallowing a lot, thinking that the final show will be the most difficult. It is always the second-last show that catches me by surprise.

Kent took the bus out to the Chez Moritz with me for the last night. I blinked my tears and stared through a reflection of snowy lights, not knowing where we were. I couldn't look at him when I spoke. "Can I ask you something—without starting an argument?"

"Shoot."

"Why did you bring my parents to the club?"

"That's been bugging you?"

I swallowed and spoke. "The truth did them good, I guess."

"Did you good."

"Why do you say that?"

"You were hiding. You still are. Afraid of the truth."

"Not again."

"I'm here to remind you."

"That's why you brought them?"

"No. No, I knew you would never introduce me as more than a waiter friend."

"It's that important to you?" For a moment I had a deep and searing feeling of belonging to someone.

"You're secretive. Gay is still gay out there in the real world, even though everything may seem fine and dandy in our little land of make-believe, bars, strip clubs, cafés. It's not a joke." He stopped as if something was caught in his throat. "Okay. To know you is to love you. I think your mother understands, but your father doesn't get it."

"You're a softie beneath that tough exterior."

"You know, in some parts of the world they have honour killings. Here they have no trouble with honour *ignorings*. Yes, I am a softie."

"I'm sorry."

"You have to be authentic to those closest to you."

"Stripping?"

"You're allowed a secret or two. What did they say about me?"

"It's important to you?"

"In some respects."

I knew then that what had been growing in me was mutual. "Nothing. My mother said you were nice." I could never tell him my father's request to not bring him along. "Nice means a lot in my mother's world."

"Hmmm."

"See, you're more than a 'waiter friend.' She knows that."

"So?"

"I know that, too."

That's mostly what I remember from that bus ride. I wonder now—hanging out at the fifth-floor exit—when it was I started to have an effect on him. I never asked him. But the fact that he was at my side, then, made the ending of the show at the Chez Moritz that much more bearable—as if he had been through all of it with me. And he had. "I can't believe you take that bus every night," he said, as we walked single file along the shoulder of the highway.

"I've only missed the stop once and it wasn't because I was asleep—I was keeping myself busy by making eyes at some guy. Imagine." When we finally arrived at the club they were all asking if Kent was *mon blond*, my *man*, since some of the girls recognized him from before. The girls, even Steve and Guy, most likely needed to believe there was something more to keep me company than my misguided ambition. I could see it in the way they looked at me—loners are intimidating.

The evening show felt similar to trying on an old, out-of-style, too small, never-to-fit-again pair of jeans. And we performed with less enthusiasm than corpses, with barely anyone in the audience to witness the dirge. Sugar's beau from Montreal, a machismo Latino who made his living as a lead drag queen in a big Montreal club, had come to watch. I made the mistake of thinking her guy was the miniscule hairdresser friend he had brought along. This put Sugar off.

If Bichon were a woman, I would have said she was on the rag. And the other girls were speaking in an angry, fast Québécois about a girl who got the boot for letting a client touch her. There was also an outbreak of "box rash"—severe goosebumps on anyone whose bum had come in contact with the boxes we used when stripping. At one point, all bent over, it looked like we were searching for a lost contact lens, when in fact we were examining each other's *derrières*. It was definitely not a love-in that last night.

Patrice hadn't talked to me for about a month. He'd long given up hope of a fruitful encounter and our drives had been silent, moody and dutiful. He made sure he got me home for the good of the show, that was it. He was the only performer not losing his job; he would continue to pull fake rabbits out of top hats while some new topless assistant posed like a deer in the headlights and held his props.

By the end of the third show, we were drunk, sad and forgiving, and after we'd all hugged for the nine hundredth time and a very patient Kent was looking exhausted and drunk, it was time to go.

Being drunk made this next part easier.

"What next?" Kent asked.

"I'm not sure. Maybe thinking of moving," I said.

"So you've thought about it? Maybe you could have shared it?"

"You've been busy."

"So have you. Where to?"

I had to swallow against a huge lump that was forming in my throat. "Toronto seems logical."

"I thought so."

"Really?"

"You'd be crazy to stay. I figured it was a matter of time. I ran away. You have to run, too."

"You want me to go?"

"Of course not."

"I've pretended all along that it hasn't gone to shit."

"Me, too. I should have put your ass on a bus way before now."

This bond was odd. What had brought us together, and made it not matter that his bed was now in my kitchen, or that I loved his fingers entwined in mine on the cab ride home?

"There are decisions I have to make on my own."

"So, what will you do?"

"More of the same, I guess."

"Strip or dance?"

"Only until I can get ahead..."

"Really?"

"It's what I am."

"Then it's a waste."

"Of course I want back in. But I may never be able to do it on the same terms again. It's hard. I've lost the keys to the kingdom. It may be too late." I was trying to get him to realize what the odds were, but my own words terrified me.

"I was locked out of something," he said.

"Your roommate beating you up doesn't count."

"You knew?"

"I figured it out."

"Well, not that." He swallowed, trying to stay on track. "Once upon a time I had been a pretty boy, someone's date. Some called me bumboy to the big city's finest."

"Finest?"

"Actors, dancers, writers, musicians, artists, you name it, politicians, too. Am I bitter and old?"

"No, of course not."

"You bet I am." He laughed.

"God, dancer's years and gay years—and dog years—have a lot in common. I have got to get a move on. I mean, we both do."

"So it's still about the career?" he said.

"What do you mean?"

"You still have your eye on that one thing."

"I'd like to find it again if possible."

"There's no room for inconvenience?" he asked.

"Depends." I felt his grip tighten.

"On?"

"Well, you could be an inconvenience and that might be okay, if you…"

"I?"

"Never mind." I tried to make out his expression as the streetlight and shadows flashed across us.

"I think I understand."

I couldn't bear the ensuing silence. "And?"

"We could be inconvenient for each other," he said.

"I guess that's what I meant."

"So I could come, too, when I get my things in order here."

"Why not now?"

"Henri's sick."

"You talk to him?"

"Real sick. Don't know if it's the clubs, the poppers, too much fun or his trip to New York—but now they're calling it gay cancer. I told you. It's not going away."

"The girls have chattered about it, but it seems as real as giant alligators in the sewer."

"It's real. It's very, very real."

"Are you scared?"

"I don't know. I don't understand it."

"I've never even met Henri."

"You might never."

"So you'd come back to Toronto, if … ?"

"He's moving home. He wants to die with his family. There's not much I can do. He has friends. Real friends. And I don't want to stay. I think I'm finally ready. I could go back if you were there."

We ended up sitting shoulder to shoulder in Kent's bed, in the kitchen. At four in the morning he showed me his photo album. Pictures of people he knew in Toronto and New York. Some he'd heard were already dead from the mysterious disease. But he was optimistic, as though my decision had given him hope to start out again. "It's time to go back."

"How long has it been?"

"About six, seven years."

"Who's the cute blond?"

"Me."

"You're joking."

"Don't sound so surprised."

"I meant, wow."

"Thanks. Anyway, one of the reasons I'm not there—mileage—sun—cigarettes—cigarettes especially—booze—partying. All the things that make life fun."

"You're still a knockout."

"To you. I was hot then. I'm not now. That's okay. That photo is about ten years old. I was such a bastard back then. A real bastard."

"A heartbreaker?"

"A fucking bastard. Still would be if I had your looks."

LOUISE AND BERTRAND CAME by the next afternoon. Kent was looking in on Henri and I was trying to catch up on sleep. The bell rang and out on the street Bertrand and Louise were looking up at my window. We met in the café. I ate my Québécois favourites, haven't had them since—*tarte au sucre* and *chocolat chaud*. I could tell this was going to be one of those conversations where everyone sits and bitches about Madame, but I had nothing left for Madame. "It's time to move on," I said. "I'm leaving, soon."

They sat with their mouths open, just staring. I wasn't sure if they were going to punch me or hug me.

"But you must," said Louise. "That is what I told Bertrand from the moment I met you."

"That I must move on?"

"It's her spirit. Madame's spirit will eventually crush someone like you."

"You think I'm weak?"

"Not at all. She is just incapable of recognizing your talent. You have so much to offer, but somewhere else."

I wondered about her scene in the studio lunchroom, but at that point none of us were behaving well. I didn't mention the end of the Chez Moritz, just let them believe I'd had it with Madame, half of the truth. I counted on my comments getting back to her. Louise held my hands. Bertrand squeezed Louise's hands. Through it all Bertrand had been so sweetly innocent and so focused. I regretted not spending more time with them in their uncomplicated lives. If Madame had paid us, then there would have been time for talking and tea and beer and sleep, I suppose.

Louise told me that Madame had hired the old English woman who had been teaching the beginner children and adults to teach company class, until things blew over. It was useless. Chantal and Maryse had refused to return. Then the new ballet mistress put Jean-

Marc's nose out of joint by pointing out that he was cheating his technique. It was true: he muscled his way through lots of things and looked great doing it, though too athletic, but that was why Madame liked him as a dancer. So Madame returned but, Louise said, had changed—from cruel masochist to indifferent victim.

"She made it clear from the start that she wasn't interested in me," I told them, but there was no look of surprise. "Look at me, je suis *Le Maudit Gai Grand Blond*. I remind her that she can't manipulate every single man." Bertrand didn't understand a word I was saying, but Louise laughed. Then Bertrand laughed and Louise and I laughed at him laughing and then we were all laughing at everything that struck us as absurd, which was everything. It seemed to me that I had single-handedly destroyed a young ballet company. Bertrand babbled like he had months before, when he was excited. Louise translated that Madame never had much to offer. She was a performer at heart, and didn't care about the true formation of a dancer. Then they dropped their small bombshell.

"We are thinking of leaving, too. Come with us. Edmonton has almost promised us places with their new company."

I'd heard about the new start-up in Edmonton, but being so close to my father's universe meant no margin for failure. "I'll think about it."

"Then Vancouver?"

"Haven't you heard of the green death? People don't go to the theatre when the sun shines, and when it rains they go shopping. If you have nothing original to say, Vancouver is fine. But you two are true stars. Why don't you come to Toronto?"

"Too many dancers." Bertrand mumbled and Louise continued. "He says it's either the National or something obscure and not very good. Edmonton is ready to offer us something good. It's a young company."

"What will Madame do?"

"She'll have Maryse, Chantal and her Jean-Marc. Though I think he won't be far behind."

"So much for her dream."

"It could have really been something. We both believed that."

"You will go far. If nothing else you have enthusiasm, and commitment, and you are so talented." It's strange but I wasn't jealous at all. I was genuinely happy for them. We hugged long and hard, and I went back upstairs.

When Kent got back he was drunk and weepy at me leaving. He climbed into his bed. "I drink too much," he said from under the covers.

"Too much what?"

"He's going to die. Henri is going to die. We all are. It's a gay disease."

"Henri's not going to die."

"It's too horrible to talk about."

"He has people to take care of him. He has his family. You're coming to Toronto if I have to drag you."

"What will I do?"

"You'll get a job. It sounds like you've got some connections."

"That's not funny."

"It wasn't meant to be. Look. I'll take care of you."

"I don't want you to go," he bellowed. I pulled back the sheets and kissed him and held him and we fell back to sleep as if that day had been one long, bad dream.

The next morning we had coffee and talked with the kind of optimism that gives a big move the momentum it demands. Kent told me about the friends he wanted to introduce me to. He bitched about the Cabbagetown queens, raved about Church Street, Bemelmans, the Beaches, the Island, Hanlan's Point, Buddy's, the Barn and the bathhouses—names of places that meant nothing to me at the time. And he insisted on being the one to give me that first-hand taste of the big city, after he settled things for Henri. So I packed my stuff and left Kent to deal with a flat full of furnishings.

I CALLED DENNIS, OF the famous group I'd met down south, to see if his *If you're ever in town…* was still available. He ended up offering me a room in his house, and that's where I decided to park my stripper's ass.

Nine

THE HEART OF THE dancer has four chambers that drive him from one side of the stage to the other, to each corner, into the air and onto the ground, force the dancer to catch up with the choreography, find the music, make the impossible possible, the earthbound ethereal, the fantasy a reality. It is the dancer's heart that becomes infected at some age. Catches the disease of dedication, addiction, of complete enveloping joy that blinds the dancer to any other way of being, and binds him by way of vibration within his limbs, to his dream. It can be a blessing that only finds its way out through steps danced, or a curse that finds its way out through tears cried, years later, at what might have been. Meanwhile the heart sets the rhythm. And in the end it's the heart that can be broken—not by hand, arm, leg, shoulder or knee—by less than a whisper.

WILL I FIND MY clothes after my twenty-flight stumble down the stairwell? Will someone run off with them once they crumple into some sad clump? Will I be forced to wander the streets of Toronto clad in a sheet, pleading my case: Toronto, the first part of it spent sorting out the Quebec months. I had a lot of time to think as I walked down Woodbine to the snow-and-sand-swept beaches and along the boardwalk where a painful wind whipped off that bleak stretch of Lake Ontario. Through Kew Gardens on a brief walk back to Queen Street, where overhead wires sang as the streetcars lumbered back and forth to the heart of the city. It became a regular circuit. I wondered, for a moment, about Daniel, but there was so little; no tears, no sentiment, nothing that would make sense in these new surroundings. A little resentment? Possibly. But all the Daniel feelings disappeared when I wasn't paying attention.

There was no Café Latin with *tarte au sucre*. No Belle Époque for a Brador, a glass of bubbly or a cup of tea at the Clarendon. No Kent smoking in my hallway.

No money, either.

I stayed at Dennis's house, a partly renovated little detached box. Other than the deafening squeal of the streetcars short-turning across the lane, there was nothing but a silence that had grown between us. He was seeing me at my worst while, I'm sure, hoping for a drunken romp. But it became a stilted life of suppressing coughs, silently opening and closing kitchen cupboards, and occasionally borrowing his food. I spent most of my time in my room, another mattress on another floor and rolls of wallpaper waiting to be glued to the bare walls. I stared out at the mess of wires—streetcar, phone, electrical—against the grey sky. God it was ugly. Was there any other choice for me? Did I just have to keep taking the path of least resistance? *Was this* the path of least resistance? How long would any of this last? Funny, the golden boy I was on the beach was now a pale, drawn, brassy-haired, petty, food-I-wouldn't-be-caught-dead-eating thief, no longer too good to be true.

I also spent lots of time and not much money at a donut shop near the racetrack, a stone's throw from Dennis's place. The backs of the tabloids that people left behind screamed sleaze. There were no ads for feathers, tits and sequins. Art was either highbrow or low. Ballet or bawdy. No burlesque.

Since my stripper skills exceeded my waitering ones, late one winter's day I finally decided to pursue an opportunity to start doing my *art* again. Open audition night at the Sultana was one streetcar ride, to the other end of the line, away. As I collected my crap strewn across the floor of my unfinished bedroom, the phone rang. It was Rachelle. She had gotten the number from Kent. She wanted an update. She sounded hurt. How could I begin to tell her? "I wanted to see you dance in Quebec." She told me she had moved to Toronto as well, and in the time it took me to become *Le Grand Blond*, she'd gone from soloist hopeful to a chubette, sewing costumes for the corps of the National Ballet. I told her my underwhelming news: "I've become an exotic dancer."

"Looks like we have some catching up to do," she said.

"You don't sound shocked."

"It's a popular choice for quitters. But you seemed more focused."

We arranged to meet at whatever coffee shop might be across the street from the Sultana. I didn't recognize her at first. She was right; she had traded her career for food. She had rosy cheeks instead of the standard sallow ballerina look, and there was a little double chin she was hiding with a scarf. She had given up the traditional bun tied tight enough to beat out a tune on her forehead. There she was, making it on her own in the big city. When I hugged her I realized how much I missed those who knew an earlier version of me. I knew I was starting to miss Kent, too, and the prospect of him moving here was my only mental escape. After the hugs and tears, and more hugging, she spoke. "We've separated. I left the bastard."

I figured this. "My God, you have tits; they'll make you top-heavy."

"You too, I feel biceps. Whoah, *quel horreur*. Destroy your line."

"My money-makers."

"Don't you love mine?" she said. "I never knew they were there. It's great. Guys look at me, I mean guys look at them."

"Me too!"

"I even have periods! But they're murder, I don't know how women do it—the rest of you looks like shit, by the way."

"I'm even worse in the daylight. I need a tan, someone to fix my roots. I feel fat. Doesn't matter. Funny thing is everyone flatters when they think there's a blow job in it for them."

"I've never seen a guy strip before. Not in public anyway. It's mostly the baby ballerinas who go down this nasty path. But you, my dear, are an original."

"Well, apparently you won't see any cock in Toronto the Good, I mean penis."

"Toronto the penis? Listen, cock's one thing I have seen lots of. Now penis, that's another story. God bless me."

THE SULTANA WASN'T IN any way like Quebec. It was childish. Naughty. Sleazy in an impersonal backroom kind of way. No Merla dropping by with costumes. No girls talking about broken hearts or love. No class, as in taste. No connecting. No cock (not legally anyway) to see in Toronto the Good. Rachelle looked bored sitting out there in a venue that looked more like a converted high school lunchroom than a nightclub. Everyone who danced that night seemed to have a pull-away tux, and they all looked like they were heavily into steroids. I suppose it made up for not being able to get completely naked. The lights hid the acne on their backs, but it couldn't hide the disproportionate Neanderthal shoulders that were the giveaway. And since steroids shrink the family jewels, it was just as well that the guys stayed clothed.

The night didn't go over well. I was distracted because I was sure something of mine would get stolen in the dark backstage. I had too much of an act. Too much dancing, too many tricks, and a very nice costume thanks to Brittany. I had come to rely on being naked as well, so the tease seemed pointless and contrived, kind of feminine. I had also lost confidence in my physique, and it showed. I couldn't pick my music and was stuck with Irene Cara singing "Fame," which made it downright comical, ironic and pathetic. Rachelle, God bless her, was the only one paying attention, so I went through the motions. Even so, the zipper stuck and I had to conceal the pain of quick hair removal. "You look like you had ants in your pants. Did they teach you that in Quebec?"

"Someday I'll tell you about that costume." I joined Rachelle and we drank, and bitched loudly about the old days until we were on the verge of self-indulgent crying. But something in that past didn't seem to matter anymore, for either of us.

"Why did you really leave?" I asked her.

"They kicked me out," she said. "Said I could come back if I started eating. Trouble is I did start eating."

"Coffee and cigarettes—the dancer's friend."

"And that Madame Kozachenko—'Eat red meat girls,' while I'm sure she's never had an honest-to-God bowel movement in her whole life. Screwy place. Her and Kharkov, Fric and Frac. Fuck. A dancer's age should be measured in light years." She dragged on another cigarette. "Our lives are so fucking short."

"Said Martha Graham."

"Well, they feel short."

Rachelle had ripened way too early. She had everything going for her—strength, flexibility, proportion—and like most people with all of those gifts, she took it for granted.

We ended up talking to this cute young guy. He had shown up, like me, to audition. He'd had a bad night, too; he was predictable and pretty featureless, physique-wise.

"I think they liked me." I couldn't believe he spoke these words. "This is the place to make it."

"I don't know. This place gives me the creeps. I've seen nicer church basements."

Up close he looked way older.

"This is my manager, Raquel." I looked at Rachelle, she immediately sat up, shoved her tits forward. I rolled my eyes. But then, why should I have assumed he was gay?

"Biltmore's is opening a backroom with male strippers only, for women—secretaries and working girls in the neighbourhood, open for lunches and after work." I could smell thick, old smoke on his breath.

"Thanks. Raquel, make a note of that."

"Don't forget to pick up your cheque." Then he left.

"The big city will finish him off," Rachelle said.

"It already did."

"Either that or he'll grow up real fast, end up working in..."

"The post office. I think he liked you," I said with a note of defeat. "Too bad we couldn't check out his weenie."

"He showed absolutely no interest in either of us. Very odd. Now you, my friend, have got to get back into class or you'll end up looking like him." Then she laughed, because he really did look like his only exercise had been walking to the bus stop.

"Give him a month on the juice and the city will be beating a path to his door."

"I'm not talking to you until you get back to class. Do you hear me? You did it before. Do it again."

"I'm having doubts."

"About?"

"Class."

"Oh brother, here we go. You can't not want to dance."

"What about you?"

"I had it too easy. I just did it. I mean I started when I ..."

"I know, I know. Right out of the womb. Everything is done from birth if it's going to matter."

"Not my point."

"Baby ballerina."

"I was a baby ballerina."

"I just want more. More than playing a role in someone else's ballet, you know. I'd like a bit more control over things."

"You want to be an artistic director?"

"Of course not, but something ..."

"Choreographer, like ..."

"Like?"

"Sorry."

"Sure. Maybe. Although the term has seemed so tainted recently, that I've tried not to consider it."

"Give yourself a chance. At least see what this city has to offer. This isn't it."

Rachelle was getting teary and drunk and I knew she wanted me to sleep over, wherever she happened to be living. Before we left I got the cheque, got the "Don't call us, we'll call you," from an indifferent bartender, and got out. We kissed on the sidewalk. She whined a little as I shoved her up the steps of the streetcar. She tumbled into a seat and *ding ding*, she was gone.

I WEIGHED RACHELLE'S SAGE advice, and then I headed off to the Biltmore Hotel. The guy was right about a male show. The banner above the back door announced the Shuter Street Shooters. The interviews were held upstairs in a dingy hotel room, curtains drawn, twenty-five-watt light bulbs, cigarette smoke suspended in layers like silken angel hair. For my audition, the obese manager watched me change *slowly* out of and into my costume, and after that he tried kissing my tight lips. It was like being blindsided by a mattress. He didn't get his hoped-for blow job and I didn't end up getting any decent weekend shifts. I had to laugh when all the other humpy applicants—full of themselves—showed up in the bar, post-tryout, looking like they had stomach flu.

I stripped for secretaries at lunch. We served them their food and then did our tease. They ate their burgers and fries while I slid around in my black scallop G-string, pretending it wasn't midday, trying to ignore the bright glare that shot through the room every time someone came in. There was no table dancing, but the customers could come up to the stage to stuff the lucky ones' pouches with bills. But every move by a spectator was weighted with self-consciousness. Unlike Quebec, which was reckless and intense, Toronto seemed to thrive on some kind of naive scandal. The audience was prudish; the customers watched us as if we were circus freaks. It felt as though we would all be carted off to jail any minute. It was the same looks I got from those English exchange students from Laval I danced for at the Chez Moritz, *How can they do this, compromise themselves, exploit themselves*? But we weren't even showing anything! I soon found out there was more showmanship in the men's shower at the YMCA. And any closet-cases who came in with their co-workers jumped hoops to pretend they didn't notice me. Meanwhile my neediness probably scared everyone off. One customer, equally as desperate, offered me a hundred bucks to have sex with him. But he wasn't my type. Too pretty. Too precious. Too petite. It would have been like sleeping with a lawn ornament.

One lunch hour I hadn't made a nickel. Meanwhile cheers were coming from the big front room where the females stripped, on the other side of the kitchen. Brigit Bar-None, a queen-sized stripper, was featured. The front room was usually packed with construction workers having liquid lunches watching a series of dancers who looked identical, from their big hair and waxworks features to their perfect tits. I called them silicone bombshells; nothing like the variety there had been in Quebec. Once the hollering had died down, Brigit Bar-

None, cleverly held together by a fishnet body stocking, strutted into our backroom. She pointed to me and then waved me to the side of the stage. I shimmied over, and she shoved a five dollar bill down my pouch and gave my nuts a healthy squeeze and smiled, wrinkling her nose like she'd done something naughty, then looked back at the audience. What a talent. Some customers followed her lead, and I cashed in that afternoon with a bunch more bills around my waist.

After that I had a deal with one of the regular girls (another dancer gone wrong) in the front room, who pitied me. I'd give her a tip if she came in between dances and put money down my string (money I gave her for the task). Nine times out of ten, it got the crowd going. But as soon as the manager caught wind of it, we had to stop.

Later that week, one of the secretaries (the one with the guy who made the hundred-buck offer) waved me over and asked if I would dance for her friend Margaret as a birthday present at her work. With ghetto blaster in one hand and my costume in the other, dripping with sweat after one crowded subway and two buses to Scarborough, while the temperature outside dropped and the temperature on the last bus had poached us and fogged the windows and drooped my bangs, hindering my search for visual cues like the storefront or a street sign, I took a chance, exited and ran through streaming traffic to an open strip mall. In a flower shop I found the infamous friend, Margaret, busily wrapping a bouquet in cellophane. "Are you Margaret?"

She nodded.

I got to work. The girls joined in, as did a cute little flower-arranging fairy. He was busy pretending to the girls he didn't really care for this (who did he think he was fooling?), while making sure to catch my eye. And then there was another party happening at the same time, in his pants, which helped. I stared down at the women as I rubbed my thighs, my ass and my chest, but quickly my eyes caught the reflection of something in the far mirror—my body—and I saw just how much of a fucking ghost I had become. For a moment I thought my reflection was a side of pale beef hanging from a hook.

My toes curled on the cold concrete. My pale skin rose in goosebumps, and my yellow hair flew with static. As far as I could translate, I was no longer *Le Grand Blond*, just *le pâle jaune*. My clothes lay in a clammy pile under the table. And there was nowhere to change from flower-shop stripper back into guy-on-a-bus. As I forced my damp T-shirt back over my head, the little florist whispered to me, asking if I would dance at his boyfriend's birthday party. He tried so hard to play it straight in front of the Scarborough girls. He scribbled his name and number on a gift enclosure.

TWO WEEKS LATER I walked through an old neighbourhood called Cabbagetown, a place gradually being transformed into perennial gardens surrounded by ironwork fences separating red brick homes. The flower boy's house was narrow from the outside, but yawning, open, new, all brick and bare wood, high ceilings and higher price inside. He squealed when he opened the door and said he'd told everyone all about me. In the two weeks since I'd danced at the flower shop, the little flower guy had invited every homo in Toronto.

To make things worse, he mangled my tape and I had to strip to his music—Marilyn Monroe singing, "I Want to Be Loved by You"—which most likely ended any future bookings with this crowd. If music can go wrong when you strip, it will. Since I had nothing to lose and he held the envelope with the cash in it, I let the little guy act out his fantasies on me in his bedroom while everyone sang "Happy Birthday" to his much cuter boyfriend downstairs. Yes, it was sleazy, but I felt like I wouldn't get my cash if I didn't do this encore. Then he told me how *nice* I was. Maybe the birthday boy would be looking for his own fun somewhere else. "I actually have a dance background. I just do this for fun," I said as I did up my pants. I tried to brush it off as a trifle, hoping he'd spread the word that this wasn't my chosen career path. Fun.

He squeezed my knee. "My boyfriend is a dancer," and his eyes twinkled with something mischievous. Who isn't? I mean people say stuff like that and it turns out they square dance once a month or are taking weekly tango lessons at the local community centre. Besides, a dancer with this house?

"Can I write you a cheque?"

"Sure." I couldn't tell him that a week waiting for it to clear was a pain. "John Rottam."

"Sexy name. Kind of good for a stripper."

THAT WEEK KENT CALLED. He had finally arrived in Toronto and said he'd found "us" a place through an old friend—over on Palmerston, a wide, lazy, tree-lined street with big, old brick apartments and houses. I was out of that work-in-progress place in a flash since Dennis, Mr. Vindictive Fag, had taken to spreading the word to everyone that I was paying the rent by stripping. I'm not sure if there was anyone left in the city who didn't know about me.

Kent and I picked up where we left off—in a big, old apartment on the ground floor of a building that looked like a castle, and to make things even more perfect, it had a working fireplace. I knew I belonged. After work I'd crawl into bed with him, and not just because he had a new queen-sized bed. I noticed recently that he was so warm beside me, and he had started sweating in his sleep. He snored, too, more if he'd been drinking lots or had a joint. But he'd put his arm around me to caress me and I'd eventually fall asleep.

No matter what he'd done the night before, he'd already be up and out looking for work when I woke. It was when we finally had time for a meal that he tried once again to talk me out of stripping. "Now that we're back in the real world," he said, "maybe you should have a real job. Did I tell you that you have a gift?"

"Not since you got to Toronto."

"Promise me you'll get your shit together."

"Not fair."

"Exactly."

When I was taking off my pants at Biltmore's, he was out at the Manatee or Boots or Buddy's. Drinking. Cruising. Every night. Recuperating, I guess, from pounding the pavement. Trying to relive his past. What were we doing? A few days later, on a Saturday afternoon, our paths crossed in the waking world, in our living room. "What do you do there?"

"Drink beer. Talk."

"Get laid?"

"God, no. I'm not going to go home with just anyone. That would be a commitment."

"So you…"

"The bathhouse, a backroom, whatever. I like to see the goods up front, not wait until I'm trapped on the twenty-second floor in some psycho's apartment."

But I'd seen the pictures of the people he loved in that album, with him looking so good, and I knew he had way more capacity for love than I ever would. Some of them came over. We'd sit around the coffee table in the living room, drink wine, pass a joint. Some of them seemed put off by our friendship. One woman, Ruth, took to me more than the others. She had a ruddy, freckly complexion. She had worked with Kent in the old days. I remember the night a few of his gang were over when Ruth and I were alone in the kitchen, and she confessed, "I'm glad you brought him back. You make him feel special. It's not easy being a former golden boy."

"I'm glad he came back, too."

"I think you make him feel attractive."

"Well, he makes me feel that way."

"I used to think, I mean hope, I could convert him." She laughed.

I started to see what it was that made him click. I saw how much he needed the people who were in his life. They didn't take friendship lightly.

Kent and I drank tea the next afternoon and the world stopped for a few minutes.

"Job prospects?" He wouldn't give up.

"I have to keep going to Biltmore's—for the money," I said.

"You can't wait tables like…"

"A normal person? This is easy money compared to waiting tables. Besides I'm a shittier waiter than stripper. Anyway, what I make is nothing compared to other guys working up on Yonge Street, getting blown on the floor and making some decent cash. At least I have my standards." He chuckled, but I'd lost my stamina to argue.

"Look," Kent continued, "I'll make you a deal. You stop stripping nights and I'll pay your rent. How's that? I want you to start dancing again."

"Now you're hitting below the belt."

"You have no excuse anymore."

Again I saw it, the need linked with the ability to dance, is a curse and a blessing, without a doubt the most wonderful feeling a person can experience. True, I had started to miss it. Nothing offered the absolute satisfaction, while demanding everything of me. Perhaps that was what being an artist meant. For those of you who take this path, I am warning you, you can never quit dance. It may turn its back on you or you may turn your back on it, but if art doesn't find its way out, it will eventually kill you.

I took Kent up on his offer and started trading the night shifts to get caught up on my sleep. I wasn't sorry to let them go; weekday lunches were better money-makers than weeknights, and I stopped feeling like I lived at Biltmore's. I bit the bullet and used my tip money to show up for morning class with Rado Zaitsev, the former Russian superstar and infamous alcoholic resurrected as a mediocre character dancer, but superb teacher with the National (and Kent's former short-lived sugar papa). Then I started swimming every afternoon with a group at the Y. We'd all competed at some point and every afternoon we were intent on keeping up the competition.

Soon all that I had lost as a dancer and as an athlete started to return and fill up my limbs once again. I regained my competitive spirit. I felt myself start to climb across the surface of the water again. My thighs screamed against the water's resistance, but gradually they propelled me. My feet stretched until they cramped. My back and shoulders settled. I took it all into class with me. I finally started to feel firm again. I started to get to know my body the way I had before.

I started running, too, but had to stretch for ages after to get back the flexibility. I ran in bare feet on the indoor track. I needed to feel the ground, my calves, and the soles of my feet. I found a nearby church turned into theatre and used the basement to practise endless turns and *tours en l'air*. I didn't force my turnout anymore. I fought against the Company's ideas about technique that made no sense, and found my own truths, and I felt myself become a strong, solid dancer. But it was a different body I was occupying now. It was a place (a temple?) that had been tampered with, explored, discovered and perhaps conquered.

Initially I was afraid I would be laughed out of the studio, but I knew that my steady progress was not going unnoticed. Zaitsev was a man's teacher; he knew the breadth a man had to dance. He wasn't about to force my turnout for aesthetics. He knew that jumping and turning came from the power in the trunk, and a solid landing, and that the audience couldn't give a shit about forced turnout. My enthusiasm spread to the point that I convinced Rachelle to come downtown on Saturday mornings for class, and more time afterwards for coffee and catching up. "There's a little earthy place off Yonge Street, just below Bloor where a tall, stunning redhead woman makes killer cappuccinos. You can treat me."

"Do they have muffins?"

"The size of grapefruits."

"It will be like old times. Remember? Post-Company class? The Barbeque Restaurant. Bran muffins like ..."

"Chocolate. Cinnamon buns like ..."

"Fucking Volkswagens, they were so big." I knew talking about food would get her out of the house. Our *petite rendezvous* became a routine.

"Kharkov was so glad to see the back of you," she said.

"Many are."

"Disappearing, I mean."

"He, along with everyone else, thought that you and Peter were an item. He's made Peter's life hell since you left. Poor Peter, he doesn't know if he's a lady's or a man's man. He's not Kharkov's, that's for sure."

"Has he got his shoulders under control?"

"Yeah, but when I left he was doing something funny with his feet."

"He fits the mould."

"That, he does."

FOR WEEKS ZAITSEV PAID attention to me and gave me every reason to think I could get it back—the shouting, the way he handled me physically. My strength and balance had really started to return, in my quads, my arches, my obliques, and I believed I was starting to look and feel really fine again. Then, one day in the middle of an arabesque—one of my strongest, most stable, most stretched and extended—my work and his dedication went down the drain with a nasty, "You're too old," and a swat on my calf sending me off balance. And that was all he could offer—that and a "Don't waste any more of my time."

Everything stopped. He had said the worst that could be said. He had spoken the dance god's truth. Not "You're a klutz," or, "You have two left feet." Those you can rationalize. You can't fix "too old." It's permanent and I may not have taken it to heart if I had started dancing when I was two. Despite my self-critical eye, I knew that what he saw was a perfect arabesque, and for some reason it pissed him off. Was he jealous? Did he know I was living with Kent? Perhaps Zaitsev thought I'd be nipping at his ankles for all those cliché character parts they'd given him. Every odd thought crossed my mind. This country has lost so many fine dancers, and created a generation of those more determined than ever to do it their way, all because of the collective nasty temperament and paranoia that has been passed down through generations of angry, frustrated, miserable, unfulfilled so-called perfectionists. I needed thicker skin.

That very small hope I had nursed, that he would take enough of a liking to me to somehow get me onto the radar at the National, dissipated. All I had was the last of a dead dream to belong to something great, with one and a half regional companies to my credit.

In the afternoon Kent and I met at a coffee place on Church Street with more gay guys than I'd probably seen in my entire life. He'd had two job offers, one as the manager in a café, part of a small chain, and the other as a career counsellor at a local college.

"I think it's time you get off your knees, I mean feet," I told him, and he smiled. He was so ready to sit on his ass for his paycheque. After this, I put my typical damper on things by telling him my news. "I've blown everything—except Zaitsev—to be told I'm too old."

"Maybe he can tell that to Martha Graham. Quoting you, by the way."

"I mean, too old for what?"

"Whatever it is you wanted?"

"Where are all the ones who said I'd make it?"

"Look, what the hell do you want? Stardom? Artistic fulfillment? Even I am starting to wonder."

"I've been dancing really, really well. You know that. I think I'm actually better than when I left the Company. I mean what the fuck? How much longer are you going to pay my rent?"

Kent rolled his eyes. "Do you want me to tell you Zaitsev's jealous? No offence, but I doubt it. He is like that with tricks; playing one off against the other. Just persevere. Take whatever he has to offer, as a teacher. The worst that can happen is he kicks you out. And he's not the only one teaching in this city. Now answer my question. Stardom or fulfillment?"

"I can't believe you were his bumboy. You're practically famous."

"Don't change the subject."

"You've made your point. I'll have to think about it." I hadn't forgotten how, that chilly night back in Quebec, Kent had taken the wind out of my sails by asking what I had to offer as a dancer. It continued to haunt me.

"In the meantime, my advice is to just keep doing your thing. A river or stream always manages to find its way…"

"…to the bottom."

"Just don't sleep with him."

"I'd still be too old."

"That's what happens. Look at me now, look at me then."

It was funny that in this ghetto where every man seemed attractive, and obsessed with aging, we could laugh at the superficiality of it, even though we were whole-heartedly under vanity's spell.

"Someone probably told him I was a stripper."

"He likes to take credit for discovering new talent. You…"

"Old, like he said."

He continued. "I need to talk to you."

"Is it the dishes in the sink? The candied chicken livers I burned? I'll get you a new frying pan."

"I don't care about the pan."

"I promise I'll clean it, even if it takes dynamite."

"We'll throw it out, get a new one."

"I'll pay for it."

He sighed loudly. I'd exasperated him. I figured living with me would end up being a trial. "Remember Quebec?" he said.

"Again?"

"Remember Henri?"

"Has he died? I'm sorry I didn't even ask I've been so wrapped up…"

"He died before I left."

"Why didn't you tell me?"

"I didn't want you to think…"

"You cared?"

"I have a problem."

"Well, he's dead, so you can't owe him money. Sorry."

"With him, I drank, a lot…"

"You still do."

"I thought I was just a big drinker, but it's not that." He paused. "Oh, what the fuck." He nibbled on a hangnail and then leaned forward. "My name is Kent and I'm an alcoholic. Okay? Get it? I mean you know me. You know my beers before dinner, after dinner, before sex, after sex…"

"During sex."

"Before bed."

"That's alcoholism?"

"I can't do evening hours without it."

"You fooled me. I honestly didn't notice. I always figured beer was harmless—now rye and Coke and my parents, there's boozin'."

"If I've acted strange, I'm sorry. I don't want to hurt you. You know, do something bad that I'd blame on the booze."

"Have you just decided this? Do we really have any evidence?"

"It's why I left Toronto in the first place. I used to get messy, every night. No one would talk to me. It got worse with Henri. He was a mean drunk. But it's brought out something in me."

"Does this explain New Year's?"

"It's become an every night thing. Every single night now, I can't relax without that first beer. I think that's what made him sick. I'm thinking that's what did it."

"But you don't seem..."

"Like one?"

"What can I do?"

"Nothing. I just wanted you to know. It started here. It's got to end here. I've started the meetings. Last week. Lots of meetings, for now. Just telling you is a big help."

I didn't tell him about my own dependency—on him. I didn't want to scare him or make things weird between us, or make him feel any more responsible for me than he already did. I felt like we had turned into some kind of old married couple who just did our thing without even noticing it. Someday we would celebrate it. I looked around the café at the other men. I felt for the first time like a couple, like there was a bond so strong between us it could never be broken, and I felt like everyone could see it. I took his hand in mine and I felt proud.

During those next few weeks, Kent attended meetings every night, and I decided that if we were ever going to make love using all our faculties I'd have to make an extra effort. I bought myself a dildo, I mean a sexual aid, that was about the size of Kent, I reckoned, and I practised with it every night after a warm bath. The initial pain was almost unbearable, but it got easier if I imagined Kent inside me and fantasized about what our first time would be like. I wanted this to happen. I had started to feel sexual with my changing physique. I actually felt more sexual than I had in ages, maybe ever. Knowing how he looked at me made me feel that way. I wanted to be enjoyed by him while I enjoyed him. I spent the evenings looking forward to our sleeps in that big bed—looking forward to fitting into our spoon shape, him curled around me, his fingers instinctively groping me while he slept.

The meetings helped. The bravado and prowess that I associated with him must have been the booze, because it vanished. He was all there now. Authentic. Consistent. Fewer cigarettes even. We shared the odd joint. He was less fidgety. There was a sensuousness about him. As if he had slowed down enough for me to see him, appreciate his crooked smile, his stubby fingers on a coffee cup, his sad eyes.

After several prolonged sessions with my vibrating plastic friend, I made an offer. It was after he arrived home from his meeting. I was feeling sexy and limber and lean. It was something I never thought I'd enjoy, but soon I found it, that feeling, the fabled prostate G spot that was so real and so pleasurable, that he had found months ago when we were together. I told Kent I had a present.

"Don't do this for me."

"It's for us." He was extremely sensitive and gentle, but the fact that he was so horny, and horny all the time, made it that much more fun. Although it took ages for me to relax and feel comfortable every time, we always ended up *enjoying* it. Something about the prolonged effort made him even more excited. Soon it was full-fledged mentorship (so *that's* why fucking feels so good, so *that's* my prostate). In the dark, in that hot room, he was over me. My feet stirred the air above me, or he would grasp them like he was at the helm of a ship holding the wheel, or he'd hold my legs by the ankles like a bound, captured animal. And in the shadows and the motion I saw a hint of his younger self, that sharp, devilish look that had made him so alluring.

One night, afterwards, as we were lying across each other in our customary tangled mound of limbs, he spoke. "It's like playing, isn't it?" But I was still an apprentice. I wondered if I would ever really be in control of my own pleasure. I knew it was only because of him that I was able to enjoy it.

After we got more settled we'd refer to the fun French times in Quebec, like an old couple talking about the good old days. "I 'ad to walk t'irty kilometres t'roo da blowing snow and minus-forty centigrade, to get to da strip club in time for my nightly blow job, before I waved my—how you call it—my dick in some woman's face, 'osti, you kids 'ave it so easy nowadays."

And he'd say stuff like, "Do you remember so and so?" as if I had been there for the whole time with him, when he'd always had his own life going on in Quebec.

I started to show up at his work, after class or after my lunch shift and we'd catch up on every minute that had passed since we'd last seen each other. Some nights, after his meeting, he took me out to

the clubs like he had in Quebec. He didn't feel the need to be anaes-
thetized. I did, but I'd sip a beer, and he'd have tonic water. We'd stay
in the dark and sometimes neck, or check out the parade of guys and
talk about taking one of them home.

"How about him?" he'd say.

"Too young. I like them older. You know."

"As old as me?"

"Experience turns me on."

"I guess we have complementary tastes. I like them young. Like
you."

Most of the time we left together. Once, he took off for a quickie at
the bathhouse, a sore point for me, but it was becoming rare. He said
he liked to sit in the dark and in the steam. For him it was a complete
escape from the real world—he wasn't looking for much more than
that and the odd thrill—but he admitted that it killed him to see me
go home alone.

After a few weeks of moaning about the bomb that Zaitsev had
dropped, I decided that it wasn't going to stop me. Other dancers wit-
nessed the jab and told me he was full of shit, and that it wasn't the
first time. At about the same time, I overheard that DDT was holding
open auditions the following week. They were looking for a classic-
ally trained male with modern dance experience. I thought I stood a
chance, in fact more of a chance than anyone I had seen recently. One
of the Company's pillars had been the investment they made in modern training to keep their repertoire broad. Graham contractions, Ail-
ey lunges, Taylor, Cunningham, Limón, Tharp choreography. Corner
to corner. Shoulders to the side. Hips to the front. Breathe low, from
the solar plexus. A modern dancer could last as long as the best of
them. Your weight travelled through muscles and bones, solidly into
the floor. It was the function first, then the form.

It was a Friday morning when I went to DDT's studios in the heart
of Cabbagetown. I walked by that same house where I'd stripped
and had humiliated myself weeks earlier. At DDT, other dancers were
stretching on the studio floor, checking out the competition. I saw
some familiar faces from class, and was eager to show what I could
do. I took my place and am able to say I looked good in the mirror.

The panel was comprised of three men—at least one I recognized, and the other two seemed familiar, but how would I know anyone from anywhere? Yes, of course, the birthday party. I suppose at that moment I could have either left, or stripped, but I persevered, trusting their professionalism. A female regisseur called out the floor barre and then the choreographer, the one who had been the birthday boy, showed us the choreography.

That day, I flew across the studio. I found that any anxiety had turned to absolute joy. I was dancing again. I was in the floor with control, steadfastness, and I felt beautiful. I was everything I had learned up to that moment, from ballet to Brittany. My fear at being misread collapsed and reinvented itself as an egotistical look-at-me-and-what-I-can-do in a joyous ecstatic burst of energy. I led the class from the front, from the back, from the corners, no fear, and soon it became clear that I was leading the battle.

When the audition ended, and we were all changing in the hallways, one of the assistants came over and whispered to me to stay behind. Some of my classmates looked up at me and smiled or winked. As if the whole room was with me. I was taken to a room where the artistic director, the regisseur and the choreographer waited. They smiled. They were nervous. We were all giddy. I sat on my hands.

"I enjoyed the class."

"Thank you. We could tell. It was obvious, and refreshing. We'd like you to work with us," said the choreographer. He looked at my eyes, not my crotch. "John Rottam, we'll have a contract ready for you on Monday."

That was it. Everyone had left by the time we finished talking. Only me left with my glory. I waltzed down Winchester to Parliament. I wanted to explode. With my feet off the pavement, I flew. Fuck! Finally! After all the shit and mess-ups. This was it. I couldn't wait to tell Kent. I called him at work and at home but there was no answer.

It was early Friday afternoon, and after Rachelle stitched her last tutu of the day, she joined me for celebratory drinks at Bemelmans, both of us feeling superb at last, both with real jobs—*and* in the big city. I would be part of a privileged elite of artists who were the heartbeat of that city. It was a superb feeling. I made a detour on the way home and stopped in at Biltmore's to tell the fat fuck I quit, only because I hoped there might be a paycheque to be had, which there wasn't. Otherwise, I just wouldn't have shown up ever again.

When I got home I called out for Kent, looked for a note or something on the table, for a message to meet him somewhere after his AA. My mind raced with the options for celebration. Ginger ale? Perrier? Great food to make up for no booze? The answering machine blinked and when I pushed play there was woman's voice telling me to call Toronto General Hospital. I was put through to a wheezing voice punctuated by heaving breaths I didn't recognize on the other end: "I... was... just... walking... down... Church... and... I... couldn't... breathe... fell... on... a... car... ambulance... came... I'm... okay... now."

I got to the hospital with minutes left before the end of visiting hours and looked for Kent. I was sober now and my energy tumbled from the highs of the day. I was so ready with my good news about the audition but there he was, eyes closed, wearing an oxygen mask. I reached under the sheet and held his hand, his rough fingertips that had tickled me so often. He dozed and I couldn't figure out how he was, or what was happening. Soon he came around and tried to talk. "I've always loved you—you know—the way it is now, what we have—us—that's the way I dreamed it."

"Please don't talk."

"I thought it would be like that. Just like that, from the first time I saw you. When I saw you in Quebec. When you opened the door to your place. I bet you didn't know that."

"Mother warned me about men like you." Maybe she had. I tried to laugh. "I love you, too. I think I love you the way you love me—I wanted to tell you when I got back from down south but I didn't want to cramp your style. I was afraid you'd be scared off, not know what I meant. I was so anxious to see you."

"It all comes out now."

"Someday we can go there together. Down south. When you're better."

"When I'm better."

We sat there for a long moment holding hands while the rush of the rest of the hospital passed by the door. I leaned in close. "Hey, don't get excited now, but I love it when you you-know-what me. Wait. That sounds bad. I mean it feels great physically, but what I mean is that to have you in me is…"

"You mean, *fuck* you?"

"*Sodomize* please, we are in a hospital."

"You're killing me. Sodomy's for churches, anal intercourse is for hospitals."

"Feeling whole. I feel whole. You know." He looked so peaceful when I said that. His faced relaxed as if I'd said the magic words. "Oh, something else… DDT wants me."

"You really are trying to kill me."

"That means I can't say *cock* anymore, at all, ever again. It's always *penis* from here on in."

"I knew you could do it. I… knew… it."

"Don't talk. Once you're better we'll celebrate. Tomorrow?" We had talked so much about the past, our shared past and our private ones. It was now time to talk about the future. "We can make plans."

He squeezed my hand hard. I hoped that he knew I had broken the curse. I could go back into the world of the artists and creators. Things could only get better. "Look, I brought you Nelligan. I'll read to you tomorrow."

IN THE MORNING I woke, my head in his lap, my neck stiff, and the nurses had already gotten to work around us. It took me a long, incomprehensible moment to realize I had been wrong. Things could always get worse; Kent had died sometime in the night and I cursed myself for having said I hated goodbyes. Even with the life gone out of him, he looked so peaceful, as if the ravages of the years were held at bay for a few more moments. The nurses said it was some kind of new pneumonia that they couldn't control. He had likely suffocated or something. I wanted to hate myself at that moment for letting the universe see how much joy there had been in my life for those few moments the night before—too much. That morning I sat—curtains pulled around the bed—with his body for hours, and wept, and dried my eyes and wept and wept and wept, until the nurses told me they needed the bed. They had called his family and he'd be kept in the morgue until they arrived. I left, and something about the clear sky said that there would be nothing, nothing at all to give me comfort. I sat in Queen's Park while traffic whirled, uptown and downtown, around me, and I cried. I cried so much that I felt as if my ribs would collapse. I hoped that from somewhere he could see me. I hoped he was there on the park bench with me. I wanted to believe anything and everything. I thought that crying about Daniel had been the ultimate broken heart and the depths of emotional despair, but I had been wrong. This pain was the kind that you curse the universe for; it's the kind you say you had never agreed to as part of your life.

From Queen's Park there was nowhere to go. My day was spent looking for places, small spaces next to dumpsters or vacant lobbies where I could crouch, pretend I was tying my shoe, and then cry. I had never cried that way, where the breath is gone, and the sobs shake your back. I had lost my frame of reference, my anchor and my reason for being. Not much made sense. I phoned Rachelle, tried between sobs to tell her what had happened.

"I wondered why you weren't at class this morning. I really missed you." But she couldn't say much about a man I said I loved, whom she had never met.

I called Kent's family when I got home and they told me they didn't want a service. Nothing. As though they were suffering more from embarrassment than from grief. Were they afraid his friends might show up at a funeral?

I called Ruth, and after the silence she came across as so much more together than what I was trying to be. She more or less took over. She wanted the parents' phone number. "Don't worry," she said, sniffing and blowing her nose into the phone. "I've done this before. There will be a funeral even if it's over my dead body."

The family had gone ahead and made their arrangements and that day everything that was Kent, including his bed—our bed—was taken by a relative with a truck. I stayed in my room and nursed a killer headache. When they were gone, I was left with that book he had shown me, of his friends, and the frying pan I never washed. I never did.

That night Rachelle came over and we lit a candle for Kent and then she smoked some of a joint I had found on the mantle while I drank a six-pack. Rachelle was quiet for a while and then she started to cry, too, mourning her own separation. "I never met him," she sniffed. "He must have been a great guy. I admit, I was a bit jealous."

"I thought we'd have a laugh. You would have liked him. He would have liked you. I wanted you to meet."

DDT seemed like a far-off victory by then. I made an effort that weekend to tell myself that our dream was finally coming true, and that anything I did for myself was for our dreams.

On Sunday, the rain uncovered piles of black snow, but I rode the streetcar out to the Beaches anyway. I needed to get out of the empty space that was no longer us. I needed to walk and walk. The tears flowed silently as I looked out the window. My nose was getting raw from wiping it, and when I got to the beach I let go and blubbered like a baby, since no one could hear me.

Monday morning I phoned DDT, told the woman who answered that it was "the new kid in the company," and asked what time company class started. The secretary told me 10:30. When I arrived, the artistic director and the secretary met me at the door. They were there to welcome me, no doubt. So this was what my new life would be like. Something of the ease and the respect of being a true professional again. I told them briefly and quickly about Kent, that later in the week I needed to go to the funeral, when I knew the details. It would be close by, I assured them. It was a bitter sweetness, and sad as I was, I wanted to believe he was right there, close by, cheering me on.

The three of us stood in the cold for several minutes, them only in shirts, and I was wondering why we weren't going in. The director started to say something about a misunderstanding while the secretary looked at me with a forced sympathetic wrinkled brow. The director said I had referred to myself as the new kid in the company but that they merely wanted me to start taking class in their junior school. Once they had broken through my delusional cloud, I was overwhelmed with the feeling they were hiding something. Politics perhaps? I remembered our conversation quite well, and there was nothing about signing a contract to take dance class; that audition had been on the lips of every dancer within a hundred-mile radius of downtown Toronto, and it wasn't to take class in the junior school. The proof was right there in the newspapers.

Can we talk politics? Can we talk competition? Nepotism? Who went down on whom over the weekend to turn my world on its head? Was it my indiscretion at the birthday party? I was baffled and speechless. There I was, back on Parliament Street on a Monday morning without a job. My fortunes were almost laughable.

I walked along Wellesley as the traffic shunted by, until I got to that coffee shop where we had felt so comfortable.

I had to find a reason to continue.

THERE IS A MOMENT during a funeral, and if you aren't too caught up on your own grief you will see it—the mother, shamed in life by her gay son, approaches the altar and takes up the picture of him his friends have placed there. She holds the picture, looks at it, wonders if she ever really knew him, wonders if she ever let herself know him. Wonders if she knew him too well and denied it, to herself and others. She realizes in a split second that there really was nothing more keeping them at a distance than her own ignorance. You'll see a tear run down her cheek when she realizes her grave mistake.

RUTH HAD ORGANIZED SOMETHING between a shindig and a spectacle; the small church was packed, and Kent's family was there in the front row where Ruth had parked them. She wanted his parents to see just how loved he had been. There were dancers, actors, models and a ton of good-looking men. There were a few looking gaunt, leaning on canes or being pushed in wheelchairs. Everyone seemed to be starting to wilt, like late summer flowers. All had been so vital and full of intense colour, then waking up in the morning and finding that the frost had gotten them. What was this thing?

Ruth came and shoved herself in beside me. "Why are funerals always such short notice? They don't give you much time for planning." We had to chuckle. "Did you see the parents? They're right up there." She was buzzing. "Wait until the grand finale." The speeches filled in all the things I didn't know about Kent but all of the things I suspected. He was so loved, and such a gentle being. No wonder he loved that album with all of his friends. I could never see myself living such a selfless life. Would I ever know any of these people?

And, as promised, at the end of the service that included tributes, poems, readings and reminiscences, one of Toronto's most famous jazz singers, a beautiful, big black woman, sang, "Somewhere Over the Rainbow" from the balcony above and behind us. I held Ruth until my head was on her chest and I was weeping like a baby. After, everyone gathered in an extremely tasteful old apartment, again in the depths of Cabbagetown, but no one seemed to want to face their sorrow about Kent. I left early. It wasn't how I wanted to remember him. The only mourning I do now is in moments like this, when there is no shoulder to cry on.

Ten

A DANCER'S STEP IS light but definite, on the ball of the foot, toes gripping the earth. A dancer moves through the music, on or off the beat, a waltz, a two-step, broken into counts of eight or triplets. The steps carry them somewhere upstage, downstage; they fly and launch into a *tour jeté*, a split *jeté*, a *saut de basque*, or any number of trajectories through the air that leave steps far behind—that leave others earthbound.

HOW DID I GET here, to this place where I am wondering if I will be dressed like Nero fiddling as Rome burns, in my bedsheet toga, on the subway on the way home?

WITH KENT DEAD AND my contract at DDT mysteriously gone, I wondered how I would pay my next month's rent—like I did when I left the Company, like I did when I arrived in Quebec City, like I did the first time I stepped off the bus in Winnipeg, like I did the first and every subsequent time I was fired from every job I'd ever had because I'd eaten ice cream out of the tub in the cooler, or eaten off some customer's plate, or stuffed a whole slice of carrot cake in my mouth (as the boss appeared in the kitchen) in order to support this nasty habit called dance, that demanded the furnace be stoked constantly.

I thought it was dumb luck to get that call yesterday. No, it wasn't another audition or a contract. There was some male bedroom-voice who was a friend of a friend of someone at that party where I had stripped, who wanted a private showing. I slept on the idea. I tried to call on my departed Kent for guidance, but I think we ended up having an argument, and then a kind of esoteric sex. I'm not sure, perhaps he understood. Perhaps he was just plain gone. Wine finally helped make the decision. I didn't get teary or maudlin as I had in the past when I drank during a depressed state. Wine kept me from it all. Thankfully I slept. Tears only came in the early morning as I stumbled to the bathroom and remembered where I was, who I was and who was gone.

A FEW HOURS AGO I hauled my crap to a rendezvous at the corner of Yonge and Bloor. Once again I felt like Kent was likely somewhere nearby shaking his finger at me and telling me I was better than this. He felt so close.

And there it was, a Corvette parked up on the sidewalk. The client, Harrison Ford's long-lost twin brother, was already stoned but he smoked another joint with me at his side, and then he revved the engine, spun off the sidewalk and tore down Yonge Street doing at least ninety through a bunch of red lights. We raced out to the Beaches on the Lake Shore and his weed had got me blathering. I was happy. I was going to have a bit of cash to get me by. I had also never smoked this much and it brought a kind of peace within, for a moment. Then I started imagining I was in an adventure flick with Indiana Jones. We stopped at Johnny K's and ordered sundaes. Everything became snapshots, no memory was joined to any other. I saw that Rachelle was there with a friend, and all I can remember is her big face saying, *Are you okay? Are you stoned? Call me tomorrow.* I just giggled back. I squinted, and even though I felt like I was all mouth, I couldn't taste the sundae I'd ordered.

The next snapshot was us as we sped up Mount Pleasant to those prison-like, whitewashed high-rises on Davisville. How the hell was I going to strip with a sundae in my stomach and a big stupid smile on my face? Maybe someone could lend me sunglasses. Maybe someone could hold me up, too.

He told me I was going to strip there, for him and no one else. I had my ghetto blaster and the sleaze I was wearing, the jeans with buttons, my tux shirt—basically whatever you find at the bottom of these stairs. I knew where this was all going. He wasn't going to take me in his arms and hold me while I cried buckets over Kent and found comfort in this guy's big, hairy chest. I could never share that with anyone.

It was a nice place. Nothing I was used to; nothing from a garage sale or the consignment store. It was all black leather chairs and white walls. Minimal. I put my tape in his wall-mounted Bang and Olufsen instead of my shitty boom box and, surprise! It was cued to play "Gloria."

I started moving, and he sat back in his black leather recliner, with nothing on but his white Fruit of the Loom hiding the lost ark.

SHIT, WOULD YOU LOOK at this, everything here at the bottom of the stairs. It's all travelled in a neat clump, it must be my lucky day.

Look at my hand. There should be a pinkie ring if he didn't go through my pockets. Here we go. I got this when I was twelve. Eaton's in downtown Edmonton. For Christmas. It's been refitted a few times. In Quebec when I realized I could use it in my act, I called on a jeweller around the corner from Sainte-Ursule, near that church. It's a great little time-waster.

This is how it started, upstairs. Same as always: I lick my finger to lubricate it, and then I press my finger into and out of my mouth in slow motion like it's a you-know-what, going into and out of some part of someone. I try not to rush. It's the slow motion that is going to get his juices going.

I got into the slow part, like always, my hips revolving, slowly, but they never stop. Maybe figure eights, just to keep them moving to the beat. That's innocent enough. By now my fingers are in my mouth and my ring is slipping off my finger and between my teeth. I didn't hand it to this guy. I just stuck it in my pocket.

My watch, too. I played with my watch a little, undid it like I was trying to unbind my wrists. Hands up here. And my wrists in front. They're a little thick at this angle. And my forearms were tight against my cuffs. All these master-slave innuendoes trigger those pheromones, leaving the skin prickly.

The watch was off. The strap was in my mouth. I licked it like it was a tongue meeting my tongue. Then I held it out so he could get a better look at it. Right near my crotch. Like some guy gently stroking himself.

I dropped it in my pocket.

It worked with cufflinks, too. There is that suggestion of bondage again and then I break free, like this, to show the backs of my wrists. I don't roll my cuffs up right away. I let things like cuffs just hang for a while. Carelessly. A watchband near the crotch, an undone cuff. Lips that are loose and glistening. The pout. The help-me-I-don't-know-what's-become-of-me pout. The I'm-too-stoned-to-care pout. The save-me pout.

At this point, in private, I would have asked him to hold the cuff-links. But up there, in the penthouse, I stuck them in my pocket.

It's funny I could go on and on about executing the perfect plié or a *tendu*, or the incredible focus to take you through a pirouette, or what it is you have to believe in order to play Tybalt or Romeo. But they would just be words. You can never be part of that dance, not like you can be part of this one.

So I did the ring, the fingers, the watch and the wrists. Here's the tie. I'd wear a long tie for a businessman theme; men get hot for the straight businessman look, or the bowtie like this one, for the classic tux that makes women drool. A jacket would have been the first thing out of the way, but I didn't wear a jacket today. I loosened the tie to show that the temperature was rising inside my shirt and then I just pulled it away and tossed it, and got down to business.

I undid these buttons. Here. At the top of my shirt. Worked my way down, still with the cuffs loose. The buttons on the shirt and on the crotch of jeans are about the best way to draw out a tease to someone. It's the Pandora's box that contains all of your x-rated dreams. By the time I reach the buttons, people have given in to their desires. They have crossed over the line and will go with whatever happens.

Tell me if I asked for it.

I just undid the buttons like this, one by one. Slowly. Until they were all undone and there were…

No.

More.

Until the shirt is open, and he got a glimpse of my nipples, my pecs, my abs. It might not look like much in this light but I can tell you with good lighting anyone can look amazing.

Imagine the fabric as it falls open here. See my nipple touching the edge. I wait for that. I know when an audience can see it, because I can feel it. My nipples are small, tight and hard. They don't have the plummy, soft texture of some you see. No, but they are nipples and they have feelings and they will respond if touched, and best of all they get erect in a situation like this one. I open the shirt. Reveal my front. The firm sight of it bared and vulnerable. My chest is nothing spectacular. I've shaped it. It looks a little beat up now. But it has depth, thanks to swimming. It has a heart, thanks to…

Yes, those are moles across it.

Don't touch it. Not now. Not yet. That's what I said up there.

Don't worry, I didn't touch him. I promise, it never came to that.

I took off the shirt and made sure he got a good view of my back, my lats, my traps, the wideness, the I'm-going-to-protect-you-ness of it. I flexed because from behind it suggests that I'm doing something crude and secretive.

So it's the back first and then the full-on front, which is what he waited for and, by God, I better give him that, all of it.

But he wasn't patient.

And I held my arms back, before the shirt came off—it's easier to flex my chest and biceps with the sleeves pulling at me from behind. And then my shirt was off and my hands were where he wanted my hands to be, on my chest rubbing myself down that line of hair, below my navel. Then my hands dug into my waist to grab this belt. Remember, I kept the hips moving, grinding, *really* grinding. Closer to the floor because that's where I was going to end up.

The belt first, it got a lot of time. I pulled on the belt to get it undone. Like I was pulling on my penis, my dick, my cock. I pulled until it pulled me off my heels. Like this. Then I whipped it out from the hoops, fast. And presto, just like when I was a kid and dried my crotch and ass with a towel, in and out, pretending I was the Lone Ranger, rocking back and forth, then side to side over my cheeks with my back to my audience. Sassy. I folded the belt and slapped my ass like heigh-ho Silver, like I did in that little cowboy outfit. And if he was into ass, which he must have been, he got a thrill, didn't he? That belt is a good part of the act.

Pretend you're holding the belt.

And then it was my pants. These ones here, so much nicer when on.

The buttons on Levi's are God's gift to strippers, otherwise a zipper will do for more formal occasions. (If it's a zipper, I pull back in the hips and pretend there is pain in my crotch because a sudden erection has crippled me and made it almost impossible to get my fly undone.) With my pelvis still retracted, I got my greedy, needy hands in there. Then I shoved the hips forward like a blatant invitation.

He showed such restraint in that chair.

I definitely had to get my hips forward as far as possible. You know. Shoved forward as if I couldn't help but have something fall out, flail wildly, and oops, I'd forgotten that there was a G-string and some clean underwear to go along with it. I shoved my pants to the floor and stepped out of them.

"Here," I said. "Hold my jeans."

Then I ran my hands up and down the inside of my thighs with my legs open. Crotch to knee. Knees to crotch. Crotch to knee. Like so. I like that sensation too, to be honest. It got to him.

He wouldn't let on if he was enjoying it, though. And neither did I.

So there, in my G-string, it was time to give him the angle shots: the hips twisted to the right and the torso square toward him so it looks like I have a twelve-inch waist and massive shoulders. Smoke and mirrors. A universal turn-on.

Sorry, I'm straying. But look in any porn or fitness magazine. You either have the broad shoulder shot or a crotch shot in your face. Let me continue.

Nine times out of ten, I get onto the floor on my knees, legs spread and go for the juice. Lots of rubbing now. I limbo onto my back. The socks come off for the foot fetishists in the crowd. (I have to please as many people as I can.) It's a good idea to have well-tended toes, not filthy black soles. My feet are okay and good with cream on them the night before. Sure, let them see your soles, too. That's a big turn-on for at least sixteen percent of your house, although they won't admit it.

I went for the G-string, and though it left enough to the imagination, with the cock ring on and the equipment on the swollen side, I didn't want to give too much away too soon. Besides I'm pretty quick about pulling at both sides and then playing with the clips until, flick, flick, flick, it's off like magic. He was going to have to see me this way anyway. I could have been just a piece of meat to him, couldn't I?

Speaking of meat, I've definitely got nothing to complain about. It's cut. Liars translate seven to nine, but honestly they rarely get bigger than this. Nice girth. When I was a kid, I thought there was something wrong with the way it stood diagonally at attention. I thought horizontal was perfect.

If all you want is to see the guy's cock while he's up there, there it is, a spiralling hose, a stumpy mushroom or a thick sausage trying to free itself of the foreskin. Some are so big they are veined, to carry the supply of blood the length of the member. Some men faint when it's erect. When flaccid, it might recoil into a warm crotch, creating the forward bulge. On hot days it swings in shorts and track pants, the sensitive head rubbing against the fabric. It gets stroked in the shower or at the urinal, shaken lightly or tugged by a lingering hand, tickled by fingertips while someone watches. It provides both fascination and joy, this taboo tool changing shape every minute of the day as it's jostled, squeezed, tossed, grabbed, sniffed, sucked and shoved, or just thought about. The dick can be a daisy chain that connects generations. It's a source of amusement, and occasional annoyance. It can be a best friend or a dangerous weapon, depending which end of it you are connected to.

You still hear it—big nose, big hose, big feet, big whatever. Daniel confirmed that old wives' tale. (Can you see old wives standing around the washtub sharing that information? Then a laugh, a nudge, a wink and the twinge of excitement or fear at the prospect.) And no, you don't need a nose to dance. But the nose of a man may be one of the sexiest of appendages, whether it curves down like an Arab's, has a Frenchman's bump, is severely aquiline like a German's, a big honking noble Roman thing or a brooding Jew's. It is nature's cruel joke if it disappears into his profile. The bigger it is, the more the heartache. Of course after what just happened up there in the penthouse of the depraved I see that size definitely has its drawbacks, makes it that much easier to hit—when it's yours that has come to blows—with the sharp side of a ring, the jewels, the family jewels, used as a weapon to set you straight.

And my balls. They've always been an asset. Some guys just don't have the volume. But mine are nicely grab-able and very sensitive, like I've got this extra organ flopping around down there. One big tickle-fest in my pants. I keep them shaved. Most people like the look, and the thought. People don't want to be picking pubes out of their teeth.

And that's it. The whole package. I don't want to throw cold water on you, but that's kind of how it went upstairs, like I told you, with the ring, the watch, the belt, the shirt, the tight jeans and then just the G-string and, and, and, my dick was feeling big and getting bigger. Sensitive. I pulled it earlier, cock ring and all, to make sure he got a good show.

I went for it.

I was stoned, but I am so cold and clear now.

Was I gyrating too much? Was I worrying about gyrating too much? Was I just too out of it? Or was I worried that I was too out of it? His looks made me harder, too, till I was full-fledged *tumescent*. I've heard that word enough since leaving Quebec. It has a real porn-mag sound, you know, like those guys' dicks are so painfully large, you'd touch them and they'd explode. Penis juice everywhere. So the cock ring and the pot gave me that swollen, cartoon character cock, cripplingly huge feeling in my dick. My skin was stinging. And there he was over on the recliner with fireworks in his underwear. Big, naked feet twitching like he was a little nervous or excited. I got too close. He touched my ass with his fingers, you know just a tickle but it really drove me nuts being high. He touched my balls. Batted them around a little. Then he got a little rough, a little wrestly and we were into the bedroom and on the bed and he was all over me, grinding his crotch. It was a pretty horny scene. I was thinking I was a lucky guy because boy, was he built. He pulled his underwear until it ripped and I caught the flash of too much dick. But whose show was this?

I tried to get a mouthful of that package, "his manliness," as Kent would want me to say, but that's not what he wanted and then maybe it was too late. I don't remember. He was on my back and I was on my face.

"I'm not queer," he said.

I struggled.

He shoved against my tight hole and then it wasn't fun.

I was dry.

He was strong.

It burned. Pulled.

I tasted his arm in my mouth. Yeah it was his arm, hair flesh.

Some blood too, come to think of it, to go with the pain and his big Indiana hands and a ring against my face. Something cracked in my neck as I struggled. I left behind being excited and accelerated into a fight for my life when suddenly I exploded and was outside my body. I see it all:

HE'S INSIDE ME.

The pain splits.

Me.

Apart.

The boy with the soapstone face, the blank eyes, the perfect teeth, the pouty lips, the swoosh of blond hair and the thighs of steel shot right off the bed. I landed somewhere between there and the wall, grabbed the sheet and fled—down the hall. Tears of pain blinded me.

Let me catch my breath.

And now, here I am at the bottom of the stairs. Explaining the art of taking off wrinkled clothes. Good he didn't chuck my ghetto blaster. I'm dragging myself down the hall now, to a wished-for laundry room where there will be an adjoining bathroom or closet and I can shove enough toilet paper in my ass and up my nose to keep from leaking on the subway on the way home, but God help me if I shit, fart, sneeze or even cough.

I DON'T REMEMBER GETTING home. It must have been a cab. But then I dream. I dream of a man I love so much I sleep with his cigarettes under my pillow. He didn't die that March when I wasn't there to lose him. In my dream he is how I knew him for six months when I was unaware that I would never be this happy or this in love again.

I wake. My dream's puppet. I eat just enough. Dress myself. Wander on foot to Cabbagetown, as a late spring chill wanders through me. At the Necropolis Cemetery his warm ashes elude me. I find no rock or name to get heartfelt over. A young man with thick hands and a round ass cradled into the seat of his pants tells me that the parents have the ashes. There is no evidence, no record, nothing for me. I turn. Begin my wander homewards. My dream has lied. Instincts have betrayed me as much as good sense did, in the beginning. I enter a corner shop on Parliament to squeeze the last chill out of my flesh and garments. An old hippie with a swollen, pitted nose sits behind a desk, asks my name, my profession. He hopes it's his mind that will impress. Chats me up. Nothing. He noticed me going to the cemetery. He tells me all of the things I heard once from other strangers—and wanted to believe. All about me being a fine cut of a man and handsome, too. He's arrogant. He wants dinner, *perhaps lunch*, he says, unconditionally with no strings, genital, oral or anal, attached. I bare my teeth and the smile protects me from the beast. I imagine what his beard is covering must be even uglier. He gives me his card. I leave, trembling, and the cold races into places it had overlooked.

Epilogue

THERE WAS BLOOD ON the sheets after. That was my first clue. But what's a little blood? It could have been my nose. When I reached the basement, I found the hoped-for laundry room, but it was secured tight. It was in the janitor's closet that I realized it, washing myself down the drain in the floor. To that moment I could have recited the choreography for *Raymonda* backward and upside down, as I stumbled down that stairwell, but it was the searing pain that changed that. I don't remember the ride home, or calling Rachelle after two days curled on my floor. Yes, the doctor gave his clinical explanation for the pain, looking over his glasses, eyebrows raised in sober doubt and judgement.

There was a warning about how things were being transmitted. He said something about blood. That's what it has boiled down to—other peoples' fluids. People could be dying at our feet and we'd be worried about not getting their spit in us or on us. Maybe it's a miracle I'm still alive. The monster could have cracked my neck and tossed me down the garbage chute. I can't fantasize about revenge. Did this one human not understand the excruciating pain that could be inflicted upon another? Did he think I would somehow give in? I only think of him now because a few weeks later I saw him at the grocery at the end of his street, with his wife and kids who I doubt knew of his pad on the twenty-eighth floor. He is still up there, in that nasty place.

I am here on my steps, staring at trees bigger than houses, just starting to turn shades of red and orange. No, I am not in Cabbagetown. The guy who got the position with DDT is. He can barely call himself a dancer. How long had it taken the choreographer to take a shine to him? I remember the reflection of his angry glare at the audition. Jealousy, I thought. But now he's in like a dirty shirt. And now, in fact, living in Cabbagetown with the choreographer, the florist's ex, dancing badly, trying to make up for a lack of training and care, and love of dance. He will never bring to that company what I could have brought to it.

IN SPITE OF THE pain I felt every time I so much as thought about sitting on a toilet (worrying if you're going to die when you take a shit is a great distraction from mourning the death of a friend), I had to figure out what to do next.

In the days that followed, Rachelle put me on what we called "the home plan"—a self-imposed seclusion inside my apartment with myself, my memories of Kent, an empty notebook and a pen.

"I don't want you going out," she said.

"With this sore ass?"

"Call me at wardrobe. I'll come by on my way home."

For two weeks she dropped by with liquids, yogurt, soup, smoothies. For four weeks I had a brow that was permanently wrinkled from the pain, but gradually over several nights it let up, and the more I slept the better I felt.

After four weeks, she came by with a bottle of what we called bubbly booze, since it wasn't wine and we weren't sure what it was made from. "I have news. I have a plan. I want you to hear me out," she said.

"Let me guess. You're going to audition as an alternate for the National?"

"Yeah, for their fat corps."

"Corpulent corps."

"Oh shit off right now."

"You insensitive bitch. Don't you know pooing hurts? I can say whatever I want."

"Fine. Be that way. I can go home and you'll never know."

"Okay. I'm more than sorry about that. *Pleeeease*, tell me your plan."

"You sure?"

"Sure. Speaking of, I had a better movement today. I'm feeling up."

She clasped her hands and put her knuckles to her lips. "Well, our friend Peter..."

"As in *Peter* Peter?"

"The very one."

"He's quitting, right?"

"How did you know?"

"I didn't think he could do it."

"Well he's quitting and..."

"And?"

"And if he comes here, and if I start dancing, and if we can get a few more bodies..."

"Bertrand and Louise?"

"Sure, your friends from Quebec?"

"Yes. Then?"

"Then guess. Oh Jesus. We could have a company."

"Who'd run it?"

"Us, you idiot."

"I could..."

"You could do whatever you want."

"...choreograph?"

"Why not? You said it was all that made sense now. Peter wants to dance. I want to dance. You want control? Here, I hereby give you control. Do it. Do it for us. Do it for five, maybe six, maybe more people who are desperate to dance. Do it for yourself. Look at you. You have come such a long way. You know you're a beautiful dancer. You're smart. What else is there? Of course there's still time to be a dentist. You want to be a dentist? Do you want to change people's lives, or just their fillings?"

"A nice smile can go a long way."

"This is important. We could be important."

IT'S NO SURPRISE IF you thought I'd be on my way back to Bilt-more's, maybe to get a shift or two, like a moth to flame, after the mess I'd been in. But I only went because I noticed Brittany's picture in the

Toronto paper as a Sunshine Girl. They'd used a stock photo I recognized from the Chez Moritz and that's what caught my eye, looking over someone's shoulder on the streetcar. I wouldn't have shown my face in that backroom, but I was still on good terms in the front room; they recognized me.

"She's history, pal. She missed last night. Aren't you the *Grand Blond*?"

Brittany unlocked the door. The room was dark. I could make out the silhouette of a sheet wrapped around her. "Come in." Her voice was a little rough, like it would be from sleeping, not from eating chocolate. But I could tell she was more or less straight. I sat on the bed and she touched my arm while we talked. "I can't believe you're here." But there was a monotone to her voice and I got the feeling she couldn't really remember me. I tried to jog her memory about the Chez Moritz. She said everything had started to blur. I told her about the shitty audition, Kent, stripping, and then she perked up. I told her my impression of the stripping scene in Toronto. "It's just sleaze bags trying to take advantage of everyone, selling drugs, selling whatever they can, to pay off others." But there was no sound. I went on. "I don't mind. There are lots of waitering jobs."

But silence soaked the room.

"They said you missed a performance?" Did she know she'd missed a night? Did she know where in hell she was?

"How did your friend die?"

"I don't know. They don't know."

"This gay cancer thing is weird."

"I don't think it was that."

"I think I know some girls who got it, or something. Seems the sinners are all being picked off one by one, the good ones, too. Do you mean it, about being a waiter?"

"If I'm lucky."

"God. Look at you."

"Yeah. Wow."

"Do you want to tell me what being a waiter has to do with anything you've ever done before?"

"Well, I'm great at giving people what they want. I blend easily into the scenery. My parents would be thrilled that I'm not taking off my clothes. Hey, I'd finally have something in common with them. They love eating in restaurants. I love food, booze, fags. Undeclared tips."

"Wiping out ashtrays? Scraping half-eaten crud into the slop bucket?"

"You've been there?"

"I'd rather die stripping."

"Those are my options. Rock-bottom Rottam."

"What day is it?"

"Saturday. You missed last night's show."

The phone rang. I listened while looking into the dark. "Yeah, yeah. Well, fuck you very much. I already paid my bill." She slammed the phone. "I guess you know what that was."

"I guess."

She sobbed into her pillow. "Fuck."

She told me she was broke. That since Quebec almost everything she'd earned had gone up her nose, with a guy she'd met in Montreal, but then he ended up like all the others. And no one was out there to help her. Her Romanian asshole Chippendale stallion fell off the face of the earth. Her brother had hanged himself. Why bother trying to stay sane? After she downgraded the Cadillac to a rusty Malibu to nothing, she went back to cold turkey.

"Do you have any money?" she asked.

"Barely."

"I just want to get back to Chicago. If you can get me back to Chicago, I'll do you a big favour someday. I don't know what. But I have friends. I do. You can come to Chicago. Just a bus ticket. I swear that's it. Okay, a bus ticket and a sandwich."

"Kent had friends. Lots of them."

"Friends are everything."

I had to find a bank.

FOR YEARS I'VE BEEN an instrument to someone else's agenda. Dancers are. Dancers are cogs in a huge choreographable universe. Dancers are the tools, instruments used to create stories. That morning after Kent asked me what I had to offer and it all stopped making sense, I knew that I could never turn back. I knew that the time had come to take the next step. I tried to hide from the truth. I could have turned my back so easily on everything but I knew that I would be running away. I had to honour a very real need.

I TURNED MY BACK on dance, then dance turned its back on me. But I was merely an instrument in the grander picture of what others were communicating. No one is indispensable. Anyone could have filled my role as second soloist. My body was a vehicle possessed by my ego, while doing the bidding of others. Dance is *my* tool now, like I was dance's for six or seven years.

You think you know the path the process will take. Last year, searching, meeting someone who helped me like Kent or Brittany, explaining to them where I'd come from and letting them help me get to the place I was going.

Someone believing in me.

Someone finally listening.

I have to remember that we're everywhere. Those who didn't quite make it for that sliver of what we thought was the only opportunity available to us. The women and men who devoted a young lifetime to the pain in exchange for a moment of glory or fulfillment on that stage, or in the studio. Others who teach it now, or design, score, light, or are professionals in office towers with their backs to the sun, or alcoholics deep into twelve-step programs pushing strollers, waiting tables, working the checkout at the grocery, four decades after they were told they were star material, and all the others in between. The cities are full of us, sitting in the good seats or sitting in the cheap seats, when we can afford it or when someone else takes us, takes pity on us—but showing up in spirit or in form when the Company comes to town.

None of us give in. Who didn't go down screaming and raging? There isn't one of us with broken dreams who doesn't burn to their toes to be given another chance to make it. Why? We're only here for a moment, but it's then, in that moment, that we want to let the universe speak to the world through us. We are the mediums, sylphs for the projections of the stratosphere, and will do whatever it takes because it feels so damn good and bad. It just feels, period. Chances don't slip by easily. You can't be exposed to the power, the beauty and the strength of creation, music, art, the human form, and not let it affect you. You can turn your back, but you will always regret it.

I can say it now (I couldn't then) that if you dance, or do any art for that matter, you'll leave yourself wide open for opinion. You won't please everyone. Dance flows. Dancers are dancers whether they like it or not. Dance, by its nature, is a function and a process. And if you think the only pleasure you will know is your own, then stop. You have to be generous or it will not thrive. Art is not perfect. The process is, but the product isn't unless you can change someone's life for a moment or forever. You will have to be crystal clear to your audience or you will make no difference. At least do your colleagues a favour—show perfection, show expertise, show originality. You will never be allowed to sit back on your heels or your sore, tight ass or hurting ego, because you have to dance all the goddamn time; that is its nature, like scaling a cliff with no rest stops. Like a shark that has to keep moving to keep water flowing through its body. Like Moira Shearer in *The Red Shoes*. You will never relax, let go and think, *Look at me*. You only get a few moments to enjoy the applause. If you think it's that moment to appreciate yourself, you'll trip up. You miss a beat and that's it: you stumble, fall and disappear. An inflated ego is a fleeting reward. It does no one any good.

OUR TOUR STARTS NEXT spring in Chicago: performances and workshops. Then on to Ann Arbor, then Windsor where I will look up Kent's parents. Then the universities in Toronto, Kingston, Ottawa and Montreal, and finally Laval in Quebec City. We will perform a ballet I have been working on based on one of Nelligan's poems. I don't know who will be there. After that, who knows, a western tour perhaps?

IN THE SUMMER I went to Chicago and New York, but the number Brittany had given me was out of service, and any enquiries yielded nothing. I wished her the best, hoped she was still alive somewhere and being loved by someone good.

I did a pilgrimage with a small sum of Kent's money that Ruth gave to me, with orders to use it. I saw the masters: Pilobolus, Eliot Feld, Graham, New York City Ballet, ABT, Joffrey, the Dance Theatre of Harlem and Merce Cunningham at the Brooklyn Academy of Music. (Did Madame still fantasize about New York?) I took class when I could, attended workshops, master classes. As my body distilled itself back to the essentials, I felt the reservoir replenish itself, this time to overflowing. All of it is now part of my vocabulary as I continue to invent my own language and definitions. I am a small part of that magic that people pay to see and share, wherever I work. The stories tell my truth.

Rachelle loves to say, "Your eyes have lost their… blankness"— one of her favourites, just to keep me humble, just to remind me that it returns from time to time. While my musculature went from tight to taut, my heart burst and broke and broke again. Kent knew the bigness of the dance world, more so than I. He feared I would be naive enough to think the world offered nothing, if not stardom. Stardom is for Baryshnikov and Kirkland. My dancers and I have a more important calling.

It is the stories in bodies, shapes and shadows that reveal themselves. I point my dancers and my intentions in a direction and tell them to fly. Sometimes it's careless. Sometimes the ground we tread is uneven and precarious. Whether the inspiration came to me in my sleep as a nightmare, or as the image of someone's reflection in the window of a bus that reminded me of someone else, a friend, living or dead, someone spiralling down a stairway, or loving an older woman or two men, or breaking someone's heart, or washing amongst the ebb and flow of tide and waves along the shore, or on a wheat field with the wide-eyed innocence of an adolescent, or the narrow squint of doubt that comes with age, set against a summer prairie sky or an approaching blizzard, it is true.

And sometimes a simple tune means absolutely nothing.

There's a space at the back of the bus, the back of a plane, the back corner of a café, or the back of my mind, that is my own rehearsal hall where my ideas expand—on seat backs, tabletops or scraps of paper. In the end it isn't about the dancer or the choreographer or the music or the applause. It is about the dance, a language we badly translate but seem to understand. The best I can do, the most comfort I can offer myself is to know I am a part of it.

From the moment I got those university girls into their tutus and onto that stage, to having a chance to dance my best Tybalt, from the moment I used all that I knew of the body and its static form, magnetic emotions, repelling electricity, wayward poles, short-circuited auroras, gleaming auras, fermenting stories and crippling genetics, to having a few dedicated people dance the story—from all of those moments—my dreams have come true. I can affect people, dancers, audiences.

For every Lisa, Marcel, Bertrand, Guy, Daniel, Patrice, Brittany, Nadine, Madame Talegdi, Kharkov, Rachelle and Kent, there is a dance.

They'll all be there, in the theatre. You'll also see me watching from the wings, spinning or tumbling across the stage, or hiding somewhere among the audience. I may be seated right beside you. I'll strive to show that love—however painful, overblown, dangerous, satisfying, obsessive or nurturing—is never wrong. Maybe a piece of the puzzle will fit back into place, and make things a bit smoother, or maybe not quite.

I'm dancing now.

Only for a moment, "Gloria" was my song, and the dance, my life.

Acknowledgements

MANY THANKS TO THE caring guidance once again from Nightwood Editions, Silas White and Lizette Fischer, for their kind support and attention to detail. I must thank the late great playwright and friend Elliott Hayes who took my early efforts and created the play *Strip*. Thanks always to Keith Maillard and Maureen Medved whose wise mentoring helped me to set out on this fascinating journey along the road less travelled. Thanks to those who read and provided feedback to early stages of this manuscript: John, Carol, Alaina, Donnard, Emily, Nilofar, Ben. And thanks to others who have yet to read it and are always there with an encouraging word, including Kim and Susan. Thanks to Louise and her feedback at the self-directed Estapona writing retreat. Thanks to my caring mother and father, for their patience and love, and thanks to my family, brother, sisters, in-laws, nephews and nieces as well as dear friends, for their love and support. Thank you to those amazing souls who have danced through my life and inspired the characters in these pages. And thanks especially to my partner Bernard and my muse Hugo, who challenge me to do my best, bolster me when I need it, and are here throughout.

PHOTOGRAPH: BRYAN CANNON

About the Author

ANDREW BINKS IS A graduate of UBC's Master of Fine Arts program in Creative Writing. His first novel, *The Summer Between*, was published in May 2009 by Nightwood Editions. His work has been featured in Joyland.ca and the Harvard Square Editions anthology, *Voice From the Planet*. His short fiction and non-fiction has appeared in *Galleon, Fugue, Prism International, Harrington Gay Men's Literary Quarterly, Bent-magazine, Globe and Mail, Xtra* and *Xtra West,* among others. His poetry has appeared in *Quill's* 'Lust' issue and *Velvet Avalanche Anthology.* Two of his plays received public workshops in Vancouver and Toronto in 2010 and he was one of the contributing writers to the Festival Players of Prince Edward County "Sounding Ground" audio plays.

www.andrewbinks.ca